THE VISIT

ROBERT W. KIRBY

INKUBATOR
BOOKS

Published by Inkubator Books
www.inkubatorbooks.com

ISBN (eBook): 978-1-83756-118-6
ISBN (Paperback): 978-1-83756-119-3
ISBN (Hardback): 978-1-83756-120-9

1

He awakened, but he didn't dare to open his eyes. Every time he moved, even a tiny bit, an awful wave of stomach-turning sickness swept through him. He'd been having the most realistic dream where he'd been falling endlessly into an abyss, making his mind whirl and his brain throb. It seemed to go on forever. It was awful. His eyes were closed, but he sensed it was night-time. It was silent, too. *Where am I?*

Alarmed, he snapped open his eyes. Blackness. Total pitch blackness. He didn't move for a long time, unsure if he'd even be able to. Was he glued to the spot? It seemed like it. He started flickering his eyes in the hope his vision would adapt and he'd regain some focus. It didn't help. Then he noticed how hot he was. His skin seemed to be burning up, but accompanying that sticky hotness were shivers so intense it was as if his bones were frozen inside of his body.

He coughed out a weak, 'Hello. Is anyone there? Hello?'

Nothing. Utter silence.

He sat up, but then that terrible silence became replaced by a low buzzing noise. Like an angry wasp had somehow got trapped inside his skull and was desperate to escape. He moved to a low crouch and felt around in the surrounding darkness. He couldn't even see his hand in front of his face. An awful thought hit him. *I'm blind... I've lost my eyesight and I'm bloody blind.* He dismissed that idea, fearing that thinking this would cause uncontrollable panic, and instead he tried to recall what he'd been doing, where he'd been, and with whom. It was all a jumbled mess, and it made him queasy to think.

He stood up, slowly raised his arms and pressed against... against something. Dust fell into his face and mouth. He winced, coughed and spluttered, 'Hello! Is this some kind of joke? What is this? Help me!'

It became hotter. Unbearably hot. So stuffy and insufferable it made his chest go tight. He was burning up, and he was overcome with a crushing dread. He closed his eyes and slammed the palms of his hands upwards. Then let out a desperate scream as he shoved and pushed. Whatever was above him moved slightly, so he shoved harder until it gave way.

A few seconds passed before he heard a mighty thump that shook the floor under him and showered him with more choking dust. With that thump came a blast of cooler air, and more darkness, although it seemed to his fuzzy eyes that it was not so complete. He climbed up. It took everything he had to do this, and the exertion caused him to drop to his knees and enter a coughing fit that made his throat feel like he'd swallowed a bag of razor blades. Then he noticed the blood in his mouth. Or at least he tasted it. He spat out a massive mouthful of the thick, clumpy stuff and whimpered, 'Please, is anyone in here? Answer me.'

Now he was able to take in his surroundings. He was in some type of derelict hut or neglected store shack. He gazed at the floor, at the chunky hatch he'd shoved open. Saw the black pit he'd crawled out from. There were several broken bricks strewn about him, and crumpled plastic sheeting lay underneath the floor hatch. Had someone buried him down there? Tried trapping him in that filthy hole? The plastic and bricks suggested that. Christ, why wasn't he able to remember? He spat more blood and wiped a dribble of stringy claret from his chin. What was the last thing he could recall? He coughed again. This time violently, and sick exploded from his mouth and nose.

After emptying his stomach, he staggered through a broken doorway that led into a larger space. It smelt foul in this part of the building. Like the stink of a rotten animal carcass left to fester for weeks, possibly months. At the end of the shack, he made out piles of broken wood, and stepping closer, he realised that this was part of the roof, long ago caved in.

He peered up at the sky, seeing a scattering of tiny stars and a bright half-moon. Had he been here before? He couldn't recall. He studied the floor. The planks were moss covered and broken in many places, revealing more dark holes leading into the unknown – into the grim belly of the building where he'd found himself just now. Faded beer cans, bottles and takeaway cartons littered the place. An old, threadbare sleeping bag was unfurled in the corner, positioned on some thin squares of tatty cardboard.

A noise snapped his attention away from the filthy bedding. A car engine. Or at least that was what it sounded like. Seeing no obvious way out, he headed back to the hatch. The vehicle's headlights streaked through the splits on the side of the building. This gave him a clearer glimpse of the place. He studied a network of large cobwebs stretched out in every corner... Lichen-covered beams, and – he laid his eyes on all the blood. Not just the blood he'd coughed up, but huge puddles of the stuff over in the far corner. And bandages... They lay everywhere, and most were stained with gore. *Shit, someone died in here... surely they have,* he thought. He could now smell the metallic blood and hear music coming from outside. It was coming from within that car. A thudding, catchy beat...

The mess on the floor triggered something in his muddled mind, and he considered that the blood might belong to him. He feared to check but knew he must. So, he raised his hand and placed it on top of his head and touched upon what was a swollen, gunky mess. His hair was matted and crusty in places, and his entire head felt misshapen, mangled and grotesque to the touch. There wasn't much pain, though. Why was there *no* pain? What the hell had happened? The tune went on – *doop, doop, doop.* He swooned and smashed down. The floor creaked under his weight and chucked up a cloud of swirling dust as he landed.

He noted two car doors slamming shut. And voices. Two different voices – two people having an informal chat. Like everything was normal. Still, that track played. His vision blurred. He heard voices and sensed the people were now in the building. He tried to call out but his eyelids fell shut and, as if back in the room below, he knew only complete darkness again.

2

Vanessa stopped swimming, wrapped her arms around her orange swim buoy and took a breather. She'd never been much of a sea swimmer, but now, living a mere stone's throw from the coast, it seemed like the perfect time to ditch the busy pools and take the plunge into the world of open water swimming. She'd noticed a difference straight away – it was tougher for a start, and after just one session she'd purchased a decent floatation aid, shortie wetsuit and nose plugs, which she hated, but not nearly as much as snorting up a pint of salty seawater.

As she bobbed up and down, she pulled her goggles onto her forehead and gazed back to civilisation. She could see their new home and smiled as she viewed the stunning property. It really was something else. It stood apart from the neighbouring houses. From here, it reminded her of a Mediterranean holiday home. She'd already spied plenty of people walking along the beach and admiring the place. She'd even waved a few times from the balcony, though she'd felt a tad silly in doing so. How had her husband described it to everyone? *A contemporary, cubist style with an abundance of natural light and open-plan living space.*

A month since they'd moved here, yet she still felt like she needed to keep pinching herself, because it was like a dream. It seemed impossible to be *this* happy. That first morning she'd woken up to the noise of the seagulls and opened the blinds, pushed the huge folding doors, smiling as they silently glided open as if by magic, and was welcomed by a stunning blue sky and calm sea view. Vanessa had stepped out onto the balcony, wearing only her thin Hawaiian-style dressing gown, and took in the panoramic view. She'd let out a happy sigh and stayed out there for ages, enjoying the fresh morning wind swishing her hair about. She'd taken in that natural air for ages – breathed it in deeply. The air was cleaner. Crisper. She'd already guessed she wouldn't miss London, but in that moment she knew it for certain. Not one bit. Curtis had joined her. He'd brought out a tray of pastries and two lattes. They'd sat there, hand in hand, nibbling at their breakfast in a blissful placidity.

They knew it wouldn't be like this every day. The winter would be bleak. Strong winds would likely batter the place, and it would be harsh and chilly. But Vanessa told herself that she'd never stop appreciating how lucky they were. She'd never take what they had for granted. She'd rested her head on his shoulder and closed her eyes.

'Guess this place will do,' Curtis had said.

'Yeah. It will do,' she'd replied with a big grin. 'I won't miss that noisy road behind the garden, that's for sure.'

'Nope. Even on a Sunday it was like a racetrack.'

'Not sure I'll ever tire of this sea view.'

'Technically, it's an estuary, Vee.'

'Oh, sorry. But somehow, "Hey, guys, come out here and check out our smashing *estuary* view..." doesn't quite have the same ring to it... Shall we dip our toes in the *estuary*, dear?'

'What... right now? Shall we finish these first? And... aren't you naked under there, Mrs Pascall?'

'Wouldn't *you* like to know?'

Vanessa smiled at the recent memory and slid her goggles back on. Then, releasing her grip on the buoy and letting it float behind her, she set back off. She'd drifted further out than she'd realised and now had her work cut out to swim back to shore.

3

Vanessa spread the chequered blanket out onto the pebbles. The beach was heaving this afternoon, as she guessed it would be. The temperature had hit thirty degrees by lunchtime and the day trippers had arrived in droves to make the most of the uncustomary blast of late June heat. Everyone, from groups of rowdy teens drinking cocktails out of cans to pensioners reading their papers under giant sun hats, was out enjoying the fabulous weather. She wondered how many people must be absent from school, college, and work today. Lots of convenient illnesses must have been doing the rounds.

The tide was right out now, and the baking sunshine cast a hazy shimmer across the water and the tiny figures frolicking about in the surf. She heard the distant thrum coming from the engines of jet skis zipping along in the far distance. She'd stayed close to the walkway near a row of tall, converted fisherman's huts, one of which was occupied by two couples in their thirties who were watching the goings-on below with a quiet superiority. A bottle of champers sat chilling in a cooler on their table, but Vanessa noted all their glasses were empty, and she decided the drinks were likely just for show. She'd picked this location so Delphine would spot her when she came along the walkway.

A large gathering of teenagers had congregated along one of the wooden groynes. They were Londoners, Vanessa deduced straight away. They were loud and a bit aggravating, especially the girls, but weren't doing anything wrong – unless you counted being obnoxious and using too much profanity.

A smashed bottle lay on the walkway close by them. Beachgoers deftly passed the shards, many scowling at the youths or throwing them a judgmental glance in passing. She watched a mother struggle with a pushchair across the pebbles in an attempt to avoid the glass on the path, her partner way too busy moaning and pointing out the mess to lend her a helping hand. A tall woman with a shaved head, walking several white terriers, danced around it. The dogs were panting in frantic rasps and looked about ready to keel over as she dragged them further on, despite their clear resistance. A skinny guy zigzagging through the crowd on a push bike stopped dead, snatched up his bike and carried it over the glass. But no one attempted to pick it up or move it to the side. The teens were oblivious to the attention this was bringing them, far too engrossed in themselves as they took selfies and sipped on cans of passion fruit Martini to give a damn.

Vanessa slipped on her flip-flops and decided to move it herself, at which point a big man with leathery skin and a mass of thick black tattoos on his arms bent down and collected up the shards.

Seeing this, one youngster, a slim Asian guy, said, 'We didn't do that, mate. Weren't us.'

Another youth, a smug-looking girl in a tiny pink bikini with white spots, added, 'No, defo weren't us! Two piss-heads staggered past and one dropped it up the floor. He laughed and kept going.'

Up the floor. It grated on Vanessa when people said that. She wanted to shout – *dropped it... ON the floor*. But of course, she refrained.

In front of Vanessa, a young guy wearing wetsuit shorts stopped pumping up his paddle board to watch the exchange with a gleeful smile, as if hoping an argument would erupt.

But the tattooed man didn't even acknowledge the youngsters, let alone dispute the matter with them. He just tramped off with two big handfuls of glass, his sweaty face set in a mask of stony vexation and his spectacles slipping down his nose.

The youths started muttering to themselves, pointing this way and that, as if discussing where to go next. Some appeared sheepish, as if now aware they were the main focus on that part of the beach. They all shuffled on, some giggling and others strutting, heads held high, as if daring any of the beachgoers to give them a mouthful.

The tattooed man had removed the worst of the glass, but plenty of tiny, shattered pieces still lay scattered on the walkway. Vanessa was tempted to go to one of the local businesses and ask to borrow a dustpan and brush. She hated seeing litter. Vanessa couldn't comprehend why some people were such thoughtless arseholes. Why they went around thinking that it was fine to leave their rubbish strewn around for everyone else to tidy up.

This, she knew, was a sore subject for many of the galled residents who had to contend with this kind of inconsiderate behaviour on a daily basis. Some locals weren't shy with airing their views about the disrespectful out-of-towners and day trippers. They just didn't like them. Vanessa recalled overhearing one sour-faced pensioner in a local chippy when they'd been visiting during the time of the house renovation.

'Those middle-class London pricks and their spoilt, bratty, vulgar children... Wish they'd all piss off to Ramsgate or Deal and leave us in peace,' he'd spat.

Vanessa told Curtis about the boorish man, as she'd started to worry if they'd made the right decision. But he'd chuckled. 'Don't worry, Vee, idiots like him are in the minority. Besides, my dad purchased this house back in the nineties. And I have been visiting this town since I was old enough to pick up a bucket and spade. I'm practically a local myself. Believe me, there are plenty of businesses in the area that are thriving because of its popularity. So please, ignore those jealous pessimists.'

'Where do this lot think they are, Ayia Napa?'

Vanessa realised she'd been gazing at the glass, lost in her thoughts, and hadn't seen Delphine approach.

'I think it's hotter than Ayia Napa today!' replied Vanessa.

Delphine handed her a tea in a polystyrene cup. 'Bit of a queue for that. Where are the two monkeys this afternoon?'

Delphine was wearing a vibrant pink and black kaftan, a tassel sarong with a tropical print, and a white canvas sun hat that was fraying at the edges.

'Lovely, thank you. Curtis picked them up from school. He bought them a blow-up paddling pool and was super excited. He couldn't wait to get them home to set it up. Sofia won't go near the sea at the moment, because a delightful child at school informed her that so much poo gets pumped into the sea here that if she swims in it, she'll smell like foul sewage for days.'

Delphine made a hole in the pebbles and placed her cup inside. 'Aw, aren't kids so sweet?'

'His dad told him that.'

Two topless guys strolled past. One spotted them, nudged his mate, and the shorter of the pair gave them a look – a look that he no doubt considered an irresistible stare but was more of a dorky grimace. Vanessa decided she should be flattered, because the cocky lads must have been a good twenty years younger than her. Vanessa averted her eyes from them, not wanting to encourage the young lads. She heard one say, 'Cor, nice. You're taking the oldie, mate.' They sniggered and walked on.

If Delphine had heard the comment, she didn't react. She was now busy applying sun cream on her shapely legs.

Vanessa had to admit, for someone in her early sixties, Delphine looked dazzling. She remembered their first meeting a couple of years back. They'd been renting Delphine's converted boat house for a few days during the renovation period. She'd assumed Delphine was in her mid-forties and was shocked to learn her actual age. The pair had a connection straight away. They'd conversed like they were old friends who'd known each other for decades. It was weird, but Vanessa felt like she could talk to Delphine and enjoyed her company. This was quite unusual for Vanessa, as she wasn't one to strike up friendships easily. She'd even been informed, more than once, that she was sometimes rather reserved and even antisocial at times.

When she'd found out that Delphine, in addition to running the boat house, also practised as a clairvoyant, she'd not been shocked by the news, because there had been something about her. Something... well, mystical, she supposed. Delphine had told her she offered her services as a romantic medium, and dealt in matters involving jilted lovers, matrimonial affairs and missing loved ones.

'Have they settled in at their new school? Apart from that little rotter telling Sofia fibs, I mean,' asked Delphine. 'Although, from what Surfers Against Sewage are reporting, maybe she has cause for concern, Vee.' She said this last sentence in a low, conspiratorial tone.

'They love it here. They adore the house. Their faces when

we showed them around. Oh, it was unreal. Jude was super impressed and Sofia said, "Mummy, how long do we get to stay here on holiday?" When I told her we were staying forever, her eyes went wide, and she just gasped.' Vanessa smiled. 'I have to keep convincing myself that it's all real, too. Our house in London was nice, but this place is different. It's like something out of a glitzy magazine. I have to keep pinching myself.'

'Mmm, I get the sense that you don't feel that you deserve what you have. It's nice to be humble, but you shouldn't beat yourself up that you've landed on your feet, angel.'

Vanessa smiled. 'I know, it's... I'm being silly, but, I dunno, I guess... sometimes I don't *feel* like I deserve it. That I haven't done enough to warrant such a lifestyle.'

'Yep, you are being silly.'

'I owe it all to Curtis. Everything.'

'You married a cracking man that's done well for himself. You've got ya head screwed on, girly,' said Delphine with a wink. 'And *he* appreciates everything he has in his life. You and the kids included. You'd never find a better fella in a million years... Lucky so-and-so.' She chuckled and squirted some cream on Vanessa's neck. 'Your neck's burning, lovey.'

'Oh, thanks. Didn't notice.'

'And trust me... he's a lucky sod to have you, too. You, my angel, are a little goddess.'

Vanessa beamed. Delphine always knew how to put a huge smile on her face.

They sat drinking their teas as the noisy hustle of the beach buzzed around them. It was scorching hot now. Delphine's mood seemed to shift. She opened her mouth as if to speak, then stopped herself.

'What?' asked Vanessa. 'What were you about to say?'

'It doesn't matter. I...'

'Delphine, what is it?'

'Well, OK... I had it again. It was... much... clearer this time.'

Vanessa sipped her tea and said nothing.

'Sorry, sorry... sorry... I know you don't like—'

Vanessa let out a nervous laugh. 'Delphine, I thought we agreed. We don't *do* this.'

'Yes, but what sort of friend would I be if I kept it to myself?'

'Um, the kind of friend who respects my wishes.' Vanessa shifted around, uncomfortable now. 'Sorry, it's just... I don't like the idea of...' She didn't finish the sentence. What she wanted to say was she couldn't bear the idea of someone probing into her mind and delving into her personal thoughts... *her memories*. It didn't sit right with her. Even if Delphine was a close friend.

'I know, I know... I just wanted to warn you, that's all. Just in case!'

'Just in case of what? Your prediction... vision, or whatever, is true?'

Delphine took hold of her hand. 'It was a dream... Well, initially a dream...'

'Delphine, come on—'

'OK, let me just say this. If anyone from your past comes back into your life, then you need to get rid of them. Don't let them back in. That's it. There, that's all I wanted to say.'

A cold shudder shot through Vanessa's entire body, causing her to twitch. She forced a smile. 'OK. Thanks. Duly noted.' She almost added, *now, please stop having strange visions about me. Save all that for your paying clients,* but decided against it.

'I will not mention it again... Fancy some oysters from The Forge?'

'Won't there be a mega queue?'

'There was earlier. But I don't mind. I'm sure I'll get chatting to someone... I normally do.'

'Oh, God, I almost forgot. I wanted to ask if you'd join us for dinner next Saturday. We have Jonas coming too.'

'Jonas? The South African guy?'

'Uh-huh.'

Delphine gave her a mischievous smile. 'Didn't you say he was a divorcee?'

Vanessa shrugged. 'I might have.'

'Mm. Guess I could check my schedule. But only if you bake me a cake!'

'Sure, I will bake you a cake... but you should lower your expectations. I am not renowned for my baking skills.'

'I'm sure it will be delicious. So, how do you know this Jonas, Vee?'

'I was his account manager back in London. His company in the city used to lease vehicles from us.'

'And he lives here? In Whitstable?'

'He does now. He's got a place along Marine Terrace. Curtis hooked up with him as soon as he established Jonas was a member of one of the local bike riding groups. I reckon you'd like him.'

4

Curtis walked up the driveway of the neighbouring property, package in hand. He spotted a man watering his pot plants by the front door. He assumed this was the parcel's intended recipient, Mr A Gates. He'd yet to be formally introduced to his neighbour. The package had been mistakenly left at their house with a bunch of others.

'Hey, how are you doing? We had your package left next door. I'm Curtis. Recently moved in next door.'

His well-tanned neighbour was wearing nothing but a pair of red and white striped boxer shorts, bright yellow crocs and a faded white baseball cap with a *Disneyland Paris* logo on the front. The man peered up, not bothering to switch off the hose, and said, 'Stick it by the door.'

Curtis had to bite his lip to stop himself sniggering. The guy's getup might have come across as cute on a cheeky toddler, but on a bloke in his late fifties with a big flabby stomach and a pair of misshapen moobs, it looked a tad creepy.

Curtis placed the package by the door. 'Sure, I'll pop it here.'

Gates gave him a curt nod by way of thanks as he continued watering his pot plants.

'See you around then,' said Curtis.

Vanessa had suggested that Curtis use the exchange as a way of breaking the ice. A way to get a feel for what their new neighbours were like. He didn't foresee matey booze-ups and day trips to the park. And next time, the ungrateful old goat could collect his own package, he decided as he made his way off the bungalow's drive.

Curtis went home via the back gate and found Jude and Sofia shooting each other with water pistols, which they instantly fired at him as soon as he'd stepped through the gate. He threw his arms in the air. 'You can't shoot an unarmed man! It's against the rules, guys.'

The pair chuckled as they each dunked their miniature Super Soaker in the pool to refill.

'Ten seconds... then we're coming to get you good,' sang Sofia, her long, brunette hair dripping wet and plastered against her face. 'We're counting, Daddy.'

'Wait, wait... I have a proposal, kids... just don't attack. I'll make you an offer you cannot refuse. Hear me out.'

Jude pumped the pistol. 'I think we should get him. It's a trick!'

'A giant ice-cream sundae,' said Curtis. 'With whipped cream. Loads of whipped cream! And chocolate shavings too. Deal?'

The pair nodded eagerly.

Curtis nipped inside via the sliding door and found his wife walking around the kitchen island with her laptop facing outwards.

'It's a negative on those neighbours, Vee,' said Curtis,

wiping water from his neck. 'I recall the builders saying he was a moaning pain in the backside too.'

'Oh, he's back now,' said Vanessa. She spun the laptop around.

Curtis saw a man's face on the screen. He almost didn't recognise Michael at first. He'd not seen Vanessa's father for many months, and he was now sporting a huge bushy beard that made his own resemble a scatter of bumfluff in comparison. But despite the beard, he registered those large brown eyes that sparkled with amusement and the heavy laughter lines etched around them. Curtis thought Michael's face appeared rounder and wondered if he'd put on a bit of weight, or if this was a combination of the shaved head and bushy facial hair, or the camera adding a few pounds.

'Big C! Oh, yes, love the beard. Makes you look butch. Like that Tom Hardy in *Taboo*,' said Michael.

'If only,' said Curtis.

Vanessa laughed. 'Yeah, if only.' She flashed Curtis a teasing grin.

'JB has just started giving me the tour. This kitchen... oh, gosh, it is stunning. I can't wait to see the rest of the house. Show me everything. I want to explore every single inch of this magnificent pad,' said Michael.

'So, how's Tenerife, Michael?' asked Curtis.

Michael puffed out his cheeks. 'Well, it's super crazy at the karaoke bar. But I love it. Love every minute.'

Sofia charged in waving her water pistol, screeching, 'Water fight, water fight... Time to have a water fight!'

Jude strolled in, swinging the pistol at his side and looking bored now.

'Come and say hi to Grandad,' said Vanessa, lowering the screen to put Michael level with the kids.

Michael let out an exaggerated gasp. 'Holy bananas! Who are you two?'

'Hello, Grandad Neal,' squealed Sofia.

'Hiya, my little walnut whip. Goodness, you've grown. You must be at least twelve now!'

Sofia chuckled. 'No. I'm only six, Grandad.'

'What about you, cool cat? You old enough to drive your dad's car yet?' asked Michael.

'I'm nine soon,' confirmed Jude with a proud smile.

Michael lowered his voice to a secretive tone and said, 'You know, if you squirt Daddy in the shorts, it will look like he peed himself.'

Sofia and Jude shared a wide grin, but before they had a chance to raise their pistols, Vanessa said, 'Um, no way. No water pistols in the house. Wait until Daddy's outside and then feel free to blast him in the shorts as much as you like.'

Curtis shook his head and feigned an expression of pure indignation. 'Outrageous. I might have to reconsider making these ice-cream sundaes.'

Jude hid the pistol behind his back and smirked. Sofia followed his actions, though with a big, toothy grin.

'JB, that little lady is the spit of you when you were that age,' said Michael with a fond smile.

Vanessa grinned coyly. 'Yes, Dad.'

'Daddy, can we show Grandad Neal the cinema room? Can we? Please?' pleaded Sofia.

Michael gasped. 'Wowser! Did you say a cinema room? No way. This I have to see. Take me there immediately, guys.'

'It's the next room on the tour, Dad,' said Vanessa.

'I'll whip up these ice creams before I get ambushed,' said Curtis.

'Yummy and scrummy,' said Sofia.

'Chocolate and vanilla for me, Big C. With a big fat juicy strawberry on the top,' said Michael. 'Aw, ooh, we're on the move again,' he continued as Vanessa walked out of the kitchen and past the dining room. 'Oh, God, love, love, love that table. This place is so voguish. It's like I'm being shown around a famous footballer's swish abode.'

Curtis chuckled. Michael Neal was certainly a character. He'd always thought Michael resembled the type of man you'd expect to open his mouth and speak with a huge, strident voice, something akin to Brian Blessed, but he spoke in a soft, camp voice which didn't seem to fit his huge, bear-like appearance. Curtis enjoyed seeing the happy, almost childlike beam on Vanessa's face whenever she connected with her father. He only wished the man was closer so he could be a regular part of Vanessa's and the children's lives too. They all adored him.

VANESSA FACED the laptop towards herself and grinned at her dad. 'Well, here we are, third floor. I've saved the best for last. Ready?'

'The suspense is killing me. But surely nothing can beat that lounge room and that awesome chill-out balcony...'

Vanessa spun the laptop so he could see the open-plan bedroom. She'd nipped up earlier and opened up the doors, so the view struck him immediately. But she guessed it wasn't just the view that had grabbed his attention. It was the deep, free-standing bath in the corner that was causing his silent astonishment.

'Interesting feature. What do you think, Dad?'

It took a while for her dad to respond, then he said, 'I... I stand corrected. This is the cherry on the cake. Oh, my, you're so lucky. A bubbly bath with a sea view and a fresh breeze on your face. I'm... it's... it's... divine.'

'It's a lovely touch, right?'

'Ooh, I need this in my life.'

If Vanessa was honest with herself, she'd not been as struck on the entire *bath with a view* idea as Curtis was. It wasn't so much the *view* part – more the *bath in a bedroom* idea as a whole. Vanessa enjoyed long, private soaks where she got to escape the world behind closed doors, and she didn't think she'd get much privacy taking a dip in here. Plus, Curtis liked showers, and she couldn't foresee him jumping in there too often. She hardly had cause to complain, as the bathroom on the second floor was fantastic, but this tub seemed rather superfluous to her. But her husband had been so ecstatic when he'd revealed the plan, she'd not wanted to burst his joyful bubble and agreed it would make a pleasant addition to the room. In principle, the idea was a good one, but only for a room in a swanky hotel for a couple's weekend retreat. Although she'd known that her dad would be blown away by this focal point.

Vanessa walked out onto the wide balcony, pleased the afternoon had stayed clear and bright so her dad would get a proper sense of what the scenery was like from the top floor. She'd have preferred him to be here in the flesh. She'd have loved that more than anything.

'I'm paranoid about the kids coming up here alone. I might have to put a lock on the bedroom door. Sofia's like a bloody kangaroo sometimes, and it's a long way down.'

'Mm, now I wonder where she gets that from. Wow, would you look at this?'

Vanessa walked to the right of the decked area and positioned the laptop on the glass balcony so he could see the beach line stretching out into the distance. After a mile or so, the land curved inwards where you were able to make out the long row of multicoloured beach huts on West Beach.

'So where is the harbour from here?' he asked.

'Can you see that tall grey building? That's the asphalt plant, which is where the Harbour Market is.'

'Hum, not really.' He chuckled.

'Well, you'd love all the Seaford restaurants there, Dad.

You really would.'

'I have heard it is marvellous. One of my regulars lived there for a time. He said it's a real trendy, hip place. He's a bit of an art fanatic. He sold a few pieces that he'd painted of the area. I can't wait to get over. If it wasn't for that blasted pandemic...'

'Dad, I understand. Don't be silly.'

'Things are getting better, though. The scene is hotting back up! I'll soon have a bath with a view to rival your own... No, sod that... a giant hot tub with sparkling lights and built-in speakers!'

'I don't doubt it.' Vanessa moved the laptop back to face her. 'So, any special guy... or gal, in your life at the moment?'

'Nooo, not at the moment. And no gals... I think that faze of my life has now faded way into the past. Just distant memories. I have lots of friends... lots of fabulous friends, and that's all I'm looking for these days.'

'As long as you're happy.'

He kissed his fingers and placed them on the screen's camera. 'I'm glad *you're* so happy, Jellybean. I'm over the moon.'

Vanessa laughed. Her dad hadn't called her *Jellybean* since she'd been in her early teens. The name embarrassed her as she'd got older, and so he'd started calling her *JB* instead. He'd never called her Vanessa, and she'd often wondered if deep down he didn't like the name. She knew for a fact that her mum had been the one who'd chosen it, so maybe that was why. But hearing the nickname now filled her with a feeling of warm nostalgia.

'And you're well... in yourself? With... with... everything?' he asked.

Vanessa nodded. 'Everything is fine. I'm fine.'

She'd always been able to rely on her dad. And she always would.

He interlocked his fingers and bent them back until he heard a satisfying click as he viewed the photos on his laptop. The house was nice. *Really* nice. Maybe Essa had won the lotto or something, he pondered.

He didn't know the area, though a bit of quick researching confirmed that this was an affluent part of town where some of the priciest houses in Kent could be located, although he suspected this house still stood apart from most of the other properties on the parade. The photos were taken from the front of the house and the unusual, dissymmetrical building wouldn't have looked out of place in a luxurious Spanish complex with its cube design, glass balconies and sea-view location. The bottom of the property had a rustic brick exterior, the middle was painted dove white, and the top floor overlaid with cedar wood siding. It dwarfed the neighbouring properties, one of which was a bungalow, the other a chalet bungalow.

The original buyer, a John David Pascall, had paid just ninety-five thousand for the house in the mid-nineties. The estimated price now... One... point... four... million. He puffed out his cheeks and re-read that. *Wow, Little Essa, you cheeky fucking cow*, he thought.

Curtis and Vanessa Pascall purchased the property three years ago – or at least they were added to the deeds, as no purchase price was mentioned here. Had old man Pascall signed the house over to the son for him to renovate? *Lucky swine.*

He slammed down the laptop and drummed his fingers on the table. He now fancied a huge blood-soaked fillet steak and a mountain of crispy fries drenched in Frank's RedHot Sauce.

Delphine exited the phone shop and stepped onto the busy High Street. She'd chuckled when she'd spotted the yellow iPhone case with a confused cartoon duck printed on it. She'd not even bothered seeing what else was on offer and opted for that one straight away.

Delphine observed the hustle and bustle of the town centre and when several classic cars rolled past her in the stream of heavy traffic, her mind flashed back to when she'd been a teenager here. The town sure was a different place back then. She enjoyed buzzing about in a car in those days. Her papa's dazzling red Spitfire Triumph, which she adored. She pictured herself cruising along the High Street, roof down, wearing her floppy velvet Baker Boy hat, her long dark hair flying out wildly from underneath it. *Good times.*

She'd not been behind the wheel for almost two decades now. Her nerves could not cope with driving these days. Too many cars on the road for a start, and everyone seemed to be in a frantic rush. Manners were non-existent. If you dared to get in the wrong lane, or made a small mistake, drivers were so quick to get aggressive, it just seemed so daunting and relentless. This little town struggled to cope with the number of vehicles that ventured into it, and often the tight lanes and slender streets were choked with frustrated motorists. She got around on foot, bike or by taxi nowadays.

Many of her friends had long since moved away from the area. They'd moaned the town had become a victim of its own success. Too rowdy, crowded, and overpriced. The quirky town wasn't big enough for all the hordes of people and vehicles that descended on the place, but if she was honest, she loved all the hullabaloo and buzz that the diverse crowds brought to the area. She enjoyed meeting all the new people that came to stay at her boat house. Just these last few months, she'd had guests from Germany, Canada and China.

Unfortunately, her last visitors, two cocky lads from Brighton, pinched one of the framed pictures out of the property, so her next stop was the Harbour Gallery to find a replacement piece for her guest house. The sketch taken, a vibrant image of a shaggy dog sitting outside some retro beach huts, had set her back three hundred quid many moons ago. Delphine enjoyed shopping for new prints and portraits – *so every cloud*. She decided she'd also nip to the florists and see if anything took her fancy, too.

Delphine waited at the pedestrian crossing. The line of cars stopped, but several mopeds with 'under instruction' hi-vis jackets zipped past without stopping, forcing a young woman with a pushchair to halt. Delphine caught the woman's eye and raised her eyebrows.

The woman paid no heed to her, scrunched up her face at the riders, and griped, 'Fall off and die, pricks!'

Such hostility, thought Delphine, as she crossed the road and hurried off toward Harbour Street, which appeared just as busy.

As she walked, her mind kept wandering back to her conversation with Vanessa, and it caused a grim sensation to wash over her. Just like an immense, gloomy cloud that hovered above her and refused to dissipate. Delphine knew her friend thought her gift was silly nonsense, but the idea of Vanessa not heeding her warning made her feel rather sombre.

The vision of that beach with the high sandstone cliff had been tormenting her of late. She often saw it so clearly in her mind since that initial dream... The subsiding yellow rock... The piles of crumbled rubble and crashing surf... Vanessa running barefoot across that beach... Of course, she didn't know *where* this place was, but in her mind's eye she'd been standing on that beach watching the scene with an intense feeling of sorrow and regret flooding her senses. The dream itself had been so oppressive it left her drained and queasy. But Delphine knew what she'd witnessed was no premonition. That event had already come to pass... A long time ago. No, this was a forewarning linked to the consequences of this past incident.

Delphine hadn't identified the other person present in the dream. The person she'd witnessed a young Vanessa escaping from. She'd viewed them only as a dark, threatening shape. But she knew that if preventive measures were not implemented to stop *that* person clawing their way back into her friend's life, then Vanessa's entire world would come crashing down around her and hurt everyone in her very orbit.

They would come soon; of that she was certain.

7

It was a cracking day. Todd sipped his vodka, stretched out his legs and gazed over the restaurant's balcony. *South Beach – heaven on earth*, he decided. The white, sandy beach below was packed out with bronzed bodies, and his eyes hunted for something tasty to focus on. With plenty to choose from, selecting wasn't a straightforward task.

He settled his eyes on a petite blonde with short hair and a tangerine-coloured bikini. He let out a content sigh and decided he'd be happy to stay here all day and get ripped. Unfortunately, his three o'clock meeting with the board of directors would screw with that plan. Work was a total bitch, he concluded, but he'd ordered the lobster special, would have a potent cocktail for his afters, and make the most of his mid-week boozy lunch. The minx in the bikini started slathering sun cream on her sun-kissed thighs. Todd popped a chunk of ice in his mouth and decided he'd like a piece of *that* for his dessert instead.

A waiter appeared at his table, a gangly fella with a toothy smile. 'Can I get you another drink, sir? Same again, perhaps?' He sounded like a Bostonian, or possibly a New Yorker.

'Yeah, sure, same again,' said Todd.

'You on holiday, sir?'

'Nope, I live here. I work in the business district. Biscayne Boulevard. I'm a construction manager.'

'Oh, but you're from Texas, right, sir? Where about're you from?'

'Woodville. But born in Lubbock. You know it?'

'I think so... Wait, wasn't that where Buddy Holly was born, right?'

'Uh-huh.'

'It's a real friendly place, right? That's what they say.'

Todd grinned at him. 'Oh, you bet, son. Friendliest place on the planet.'

The woman yanked at her bikini bottom, giving Todd a brief flash of whiter flesh beneath the tight swimwear.

Todd grinned. 'Oh, man, I'd give my left arm to have that slut riding my dirty dong. I bet she has the gusto of a spirited teenage horse-rider breaking in a plucky, untamed, Chickasaw pony.' He said this more to himself than to the waiter. Though he knew the puny jackass had heard him. He'd wanted him to hear.

The waiter peered over the railings. He saw the woman, then pulled a *that is not appropriate* face, and continued to wait for Todd's order, his cheeks reddening.

Todd enjoyed dropping inappropriate and lewd comments to strangers. He did it often, just to see them cringe. But he'd met a few good people this way, too. Like-minded folk who shared the same sordid interests he did. It was always nice to have friends who liked the same passions and hobbies you did. That was his way of thinking, anyway.

Todd tossed another ice cube into his mouth, crunching it in frustration – the fact that he'd never get to ride that delicious little mare on the beach was now annoying him. 'Man... slap my tinker balls,' he muttered.

The waiter appeared super embarrassed now. His cheeks were glowing the colour of a fat, juicy tomato.

Todd chuckled at the weedy runt and almost choked on the ice. 'Just get me a melon and raspberry swizzle. And don't be shy with the vodka, son. And what's the story with my lobster, hey? Did someone send the cook out to catch the damn thing with his bare hands? Or has he taken the fucking crustacean out on a damn date? I don't have all afternoon to sit around on my fat tush licking ice cubes like a mental patient.'

'Um, OK, so one swizzle, extra vodka. And I'll chase up your seafood, sir. Shouldn't be long now.'

'Good man,' said Todd, focussing back on the beach. *Hurry the fuck up, or I'll shove that lobster up your keester,* he considered with a one-sided grin.

'Motherfucker,' Todd muttered, seeing that the tangerine bikini hussy had vacated the spot. He caught sight of her walking away, weaving through a row of skinny palm trees. Adding to his irritation was an email buzzing through on his phone. He grumbled to himself and read the message, a sudden vision popping into his mind of the waiter mixing his cocktail with his pencil-like dong, with a big, cunning grin on his face. *Well, it all adds to the flavour, so screw him,* thought Todd. He'd had much worse things to pass his lips than a cock-stirred melon swizzle. Just so long as the stupid piss-stick didn't forget to add the raspberries, or... *What the hell is this?* It took several moments for Todd to comprehend what he was seeing on the screen. He squinted in the sun to view it again. What exactly was he looking at here?

He stood up so fast he sent his seat clattering down behind him. Then he raced from the establishment without paying his bill.

. . .

TODD JOGGED TO HIS CAR, stuck the engine on, and cranked up the AC. He viewed the email again. Maybe he'd taken the contents out of context. Sweat poured down his face. His shirt was stuck to his body, the perspiration soaking his pits. Even his hands were slick with sweat. This was a total fucking disaster. No, it was an absolute, ass-banging master fuck of all proportions.

Todd selected Ritchie's number.

He answered on the second ring. 'Yo, how you doing, bro?' asked Ritchie, sounding like some bloody Californian stoner or surf bum.

'We need to meet. Right now!'

'But, Todd, I'm busy—'

'NOW, Ritchie!'

There was silence on the phone, and Todd assumed Ritchie had hung up. Then he said, 'As you're asking so nicely, OK then, Todd.'

8

'Let's hope she eases off the predictions tonight. We don't need any foresights, or any of that psychic stuff, whilst we're pigging out on our spicy fajitas,' said Vanessa.

'It might make the evening more interesting,' said Curtis.

'Or it might make Jonas feel uncomfortable if she starts foretelling his future whilst he's tucking into a slice of cake and cream.'

Curtis laughed. 'Come on, you know Jonas better than I do. Not much would faze him. He's an open-minded guy. It's just a bit of fun. Anyway, didn't you say she wasn't even that good at forecasting the future, so why does it matter?'

Vanessa flicked him with a tea towel. 'Stop it! I never said that. I think the world of Delphine.'

'Mmm. No, wait. I might've said that. To be fair, she didn't see her own divorce coming, did she? Or have an omen that her hubby was bonking his way through his entire admin team at that media firm.'

'Curtis, don't be mean! That's because she's always too wrapped up in her clients' love affairs. I feel sorry for her. She actually has a huge following with thousands of happy customers. It's not just "a bit of fun" to her. She takes it very seriously.'

'I'm just kidding... But I'm still not sure you should play cupid here, Vee.'

'Delphine and Jonas are both lonely. I bet they will really hit it off. They are both a bit... I dunno...'

'Bonkers?' Curtis peered into the plastic cake container, admiring Vanessa's work.

Even she had to admit that she'd been over the moon with the results of her little baking expedition. She'd never been much of an artist in the kitchen, but her raspberry tiramisu cake looked rather impressive.

Curtis pretended to lift the lid. 'Yum. Just a quick cheeky taste.'

'Don't you dare. And no, not bonkers... eccentric. I'll also tell her you said that.'

'Please don't, Vee,' said Curtis with a big, daft smile.

'Best behaviour, you. Or I might. Then you'll be in trouble.'

Curtis drummed his fingers against the lid of the container. 'Good job the kids aren't here. That cake wouldn't be safe from Sofia's sweet tooth! We could eat it now and serve the guests that toffee cheesecake that's stashed in the freezer. I'm game for that plan.'

'I bet you are. But I've sent Delphine a photo now, and she has already messaged back saying how wonderful it looks. So mitts off, buddy.'

Curtis let out a long whistle. 'Wow, sending cake snaps. Now I know you're proud of this masterpiece. You'll be on Bake Off soon, Vee.'

Vanessa placed the tea towel over the top of the cake container. 'No chance of that. I couldn't handle the pressure. I'm way too flaky to be on TV.'

Curtis gently pulled her over to him and kissed her neck. 'Well, we have a few hours free. We could make the most of the kids being away.'

She let him kiss and caress her for a few moments before chuckling. 'That will just have to wait. You have jobs to do.' She pecked him on the nose. 'We need two bottles of red. We don't have any. That's the only thing Delphine drinks.'

'Ahh, can't she bring her own? She probably will.'

'And if she doesn't? What's she meant to drink?'

'Champagne, chardonnay, beer... tap water?'

'Red, Curtis.'

'Um, can't you just ask her if she's bringing some?'

'Curtis, I'm not asking our guests if they intend to bring their own plonk! And I don't want to be the one to tell her there's no wine because my sex-mad hubby wanted a fruity afternoon and so refused to go to the shops.'

Curtis let out an exaggerated sigh. 'Hmm. Fine. Which one does she like?'

Vanessa smiled at him, gave him a seductive wink and said, 'I'll text you the names. I'm going to get the starters prepared. Then attempt to make myself beautiful.'

Curtis pinched her bum. 'You're always beautiful!'

She flashed him a playful grin. 'I see what your game is here. Go easy on the sherbets tonight. Perhaps they'll both leave early... and—'

'I'll be pushing them out the door by ten pm!'

'Yeah, more like you'll be pissed as a badger and chewing their ears off until gone midnight.'

Curtis pretended to be offended. 'I will *not* be pissed as a badger... Why a badger, anyway? Who says that?'

'Isn't it a thing?'

'I believe it's mad as a badger and pissed as a parrot.'

Vanessa shook her head. 'Well, I prefer pissed as a badger.'

'We could've been upstairs and finished by now, instead of debating which animals are more likely to be pissed.'

'You're right. And had a shower. Um, and a coffee.'

Curtis wagged a finger at her. 'Right. I'm not taking the bait. I'm going to the shops. I'll take my bike. It's another scorcher, so I reckon the roads will be jammed with visitors heading into town.'

'Go to the M&S Food Hall. Grab a few baguettes too. Oh, and creme fraiche for the soup.'

'Two bottles of red and three baguettes? On my bike? Maybe a string of garlic, too?'

'I've got plenty of garlic. Be quick.'

Curtis winked and, using a coarse French accent, said, 'Well, madame, I shall be faster than a mad, bladdered badger!'

———————

9

C urtis stood in the hallway, sipping on a bottle of beer as he watched his wife descend the stairs.

Vanessa got halfway down, stopped, and smiled at him. 'Well, what do you reckon?'

Curtis shrugged, pretended to pull a disappointed expression and said, 'I dunno, Vee, I just thought you were going to make an effort tonight. No time to change now, though, I guess. Wait, let me get a proper gander.' He made a show of rubbing his eyes, opened them wide, and gaped in shock. 'Wow! You look... I can't find the words... I'm speechless.'

Vanessa laughed and continued down the stairs. 'Yes, that'll be the day.'

Curtis couldn't take his eyes off her. Vanessa looked sensational. She wore a body-hugging dress that showed all her wonderful curves. It was light blue with small daisy prints, and tied at the front with spaghetti-like straps. She had her warm blond hair down, flowing in wavy locks and swept over to one side. Her feet were bare, her nails a pale pink colour with a tiny sparkle of glitter on them. He felt underdressed in his grey chinos and boring blue, short-sleeved shirt.

'I have poured you a glass of white wine, m'lady. It's on the lounge table.'

Vanessa planted a long kiss on his cheek. 'Why, thank you, sir. But I'll take it on the balcony.'

WHILST VANESSA PREPARED THE STARTERS, Curtis had made the introductions and Jonas and Delphine were already making small talk and seemed very relaxed in each other's company.

Delphine wore a berry-red off the shoulder lace dress and a white knitted hat that had beaded strands flowing down from it, which were entwined with her long, ringleted hair. Delphine's hair appeared a different colour than her normal dark brown. It seemed to have a reddish tinge under the light, and Curtis wondered if she'd dyed it especially for this gathering.

He'd tried dying out the greying patches on his own dark hair, but it was becoming a losing battle and he knew it would only be a matter of time before he'd have to succumb to the fact that he'd be a proper silver fox, just like his old man. Not an issue Jonas needed to concern himself with, because his head was totally bald and seemed to shine as though he'd polished it tonight. He wore a short-sleeved shirt with a loud Mexican skulls and red roses design. A shirt, Curtis considered, that most guys could never pull off, but Jonas managed it. He looked quite sharp in it. The South African had a big, wide build, and the tight shirt made him appear like a burly rugby player. He also wore a big pair of round designer spectacles.

Jonas scanned the room and chuckled. 'I think you under-sold this place to me, Curtis.' Jonas turned to Delphine. 'You know what he told me, Delphine... He said, "It's nice, because we get a touch of natural light in the house." A touch? Wow, it's more like an avalanche of light. This pad is simply beautiful.'

Curtis, using a fake plummy voice, said, 'Thank you. Now, please, come this way. I'll prepare us all some drinks.'

Jonas let out a big, infectious laugh. 'Sounds like a plan to me.'

CURTIS CRACKED open his fifth bottle of beer and joined the group on the lounge balcony. He'd need to take it easy on the beverages, otherwise he'd be legless by ten. He had plans for a romantic midnight soak in the tub with Vee. Curtis wanted to watch the storm from their bedroom whilst sipping a glass of bubbly in the foamy bubbles with his wife. The predicted storm had yet to materialise, although the shifting clouds appeared dark and threatening now.

Jonas and Delphine had been deep in discussion about social media posts for twenty minutes. They were now debating some video they'd both seen about some young guys in Bangladesh who practically kidnapped a homeless man in order to cut his hair, wash him and clothe him in clean clobber.

Jonas shook his head. 'Don't get me wrong, Delphine, I'm all for seeing the good in everyone, but I see stuff like that as self-glorifying. You wanna help a guy out, excellent... but why the need to film it and post it all over social media? Surely it's so those egotistical people can sit on their high horses and brag about how amazing they are. Right?'

'They might just want to share their experience. Or they do those things to enlighten people and encourage others to do good,' said Delphine.

Jonas chuckled, showing the sizeable gap in his front teeth. 'Eish. Yeah, guess I'm too cynical. Taking a favourable view is nice, Delphine. Keep the faith. Good on you.'

'Yeah, I'm on the fence on this one,' said Curtis. 'I mean, I've not seen the particular video, but... I'd say... well, I guess it seems that if someone helps an old lady across the road these days, they need to shout about it. The act alone should be enough. In my eyes.'

'What about you, Vee?' asked Jonas.

Vanessa gazed out across the balcony, sipping on her wine. 'I don't do social media.'

'Yeah, but what's your view?' asked Jonas. 'Self-promoting... or virtuous?'

Vanessa shrugged. 'I think helping to better someone's life in any way is a fantastic thing to do. And if the person involved has no qualms about the experience being shared, then I guess there is no real harm in it.'

Jonas nodded thoughtfully. 'What if *you* were the homeless person? Would you want it shared?'

'No. No, I wouldn't,' said Vanessa.

On the horizon, Curtis spotted a vivid flash of light. 'The storm is here,' he announced, holding his beer up high.

'You like a storm, bruh? I'll have to take you over to Johannesburg... Woo, the storms we get over there are phenomenal. The Highveld creates some batshit-crazy lightning storms. We're talking like bolts of angry lightning that are like special effects out of a movie. Like the end of days is coming. Stunning to witness, yet quite terrifying too, especially if you get caught out in a bad one.'

'Sounds pretty crazy,' said Curtis. 'I'd love to witness that!'

'A guy that worked for us got struck in Boksburg. Killed him. He got collared stepping out of his car. A witness clocked it from their window and said it was like an angry finger of the Gods smashing out of the sky. Bloody awful.'

'Christ. Is that common?' asked Curtis.

'There are plenty of deaths and injuries in the Gauteng provinces, Curtis. It's no joke. Sometimes there'll be plenty of electricity in the sky, yet no power to put on the lights. Mad, huh?'

Another flash hit the horizon, brighter than before.

'You ever hear about people changing after being struck?' asked Delphine.

'Changed? Well, yeah, getting scarred... spinal cord issues, weakness of muscles and even brain injuries are common,' said Jonas.

'No, I mean changed... in a good way. Beneficial changes,' said Delphine.

'What, like turning them into a superhuman?' chuckled Jonas. 'Not personally. I have seen some pretty unusual burns left by the strikes. Patterns that have the appearance of tree branches. The lightning bursts the blood vessels and as the electric surges through them, it imprints on their skin.'

'I remember a story that another clairvoyant told me. About a woman in Croatia,' said Delphine.

Curtis caught Vanessa's eye as he sipped his beer. She gave him a quick, comical grin and raised her eyebrows. Delphine had at least made it to nine thirty.

Delphine continued. 'A young woman. A market trader in Zadar. This power cable on her stand got hit, and she suffered some awful injuries. But she survived and a few weeks after the incident, she started getting powerful visions. It's said she's now one of the most respected psychic practitioners in Europe.'

'Wow, that must have hit the spot!' said Curtis. 'What's she called, Madam Flash? No, wait, that sounds more like a stripper!' He chuckled at his own joke.

'Come and witness the amazing... the electrifying... Madaaam Flash!' bellowed Jonas, which he then followed with a bout of uncontrollable laughter.

Delphine giggled. 'Hey, I never said it was true! But stranger things have happened.'

A crack of vivid purple lightning streaked the horizon. No sign of a drop of rain yet.

Jonas started clicking his fingers to the music. 'Cool tune. What song is this?'

'Oh, it's "Hail Bop" by Django, Django. Me and Vee watched them live about five years ago. Amazing band.'

'Turn it up, bruh,' said Jonas. 'Let's get this jowl started!'

'I dunno about you guys, but I'm about ready for dessert now,' said Delphine, clapping. 'Cake, cake, cake... Come on, let's get a glimpse of this masterpiece, Vee.'

'I'll go down and grab that, Vee,' said Curtis.

'Hold your horses. How many beers have you had?' asked Vanessa, flashing him a teasing grin.

'I won't drop it!' said Curtis. 'At least I'll do my best *not* to.'

'Don't trust him, Vee. That's too much of a risk,' said Jonas.

'You just get the drinks. I'll deal with the cake,' said Vanessa, heading back inside. 'Anyone want cream?'

Jonas patted his stomach. 'Probably shouldn't, but what the hell?'

'I'll take a splash,' said Delphine.

'I'll bring it up,' called Vanessa.

'Drinks, guys?' asked Curtis, using his phone to turn up the Bluetooth speaker.

'Red for me, Curtis. Would you be a star and bring up my bottle? I left it in the kitchen,' said Delphine.

'I'll take a beer, cheers,' said Jonas, now bopping to the track.

Curtis stepped inside, grinning as he left the pair laughing and boogying.

· · ·

CURTIS POURED DELPHINE'S WINE, humming to himself. Vanessa was busy clanking about and seemed to be avidly searching every drawer in the kitchen's island.

'You could be right, Vee... they seem to like each other.'

'Uh-huh.'

'Told you Delphine would bring red wine,' he sang.

'You did.'

'What are you looking for, Vee?'

'The cake knife set. I'm wondering if we left it behind. Who packed the kitchen?'

'The removal guys packed everything, Vee. Didn't you notice it when you unpacked?'

'Not sure.'

Curtis walked over to the wooden knife block and pulled out a chunky steel knife. 'What's wrong with this big, bad boy? A knife is a knife, isn't it?'

'No, Curtis. It's a two-piece set that has a server too. An anniversary gift from your folks. It's dated. Our names are on it and everything.'

'Yeah, I knew that,' said Curtis, hiding a silly grin under his hand. It was the first he'd heard about this set. He'd most likely been chin wagging to his dad when Vee opened that present.

'Mmm, I'm sure you did, Curtis... Just pop that one on the tray. I'll use that instead.'

Curtis placed the knife onto the tray between the cake container and cream, then trotted over to the fridge to retrieve the beers. The doorbell chiming in the hallway stopped him. 'Who could that be?'

'Mr Gates probably wants you to turn the music down on the balcony. We should go inside now.'

'Sod that. It's not that late. Plus, it's the weekend.' Curtis opened the fridge. 'I'll just ignore it in case it's a salesman.'

'There wouldn't be anyone traipsing about down here now. Best check. Have a quick nosy on the screen first.'

'Go up, Vee. I'll take a gander.'

'Hurry then.'

Curtis strutted along the hallway towards the front door, humming as he walked. He considered going into the study to check the security camera on the driveway, but decided not to bother and just opened the door. A man stood between his cars. He had his back to Curtis and seemed to be admiring the Jeep Wrangler.

'Hey, you OK?' asked Curtis. 'Can I help?'

The man turned to him and smiled. 'Aw, how are you doing? Sorry, just checking out the monstrous tires on this motor. They are beastly. Is this the Rubicon, or Sport?'

'Rubicon. It's not mine... Well, my company just purchased some to lease. I've always fancied one, so thought I'd borrow her for a few months.'

'You tried it off-road yet?' asked the man, now eyeing up Vanessa's green Mini Cooper. 'I take it this must be the wife's motor?'

The man, despite the sticky weather, wore a tanned leather jacket, black jeans and had an old canvas bag hanging from his shoulder. His hair was shoulder length, dishevelled and shaggy. He stood shorter than Curtis at around five foot eight. The guy did have a rough around the edges vibe to him, but he seemed amicable enough.

'Nope, not really had the opportunity to take her cross-country,' said Curtis, wondering why the hell he'd started discussing his Jeep with the guy and not determined the reason for the stranger's appearance on his doorstep, and his sudden interest in his vehicles.

His expression must have conveyed his confusion to the man because he held out his hand and said, 'Hayden Knox. You must be Curtis?'

'Um, hi,' said Curtis, accepting the firm handshake, even more confused now the strange guy knew him by name.

A patter of rain started.

Hayden scratched his unshaven face and offered a welcoming smile. 'I'm looking for Vanessa. I know her from Bournemouth. We kinda grew up together.'

'Oh, I see. Is she expecting you?' asked Curtis, knowing she wasn't.

'No, no, nothing like that... I'm staying in the area for a while and thought it would be a crazy surprise for her if I turned up out of the blue to say hi. We haven't seen each other for like, cor, twenty-something years. How's her dad, Michael? He still doing OK?'

'Yeah, good. He's living abroad now.'

'A right character, hey? Essa was always close with her dad, so it must be difficult if he's not about.'

'Oh, yeah, he's still a character alright. I'll give Vee a shout,' said Curtis, stepping outside, pondering over the name *Essa*. His wife hadn't mentioned using that name before. Curtis expected to see Vanessa and the guests up on the balcony, but the sliding doors were shut and he couldn't see anyone in the lounge, yet he could hear Jonas's booming laughter and some funky jazz music playing. He assumed his wife had taken the small party inside, fearing that they were upsetting the neighbours.

'I saw some big, bald black bloke dancing out there, but he didn't see me,' said Hayden.

Curtis could see Delphine at the window and waved up, but she was too busy eating the cake to notice him. Then the rain came down properly. A really heavy battering. 'Step inside,' said Curtis. 'You can't stand out there in that!'

'Thanks. I can come back tomorrow... if it's a bad time,' said Hayden as he followed Curtis into the wide entrance hallway.

Curtis walked to the stairs and called up, 'Vee, Vee!' After getting no reply, he turned to Hayden. 'I tell you what, wanna pop up and say hi?'

'If you don't mind? It would be brilliant to say hello.'

'Can I get you a cold beer?'

Hayden smiled. 'Oh, defo, thanks. Amazing.'

A flash of lightning lit up the world outside and the rain started smashing down. Curtis could see Hayden clearly now in the lit hallway. The man appeared a few years older than Vanessa. He had heavy lines and dark circles around his pale blue eyes.

Curtis grabbed the beers and led the man up to the second floor.

'Awesome. I like these,' said Hayden, referring to the LED staircase tread lights. 'These steps walnut?'

'Um, yes,' confirmed Curtis.

Jonas's loud voice boomed out saying, 'I'm gonna be questioning your husband on this, Vee. Time to confess... are you sure you didn't buy this from the cake company in town?'

Curtis walked into the lounge and found the trio sitting on the sofas tucking into the cake. The mood was jolly, and everyone looked chilled and merry.

'Oh, yeah, it's lekker,' said Jonas.

'So tasty,' agreed Delphine.

'I don't know if I should be annoyed or flattered by your disbelief in my cake-making skills, Jonas,' said Vanessa. She caught Curtis's eye and gave him a sweet smile. Her cheeks were glowing a pinkish colour and he couldn't tell if this was because of the wine or the compliments about her cake. Probably a touch of both.

'I hope lekker means good, Jonas,' giggled Vanessa.

'Sure does,' confirmed Jonas.

Hayden unhurriedly came up the stairs behind Curtis,

running his hand along the glass balustrades. He seemed to be overwhelmed by the house.

'Hey, Vee, there is an old friend here to see you. Um... Hayden... Hayden... Knox.' Through his alcohol-induced haze, Curtis had almost forgotten the man's name.

Hayden stepped into the lounge. 'Hope you've saved a slice for me, Little Essa... It's been a long time. How you keeping?'

The music stopped at that moment and a rumble of distant thunder sounded from outside.

Vanessa's face went from a jolly pink flush to a chalky white colour. She appeared utterly stunned.

Curtis knew straight away he'd made a grave error in inviting this man inside their home without first consulting her.

It seemed clear to everyone present, too. The atmosphere in the room shifted the moment Hayden had stepped into the lounge; the moment they'd all witnessed the expression on Vanessa's face change from joy to something akin to shock, with a clear hint of outrage.

His wife now fixed Curtis with an expression of total disbelief. He knew that look. It said, *what the hell do you think you are doing, Curtis?*

Jonas laughed, but even that had a nervous edge to it. He stepped towards Hayden and shook his hand. 'How you doing? I'm Jonas Nangola.'

Hayden accepted the hand and grinned at the big South African. 'Alright? Good to meet you, mate. Boss shirt, by the way. Weirdly, that suits you.' He then turned to Delphine. 'Hello.'

Delphine gave Hayden a thin smile, with an accompanying look that suggested she didn't trust the man as far as she could throw him. 'Hello, there. I'm Delphine.'

'That's a pretty smart hat,' said Hayden.

'Thank you.'

'You knit that yourself?' asked Hayden.

Delphine flashed him a sarcastic smile in response and, with her eyes narrowed, stuck the fork into her piece of cake.

Curtis caught his wife and Delphine sharing a funny look... as though they knew more about this visitor than he did. He guessed he was no doubt reading way too much into the situation. Hayden was clearly an old flame whom Vanessa hadn't expected to see, and she most likely felt super embarrassed by his sudden appearance. He could understand that. Talk about mega awkward, especially with guests over.

Hayden smiled guilefully. 'Well, well, Essa... now who would have thought you'd end up in a tremendous gaff like this? What a magnificent home.' He turned back to Curtis. 'You have this built to your own specifications? Honestly, it's one of the best-looking properties along here.'

'Thanks. Yeah, I... well, we both got involved with the makeover. The kitchen was all Vee,' said Curtis as jovially as possible. He was desperate to morph this cringey, uncomfortable atmosphere he'd created into something more upbeat. Thankfully, the music came back on. He wasn't keen on the track but welcomed the noise from the bouncy house music. Some Ibiza classic Vanessa liked.

'Do you mind if I grab a seat? I have been walking a fair bit tonight,' said Hayden, plonking down next to Jonas before getting a reply. 'A cracking day earlier. Shame it's pissing down now, huh?'

'Take a load off,' said Curtis, avoiding Vanessa's laser-like glare. He wondered if he should ask Hayden to leave, but he'd given the guy a drink and it was belting down outside. He'd look a right arsehole if he did that. No, let him finish up, offer to order him a taxi and then ask him to vamoose as politely as possible – that seemed like the ideal plan of action here. If he explained to Vanessa that *he* didn't care who the guy was and that he knew they obviously had some history but wasn't worried... maybe then she'd relax a bit.

'You don't look very pleased to see me, Essa. Sorry, I know it's been such a long time. I had a few drinks in town and found myself walking up to say hi. Curtis said Michael's moved away. I bet you miss him.'

'Oh, did he?' said Vanessa in a monotone voice.

'He *come out* yet?' asked Hayden with a wry grin.

Vanessa ignored that question.

'Everyone was adamant Michael batted for the other side,' said Hayden, to no one in particular. 'It was a bit of a running joke, right, Essa?'

No one responded.

The excruciating quiet, filled only with the beat of the background music, made Curtis want to scream.

Hayden broke the awful, voiceless period. 'You ever go back to Bournemouth, Essa?'

Vanessa shook her head. 'No. Never.'

Hayden nodded at the family portrait on the wall. 'Cracking-looking kids, Essa. How old are they?'

'Six and eight,' said Vanessa.

Hayden smiled. 'I'm so pleased you're doing well. It's so good to see you again after all these years. Again, I'm sorry for dropping in unannounced. Perhaps I could take you and Curtis out for dinner one night?'

'No. That won't be necessary,' said Vanessa, her voice cold.

'So, Hayden, where do you live?' asked Jonas.

'I've been living in France for six years. Near Lillebonne. Came back last year,' confirmed Hayden.

'That's in the Normandy region, right?' said Jonas.

Hayden nodded and seemed surprised that Jonas knew this.

'I passed through there once. What the hell does a Brit do for work around there?' asked Jonas.

'I was working for a logistics company based near Le Havre Port. What about you guys?'

'I set up an insurance brokerage firm in London a few years ago,' said Jonas. 'I was a manager for a major recruitment company in Jo'burg, but I moved to the UK with my wife. But that all went... eish... wrong.'

Hayden turned to Curtis. 'What about you? I'm guessing from this place, architect... lawyer, or... I dunno, film director?'

Curtis saw Vanessa gulping down her wine and instantly refilling the glass.

'Vehicle leasing,' said Curtis. 'We have three branches in the UK. It's my old man's firm, but he's semi-retired now, so I look after things.'

Hayden raised his bottle. 'Good for you. Cheers.' He drained the beer and smacked his lips.

Curtis was about to offer to see the man out, but Hayden was now chatting away to Jonas and asking if he missed Johannesburg, and the moment passed.

CURTIS HAD drunk way too much and was struggling to keep up with the conversation between Jonas and Hayden. Vanessa and Delphine were on the balcony, chatting in conspiratorial tones, and he kept getting the odd bitter glare from his wife, obviously due to the fact that instead of frogmarching Hayden from the premises the moment the weather had eased, he'd instead let him drink three beers, several shots, showed him the cinema room, back garden and allowed him to use the toilet more than once.

Every time Hayden tried to engage Vanessa in small talk, she'd replied with quick, sharp answers, and Curtis knew he'd be in for a major scolding for letting him outstay his welcome. Or for letting him past the front door, period. Jonas wasn't helping the situation, as he'd been chewing the guy's ears off and was waffling on about his travels in France and how he'd considered moving to Bordeaux a few years ago.

Delphine had ordered a taxi and seemed offish and quieter since the new arrival, and it was obvious enough that she was only leaving so the other two would follow suit. Yet the other two men hadn't taken the hint and were a bit too comfortable. They had made no mention of leaving.

Delphine and Vanessa came back inside.

'Hey, Delphine, so you rent out a place on the beach. A converted boat house, right?' asked Hayden. 'Any availability?'

Delphine laughed, as if the very idea of her having any space was ludicrous. 'My place is booked solid until mid-October.'

'So where do *you* stay?' asked Hayden.

'I own a static caravan. Out of town,' said Delphine, eyeing him mistrustfully.

Curtis didn't know Delphine as well as his wife did, but he knew her well enough to know that the hostility she'd been showing Hayden seemed out of character.

Delphine and Vanessa's little furtive glances and chats were annoying him now. Had his wife confided in Delphine about this man? But why hadn't Vanessa just dragged *him* to one side and blatantly told him what her bloody problem was? It was like she'd been humiliated by Hayden's visit but she was blaming it all on *him*.

Curtis had also seen the peculiar, brief glances Vanessa and Hayden had shared... like they couldn't quite tell if they wanted to kill each other or jump into bed together... Alright, he'd surely imagined the latter. But *so* what? They had history together – big deal... It was a lifetime ago, so he didn't care. It was all this stupid tiptoeing around the subject that he didn't like. In fact, he decided he couldn't stand this nonsense any longer. He fixed his eyes on Hayden, who was nodding at something Jonas had just said to him.

'So, Hayden, were you and Vee... like... going out?' asked Curtis in a breezy tone.

Vanessa looked as though she wanted to punch Curtis straight in the face after that question.

Curtis bit his lower lip and avoided eye contact with her.

Hayden sniggered and sniffed. 'You could say that. Isn't that right, Essa? You sure you want all the juicy details, Curtis?'

Curtis had been noticing the change in Hayden. His mannerisms had altered dramatically in the last ten minutes. Any civility he'd possessed seemed to have evaporated, and his voice possessed an edge of mockery that hadn't been there earlier. Or at least, he'd been oblivious to it.

'I was a few years older than Essa... She was only sixteen. Well, nearly seventeen.' He gazed at Jonas and whispered, 'I stole her cherry. But I'll tell ya this... It was as sweet as that raspberry cake over there! We were at it like bloody horny rabbits. We'd screw all day sometimes.'

Jonas's eyes widened in shock, but he didn't reply.

Curtis necked the rest of his beer in one big gulp, wishing to God he'd not opened *that* door. Or the front door earlier that evening.

Hayden smirked at Vanessa. 'Hey, Essa, you remember that club we went to? The one where we snuck off into that cramped cubicle... Funny story, this...'

'No!' hissed Vanessa.

No, she couldn't remember... or no, don't tell the story, considered Curtis.

Hayden continued. 'So, Essa's straddling me, and we're right in the moment. She's going up and down like a lunatic, when this hand reaches under like a crawling spider and snatches up her knickers that have slid down her leg and dropped onto the floor! This happened right at the moment when we're both about to... you know, go whaaaam! Little Essa's screaming in elation and shouting, "Ahhh, ahhh, oh my God.... someone just pinched my fucking thong!" Oh, I ended up pissin' myself.'

Delphine started coughing and choking on her wine. 'Oh, Jesus!'

Vanessa's face dropped, then she walked out. Curtis heard the thudding of her bare feet on the steps as she raced up to their bedroom.

'Well... I guess you had to be there,' said Hayden.

Jonas gasped, 'Ag, no, man, you can't say that! That's the man's wife, bruuhh!'

Hayden shrugged and pulled a face. 'Ah, well, I kinda just did.'

'Aikona! That's too much,' said Jonas, gazing at Curtis, stunned that he'd not responded to this.

'Curtis knows I'm only messing. This is all ancient history. Sexed-up teenagers mucking about. Screwing each other stupid. We were all young once, right? There's another story about a bus journey, but—'

'Whoo, I think that's enough. Come on, Hayden. Let's take a walk,' said Jonas, struggling to get up. 'Great evening, Curtis. Tell Vee thanks so much for her hospitality. Smashing cake.'

'Alright. Let me just take a quick slash,' said Hayden, unsteady on his feet as he waltzed off.

Delphine waited for Hayden to go and said, 'You better go and check on Vee.'

'Yeah, go up, Curtis. I'll walk him out. The guy's had too many beers and he's talking shit. I think he's just got a crass sense of humour and doesn't get he's taken it way too far.'

Delphine snorted. 'I thought *you* were the cynical one,

Jonas. You honestly think that he didn't mean to ruin the evening? He came here specifically to—'

Curtis cut her off. 'I think we need to stop letting this all get out of proportion. Unless Vee told you something I should know about?'

Delphine forced a tight smile. 'Tell Vee I'll call her tomorrow. Thanks for having me... And, Jonas, get that man out of their house and...' She then gave him a gentle smile and said, 'I hope to see you again soon.'

'I'd like that,' said Jonas. 'You fancy grabbing lunch sometime?'

'Sounds lovely,' she said with a warm grin. Then she left.

Jonas chuckled. 'Result for me. For you, man...' He sucked air through his teeth. 'I'd be prepared for a night in the spare room.'

Curtis sighed. 'There's no bed in there.'

AFTER JONAS LED HAYDEN OUT, Curtis tidied up the glasses and took the remainder of the cake downstairs to the kitchen, keeping it sealed in the plastic container. He guessed the kids would like a slice when they got back from his mum and dad's place tomorrow. Although, after Hayden's comment, he was tempted to bin the bastard thing, but decided that would be very immature. He couldn't find the knife anywhere. *Perhaps Vee has taken it upstairs to castrate me with*, he thought grimly.

Curtis trudged up to the top floor with a jug filled with water, ice, and lemon wedges. He didn't bother with the pricey champagne he'd bought especially for their bedroom afterparty.

He crept into the room and found Vanessa curled up on the bed, wearing her dressing gown.

'You awake?' he whispered.

No reply.

'Want some cold water?' he asked, now realising he'd forgotten to bring glasses.

Nothing. He guessed the romantic soak would be out of the question tonight.

'Vee, I'm sorry, OK… I shouldn't have just let that idiot in our house like that. Stupid of me.'

Still nothing.

He swigged the water from the jug, grateful for the cold liquid. His brain felt like a dry prune.

'OK, night then!' sighed Curtis. He then headed through to the ensuite, tugged off his clothes, gave his teeth a quick brush, then headed to bed.

Curtis lay there in the darkness, listening to the sound of his wife's heavy breathing. He rolled over and put a hand on her shoulder and leant in to kiss the back of her neck, but she tensed up, then shrugged him off.

'I don't get why I'm the bad guy here, Vee.'

'I've come on,' she mumbled. 'Just go to sleep, Curtis. Just go to bloody sleep.'

Curtis huffed and turned his back on Vanessa.

10

Vanessa had been in a trance-like state all night. Thinking... Dwelling on her past and what last night all meant. She listened to the seagulls outside. A streak of sunlight shone through a gap in the door's shutters. The bright beam danced inside the bathtub each time the blinds moved in the breeze. It was morning, yet she'd not slept at all. She'd not been able to shut down her mind... The cogs kept turning and the memory factory kept running constantly, the incessant memories playing over and over. An evocative movie that she couldn't switch off.

Curtis was awake and fidgeting about, rubbing his feet together and head-butting his pillows into place. Ahhh, she could have slapped him last night. What sort of idiot lets a stranger into the house like that? God, for a grown man with a canny business head on his shoulders, her husband could be a gullible dope sometimes.

He edged over to her, placing a hand on her buttocks, and left it there. She understood what that manoeuvre meant, and it riled her he'd even consider trying it on this morning. She had a mind-splitting migraine. Her skin was sore and her stomach felt bloated; the stress of last night had triggered the worst period she'd ever experienced in her adult life. After racing upstairs, she'd gone to use the toilet, and when she'd stood up and seen all the blood in the pan, she'd started having a panic attack. It was horrible. She thought her entire insides had fallen straight out of her, and she wasn't even due on for a fortnight.

Curtis started squeezing her right bum cheek, and she went rigid. Then he inched his hand further over and she sat bolt upright. 'I already told you, I can't! What are you checking? Just making sure I'm not lying to you?'

Curtis sat up and puffed out his cheeks. 'I see your mood has improved since last night!'

'Unbelievable!'

Curtis elbowed the pillows and slumped against them. 'You know, it should be me that has the hump. You get that, right?'

'Yet you don't. And you were happy to sit there and...'

'Go on, say it... I should have punched the guy in the face like some jealous hooligan. That's not me, Vee.'

'I'm getting up.'

'My dad taught me never to rise to the bait and to turn the other cheek. You don't win by losing your head.'

Vanessa rubbed her forehead. 'Righto, Curtis. You're right. Daddy Pascall is always right.'

Curtis sighed. 'Come on, Vee. I'll make some coffee and we'll sit outside and have a chat about this. I understand that was embarrassing, but, as much as that was shocking for me to hear, I'm a big boy. I always assumed you'd... you know, been with other guys. God, we can't let something like that upset us... It was years ago. It's so silly.'

Vanessa couldn't help but shake her head as she clamped down on her bottom lip in irritation. Her husband didn't have a clue. He really didn't.

. . .

VANESSA SLID in her AirPods and sat at the kitchen island sipping on a coffee. She kept running the night's events over and over in her head... The feeling that had hit her when she'd seen *him* in their house was indescribable... that expression on his face... the way Delphine's demeanour had changed. It chilled her to the bone just thinking about it. The crackling tension radiating from her friend seemed almost palpable... Vanessa had felt her chest tighten so much she'd struggled to inhale for a few moments. Outside, they'd spoken in hushed voices and Vanessa had demanded to know what Delphine meant by her previous warning... the warning she'd dismissed as psychic gibberish.

Delphine had replied, 'I said if anyone from your past comes back into your life, then you need to get rid of them.'

'Get rid of them?'

'Yes. Because they'll bring with them a terrible sorrow from a time long past... and I sense history will repeat itself.'

'Delphine, what do you mean by, "history will repeat itself"? How?'

But Delphine didn't answer and didn't seem keen to continue the discussion. She indicated they should go back inside and scuttled away as if the very step she stood on was cursed.

Vanessa shuddered at the memory and picked up her phone. She wondered why on earth she'd selected *that* song? The song that, when she'd left Bournemouth and moved to London, her dad had banned her from listening to. Banned her for her own good, because of the emotions it stirred in her.

She closed her eyes as she pressed play. Her entire body tingled as the melancholy guitar riffs of Metallica's "Nothing Else Matters" began and she started shaking at the memory it invoked – the empty beach. A place of painful recollections. The place where she'd first heard this song. As she remembered, the guitar riffs lasted a minute before those lyrics kicked in. When the singing started, so did the tears. She tried to fight them, but it was impossible. She was eighteen when she'd listened to this track, for what she agreed to herself would be the *very* last time. But even now, the poignant song triggered her emotions in the same way it had done all those years ago.

She wiped the hot tears away and saw her raspberry cake sitting on the side. Curtis must have forgotten to put it into the fridge last night. With the music still playing, she walked over to the cake and ripped back the container's lid. She glared at the sponge.

It was as sweet as that raspberry cake.

It seemed so insane, but just yesterday, all she cared about was her stupid dinner party. Her bloody perfect cake... She'd flapped endlessly about making the night so fabulous, and that seemed silly because now... *now* she had genuine worries. She knew without a shadow of a doubt that *he* would bring trouble of momentous proportion to their lives. The consequences of her past mistakes would shake their world and threaten to destroy everything.

Why now? After all this time, why now? When life was so perfect. When she had everything she ever wanted and so much more. Why did life have to be so damn cruel and unfair? For some reason, she hated that silly cake. All that fuss and it was hardly even touched. They'd all been too preoccupied with that bastard's mysterious entrance to give a flying fuck about her precious cake. All that effort to position those raspberries in the identical rows. Stupid bloody idiot.

As the music continued to play in her ears and the intensity of the guitar riffs rose, the streams of tears flowed. Vanessa balled her fist and hammered it down into the dessert. The vanilla sponge and raspberry cream splattered all over the place. She hit it again, and again and again, flattening it completely. Then, gazing at her handiwork, shocked by her actions, she sobbed and sank to her knees. She was hit with an icy dread that made her want to run away and never look back.

CURTIS CAME DOWNSTAIRS, going gingerly, as he felt rather fragile. These days, anything more than four beers and a hangover seemed inevitable. He was glad the kids were with his folks, as the silence in the house was welcome this morning. He'd had plans for a balcony breakfast. Croissants, bacon, fruit, the works – but with his wife still in a strange mood and his stomach churning, he decided a coffee and half hour back in bed would be a sensible option.

When Curtis walked into the kitchen, he expected to see Vanessa sitting at the island drinking coffee, but all he found was a pulverised cake and cream filling splattered all over the fridge and worktop. 'What the hell?' he muttered to himself as he went over to inspect the cake carnage. It looked like someone had attacked the thing with a hammer, the mess it had created.

He searched for Vanessa and found her standing on the grass in the garden. Just standing there, gazing up into the sky like she'd been hypnotised.

11

Vanessa's hand shook as she opened the file hidden in her phone's iCloud. The one she wanted was buried deep within several file boxes marked VND. Which stood for *Vanessa Neal's diary*.

The diary itself she'd burnt around fifteen years ago, when her dad moved to Spain and she'd needed to retrieve the last of her old bits and bobs. She couldn't keep the thing in her own house, yet something told her not to lose all traces of those thoughts and stories held within those tatty pages, so she'd taken photos and stored them. She'd locked them away in the cloud, much the same as she'd locked them away in her own mind.

The file didn't load up, and a pang of worry hit her. *Have I deleted it by mistake somehow? Or has the file become corrupted?* But then it flashed up on the screen and she saw the unfamiliar scrawl. Her teenage handwriting. She'd not viewed these pages in a long, long time. She'd not read the extracts at all during her adult life. God, why would she? She had to ask herself why she'd even kept these and what she ever intended to do with them.

Vanessa flicked through the pages, cringing as she caught the odd snippet here and there. The mindset, opinions and feelings of an unrecognisable adolescent. All hormones, uncertainty, and attitude. There were only a few entries contained within the scores of pages that she wanted... no, *needed* to see. June... June of *that* year... the year when her life became so complicated... so messed up... so utterly messed up. It almost seemed like the memories were not hers. Not Vanessa Pascall's... That seemed so impossible. These were Little Essa Neal's memories. And *she* was a different person altogether.

But this entry differed from the others. It had an insightful undertone to it. Deep and clearer than the ramblings of those previous entries. Had what happened that night changed her and made her more perceptive? Made her... grow up?

Notes to older me

Tuesday 13^{*th*} *June 1995.*

Where to begin with this one? It's now four days after that night. That horrendous night. Four days and I still feel peculiar. Sort of fuzzy and heavy-headed. Sad, too. Really, really sad... like everything in the world is shit. That nothing matters anymore. Maybe it's the aftereffects of what they gave me. Or perhaps it's something else. Like what happened. What they all did. Most likely a combination of both, I guess.

Whatever it is, the sadness still clings to me like a heavy shadow and refuses to evaporate. I'm still trying to make sense of everything in my head. I hope when I re-read this

*in years to come, I'll look upon that night differently. And
I'll have a different view on what happened. Like it was
just a big adventure. Teenage kicks and all that nonsense.
Though, I suspect that I won't. Things became very blurry
as the night progressed, but I'm going to write as I recall
those events.*

*Sooo – here goes – I remember drinking early. Too early.
Half a bottle of blue Mad Dog 20/20. Oooh, yeah – BIG
mistake. I'd dressed up, expecting a night out clubbing with
Hayden. He said he knew the door staff at one of the new
clubs in the centre and that he'd have no trouble getting me
in. I was excited, and if I'm honest with myself, perhaps a
little nervous too. Probably why I guzzled all that sickly
sweet booze. My stomach tied itself into knots when that
spruced-up, dazzling red Ford Sierra came tearing down
the street, its engine growling like a tank. He – Dominic
Brookes – he'd done something to the engine. The car – all
spoilers, body kits, and gleaming metal – roared deeply.
That boy and his silly car. He was in love with the thing.
So, Dominic sat there revving the throaty engine, eyeing
me with those cold, nasty green eyes of his.*

*Hayden told me to jump in the back and I found myself
sitting next to this right moody cow. I didn't know her from
Adam. A strange girl, with blond plaited hair and an elon-
gated face. When I tried to strike up a conversation with
her, she made it very clear she had no desire to partake in
small talk. She gazed out of the window, pouting as she
watched the world flash by, her face fixed in a petulant
scowl. I hoped she didn't intend to come out partying with
us. Bloody Debbie Downer or what? It would be hilarious
if her name actually was Debbie. Ha ha.*

Anyway, we got into the town centre. Dominic did some doughnuts in this supermarket car park. There were loads of petrol heads, chavs and bimbos hanging around there. They were whooping and cheering on the idiotic drivers who cruised about and then suddenly raced off to do some pointless skid or handbrake that sent streams of putrid smoke into the sky. The endless thud-thud as dozens of car stereos competed for dominance filled the air. The noisy, blended tunes, sounding unsynchronised and jarring. To my ears anyway.

I remember thinking that Hayden looked so casually dressed – not ready for a night out at all. He wore baggy jeans and old trainers, and I felt silly in my best dress and going-out sandals, surrounded by the smell of burning rubber and gangs of boisterous louts. I asked him what we were doing and if we could go. Then he informs me there's been a change of plan. He has something much better to do. Something so crazy it will blow my mind. The grumpy girl had gone by this point.

So, I got back into the car. Oh, God, thinking back to that moment, I wish that I hadn't. I'd been drinking some cider that Leanne Riggs gave me... She sat in the back with me and Hayden. Debbie Downer had also left her Smirnoff Ice behind, so I finished that, too. They all cracked jokes and shared good-natured banter. I'd always quite liked Leanne. (Sure got that wrong.) She was quite unfeminine, acted like one of the lads, and dressed boyishly. She'd treated me like a good friend in the past.

Anyway, all seemed well at this point. But then he got in the car and the vibe changed. The strange lad. I wanted to get out. I knew in my drunken haze I should, but before I had time to consider opening the door, Dominic floored it and we were racing through the streets of Bournemouth so quickly my stomach started doing wild somersaults.

12

Vanessa stood out on the bedroom balcony and gazed across to the water. The tide was high and the air hazy. Late morning sun caused it to glimmer. Her eyes stung due to lack of sleep. She'd not slept a wink since Saturday. Things had been tense for the last few days. She'd not spoken about the weekend and had been avoiding being alone with Curtis as much as possible. Even Sofia had picked up on Vanessa's dismal mood and had asked her during the school run why Mummy seemed so sad. Her daughter picking up on her emotional state made her feel even more dejected.

She made to go back inside when she glimpsed it again – *that boat*. The same boat she'd seen yesterday, though it had been a couple of hours earlier. Just before the school run. There were always plenty of boats and paddle boarders passing by. But this one seemed to stay in the same patch of water, within view of the house, just bobbing around, and that was why she'd taken heed of it. It looked like a standard row boat, and although she couldn't see much because of the distance, she'd made out the shape of one lone person on board the small vessel. The tide was already going out. She pulled up a chair and observed it.

VANESSA LET OUT A GAPING YAWN. She'd eyed that boat for an hour. She knew it was *him*. She *just* knew it. Jesus, maybe it was nothing more than a random fisherman and she was losing the plot, but, as soon as that boat drifted away with the tide, the person would sit down and row it back in view of the house again. The process had been repeated many times, and Vanessa wondered if this was a ploy to entice her out of the house. Though it was likely just a way of making *his* presence known.

She snatched up her phone and clicked on to the Amazon app. Keeping half an eye on the boat, she selected a pair of high-definition binoculars that came with a tripod. She ordered this for next-day delivery. Jude had asked for a pair anyway, and they would come in handy if *he* was intending to play games.

The figure on the boat was standing up now, and Vanessa couldn't be certain, but she reckoned that he was watching *her* through binoculars. She scowled as she squinted in the sun, willing her eyes to focus – willing them to see the figure clearly. She gripped the glass divider and mouthed, 'Piss off!'

Then she raced inside, ran across the bedroom, and made a beeline for the dressing room. In her desperate hunt for her shortie wetsuit, she threw clothes and shoes around until she located it. She heard her deep, short breathing as she tore off her clothes and got herself into the swimwear.

She steamed down the stairs and made for the front door. Not bothering with her goggles, nose plugs or buoy, she sprinted across the road without even shutting the front door, charged across the grass, and darted onto the beach pathway.

Instead of taking the steps, Vanessa jumped down hard on the shingle, which caused her to yelp.

She could still see the boat out there as she ran, but it appeared to be moving away as she hurried to the water. The soles of her feet hurt like crazy as she thundered on and sped forward in a graceless, splashing stumble. She trod on something sharp in the water and cursed. But she didn't stop steaming onward until she was at waist height and then she pitched headlong into the water, propelled her body forward and came up swimming. She powered forward using the front stroke and swam like a navy seal.

Vanessa travelled a good three hundred metres before she came to a stop and searched for the rowboat. It was heading towards Whitstable, but it had moved out into deeper waters.

'Stop,' she yelled. 'Stop and face me, you bloody coward!'

The boat was some distance away, but she kept going. She became determined to catch it up, although she had no clue what she'd do *if* she did.

Another two hundred metres and she came up again. An adrenaline rush had caused her to go off like a rocket but now she was struggling and, as she began treading water, a small wave hit her and she took in a mouthful of salty water. Her eyes were fuzzy now, and she wished she had her goggles and buoy.

The boat rocked and bobbed in the waves, about sixty metres ahead of her, and she caught sight of the figure rowing vigorously. The craft started moving in a diagonal path towards deeper, choppier waters. The rowboat was red with white writing on the side, and Vanessa made out the word *barnacles*.

She continued the chase. She knew it had become unsafe to follow, but her stubbornness wouldn't allow her to succumb that easily. But it became harder to keep her eyes trained on the craft now.

After another minute of frantic swimming, she came up again. Now, she succumbed to the fact that she wouldn't be able to catch it without putting herself at serious risk. As the boat moved further and further away, she set her sights back on the shoreline and was perturbed to establish how far out she'd swam in her irate pursuit of the boat. She took some deep breaths and tried to control her ragged breathing, and set off using more controlled, less frantic strokes. She started shaking all over when she reached the shore. *Jesus, what a stupid move*, she thought.

VANESSA CLEANED the two cuts on her foot using disinfectant, covered them in cream, and applied a small bandage. She didn't think the cuts needed stitches, but she'd left a blood trail through the hallway and kitchen, so strode off to get the mop and floor spray.

After the clean-up job, Vanessa kept herself busy for the rest of the day with paperwork, a touch of window cleaning, and prepared a spag-bol for dinner. This always went down well with both her children. In London she used to work part-time in the Finchley branch, but it wasn't feasible for her to travel to the office now, and since the pandemic, she'd become accustomed to home-office life, and quite liked it. But today, whatever she did in order to block out the flooding thoughts, bleak memories, and feelings of deep anxiety, it did little to help alleviate them.

After she'd fed Jude and Sofia, Curtis called to say he'd be late back from London. He suggested they should have a late dinner, a glass of wine and a chat, to which Vanessa responded by lying and saying she'd already eaten, felt groggy and would grab an early night. Curtis sounded disappointed, and this made Vanessa feel bad, but she couldn't face being alone in her husband's company right now. Things were too odd since Saturday's disastrous events, and she knew where the conversation would lead and what questions he'd be asking once they were settled in each other's company.

It would be high tide again in an hour. Vanessa got Sofia and Jude settled for the night and wandered up to the bedroom. It was eight thirty. The sun dipped on the horizon and the sea sat still in the breezeless evening. She stepped out onto the balcony and, just as she'd expected, saw that the rowing boat had returned. It looked nothing more than a black silhouette against a red-hued sky, but she knew it was the same one. The figure on the craft stood statue still. She stared out there for a long time. Then, she spun on her heels, aggressively closed the folding doors and shut out the world.

13

C urtis returned early from work to find the kids alone in the lounge, eyes fixed on the TV. They'd informed him they'd both had dinner early and Mummy had a terrible headache.

Six days had now passed since Hayden's unwelcome visit, and Vanessa's behaviour was becoming increasingly unusual and worrying. She hadn't been eating, she'd become distant towards both him and the children, and seemed to want to spend most of her time alone in the master bedroom, on the top balcony, or slumped in bed. Yet, strangely enough, he knew for certain she wasn't sleeping. It seemed like his beloved, chirpy wife had been replaced by a sullen, mopey teenage girl. When he tried to engage her in conversation, her aloofness was infuriating. He couldn't get much more out of her than a churlish *yes, no thanks,* or *not sure.*

She'd also purchased some decent binoculars, and they'd been positioned on the bedroom balcony on a tripod. These were apparently brought for Jude to use, but his son had informed Curtis last night that he'd yet to try them out because Mum wanted to test them first to establish if they worked properly. Then there were the nasty cuts on her foot, which she did by stepping on a shell on the beach. Or so she said.

'How long has Mummy left you two down here for?' asked Curtis.

'A little while. I think Mummy is watching the sea for bad people again,' said Sofia, not taking her eyes from the TV. Her favourite cartoon, *Love Monster*, was on. She'd be glued to that for ten hours straight if they'd let her.

'Watching the sea,' said Curtis, forcing a laugh. 'Why would she be watching out for bad people?'

Sofia shrugged. 'That's what *he* said.'

'No, I never. I said *maybe* she's guarding the house,' said Jude matter-of-factly. 'That's what it looks like she's doing.'

'Mummy doesn't *seem* like Mummy,' said Sofia. 'She's being no fun.'

'I think she's just feeling a bit... under the weather this week. But she's not guarding the house. That's silly. This is a private road for a start. Bad people can't come up here. They are... banned.'

'Oh, OK. Mummy told us not to play in the garden. She's locked the door, and we can't reach the key,' said Sofia with a gentle but melodramatic sigh.

'Come on, downstairs, you two. It's too nice this afternoon. You don't want to be cooped up. I'll unlock the door.'

AFTER LETTING the kids outside to play, Curtis went up to the top floor and found Vanessa sitting out on the balcony sipping from a bottle of water. She hadn't seen him approach and seemed startled when she did acknowledge his presence.

'Hi. You OK?' asked Curtis.

'You made me jump,' she said, gazing at him briefly, then turning her focus back out over the balcony.

Curtis noted his wife had a small rash of red pimples on her chin, which was unusual for Vanessa. Normally, her skin stayed flawless and glowing, and even without make-up, her skin appeared unblemished. Stress... this was all stress. The move... plus this Hayden guy embarrassing her... the change in circumstances... Something had gone wrong here. He wished he knew how to solve the problem.

'I can't help if you shut me out, Vee.'

Vanessa sipped her water, and he caught her chest heave as though she'd taken a deep intake of air.

'Look, whatever has got you so upset... whatever you need to talk about... I'm here to listen. You can tell me anything. You understand that, right?'

Vanessa's jaw tightened. She picked up her shades from the table and slid them on. 'Your dinner is in the oven. Spicy chicken and rice.'

'OK. Thanks. And are you eating with me?'

'I already ate.'

'Right. So, what's with the binos? You searching for something out there, Vee?'

Vanessa shook her head. 'No, just... being nosy.'

Curtis knelt down and took a peek. He scanned along the front and fixed on a paddle boarder near Seasalter beach. A carefree dog wearing a red buoyancy aid sat on the board and Curtis could see it was a border collie. 'These are pretty powerful. We should take the kids up to Oare Marshes. We could try to spot the seal colony out there with these.'

'Mmm, yes, if you like.'

'I've had them follow my kayak before. I bet Sofia would love to find them, Vee. Sometimes the seal pups go right underneath.'

'She would like that.'

'Right, I'm going for a shower. The kids are playing out the back, by the way.'

Vanessa took a deep breath and stood up. 'I'll go down with them!'

Before Curtis could respond, Vanessa charged off downstairs.

V anessa sat on the bed, hugging her knees. Curtis shuffled, grunted, and slumped the back of his arm across his forehead. He fidgeted for a bit before letting out a gentle, murmuring snore.

She picked up her phone from her bedside table, unlocked it, and scanned her emails. Then, without even intending to, she clicked on the file app. Vanessa hesitated for a heartbeat as she deliberated on whether to open the old diary file or delete the thing. She thumbed the icon and opened up the old wounds once again.

Tuesday 13th June 1995 continued...

The lights of Bournemouth glimmered behind us. I felt so wary of that other boy... I say boy, but he wasn't. I'd say he could've even been closer to thirty. Hard to tell in a dimly lit car whilst tipsy. OK, I'm fibbing... not tipsy... wrecked. He may have just appeared ten years older than

the other lads to my befuddled eyes. But he had this kinda
hard look. The type of rough lad you just knew liked to
fight and cause trouble. Like one of those lads from the
Springdean Estate. His eyes... eek, his eyes, they seriously
creeped me out. So black and empty. He had a face so
gaunt... like he... I guess he looked like he had something
wrong with him. Like he might have been sick or some-
thing. Emancipated... I am sure that word describes his
features accurately. No, wait up. Maybe it's actually
emaciated. Ah, whatever. He smelt weird, too. Like stale
sweat and... I dunno, like a wet, dirty dog. I didn't like him.
I really didn't like him or the vibe he'd brought to the
group.

Leanne produced this little sheet with tiny squares on it.
She put one square on the tip of her finger and passed it to
Hayden, who studied the tiny thing with a big, nervous
grin.

Leanne said something about Sonic the Hedgehog tabs.

Hayden showed me the tiny square. It had a blue hedgehog
on it. Hayden told me to put it on my tongue. Said it would
take me to a magical place and that I'd see insane stuff.
Most likely stuff from the folklore books I liked. Wild fairies
and crazy imps. I said no way to that. I said I'd stick with
the drink. But they all took one. Even Dominic.

I didn't have a clue where we'd driven to. My nerves were
shattered. Dominic drove like a total maniac, and I could
see he appeared a bit on edge now. I guessed he was keen to
get to our destination before those funny drugs took hold of
him. I visualised us crashing. The car rolling into the

unknown and all of us crushed as we died in a desolate ditch. I said a prayer in my head. I prayed to God to keep us safe.

Stupid, I know. So stupid.

15

Curtis and Jonas broke away from the rest of the riding group and headed along Harbour Street and through Whitstable town centre. The place had already started to get congested, the usual Saturday bedlam getting underway, made worse by the high temperatures. It was lunchtime and beachgoers were now jostling for prime car parking spots. Curtis was sweltering and couldn't wait to get out of the clinging riding gear and into the shower for a cool down.

They weaved through the traffic buildup on the High Street and left via Terry's Lane and were soon out of the bustling streets and onto a single road known as Island Wall, a residential area lined with charming terraced houses, near where Jonas lived. The sun momentarily hid behind the clouds, giving them a welcome reprieve from its harsh rays. Twenty miles in the roasting heat had destroyed the both of them. They now rode side by side at an easy pace.

'You fancy a beer this afternoon?' asked Curtis, short of breath. 'I might head back down to the seafront.'

'Sounds great, but I've kinda got a date, so I'll have to pass.'

'What... Delphine?'

'Just a few drinks.'

'Wow. Fast mover.'

'I must have a good aura or something, hey?' said Jonas, chuckling. 'Anyway, you take it easy.'

'You too. Say hi to Delphine.'

Jonas veered off onto Neptune's Gap, almost wiping out two preoccupied pensioners who stood in the middle of the narrow road deliberating their direction. Jonas aptly swerved to avoid the couple and Curtis heard him chuckle and say, 'Eish, close one.'

The pensioners changed direction, unaware of their near miss.

Curtis grinned at the sight of the big man on a bike that appeared way too small and delicate for him. But despite his beefy size, Jonas was a deft rider and kept up with the best of the group. The man also had the stamina of an ox.

Curtis upped his speed again. Ten minutes and he'd be home.

CURTIS HOOKED his bike up in the garage and went into the kitchen for a chocolate protein shake. He found Jude stuffing crisps into his gob at the kitchen island, his eyes glued to his iPad.

'Hey, tough guy. Where's your mum at?'

'Watching TV with Sofia,' he mumbled, not moving his eyes from the screen.

'Fancy a walk to the beach later? Get some fish and chips?'

'Nah. It's too far. Maybe if we drive.'

'It's too busy to drive, champ. It will do you good to walk.'

'Can you take me to Deadman's Island in the summer holidays, Dad?'

'Um, yeah. What's that, a theme park?'

'No, but the place is super haunted. They say it's scattered with human remains. It's not far away.'

Curtis shook the protein drink vigorously. 'Ay, sounds creepy. But I don't think that's an actual place.'

'Tyler has been. *His* dad took him out there on his fishing boat and he is really old. Tyler said it's a boggy marshland and if you fall overboard, you'll get dragged under by the ghosts.'

'Wow, some imagination your friend has got, matey boy,' said Curtis in a gruff pirate's voice.

'He's *not* my friend. He said you'd be too scared to take me, anyway.'

'Oh, did he now? I think he's pulling your leg,' said Curtis, taking a big swig on his shake. 'And I wouldn't be scared. Ghost stories don't scare me, pal.'

'Apparently, the ground is polluted with the plague. And if you are unlucky enough to get sucked into the mud, you could still catch it.'

'Right, well, you should have said before. Now you've added that snippet of bleak info I'm brimming with excitement.'

'So, we can go?' asked Jude with an eager smile.

'Let me check it out first. I'm not promising anything.'

CURTIS GOT SHOWERED AND CHANGED, then tried to convince Vanessa to walk down to the seafront for some food and a couple of drinks. This idea received a tepid response from his wife, because it was too hot for the kids and she was too tired to go out.

So, deciding it was much too nice an evening to stay in

and be ignored by Vanessa, Curtis ventured back out. Rather than walking, he opted for a leisurely ride on his old hardtail mountain bike, and was back on the seafront in fifteen minutes. He bought fish and chips on the beach with a pint of *Sundowner*, and had great fun balancing everything as he bumped the bike down onto the pebbles. He headed down past two rows of beached yachts, their tall, spiky masts spearing into the blue sky, many of which sat on trailers. As the beach sloped, he sat down next to an upturned row boat covered in red tarpaulin. He spilled some of his beer as he got comfortable and muttered a curse.

The tide was quite far out now, but the beach was packed despite the late hour. There were families set up on blankets around him, and a small birthday party was in full swing to his right. They had tables and gazebos erected, chill boxes laid out, and even a couple of tall speakers rigged up, although no music played. As he stuffed in a few chips, he realised how hungry he was. The party guests yakked away, their conversations blending into an ungraspable babble of noise, with only the odd, 'Oh, yeah, totally,' discernible from a tall, smug-looking woman wearing a long green dress and a wide sun hat with an enormous big pink bow on the front. Then the speakers made a spluttering echo, and a skinny guy in massive shades, sipping from a can of fruit cider, started fiddling with the sound system.

It seemed weird being on the beach on his own, surrounded by the noise and buzz of all these people. All these families.

Out in the water, kids and adults alike were messing about on inflatable boats and paddle boards, their yelling and screeching still audible from this distance.

The speakers made a thudding noise, and a song started playing. A tune recognisable from the get-go. Curtis gulped at his pint. "In the Summertime" by Mungo Jerry. Curtis hated this track... No, that wasn't right... not the track. He liked the track... More the memory it invoked. Thankfully, he heard it infrequently these days, but when he did, the song would make him remember that advert from back in ninety-two.

Even to this day, he could picture the scene with frightening clarity. The cheerful group of people at the country pub. A young black guy wearing a straw hat. Another guy with a baby. The man chugging back his beer, and his wife, or girlfriend, waving him over to the car. The atmosphere of the scene then changing – another guy drinking and his gleeful face morphing into a horrified one... and then that song slowing down and coming to a creepy stop. At this point, the viewer was treated to an eerie view of the Vauxhall Cavalier the people had driven away in. Only now it's smashed to pieces in some country lane, and as the camera pans into the wreckage, the viewer gets to see the occupants, who are all dead in the mangled mess.

It still gave Curtis cold chills. He remembered it vividly and vowed that he'd never drink and drive.

Two years later, his older brother Steve died after losing control of his own Vauxhall, though his car was an Astra. They'd been told Steve drank four pints that afternoon. He lost it on a bend doing sixty. His passenger and best mate Philip Franks had survived without a single scratch on him. It tore Curtis's world apart.

He still often thought about his brother. He wondered if he'd have been so involved in the family business as Curtis. Their dad always seemed to go on about Steve not being committed enough to the business, but that would have changed as he got older. His brother just preferred to go out and socialise in those days. Perhaps Steve would have been the one who renovated the old holiday home instead of Curtis... He sipped his beer and considered that if that meant having his brother in his life, he'd have been fine with that. He'd have done anything to change the past.

Curtis sighed and finished his beer. He closed the lid on the fish and chips, leaving them barely touched. They were delicious, but he didn't want to eat them now. His appetite had gone. The beer going straight to his head and making him come over drowsy did little to fuel his taste for food. So weird how just one beer could hit you like that on a hot, sunny day, he mused.

God, he wished that song would change. It started driving him insane. He imagined the advert had ruined that catchy song for millions. He considered moving, but didn't.

A squabble broke out in the water. Just kids having an altercation over a paddle board. One of the group, a woman in her thirties with her hair in a topknot, charged down there to sort it out. The music changed to a reggae number. The woman with the topknot had forgotten her flip-flops and strode further down onto the slope, doing a zombie-like walk as she crossed the harsh shells and pebbles left by the retreating tide. A few kids and parents were doing a similar funny walk, heading in the other direction. The current tune cut out to a chorus of guffaws from the partygoers.

Someone should sack this DJ, decided Curtis.

One man from the group, a shirtless lump with a dad bod, strutted off down the slope with purpose, grumbling something about bringing the board back in. *There goes the hero of the hour. The unruly kids are in trouble now,* thought Curtis. But he too was thwarted by the merciless rocks and Curtis had to stifle a snigger when the man almost fell over. The partygoers didn't, though; they were all in hysterics.

The speakers sputtered again, and the music came back on. He couldn't believe it... Mungo Jerry again... Curtis slugged his beer in frustration, grabbed his belongings and hunted for a bin to ditch his uneaten dinner.

· · ·

VANESSA WATCHED from the lounge balcony as a huge army helicopter flew low across the sea, its twin propellers causing a deafening noise and drowning out the sound of her kids bickering behind her. People down on the beach stopped what they were doing to crane their necks in order to observe the passing copter.

Vanessa kept on playing last Saturday over and over in her head... and each time the frustration of the situation grew and grew to an almost unbearable sensation of exasperation. Why didn't she drag *him* aside and talk with him? Why didn't she at least try to determine what his game was? Lock horns with him in order to get in front of this thing... this... solemn *predicament*.

She'd been frozen in shock. That's what she kept telling herself. None of it seemed real in that moment. Plus, anyone in the same situation would've reacted the same way, and it seemed stupid to keep reflecting on what she *could*'ve, or *should*'ve done... She needed to consider what to do next, and only one idea kept presenting itself.

It may have been twenty-seven years ago, but that didn't matter, because that bastard's hateful look had stayed in Vanessa's mind, clear as day. When she'd told him she was leaving and she'd turned her back on him for what she thought would be the last time, she'd confirmed it was over and that she intended to go away forever.

She'd never forget his nasty, bitter voice when he'd said, 'Even if it takes me years to pay you back... I'll never forget. Or forgive. Never!'

But after their twisted, unpleasant confrontation, she'd kept walking, not daring to gaze back, her eyes flooding with tears, the thick blood flowing down her face as the rain pounded down and the drab, cloudy sky turned a perfect incandescent blue as the lightning tore it up.

She remembered shivering nonstop when she'd returned

home, a slither of dread cutting through her, but also a feeling of pure relief... like an immense weight had been lifted from her shoulders. She'd been able to breathe again. A new beginning.

The helicopter had passed over and she could hear the kids again. They were still disputing some element in the cartoon and Jude kept advising his sister that many aspects of the show were silly and implausible. Of course, Jude was just *being* Jude, as per normal... a bossy smarty-pants who'd shoot down pretty much everything Sofia said, scolding her for being too immature or imprecise for his liking. That boy definitely needed an older sibling to engage and compete with, though even a teenager would most likely struggle with his precociousness.

Vanessa went out onto the balcony, sat at the table, and opened up her laptop. Then she searched for stolen rowboats in the local area.

CURTIS DECIDED another beer wouldn't be a bad idea. He ventured into a little tap-house, a quirky, open-fronted shack by the seafront walkway. A prime spot for tourists. Curtis hoisted his bike over the wall. He'd forgotten how heavy the old thing was, especially compared to his Dawes road bike. He then leant his bike against some metal railing right next to a red, upended surfboard that had '*open*' written on it in big white letters. It took three attempts to release the combination lock on the chain snaked around the bike's frame, then he secured it to the railing and wandered inside.

The place was all barrels and ropes with a rustic vibe. A seat, constructed from half a rowboat upended and decorated in fairy lights, was an expert touch. The bar had a vast selection of craft beers to choose from.

After some deliberation, Curtis opted for an Oyster Stout,

which slipped down a treat. He decided he'd spend some time here and try a few brews. So, he pulled up a tall stool and placed his drink on a wooden shelving ledge. Stacked underneath the seating area were various empty beer crates, which he used to rest up his weary feet. Curtis got comfortable, opened up his phone and searched for Deadman's Island.

VANESSA DIALLED the number she'd found on a local listing for a Greg Butler. The line rang out for ages, and just as Vanessa was about to give up, a man answered.

'Hello, Mr Butler?'

'Yes, speaking. How can I help?' said the calm but nasally voice on the other end.

'I'm calling about the boat. The one on the internet.'

'Ahh, I see. Is that *Shrimpy Cruiser*, or *The Bottom Feeder*? They are both still for sale.'

'Um, no, I'm calling about *Ms Sally-Anne Barnacles*,' she said.

'You've found her?' he asked, a hopeful edge to his voice.

'No, but I'm sure I've seen it near here. A few times. Close to where I live. A red boat with white lettering in an Old English style of text? Is that right?' she asked.

'Sounds like her. Where's *here*?'

'Preston Parade. Seasalter end.'

'Ooh, lucky you,' he said in a flat voice. 'No doubt just teens messing about. It happens. Probably DFL shit bags. It'll wash up somewhere. Not the first one that's been borrowed.'

'Right,' said Vanessa. She'd overheard the *Down from London* phrase before. Londoners got the blame for everything around here.

'Don't worry, I'm not opposed to outsiders or anything

like that. Not at all. But some of these younger crowds, they bring trouble. Little obnoxious bastards think they can do whatever they please.'

'I hear you; I really do. So, the article said it was stolen from near Whitstable... but whereabouts exactly?'

'Near the sailing club on Tankerton Slopes,' he said, now with a hint of suspicion. 'Why is that?'

'Oh, I was just wondering. If I see it again, shall I call you direct?'

'Yes, please. If you would. And notify the police. The theft is registered with them.'

'Yes, of course.'

'And can I ask your name?' he said, his voice now sounding uncertain.

Vanessa hesitated. 'Um, yeah, sure... it's Rachel Jones. Ms.'

'I appreciate you calling, Ms Jones. I would like the old *Sally-Anne* returned. You take care now.'

'You too, and I hope you get her back.' Vanessa ended the call. At least now she had an area to comb. There was a chance, albeit a slim one, that he'd be staying near where he'd stolen the boat. On Monday, she'd go on a diligent search.

She stepped inside, and the children were now peacefully watching a film. She headed downstairs and continued into the study. Her next job was to go through the CCTV from last Saturday.

16

Todd shoved the barrel of his Smith & Wesson M&P handgun under his chin and shuddered. Could he do this? Actually blow his brains out of the top of his head?

He swallowed down some lumpy bile as he visualised the aftermath. Saw in his mind some horrified maid trotting in and finding his brain pulp dripping down the bright white walls of the luxury five-star hotel he'd been living in since... since... *he* ruined everything. Todd imagined a forensics team in full white overalls, having a cheerful debate about the Miami Dolphins and Tampa Bay Buccaneers. Teasing each other about the score predictions for the much-anticipated August clash, as they assiduously raked out his skull fragments that were imbedded deep in the ceiling.

Todd got a waft of that perfume. Sweet and floral, with a musty edge... such an overwhelming smell. The call girl had left over an hour ago, yet still the scent of her lingered, as if to drive him insane and remind him of what he'd become. To remind him he'd lost *everything*.

He closed his eyes and tried to picture the Cuban. Young

and doe-eyed. Slim and beautiful. Three Viagra and his pecker still stayed as limp as a well-cooked noodle. She'd allowed him to do anything he liked to her. The amount he paid, he'd been given permission to do anything he desired. She'd even offered to give him head without a rubber. She'd even let him... 'Aahhh. Do it, you God damn coward! Do it,' he hissed at his wretched reflection. He snatched the gun away from his chin and shoved it against his right temple. 'Do it, Ericsson. End it now, you chickenshit. DO IT!'

The Cuban hadn't laughed at him. She'd been professional and tried to coach him. Tried to raise the snake. Tried to bring the old Todd back. But all he saw in that humiliating moment were his two daughters. All he could see were their outraged, scolding expressions. Crystal in her white joggers and peach top, hand on her hip and glaring at him like he was no more than a disgusting monster. Sasha, in her giraffe print pjs, her long blond hair bedraggled from sleep, eyeing him with those big, round eyes. Eyes full of hostility. Both broken beyond repair. His baby girls, barely teenagers, and having to deal with all this revolting mess. If only he could turn back the clock and make a different choice.... *If* only.

But those images of his girls wouldn't go away. No vice would remove them. No drink, drug, woman or man existed that could obliterate the terrible images that whirled in his mind. It was time. This *was* the only way. *DO it, you feeble prick.*

Todd's finger brushed the trigger and his heart thudded so fast it hurt. One quick squeeze and it would all be over. Sweat poured down his face, and he glimpsed himself in the huge mirror. *Look at you, you sad piece of shit*, he thought. You deserve this. His face appeared more bloated and blotchier than ever. His heavy jowls sagged down, and his thinning hair was almost non-existent now.

Yes, it was time. He closed his eyes and willed himself to

do it. And when he'd plucked up the courage to apply the pressure, his mobile burst into life and danced around the sink. He considered leaving the phone. He'd resigned himself to the fact that this was happening. *Today.* He'd promised himself he'd not walk out of this hotel bathroom.

But then a thought occurred to him – what if one of his girls was phoning? What if they wanted to talk to him and work through the mess? He had to be sure.

Todd snatched the handgun away and slung it down onto the white tiled side, and it thudded as it landed. He grabbed the phone. His heart sank when he saw it was not one of his beloved daughters calling. Even so, this was a call he needed to take. 'Hello,' he said, his voice sounding shaky to his own ears.

'How you holding up, Mr Ericsson?'

'Trisha, good to hear from you. I'm... OK.'

'So, I have a name for you. I had three top investigators working on this, and one of them got a hit.'

'Go on.'

'OK, we have the guy's real name now. But he's no Californian like you thought. The guy's a Brit.'

'What?' said Todd, stunned. 'Are you sure it's the right guy?'

'The investigator said she's pretty darn sure. And trust me, this lady is top notch. Highly recommended. She's even tracked a location... I'm sending you that now. This was a hit from yesterday, so it's not a live trace or anything, but it gives you a rough idea of where he is. Don't ask me how or where she obtained the data. She didn't seem too keen to part with that information.'

'Right. This sounds promising,' said Todd, hands trembling.

'My guess is she's tracking his credit card usage. Her suggestion was that she monitor him until he's back on US soil, or at least in a fixed place, such as a hotel, and then you'll have the opportunity for a face to face with the subject.' She let out a hoarse giggle. 'Subject... listen to me, using all the technical jargon.'

'So, he's out of the country?'

'He sure is. Look at the map I've sent you. I'll keep you up to speed on any news I hear from the investigators.'

'Good work... But, Trisha, cancel all the others. Just keep this one running the case. She sounds like she's got this.'

'Roger that. Take care, Mr Ericsson.'

Todd ended the call and wiped the beads of sweat from his face. *A Brit...* he'd have never guessed... Jesus.

He stared at the gun, inhaled deeply, and let out a long exhale. Another few seconds and he'd have pulled the trigger. At least now he had something else to focus on. That motherfucking, cock-sucking, soon-to-be-dying-in-tears-of-sheer-bastard-agony Brit.

He opened Trish's attachment and frowned, even more confused, after establishing where this piece of shit had been yesterday.

17

Curtis walked outside of the taproom and stood by the entrance. There was a fan by the seats here, but it seemed to blow more hot air around the place. So he opted to sit on the sea wall, where many other patrons had congregated, and gaze out across the beach.

The tide was out now, and the scores of oyster beds could be seen along the seafront. People continued to stream past... The folk who flocked to Whitstable were a diverse crowd... A real colourful mix. He decided someone could lose hours just chilling on the seafront watching the world go by. Curtis heard at least two guys get told by their partners that they didn't *need* another drink; they were practically dragged away like resentful children as they pointed at the chalkboard drinks menu. He'd seen three people, all men, trip over one of the chunky boat chains leading down to the beach, and he'd allowed a tiny snigger each time.

Someone had left two toy green cars on the wall and Curtis pictured a couple of parents enduring a relentless earful all the way home because they'd forgotten them and it was the end of the world for their upset child. *He'd been there.*

Curtis felt pickled now. The sun had started setting, casting a magnificent orange glow across the horizon, and everyone seemed transfixed by the alluring display. He decided this was the most spectacular sunset he'd seen in ages and only wished Vanessa was around to enjoy the view with him. He took a few snaps on his phone but knew they'd not do the scene justice.

A couple of dogs were sniffing about at the taproom's entrance, and one dachshund, despite its owner's calls to return, waltzed straight inside and found some patrons to make a fuss of him. The people in this town loved a pooch. Furry friends were welcome everywhere. Another dog, a drenched black labrador, capered along the beach with a massive, boomerang-shaped stick in its mouth.

Curtis finished his beer and decided to head back home before he became a danger to himself, and others, on his bike.

But a short man in flip-flops and cargo trousers stood leaning against his bike as he chatted on the phone. He wore a faded green T-shirt with the slogan *There's a good chance I don't give a shit* emblazoned on the chest, with a cartoon monkey donning a baseball cap sticking up his middle finger underneath the lettering. The guy spoke with an expressive, smooth-tongued voice. 'I know. That's my point... Uh-huh, that's where it *all* derives from... Oh, I know. Well, Marvin was excoriated and promptly sacked. Good riddance, I say.'

Curtis took another peek at the sunset and a figure caught his eye. He dismissed the figure and turned back.

The short man, now examining Curtis's bike with an uppity sneer, waffled on. 'Uh-huh, please do keep me up to speed with any consequential developments... You, too!' The man let out an annoying, phoney laugh.

Curtis turned back to the beach. The figure was a way off, standing with his back to him, but his attention had been drawn to the man because he wore a tanned leather jacket... not unlike... Hayden's. His hair was the same length and carried that same shaggy style, too.

The man peered out across the beach to where numerous people sat watching the sun setting. The groups ahead of him looked like dark silhouettes under the ebbing sun. A pack of topless teenage boys strolled past with a tube speaker banging out some thudding track, and they blocked Curtis's view of the man in the jacket. Curtis stood up on the wall for a better vantage point. The man turned around and he saw his face. Hayden... He could see him clear enough now. He stared straight at Curtis, offered a smirk, and wandered off down the pathway.

Curtis jumped off the wall and weaved through the patrons to follow him. The path was busy, so he diverted onto the beach and jumped over a low wooden groyne. He skidded on the shingle. 'Hayden! Wait up,' he called as he moved. He could see him in the distance, walking at a relaxed pace, with his hands stuffed in his jeans.

Curtis called again, 'Hey, Hayden!'

Hayden stopped on a concrete boat slipway. He stood in front of a sign that said *Private Oyster Beds* and gazed out to the hazy water.

Curtis came close to him, but as a throng of sightseers strolled around the bend and stopped to drink in the sunset, Curtis lost sight of Hayden as he merged into the crowd.

Curtis broke into a run and made his way around a line of yachts, and as he dashed from behind one, he collided into a youngster and sent the poor lad, and the collection of plastic glasses he'd been holding, flying.

'Oh, I'm sorry,' said Curtis, scooping up his scattered horde of plastic beer glasses.

The lad picked himself up. 'No drama. Where's the fire,

mate?' He chuckled. He had a big round face and grinned, displaying uneven teeth.

Curtis handed him back the reusable glasses. There were about twelve.

The youngster accepted them and held them to his chest. 'I get a quid for each one I return to the taproom. I make a decent bit of cash when it's a scorcher. Have to pick some out of the bins, though.'

'Good for you. Sorry again,' said Curtis, scanning ahead for Hayden.

'Can't believe people just toss them away and don't get their deposit back, man. It's mental. Right?'

'It is, it is. You keep saving the planet, buddy,' said Curtis as he trotted along the pathway. He convinced himself that Hayden had left the seafront, so he jumped over the wall and dashed through a tight gravel walkway flanked by fisherman's huts. They were black, wooden-slatted buildings with green doors.

He slowed to a walk and passed by huts numbered seven and eight, ending up at a place called Oggies Alley. A door lay open, giving him a view of a bright white wall and stylish low leather sofas. He considered popping his head right in, just to double-check Hayden hadn't slipped inside, but thought better of it.

Instead, he walked down the quiet street and came to a small pub with people milling around outside, drinking. He scanned around for Hayden but could see no sign of the man. Most people were in summer wear, so he assumed spotting a man wearing a leather jacket in the crowds should be an effortless task.

He jogged along a pebble-strewn track, made his way back onto the beachfront and headed towards the harbour area, his eyes continuously scanning for Hayden. He walked around the small docking area where several tug boats were moored up and headed towards the Harbour Market. A recent fire had gutted out one of the seafood restaurants here, which now stood as a depressing, blackened shell, sectioned off by temporary fence panels and barriers. A really tragic event for the area.

As he studied the damage, he caught sight of that leather jacket through the fence on the other side of the building. Hayden appeared to be heading back into town. Curtis didn't call out this time as he walked on.

VANESSA SAT on the balcony and poured a glass of Zinfandel. She'd almost finished the bottle already. Not wise considering she'd taken ibuprofen and aspirin for her perpetual period pains.

The children were fast asleep, and Curtis had messaged her, saying he'd run into a couple of his new riding buddies and had decided to stay out and have a few drinks with them. This was unusual for Curtis, so she guessed he wanted to stay out of her way.

Vanessa couldn't blame him, of course. She'd not been a joy to be around this week. She touched her chin and squirmed. The rash of pimples seemed to be getting worse. Now her arms were a mass of bumpy goose skin, too. The situation was taking its toll on her mental and physical state. If only *he'd* just make it clear why he'd come here... came out with it and stopped leaving her hanging in limbo to mull over all the awful possibilities.

This had been the longest week of her life, and now she wanted her husband to come home more than anything. Home and safe... with her.

. . .

CURTIS SAT OUTSIDE, drinking and watching out for Hayden. He'd wandered into another pub where a large group of people, mostly a younger crowd, were mooching about outside, drinking and chatting. This was no tourist bar. The people here were locals, and the atmosphere seemed to have a more boisterous and livelier vibe.

He'd found a small table and set up surveillance on a road that led down to the beachfront but also gave him a view of the routes leading in the direction of the harbour and High Street, so it seemed an ideal spot to hang out. The only issue was he'd drunk way too much and things were getting fuzzy. Being so busy, it was inevitable that he'd be joined by other drinkers, and he soon found himself chatting with a local skateboarder enthusiast called Len. This guy told Curtis he'd skateboarded every day for the last forty years and didn't intend to stop anytime soon. Curtis was flummoxed to learn that Len was fifty; he looked younger than he did.

He also spoke to a local plasterer called Paula, who mistook him for someone else called Joey, and she ended up telling Curtis her entire life story, speaking in his ear with a machine-gun-fast voice he found hard to keep up with. He found himself nodding and smiling a lot. As a bonus, he got to view around fifty photos of her girlfriend, Nora, who not only looked twenty years older than Paula, she sounded like a complete tetchy sod, and he was almost tempted to tell her to dump the moaner and find some new skirt, but he decided against this. Luckily, he'd stayed his tongue, because Nora had now shown up with a face like thunder, and the couple had gone inside for a little heart to heart.

But Curtis was enjoying himself. He couldn't remember the last time he'd gone out drinking and chewing the fat with complete strangers like this. *In fact, I never have.*

18

---

anessa checked her phone messages. She'd asked
Curtis what time he'd be home, but he'd yet to
reply. She fought back the panic threatening to rise
inside of her. Vanessa told herself to stop being ridiculous.
Yes, Curtis could be a pushover in some respects, but he was a
big man, and capable of looking after himself. She knew
that... *But* this wasn't some idiotic thug skulking in the
shadows waiting to strike. Insidious, manipulative and clever
would be how she'd describe *him*.

She opened that file again and found herself back inside
the old diary.... back inside Little Essa's head once again.

Tuesday 13th June 1995 continued...

We ended up in the middle of nowhere at some derelict
church. A sinister-looking twelfth-century building. The
doors were boarded up with notices to keep out and signs
warning that it was an unsafe structure. One even warned
danger of death.

Dominic started going on about the disused church being cursed and used by a cult of devil worshipers called Satan's Soulmates, and we were here to see if the gossip was true. I said I'd stay in the car, but Dominic had already locked the doors and said, 'Either get in the church, Essa, or wait outside on your own, because I'm not opening my car!'

Hayden told me he'd look after me and to stop worrying. That it would be a right laugh.

That older lad prised open the wooden shutter on this side door and slithered inside. We all followed. Me included. I had a knot in my stomach... a horrible fist-like knot that seemed to grow in my guts, weighing me down. Like I'd swallowed a huge rock. It smelt damp and horrible inside. Mildew and decaying wood. And the heat in there. Sticky and clingy, like going up into a stuffy loft at the end of a long summer's day. I struggled to breathe.

I remember at this point, things grew strange. Rushes of warmth passed through me. Like hot, erratic waves. I heard my heartbeat in my ears, and that seemed odd. So did the taste in my mouth, like... I dunno, it tasted nasty and metallic.

Inside that church, it was carnage. Leanne and Hayden were shining bright torches around. They were leading the beams across the old benches that were peppered with gloppy bird droppings. The poo lay everywhere. Ew, it was disgusting. Hayden shined his light up and it danced across the skinny pane glass windows. The coloured glass was cracked and parts were smeared with a thick black substance, but I did not know what... The torch light moved across the lumpy stone, revealing huge spots of moss and moist patches.

The older boy now stood on the pulpit smoking a cigarette, his face grey and bony. He almost appeared skeletal... otherworldly. I kept staring at him. Like I was hypnotised or something. I started trying to figure out who the hell this stranger was. What were we all doing in this freaky place with him?

Hayden and Leanne found all these markings on this bench. They appeared to be symbols etched into the wood with a knife. Satanic symbols and bizarre runes and signs. One marking said The Soulmates will destroy the world.

Hayden didn't like seeing these markings. He freaked out, saying, 'I reckon we should go... This shit is real and we're not safe here. They will curse us! They have decimated a church. That's unholy... that's so bad.'

But Leanne and Dominic laughed at him, calling him a superstitious idiot. After his rant, Hayden joined in and pretended he'd been joking. Only I knew he'd been serious. Deadly serious.

It must've been around this time when I started to... see things. The torch lights were all changing different colours, and they seemed so bright... so mesmerising. The older boy's cigarette glowed a funny bright green colour, and the smoke became thick, like swarms of clouds engulfing him. But he looked more and more sinister with each drag he took. Evil. Yes, he looked evil and intimidating. Hollow-eyed and ghostly.

The others were talking about going up to the bell tower and they were shouting and making cackling noises. I followed them, as I did not want to be left alone with the stranger. I passed another sign. One that read danger of collapse. But I kept walking. Things were getting slow. My perception seemed to have increased tenfold. Like I'd gained a superpower. Like I had supersonic senses and I could detect every tiny creak, knock and... murmur... I even caught the sounds of whispering voices. Ghastly voices. I convinced myself that it was them... the Soulmates... these devil worshipers. So I went faster, but my legs no longer felt like they belonged to me.

I noticed the crumbled steps ahead of me. The spiralled stairway was demolished. A dark gap lay at my feet and I swear if I'd taken one more step... I'd have fallen into the gloom below. I peered into that darkness for what seemed like an hour. Then the bottom appeared as if by magic – dotted below I saw rubble and broken furniture. That fall would have likely killed me.

Someone called my name and I only then realised that Hayden was shining his torch into the hole in the stairway, allowing me a glimpse of what would've been my fate. 'It's not far, Essa. Jump over,' Hayden shouted with a big, reassuring smile on his face. His eyes seemed odd, I recall noticing. Big, round and dazzling. I made the jump. He snatched my hand, pulled me to safety, and I followed him up the unsafe steps.

We found Leanne and Dominic at the top of the tower, laughing like loons.

Leanne was gazing at her hands, grinning childishly and going, 'Woooo, mental as fuck, man. Mad, mad, mad.'

Dominic peered out of a small window, making a sound like a sheep. Or perhaps it was meant to be a goat... His head seemed huge to me, like he'd shoved a huge fuzzy, pulsating wig on. The hedgehog tabs were hitting the boys now.

That's when it became very clear to me... I'd put the weird feelings down to booze and nerves... but I knew I was out of it, too. I'd started bloody tripping out of my skull. I don't know how, or when, but they'd spiked me in that car and a wave of sheer panic, desperate dread and fierce anxiety hit me all at once. My heart thudded so hard it sounded like a drum beat echoing around that entire tower. I wanted this to stop. The rushing sensations, those intense, fuzzy images, the mysterious noises.

But Dominic and Hayden were now complaining that they'd taken duff tabs, because they were getting no effects at all. Then Dominic turned to us all and spoke all cold and dark and goes, 'There is a lone figure standing out there by a gravestone, pointing up at me.'

I was shaking my head. Shaking my head and saying, 'No! It's the older boy. It's just the strange boy who came here with us.'

Dominic made this contorted face. 'What you on about, Essa? What older boy?'

Leanne giggled. 'Little Essa's having a baaaad trip. She's gonna freak.' And she started laughing and chanting, 'Freak, freak, freak... freaking out! Whooooh, yeah.'

So I turned to Hayden and pleaded with him. Told him to stop them from teasing me. To tell them to stop being horrible arseholes.

But he says, 'It was only us in that car, Essa. I reckon you might be in trouble. Real trouble. Do you think it's... him? Has he come to take you away?'

He said this so solemnly it made my blood run ice cold. Like I could feel it racing around every single vein and freezing every part of me as it hurtled around my body. My skin prickled with goosebumps and a few tears left my eyes. 'Who?' I asked him.

'The troll,' he said, so quietly I barely caught his words. 'That troll from your garden. I think he came here with us. Followed you. To take you for his own, Essa. The... Whisper Troll.'

My pen is shaking in my hand as I write all this. Just thinking about Hayden speaking of those things... things I'd told him in total confidence... My fears and... my... private affairs... To say I was enraged would not even come close.

'It's not called the Whisper Troll!' I growled at him.

n my drug-induced state, I glared at Hayden for a very long time. Gazed into his sharp, unwelcoming orbs. I saw him in a different light. I saw him for the weak, nasty bully he was. How the hell had I let him treat me like this?

I'd been like his little lost puppy... his Little Essa... hanging around him like some sad, fawning puppet. And for what? For his amusement. Just so his arsewipe friends could jeer at me and make me feel insignificant.

Any decent human being would have calmed me down and told me I'd be alright. Lie and say that the drug wouldn't last long and freaking out was normal. That I'd even enjoy the high if I'd only free my mind, let myself go and absorb the euphoria.

But he wasn't normal. Because drugging your girlfriend in order to scare the utter shit out of her for a laugh with your mates... wasn't normal. The fact that they had purposely taken me to that bad place. It was twisted. All of it... I saw it all so clearly in that one single moment. It seemed like I'd had... I dunno what you call it... a revelation, or perhaps (here I check my tatty dictionary) yes, an epiphany... That's what I had in that moment. I'd been so besotted with him, and so I'd let him treat me like a fool. I had convinced myself he was magnificent, handsome, and kind. I'd told myself I'd hit the jackpot landing myself a boy like Hayden Knox. But now things were clear. I saw through all his lies and deceptiveness. It's super hard to describe now, sitting here writing this, but everything fell into place. I'd been fooled, but I would no longer be conned by this monster.

My limbs had become so heavy and my heart beat so fast I considered it might rip straight out of my chest. I held my hand against it. As if doing so would hold it in place. It seemed to ache, too. My entire chest did.

Then Dominic fixed me with a sinister glare and told me

the Whisper Troll was waiting for me down in the grave-
yard. That they'd all seen my headstone. Because I was
already dead. This place was purgatory and if I didn't let
the troll take me, I'd be stuck here forever.

Dominic said, 'You took your own life today, Essa. You
drank a bottle of neat vodka. You used it to wash down all
those pills. Your dad found you collapsed in the back
garden. But it was too late. You ARE dead.'

I didn't want to believe him. But by this point, my mind
had gone into overdrive. The walls closed in. The smells,
the heat, their mean faces, and my own hoarse breathing...
all became infused into a medley of utter madness that
made my brain feel like it was pulsating... like at any
moment it might pop... explode, sending fragments of my
brain matter into the blackness below. I wondered if I was
going mad... No, I was going mad.

VANESSA STOPPED READING and her heart seemed to
physically ache at the memory of that night in the church.
She closed the file and promised herself to stop reading the
contents. Told herself to delete everything. She didn't, of
course.

19

When Curtis peered up, he saw Hayden sitting where the skate boarder sat a moment ago... just enjoying a beer like he'd been there the entire time. Like this was his table. He nodded at Curtis and raised his glass. 'Down the hatch.'

'You're still staying in town, then?' asked Curtis, thinking, *what a stupid question.* He prepared for a snarky reply.

But that didn't come. Instead, Hayden offered a wistful smile and said, 'I need to apologise, Curtis. You invited me into your home and I was a total dick.'

Curtis puffed out his cheeks. 'Well... I guess we'd had a few, but—'

'But nothing. There are no excuses. I can be an idiot when I'm out of it... but my comments were unnecessary. I hold my hands up. I was out of order. So, I'm sorry. Please tell Essa I'm sorry. I'd tell her myself, but I'm guessing I'd not be welcome back anytime soon, hey?'

Curtis wanted to say that the man's visit had resulted in his wife changing into an almost unrecognisable, sullen stranger. He wanted to ask what happened between the pair to have triggered such a reaction from his wife and why Hayden was still lingering around the town. He wanted to ask why he'd not stopped earlier and spoken to him. Why he'd stridden off and lost him on purpose. But Curtis acknowledged, even in his clouded, drunken state, that if he wanted the answers he sought, being blunt would not be a sensible option. Subtlety would be required here. 'I think she was a tad... surprised, Hayden.'

They spoke for a while about general stuff, and Hayden started opening up about the situation with his mum. About how she'd suffered a serious stroke several years ago and so he'd left France behind and returned to Bristol where his mum now lived to help care for her. That this trip had been his first breather for over a year now and that the situation was suffocating him. 'I love my mother, Curtis, but she needs full-time care. I can't afford it. So it's down to me to look after her.'

Curtis saw the anguish in Hayden's eyes. It struck him that everything about this man seemed so much different to the confident, outspoken individual who'd upset Vanessa around this time the previous weekend. Curtis questioned why he'd been so worried, if he even *had* been, that Hayden posed some sort of threat. Under the opaque outside lighting, Hayden appeared somewhat pathetic and fatigued as he sipped his drink. He didn't really believe that he'd seen a spark between Hayden and Vanessa... did he? Surely all that nonsense had been imagined.

The conversation faded and Curtis felt the need to resume the small talk. 'You got kids yourself?' Curtis asked.

'Um, no. Not sure I'm firing real bullets, if you get what I'm saying.'

'You've tried?'

'With two partners. I've never had tests or anything, but I'm sure I'm the one with the problem.'

'That's a shame. Sorry.'

Hayden laughed. 'I'd be a shitty dad, anyway.'

'I'm sure that's not true.'

'Your kids are lucky. To have the life you've provided them.'

Curtis waited for some mocking comment to follow, but it didn't come. Hayden seemed sincere.

'I didn't do well in school, Hayden. I'm not what you'd call an intellectual type... And I'm not the best with numbers,' said Curtis. 'But from the age of twelve, I knew I wanted to earn. So I started pestering my old man for work even whilst I was in school. As soon as the day was done, I'd be out of those doors and riding my bike to his yard. I'd offer to clean up the vehicles, run errands, and stuff like that. During the summer, all my mates were out having fun and getting up to mischief. Not me. I was busy proving myself to my old man and making some dough.'

Hayden raised his glass. 'I guess it worked out well, Curtis. Now you're the big boss man.'

'Yeah, I mean, having good work ethics was drummed into me. I want my kids to be the same, you know? I don't want them to think they can have it on a plate like entitled brats.'

'Uh-huh. Guess it's the school holidays soon. Bet you've got a ton of stuff planned, right?'

'Yeah. That reminds me, my cheeky git of a son called me a scaredy-cat today. How about that?'

Hayden flashed an amused grin. 'What? Why? What's a big, strapping fella like you possibly scared of?'

'He wants me to take him to some creepy island during the school break. I thought he'd made the place up, but it's real.'

'Sounds intriguing. Where's that?'

'It's called Deadman's Island. Near Queensborough.'

'Never heard of it.'

'On the Isle of Sheppey. You can see it from our house.'

'Deadman's Island?'

'No, no, I mean Sheppey... Queensborough is on the other side. A thirty-minute drive.'

'Got you. What's the deal with that place?'

Curtis sipped his drink and lowered his voice. 'Get this... So, they found around two hundred human remains on this island about six years ago. It is believed they are the bones of men and boys who died of the plague on board prison ships. These floating hulks that were moored up on the Medway about two hundred years ago.'

'What, and the bodies are still there?' asked Hayden, engaged in the tale.

'They were buried in mass graves in the marshes, and coastal erosion and the change in sea levels caused all the coffins and remains to rise to the surface.'

'Shit. Sounds like it's a cemetery.'

'Ah-huh. It's forbidden to go there. At least, prohibited without permission from Natural England, who own the site. But I've seen footage of kayakers and fisherman who have ventured around it.'

'Why would your kid want you to take him there?'

'One of his friends planted the idea into his head. Plus, he's obsessed with everything pirates. He loves all that swash-buckling and adventure stuff. You should see his bedroom; it's all pirate Lego and skull-and-crossbones flags... It was obvious a place called bloody Deadman's Island would pique his interest.'

'You should take him. Be something cool to tell all his school buddies,' said Hayden. 'It'll be fun. Something different.'

'It's a short boat ride. Less than a mile to cross over from Queensborough, but—'

'But?'

'It's in the mouth of a small estuary. Across an area where tides move quickly. It can get choppy out there. Plus, it's a shipping lane. He's only eight.'

'He'll be fine with you.'

'I might go alone next week. To scope it out and see if it would be suitable for him to go across.'

'I'll come with you... I mean, if you wanted. Might be safer. To be honest, it sounds pretty fascinating,' said Hayden.

Curtis, surprised by this offer, stammered, then said, 'Um, sure... I guess... If you'll still be about. I'll need to monitor the tides and weather, of course. Perhaps if I could take your number, we can arrange everything via text?'

'Give me your mobile. I'll pop my number in.'

Curtis handed over his phone. He didn't intend for a moment to arrange any such trip with Hayden, because he knew Vanessa would go ballistic. She'd be super annoyed when she found out they'd spoken tonight. Not to mention it would be way too weird socialising with his wife's ex. He wasn't jealous of the guy, but it didn't seem right. There was one thing having a cordial friendship with your wife's ex if you were forced to see them because of parenting rights or whatever, but in this situation, it would be downright odd.

'Drop me a text, Curtis. I'm about for another ten days, but then I need to return to Bristol.'

'For your mum?'

Hayden nodded and wandered inside to get them both a drink.

HAYDEN ENDED up convincing Curtis to join him at another bar and the pair ended up quite comfortable in each other's company as the boozy night progressed. Curtis, despite himself, found the other man likeable and easygoing. But boy, he could tuck the booze away. Curtis struggled to keep up with the heavy drinking session.

They'd found a place with live music playing. The band was banging out great tracks and the place was crammed and lively. He'd spotted Paula and Nora there, and the skateboarder guy, Len, propped up at the bar, nodding away to the music. The band had played tracks from Skid Row, Soundgarden and Counting Crows, and they were fantastic.

Hayden, now blind drunk, pumped his fist and whooped along. He seemed like an excited teenager with a gleeful grin plastered on his face. He kept patting Curtis on the back, laughing and encouraging him to join the madness. Curtis couldn't recall the last time he'd had such a blast. Hayden even took a few photos of them pulling stupid faces and dancing about the place.

The band's lead singer was a slim chap in his early sixties. He had a long, straggly beard, thinning hair, and wore a salmon coloured top emblazoned with two palm trees and the slogan *California Dreaming*. As the singer swapped his electric guitar for an acoustic, the tempo changed. Mellow rock ballads replaced the earlier heavy beats. The music morphed the rowdy punters into a sedate, watchful audience. Some drinkers mouthed the lyrics. A few couples huddled up together, held hands, or wrapped their arms around one another.

Hayden's eyes were like slits and he gazed about in an exhausted daze. He struggled to stand without holding onto a chair for support. He slumped down at their table, rattling the many glasses cluttering it, some of which were full pints scarcely touched by Curtis. Hayden kept buying him a drink every single time he staggered up to the bar, regardless of his protests that he'd not wanted another.

'May I?' asked Hayden, reaching over to pick up one of his

untouched beers. 'Seems like you need a hand, my good man.'

Curtis stifled a yawn. 'Help yourself. I've drunk way too much already today.'

'The night's just getting started,' slurred Hayden. 'Let your hair down, man. Have some fun for once. You deserve it.'

Curtis raised his own glass, thinking the night was now wrapping up, but he didn't think Hayden would listen.

The lead singer finished his song to a wild applause and a chorus of loud cheers.

A woman's booming voice called out, 'More! One more.'

The singer took a swig of his beer, and said, 'One of my favourites... Pearl Jam's "Better Man". Ready?'

This got more cheers and hoots... As the singer started thrumming his guitar, a hush washed over the crowd.

As the singer played, Curtis found himself quite touched by the stirring piece. He'd never heard of the track, nor could he recall ever listening to the band Pearl Jam. The guy sang in a beautiful voice. Both husky and silvery. Curtis, drawn right into the music, listened intently to the lyrics. As he nodded away, lost in the moment, Curtis caught a glimpse of Hayden and was taken aback. The man appeared to be altogether fixated on the singer. His mouth had dropped open, and his face carried this peculiar, haunted and drawn countenance.

As if in slow motion, Hayden placed down his drink, spilling much of the contents as he did. Then he started mouthing the song's lyrics... but he looked bewitched, scared and woeful. His eyes became red and watery. His shoulders slumped and his posture sagged.

Curtis, about to ask him if he was all right, stopped himself... because in a sudden movement, Hayden raised his hands. He started moving his fingers. The act was barely noticeable, and Curtis thought he was drumming his right fingers against his chest. But then Curtis comprehended what Hayden was doing when he outstretched his left arm and wiggled those fingers too... he was mimicking playing the guitarist's cords. His fingers began moving in rapid, erratic motions, as though he really did hold a guitar in his own hands.

Curtis observed in awe as Hayden continued to strum his imaginary instrument, his knee raised as if resting it on his thigh. This wasn't just someone messing around playing air guitar. Hayden had gone somewhere else. He'd been transported to another place. He was acting like he'd been possessed. Or as if... he was stuck in some meaningful memory.

Whatever had gripped the man now consumed him and had taken him right out of this moment and placed him deep into another. There was an unmistakable, deep concentration on Hayden's face as he continued to play, his left hand moving up and down the phantom guitar.

Hayden closed his eyes and a few tears slid down his cheeks. Curtis, now captivated by the man's behaviour, watched openly, and even when Hayden opened his eyes again, he still didn't notice Curtis gazing right at him.

As the song progressed, Hayden's features grew darker. His face twitched and his lips quivered. His body shuddered, and for a moment Curtis expected the man to topple and fall from his chair, so prepared to catch him.

As the song reached its end, Hayden's eyes flickered, and he surveyed his surroundings with an expression of shock and unease. He swallowed hard and caught Curtis's stare. He eyed him with confusion, as if struggling to register *who* he was. For a brief moment, he looked furious. His eyes blazed with anger, and his lips curled into a snarl. But then he coughed and gave Curtis a lopsided smile. 'Hey, sure is hot in here.' He snatched up a beer and gulped it.

'OK?' asked Curtis.

'Gonna take a leak.' With that, Hayden staggered off.

Curtis, mystified by what he'd witnessed, took a deep breath. *What the hell was that?*

AFTER FAILING to locate Hayden once he'd wandered off to the toilet, and now grasping how the evening had flown by in a blurry, drink-fuelled flash, Curtis trundled off to locate his bike and found himself back down in the harbour area. He'd never explored the seafront during the twilight hour and found wandering through the empty Market Harbour quite a curious experience, as he'd never once seen the place so quiet. He'd walked for a while and not encountered a single person. The wind had picked up and the entire place seemed full of rattling and whistling sounds. Chains clunked and yacht masts jangled and swayed.

He stood on a wooden boat ramp and viewed the horizon, the far-off lights of Essex and Sheppey only blurred smudges across the water. Red and green beacons flashed out at sea, and a sudden hoot from a group of youngsters filled the air, although he could not see them. They started howling, and some crowed and called out as if they were American Indians in some old Western movie. No doubt a group of drunk teenagers either camping on the beach or having a late one.

But their noise soon faded into the night and Curtis felt a sudden apprehensiveness. A deep paranoia fell over him, accompanied by a shiver. It wasn't even that cold tonight. He started down the path, wondering how on earth he'd ambled off as far as the Market Harbour. His bike was in the other direction. He didn't intend to ride; he'd retrieve it and push the old thing home.

Then that feeling again... and another shiver that caused him to jolt. Something made him turn around – and when he did, a shape caught his eye. Unless his drunk vision was deceiving him, which couldn't be ruled out, he thought he could see a figure standing on the beach some thirty feet away.

Curtis rubbed his beard as he eyed the shadowy form. Was it a person? He swallowed hard and couldn't shake the fear rising in him, making his legs heavy and his heart race.

The shape didn't move. It seemed frozen in time.

Curtis tried to call out, but the words wouldn't leave his mouth. Whoever stood down on that shingle wanted him to be afraid. They'd succeeded in that, yet Curtis would not empower them. He was loath to appear intimidated, yet he knew he'd better not approach.

After a couple of minutes of fixed staring, Curtis reached for his phone and called the number Hayden had furnished him with early that night. It rang for a while, but went to the O2 voicemail. The figure didn't move. Nor did they make a grab for a phone. Curtis heard no ringing either, but then it may have been set to silent.

The wind whipped across the beach and the yacht masts clinked, and somewhere a metal dinging sound rang out. The figure's clothes fluttered, giving the appearance that they wore a long jacket or cape.

Curtis next dialled the number for Whitstable Cars. The line kept ringing and ringing and he considered they might have called it a night. He willed somebody to answer.

The figure dropped onto their haunches and Curtis strained his eyes to get a better view.

'Whitstable Cars,' came the voice from the phone.

Did the figure bury something in the shingle?

'Hello?' said the taxi operator.

'Um, hi. Pickup from Harbour Street, by the entrance to the aggregate works... please.'

'Going to?'

'Preston Parade.'

'Be twenty minutes. Is that OK?'

Curtis still watched the figure. They'd stopped digging, but not stood up. 'Thanks.'

'What's the name, please?'

'Um, Curtis Pascall.'

'OK, great. Got you all booked in, Curtis.'

Curtis still watched the figure. They'd not yet stood up. 'Cheers.' He ended the call and headed back towards the harbour area, walking as fast as his fear and alcohol-infused legs would allow. He could walk home in half an hour, but not in this state. The wind seemed to get fiercer and his breathing was even more ragged as he bumbled along, overcome with anxiety in his rapid need to flee the beach area.

CURTIS COULD SEE the giant arms of the excavators parked in the nearby asphalt plant looming up behind him. The plant itself, grey and clad in corrugated metal, stood like some monolithic tower from a grim fairy tale, dominating the skyline. Curtis waited on the main road, willing a set of headlights to approach, as he kept intermittently flicking his eyes back to the far side of the harbour – waiting for the figure to appear in the distance.

He felt so spineless, but he would have been lying to himself if he'd not admitted to wanting to jump for joy when the taxi pulled up. Curtis trembled as he sank down into the passenger seat. He'd never been more pleased to see another person as the young driver greeted him with a warm smile.

As the car headed back towards the High Street, Curtis was certain he caught another sighting of the shadowy figure lurking in the courtyard of the burnt-out restaurant, and wondered if he'd lost the plot and was seeing things.

20

Vanessa sat at the end of the bed. She hadn't slept a wink. Her swimming stuff lay all over the bedroom tub, left to dry from yesterday's swim. Curtis's clothes were scattered over the floor and he remained in the same spot he'd face-planted the bed at one am, naked save for one white sock.

The stink of sour booze lingered in the air, so she padded across the room, unfolded one door and slipped out onto the balcony. She took in the fresh morning air and scanned for the boat in the hazy dawn. No sign today. Not yet.

CURTIS APPEARED downstairs just after nine. He slumped at the breakfast bar, sheepish and drowsy. Vanessa considered he was doing a class job of imitating last Sunday's disgraced, in-the-doghouse demeanour.

'I've made you a smoothie. It's in the fridge. You could use some vitamin C.'

Curtis grimaced. 'Maybe later. I need a coffee first.'

Vanessa sipped her fruit smoothie, not taking the hint and offering to put the kettle on. 'Good night?' she asked.

'Sorry I didn't text you back. I've only just seen the messages.'

Vanessa shrugged, sensing her husband needed to get something off his chest.

He kept scratching the back of his neck, smoothing his beard and avoiding eye contact.

'What?' she asked.

'I saw *him* last night... I bumped into Hayden.'

Vanessa tensed and it seemed every muscle in her body became taut.

'We talked for a while. Well, for a few hours.'

Vanessa gritted her teeth. 'Oh. I see. A few hours. Wow.'

'We ended up at the same bar and—'

'And you bought him a few cold ones? What, as a thank you for ruining last weekend?'

'He said to send his apologies. He feels bad, Vee.'

'So, you had matey drinks? Are you best pals now? What next? Is he joining the riding club?' She let out a dry laugh. 'I know you're desperate for friends, Curtis, but this... this is absurd.' The forlorn expression forming on her husband's face made her regret that comment.

The truth was, Curtis didn't have many friends. Not good ones, anyway. He'd spent most of his adult life so focussed on the business, he had allocated little time to enjoying a satisfying social life. His dedication had gained him plenty of money and respect, but that came at a cost. He had lots of work colleagues and associates back in London, but he was the boss. That meant a certain distance was always kept. That just seemed to be the way it worked. She knew he was keen to change things, and the move to Whitstable, as well as being a chance to disengage from the constant grind of work, was meant to give him a chance to live a better life. That included a decent social life outside of his unremitting, utterly consuming business.

'I think the guy seems genuinely upset with himself for the things he said, Vee.'

'And what else did you talk about?'

'Just this and that. His mum had a stroke, and he looks after her. They live in Bristol. Um, he's going back in ten days.'

'What else?'

Curtis drew in his lips and crinkled his nose.

'What?'

'Vee, I think the guy has some issues. Like, perhaps he's... you know, not quite the full ticket?'

Vanessa sipped her smoothie again.

'Vee, please just tell me what's going on with you two. What happened when you were teenagers?'

Vanessa put down the glass and swallowed, her throat raw and tight. 'Did he say something?'

'Is it some kind of secret? Something you both did? It's clear enough that whatever the issue is has put you on edge.'

'Listen to me. Listen carefully, Curtis... *He* manipulates, twists and destroys.'

'Come on, Vee, you've not seen each other since you were teenagers!'

'*He's* poison. He gets inside people's heads and—'

'And what? What did he do? Make me understand what's going on. Why leave me in the dark like this? Why can't you even say his name?'

They sat in silence for a short while before Curtis tutted, got up and filled the kettle with water from the filter jug.

'They drugged me once,' she said quietly. 'Him and his friends.'

Curtis stopped pouring.

'They spiked my drink with LSD tabs. Quite a few,

judging by the state I got into. Then they drove me out to this derelict church in the middle of nowhere. Some scuzzy den where junkies and creepy cults used to hang out.'

Curtis put the kettle on and returned to his seat.

'They told me I'd killed myself and I was stuck in purgatory.'

'Oh, come on, Vee, you surely didn't believe that bull crap?'

'Curtis, have you ever taken LSD?'

'Of course I haven't!'

'Well then, trust me when I say that if someone says you've killed yourself whilst tripping off your tits, your brain doesn't cope well.'

'What? "Tripping off your tits?" Come on, Vee. LSD. Derelict churches and chasing around with a gang of undisciplined youths. There's a lot I don't know about your past.'

His judgmental tone riled Vanessa, but she didn't react.

'What else did you take? Next, you'll be telling me you spent half your unruly youth smoking crack cocaine and robbing old ladies.'

'Oh, I see. OK. So, what *they* did was my fault?'

'No... no, I'm not saying that. It's just... I'm hearing some things about your past that are, quite frankly, shocking me, Vee.' He huffed and tugged at his beard. 'But let's not get this all out of proportion. I'm sorry, alright? Look, dredging up the past like this is unhealthy. You should talk to the guy. Phone him up and clear the air. Get all that previous nonsense out of the way.'

Nonsense, thought Vanessa... *If only he knew the half of it.*

'I don't have his number!'

'I'll text it to you. Call him today and sort... whatever *this* is out. I can't stand you being like this.'

'He gave you his number? Why did he do that?'

'Um, I dunno.'

Vanessa scrutinised him. His guilty expression belied his words. But for now, she'd let that go. 'Send it now, please,' she demanded.

'My phone's upstairs. I need to drive down and get my bike back. I left it on the seafront.'

'You left a four-grand bike outside all night?'

Curtis shook his head. 'No, my old mountain bike. I'll drive the kids down and buy them an ice cream.'

AFTER A SHOWER AND STRONG COFFEE, Curtis felt just about awake enough to drive down to the beach. He parked up in Keam's Yard carpark next to the taproom and loaded his bike into the Wrangler. Then he took Sofia and Jude for a stroll to get ice creams from the Mr Whippy van next to the harbour. It was still early, and the harbour wasn't busy yet. Dog walkers and joggers dominated the walkway and a pungent, fishy odour hung in the air, which churned his fragile stomach.

Curtis returned to the spot where he'd seen the figure watching him the previous night. He'd presumed that now, in the daylight, with people around him, he'd feel ridiculous for his cowardly reaction to the strange watcher. But he didn't. Even now, the memory of it almost made his legs buckle. Something told him... something deep inside his gut... that he'd done the right thing. That if he'd gone to confront the individual, the consequences would have been bad. God knows how. But it was there, nagging away at him.

Whilst Jude and Sofia sat on the beach and devoured their ice creams, Curtis walked down to the place where he'd previously seen the figure crouching down. A small mound of shingle and shells marked the spot, as if they'd been purposely left in order to make the place easy to find. As if they'd known he'd come back and snoop around.

Curtis knelt down and dug into the mound. Nothing obvious here. He dug deeper and the top of a piece of what he guessed to be a crisp wrapper caught his attention. He pulled it up. But it wasn't rubbish – he'd found a photo. One from his house. A picture taken many years ago, of Curtis and Steve, both holding pool cues. A shot taken in the garage of their old family home, around ninety-two. It had been in Curtis's study, stuck on the wall, and he'd not even noticed it had gone missing.

'What's that, Daddy?' asked Sofia, ice cream smeared over her lips.

Curtis shoved the photo inside his pocket. 'Nothing. Time to head home.' He stood and took a few deep breaths.

'Are you not having yummy ice cream for breakfast, Daddy?' asked Sofia.

Jude smirked. 'Daddy had too many beers last night and feels sick.'

Curtis tried to let out a jovial chuckle, but ended up coughing and almost throwing up. 'Come on. Let's go back to the car.'

What game was Hayden playing? Now he wished he'd not given his wife that number.

VANESSA STOOD on the balcony and gazed out to sea. The boat hadn't been back. She dialled Hayden's number for the tenth time. Like the previous times, it rang for a while, then went to the O2 voicemail. She left a message. 'We need to talk. Today! No more bullshit. I want you to tell me what you want!' She ended the call, sat down on a chair, and tossed her phone onto the table.

A message beeped through on her phone. She snatched the device back up and read it.

> You have the wrong number.

Vanessa thumbed a message back:

> No more messing about! Why are you here?

No reply came.

Vanessa headed downstairs to the kitchen. The patio doors lay wide open and she could hear lively hoots and whoops from Sofia, confirming that her family had returned. Curtis didn't even acknowledge her. He sat on the doorstep gawping out into the garden, subdued. Sofia bounced like a loon on her low trampoline.

Curtis caught Vanessa's eye, pursed his lips, and flashed her a disapproving look. She considered her husband appeared older and more exhausted than ever today. There were worry lines stretched across his forehead, and his beard looked scruffy and very bushy. He gazed back into the garden, letting out a long, melancholy sigh.

21

'Have you been sleeping?' asked Delphine, passing Vanessa a coffee in a tall glass. Delphine wore a lilac turban head towel and a long kaftan gown with bright, psychedelic patterns. Her flawless skin seemed to glow.

Vanessa placed her drink on a wicker table where a crumpled printout lay. An image she'd printed from the CCTV footage. Delphine had eyed the photo but hadn't commented on it.

They sat outside Delphine's static caravan on a decking area, under a triangular-shaped sun canopy that fluttered in the light breeze. The decked-out area was painted a light charcoal colour and the little space was surrounded by big white geraniums, violet snapdragons and pink magnolia shrubs. The small garden was immaculate, the park itself serenely quiet and charming.

'Delphine, when did you first comprehend that... you could, you know, see things?'

'I guess I knew I was different by the time I'd reached nine, perhaps ten. My mother didn't embrace my gift. She assumed there was something amiss with me. That I had problems. She blamed my Greek heritage... well, my papa's mother, mainly... Grandma Lambros, the wannabe Athenian fortune teller, putting crackpot ideas in my fragile head. But my granny used to chuckle and say, "Hey, you do have the gift, my sweet Delph, but you didn't inherit it from me... because I was a total faker." Such a quirky lady. I miss her.'

'Your mother thought you had problems?'

'She'd take me to the doctor and demand they put me on medication. She'd tell the entire family to "Ignore Delphine... Delphine is cuckoo." As I got older, I stopped trying to convince her. It didn't matter what she believed.'

'Did it put a rift between you and your mum?'

'Yes. A little. But things eventually changed. But she could never resist the odd dig. She'd always believed that everything had to have a rational explanation and did not tolerate any mumbo jumbo nonsense. But... that was her opinion. We still had a decent relationship. What about you?'

'Me?'

'Your mother isn't in your life. Is she?'

Vanessa sipped her coffee and shifted uncomfortably. She'd never once mentioned anything about her mother to Delphine. She never spoke about her. Not even to Curtis.

Delphine, sensing this was a sore subject, shook her head. 'Don't talk about it. Not if you don't want to.'

'I have memories of her. But—' She stopped and gazed at Delphine, trying hard to get a read on her. She felt that opening up and picking at this scab wouldn't be wise. Especially not to Delphine. 'We had an odd relationship. She was in and out of my life for most of my childhood. Until one day she just couldn't be bothered anymore.'

'How old were you when she left, Vee?'

'Ten. I remember because it was my birthday. There was another man. Well, there were plenty of those in Heidi's life, but she'd been telling my dad about some special fella that had swept her off her feet. That this other guy was... the *one*. I can still recall his name... Gable... Gable Dankworth. A total sleaze. Just how she liked them. They moved to the Midlands.'

'Sorry.'

'So, your gift... when you see things, are they always crystal clear?' asked Vanessa, desperate to veer the conversation in a different direction.

'You can ask me. It's OK, Vee.'

Delphine's eyes flicked to the photo, then back to Vanessa. 'I see you're very interested in this all of a sudden.'

'I can't really ignore it now, can I?'

'I'm just teasing, lovey. I understand this stuff scares you.'

'I know what I said, Delphine... But I'm going out of my mind. Those things you told me...'

'I visited a place in a dream. A place where I saw you. You were very young and distraught. No, terrified. I seem to recall high yellow cliffs. I think there was a boy with you.'

Vanessa's blood turned cold. She pointed at the photo. 'Is this who you saw in your vision?'

'The images were unclear. The faces of those present... blurred.'

'Then you can't be certain it was me.'

'But *it was* you. You don't always have to see everything clearly to know.'

That's cleared all that up then, thought Vanessa.

'Do you know we all carry the gift, Vee? I believe every single person does. A sixth sense. Déjà vu. Strong premonitions. That sinking feeling that something terrible is about to happen. Some people just decipher how to utilise it in a befitting fashion. They can hone the skill and use it in an effective way. For most, it's not as obvious. It doesn't rise to the surface and dominate their every waking moment. For others – it's strong. It's oppressive. It cannot be ignored. Otherwise, it would drive them insane. I'm in the latter category.'

Vanessa fixed her eyes on Delphine and held her stare. 'That night... at my house. What did you sense? In him?'

Delphine didn't respond for several moments. Vanessa felt fixed and drawn to Delphine's light-grey eyes as though the other woman had slipped right inside her subconscious and had delved around in her memory bank. It made her uncomfortable.

'Sadness. Confusion... anger,' said Delphine.

Delphine jolted away as if an icy bolt shot through her. She appeared agitated as she sipped her coffee, her lips curling as if the drink now tasted sour. 'I think he wants answers,' said Delphine, speaking in such a quiet voice Vanessa barely heard her.

VANESSA GOT into her car and sighed. The conversation with Delphine had left her feeling discomposed and drowsy. Now dark thoughts and memories swirled in her head like an agonising tornado, intent on ripping the very foundations of her sanity to shreds.

A sudden flashback hit her like a slam of lightning and she could picture her mother standing at the end of her bed, with a look of scorn on her pinched face. 'Have you been spying on me, Vanessa?'

'Who was that man, Mummy? The one in the blue van?'

'There was no man. Silly old Billy.'

Vanessa *had* seen the man. She'd peered out of the bathroom window. Seen her mum lean into the car. Glimpsed the man's ruddy face and bristly beard. Watched them kiss. 'I saw... him. The big bearded man.'

'If you tell tales, do you know what will happen, Vanessa?'

Vanessa remembered shaking her head and her mother

stomping over to her. She could recall her gnashing her teeth and that incensed expression that washed over her gaunt features. Vanessa remembered the angst in that moment and the strong cigarette stench clinging to the woman. She'd almost wet her nightie as the bedsheets were torn back.

'The nasty Tittle-Tattle Troll will come for you, Vanessa! He'll come and *snatch* you away!'

'You're lying. There is no such thing.'

Her mother had dragged her from the bed, gripped her by the back of the neck and marched her over to the window. She pointed down at the garden. 'That dirty old wooden shed... see it? Well, that's *his* domain. That's where he takes all the children that tell horrible tales. His skin is sallow, with thick, grey hair on his back. He's gangly, deformed, and his face is disfigured and piglike. His long, spider-like fingers will rip at your flesh and if you don't comply, he'll pull out your organs and feed them to his giant pet spiders. His eyes are like fire and full of wrath. He'll drag you down there and keep you in his den. Like a little pet. He has an army of ghastly fairies. Not the nice ones you read about in the kiddie stories, but beastly little things with teeth like razors and hard, reptilian skin. They come from the bleak Norwegian forests. Dark, unfriendly places where the sun never shines.'

Vanessa had remembered gulping in terror and wiggled, desperate to pull herself free so she could run away from her. But the grip had been tight.

Still, her mum had carried on. 'The fairies guard the shed for the troll. They hide in the grass and bushes all the time, and they'll stab at your legs with their tiny spears if you go into that grass. Perhaps even bite off your toes and eat them for a snack! Sometimes those fairies will sneak into bedrooms at night. They'll climb inside the little liar's mouth whilst they sleep and make their way right down into their stomach. Then they'll eat you from the inside out!'

Vanessa had shuddered and gasped in horror, slapping a hand over her mouth. Her mother had been so convincing, so solemn in her telling of the grim story, that Vanessa believed it.

Then she pinched Vanessa's cheek, hard enough to make her yelp, and said, 'So stop making up stories, or the Tittle-Tattle Troll and his nasty, obedient minions will hunt you. And no one will stop him. He'll drag you down there and no one will ever be able to find you. You'll be there, but we won't be able to see you. No one will.'

'Why? Why won't anyone see me, Mummy?'

'Because... you'll be in the troll's dark land. Us adults can't see it. But it's there... oh, yes, it *is* there, and it's scary. Dark and stinky... a world with no colour, like an old-fashioned movie. It smells like rotten flesh. Children's flesh. The floor is made up of bones. The tiny skulls of the nasty boys and girls that tell horrid tales are littered all over the floor. Because when the troll gets bored with you, you'll no longer be his pet... you'll be his... DINNER!'

After her mum had said this, she planted a long kiss on Vanessa's cheek, led her back to bed and tucked her up as though the previous conversation hadn't just happened. Her nastiness lifted, and she gave Vanessa a playful tickle and silly smile, as if the whole thing had just been some daft game. 'But you don't need to worry about that silly, grotty old troll. Because you don't tell fibs. Do you, sugar?'

'No, Mummy. Never.'

She'd given Vanessa's nose a gentle squeeze. 'Ah, good. That's good to hear. Night-night, cheeky.'

Her mum often did that – transformed from one character to another in the space of a few minutes. It was very disconcerting. Very peculiar. Like there were two sides to her that were so different. Unfortunately, Mean-Mum had been the most prevalent character during Vanessa's childhood.

There were other stories, too. The miniature goblins that would steal her filthy teeth if she forgot to brush them. 'They'll yank them out and smash at them with tiny axes and hammers, Vanessa!' And the fierce demons that lurked in the cupboards, ready to claw out your eyes and chew off your tongue if you took food without first asking.

Vanessa didn't sleep a wink during that night she'd learnt about the troll. She knew her mum wasn't joking because she'd seen the nastiness in her eyes. Sensed her hostility. So, Vanessa didn't venture down to the bottom of the garden for a long time. Not right down there, anyway. And she never went barefoot in that longer grass that encompassed the old, tatty shed, or anywhere else out there. The garden's end became *the total no-go zone.*

Even when she was old enough to understand her mother was bullshitting her, it still stayed with Vanessa. Still echoed in her mind that it wasn't safe down there. That shed still spooked her out. She'd stare down at it sometimes. Often, she'd convince herself that a peculiar, dark shape had materialised in the window, as if something was inside, furtively watching her. It became a weed-covered patch that was so unkempt, so tangled with brambles and shrubbery, it did become the forgotten, no-go area she'd always considered it.

Their garden at Redrow Close was strange. Rather skinny, but also very long, with high fences on either side that seemed to loom above you, giving the impression you were penned in. It never caught the sun or felt welcoming. She had no fond memories of fun and laughter in that garden.

She recalled going down there drunk. Right down there, to the very end. To the rickety shed itself. She'd been about fifteen and thought, *Sod this. It's time to put this one to bed. Time to stop being ridiculous.* But even after half a bottle of stolen Archers, consumed neat, and a good few tugs on a chunky hash joint, she still got scared out of her mind. She'd heard her own breathing as she'd approached. She'd never forget how loud those rasping breaths sounded. It was like she'd started having one of those asthma attacks her friend at school, Sally Taylor, used to have. Like she couldn't breathe properly. She used her dad's hefty Maglite torch to peer in through the window, and scanned the beam over all the forgotten junk inside. Saw the rusty tools, stacks of crates and some corroded bike parts.

When she tried to open the door, she'd caught the back of her hand on a score of vicious thorns that tore right into her knuckles. One stuck in deep, and as she pulled her hand away, one toothlike thorn broke off and embedded itself in her skin. That hurt like hell. She'd gone straight back to the house to remove the thorn with tweezers and clean the nasty gash with antiseptic cream.

It now dawned on Vanessa that she'd been about the same age as Sofia is now when her mum first told her about the troll. That put a big lump in her throat.

Vanessa's dad tried to explain things to Vanessa once. 'She's just different from other mums. She does love you, Jellybean. Honest to God, she does. It's just she... she wants other things in her life, too. We are... I don't think we are quite enough for her. That's all.'

Vanessa could never recall her dad bad-mouthing her mother. Not ever. Not even when she'd treated them both like shit. Even when Vanessa told her dad the troll story, he hadn't condemned her. 'No, Jellybean. No. She was joking. She's always had a whacky sense of humour. Bonkers, that woman. But I bet she only meant it as a laugh. You were too young to understand her warped humour and you've taken it all wrong. But if you knew her like I did... you'd understand.'

He'd always defend her. Vanessa loved him for that. Because that must've been so hard to do.

Vanessa eyed the printout from the CCTV. Earlier that

morning, she'd been to every hotel and bed and breakfast along Marine Parade and surrounding streets, showing the photo to everyone. She'd used the pretence that she was searching for her brother-in-law who'd fallen on bad times and had fled the coop, leaving his distraught family worrying sick. But no one she'd spoken to recognised him.

Deep down, she knew it was a waste of time. If he didn't want her to track him down, she'd never find him.

22

The petrol station was jam-packed, and it was so sweltering in the car, Vanessa wondered if the AC was on the blink. She'd picked the wrong pump all right, and now she was wedged right in, and the woman in front hadn't even started filling up yet.

'Mummy, I'm hungry. Can we get sweets?' whined Sofia.

Vanessa cranked up the AC switch.

'Mum, Sofia keeps nudging me,' complained Jude.

'No, he keeps nudging *me*, Mummy!'

The woman in front seemed to take forever. As if deliberately taking her time to stroll to the pump. More cars piled into the forecourt. The van behind them edged closer, its engine grumbling as if the vehicle itself was as irritated as she was.

'Mummy, Jude called me Sappy Sofia.'

The woman filled up with a bored expression plastered on her face, which accompanied the two-inch-thick foundation already stuck on it.

'Ew, Mum, Sofia just wafted her fart over to me!'

The woman started shaking the pump, knocking every

tiny drip from it. The van seemed to loom closer. Vanessa's chest tightened as she gripped the steering wheel and willed the woman to move her bloody Nissan.

As if sensing Vanessa's annoyance, the woman took a leisurely stroll back to the car to get her purse.

Great, she is paying inside.

The woman flicked her bright, bouncy blond hair as she walked back past, and Vanessa caught her eye as she strutted away, a hard scowl now slapped on her morose face. There were several parking spots opposite, which they both knew she *could* have nipped into. Vanessa would have done the courteous thing and moved before paying.

Vanessa breathed in deeply, then let out a long, whistling sigh. The air-con was blowing cold now, yet she still felt hot and clammy.

'Mum! Sofia stinks,' complained Jude. 'Eh, like gone-off baked beans.'

'Mummy, I need a wee and my tummy says I'm hungry.'

'Your tummy says you need an enormous poo, more like,' said Jude, spitting out a hysterical laugh at his own joke.

Sofia scowled. 'I can only poop at home!'

In the Nissan, several young kids were jumping about, along with a small white terrier which Vanessa could see leaping from seat to seat and shaking a soft toy in its jaws. Those kids were bickering too, and one was trying to retrieve the toy from the dog.

A beep sounded from the other side of the forecourt.

Vanessa's fuel gauge was almost on empty, but if she'd been able to reverse, she would have been skidding out of the place without a moment's hesitation.

Vanessa blocked out the engines and the complaining behind her and concentrated on her breathing.

The woman eventually came out with a handful of shopping. She gave Vanessa a sly smirk as she strolled back to the Nissan, milk, crisps and doughnuts in her grasp.

When the woman plonked herself inside the car and proceeded to dish out packets of crisps to the unruly children, Vanessa tensed up and wanted to scream obscenities at her. To tell her to piss off out of the way before she rammed her stupid car straight out of the garage. She could feel her blood boiling as she gritted her teeth in anger, but was loath to react. It was as if the horrid woman wanted her to snap and lash out.

The woman started her engine, but still made no effort to move away. And why? Because the damn arsehole was lighting up a cigarette now.

That was the final straw. Vanessa watched as the woman puffed smoke around the small space and she couldn't help but picture her own mother. Even when she'd moved out and her dad had quit... even then, she'd puff that vile stink around the entire house. Even in Vanessa's bedroom. She remembered having to keep her window open all night after one of Heidi's fleeting visits.

Vanessa spun to face her kids. 'Jude, stop annoying Sofia and climb in the front with me! And, Sofia, stop farting on your brother.' She then gave the woman a long, aggressive blast of her horn, which resulted in the woman turning in her seat, giving her an indignant glare and then her middle finger.

Vanessa's heart was racing as she chewed on the inside of her mouth.

Sofia leant between the seats. 'Mummy, why did you beep that lady?'

'Um... oh, because I know her,' lied Vanessa, not wanting to admit to her children that she'd lost her shit with the sour-faced moose.

'Do you? What's her name?' asked Sofia.

'Oh, um... Debbie.'

'Debbie who?' asked Sofia.

Slowly, the Nissan moved off the forecourt and Vanessa bolted into the spot and wrenched up the handbrake.

'Debbie... Debbie Downer! Now in your seat,' said Vanessa, scrabbling for her purse, before leaping out and charging to the pump.

23

V anessa found Dominic Brookes on Facebook. Even without her own account, it had been super easy. He'd popped up straight away and, luckily for her, his account was open for all to see. She scrolled through his posts and established he was married with kids, worked as an estate agent in Southampton, and broadcasted his entire life on social media. Places he frequented, food he ate, days out he'd been on... the lot.

She couldn't locate his address, but didn't intend to turn up on his doorstep anyway. But she'd seen regular posts on a Thursday afternoon, where Dominic would tag himself as being present at a pub where he and his work buddies would hang out for a boozy post-work gathering. He'd been tagged there four Thursdays in a row. This seemed like the best place to hijack the man. Failing that, she'd call the estate agents and request a viewing. Specifically requesting Dominic.

. . .

ON THURSDAY, Vanessa cleared her day and left for Southampton just after lunch. Curtis was back early, and she'd asked him to pick up the kids from school as she was meeting Delphine to go plant and flower shopping. She'd not slept well the night before and, after spending an additional hour in traffic, had to stop at Fleet services for three strong coffees, a face wash and some paracetamol to fight off the headache edging its way into her temples.

Once back on the road, she started having doubts about what she was doing. It seemed sensible yesterday, but today, here and now, almost at her destination, she realised how insane this was. But she didn't turn back.

VANESSA STOOD across the road from the pub. The place was an impressive twelve-century building near Southampton Port. It was half-timbered, with white walls and an abundance of hanging baskets decorating the front, all of which seemed to burst with red, white and purple flowers. By the door stood a food board advertising beer-battered cod, chips, and mushy peas. She imagined the place was steeped in wonderful history and served fabulous food, but she wasn't on some jolly excursion. She was here for Dominic. For answers.

There were two motorbikes parked out the front, and by the nearest table stood two leather-clad bikers; a couple in their early sixties who were discussing their order. They'd claimed a table by putting their crash helmets and jackets onto it. Two more tables were dominated by a group of suited men, leaving one spare.

Vanessa strolled right past and stepped around the side of the building. She couldn't be sure if Dominic had been with the group, but it wasn't a busy street, so Vanessa guessed she'd have stood out if she blatantly stood there gawping at the bunch.

Vanessa walked back past the men again and hurried inside. She ordered a Diet Coke, a bag of ready-salted crisps, and went back outside. She made for the bench, picking the seat facing the suits, and got comfortable. The men were a mixed bag, some of them quite young, others clocking fifty, but she'd yet to spot Dominic on either table amongst the gathering. The sun was out and most of the men had removed their jackets and loosened their ties as they sipped beers and chatted.

TWENTY MINUTES DRAGGED PAST, and after listening to the men talk shop and waffle and moan like a bunch of fishwives, Vanessa started to lose faith in seeing Dominic today. All she'd established was that the men were from two different estate agents. Most of them disliked their wives or girlfriends, and one guy called Maddocks had broken his big toe during a friendly game of football. Oh, and the elderly couple had fussed and complained about everything, everyone, and started each sentence by tutting, sighing, or blowing out an irritating huffing noise.

Vanessa stood up, and before she even knew what she was doing, addressed the suits. 'Hey, you guys are all estate agents, right?'

Seven pairs of eyes were all fixed on her.

'We are. You want a card?' asked this Maddocks guy.

'I was wondering if any of you know Dominic Brookes?'

The name generated a few wry grins and one bald guy muttered, 'He's been at it again, the little sleaze.'

'He a friend of yours?' asked Maddocks.

'Um, no. He did some viewings for me. Helped me find a

place. I... was just going to buy him a drink, that's all. To say thanks for all his help.'

'She can buy me a drink if she likes,' said one of the younger men at the far table, plainly showing off to his companions. This got a few sniggers. But Maddocks gave him a reproaching glare. A glare that Vanessa thought said, *that's bad for business, lad.*

'Dom is on his way. Got caught up in a viewing,' said one of the other older guys with a round face and thick, comical eyebrows.

She grinned at them. 'That's... yep, that's great. Listen, this sun is giving me a headache, and I forgot my shades, so I'm heading inside. Could you tell Mr Brookes to nip in and say hi? I'd appreciate that.'

'Of course we will,' said Maddocks.

VANESSA WAS FINISHING her third soft drink when Dominic strutted in and approached the bar. As he ordered up a beer, he scanned the room with a suspicious scowl fixed on his face. Dominic caught Vanessa's eye, and she gave him a wave. He rubbed his chin and appeared confused, as though searching his memory for where he knew her from. They'd not clapped eyes on each other since ninety-five. She didn't expect him to recognise her. He paid for his drink and strutted over to her table holding his pint. She'd purposely sat out of the way in a quiet corner.

'The guys said you wanted to buy me a drink,' he said, his frown deepening.

Up close Dominic looked much the same as she'd remembered him – beady-eyed, with sharp facial features and a face you'd quite like to punch, more than once. Only now his once dirty-blond, tousled hair was short and receding and he had a week's worth of fluffy stubble on his bony face. His suit was well pressed, and he wore an eye-catching floral tie. He hadn't recognised her. He gave her a professional smile, although this smile soon morphed into a leery grin with an accompanying look that Vanessa thought said, *are you a past conquest?*

'Hello, Dominic. I'm Vanessa. Vanessa—' She almost said Pascall. '—Neal.'

Dominic's face changed. He scowled and his nostrils seemed to grow three sizes bigger. Then he laughed, spun on his heels and walked away from her.

'Dominic! I just want to ask you something. Please... It's important.'

Dominic turned, tutted and said, 'Piss off.'

'He showed up at my house.'

'Who?'

'You know who.'

Dominic shrugged. 'So? Why would that matter to me?'

'Why? What does he want?'

'Well, why didn't you ask him?'

'He's playing games! I need to find out what he's up to, Dominic. I really do!'

'And how the hell would I know?'

'Has he been in touch? Have you spoken about—'

'No and no. And I'm not interested in any of that shit. I don't want to get involved.'

Vanessa snorted. 'You were happy enough to get involved that night.'

'I literally have no idea what you are talking about. Involved in what?' he said in an innocent voice as he arched his eyebrows.

'Yes, you *do!*' she snapped. 'Don't be an arsehole, Dominic.'

'I've not even seen Knox since... um, let me think... yeah, since some big rave in Bournemouth. We saw in the millennium together. A bunch of us. He was talking about the States. Some bullshit about this massive opportunity he had... I assumed he was talking shit. But he left and I've not seen him since.'

'I don't believe you. You were his little follower. You shadowed him everywhere and were always so desperate to make him admire you.'

Dominic shook his head. 'Your memory must be all mixed up. That's all lies. You were full of crap back then, and evidently nothing has changed.'

'He thought you were a weak-minded, arse-kissing creep. He told me that one day. After he found out that you'd been buying the same clothes and trainers as him. Oh, yeah, he took the right piss out of you behind your back. And yet you still sided with him... you still let him...' She stopped and sipped her Coke. She could murder a *proper* drink now.

Dominic sniffed and pretended to be upset. 'Oh, I'm heartbroken. But I'm bored now. So, goodbye. *Do* have a pleasant life.'

'If everything comes out... you'll be in a lot of trouble, Dominic.'

Dominic inhaled, drew in his lips and exhaled out of his wide nostrils. 'Yeah, is that a fact?'

Vanessa didn't respond. She didn't like the nasty edge in Dominic's voice now. Or the flash of malice in his small green eyes.

Dominic checked behind him, as if making sure no one could hear him, then he stepped closer to Vanessa's table and glared at her. 'Who'd you think you are? Waltzing in here spouting bollocks. It was a lifetime ago!'

'Twenty-seven years, Dominic. But it still happened! You still played a part in what—'

'Shut your mouth!' he hissed, jabbing a finger so close to Vanessa's face he nearly poked her in the eye. 'Don't you dare, you stupid bitch. I bet you think you've moved on. But deep down you're still just... *Little*... stupid... *Essa*. And if you start unearthing the stuff from all those years back... trust me when I say this – you'll be in for the mind fuck of your life.' He let out a low, nasty chuckle. 'So... do... not... screw... with... me. Got that, Essa?'

Every time she heard *that* name, it felt like a knife in her guts. She hated it. She fought back the tears struggling to escape from the corners of her eyes. Dominic Brookes had always been a vile beast of a boy. And underneath the crisp suit, flashy tie and business-like smile, the nasty boy she remembered all those years back still lurked within. She'd unleashed him easily.

Dominic gulped back his drink and let out a long, 'Aaaah-hhh.' Then he smacked his lips and wiped them with the back of his hand. 'Do you know he was shafting two other birds behind your back? Oh, what was their names... Kelly and Tiff, I think. Right dirty skanks. Yeah, one of them gave him the clap or something. He was laughing and telling us all he was surprised he'd not given it to you. I remembered him saying he'd shafted one of them up the... you know? The *wrong* hole. Whoops! Then went straight to see you and made you nosh him off. Said he'd not even washed his dirty pecker. He thought that was hilarious. Well, we all did.'

'You're a sick animal. And *that* didn't happen! I never used to do—' She stopped herself. No way was she having that conversation with this bastard.

Dominic sniggered and shook his head. 'Aw, honestly, if you knew the things he said about you. You'd cry. We all laughed behind your back. Everyone did. Ickle Essa... Knox's clueless little fuck toy.'

Vanessa stood up. She'd heard enough now. If she had to suffer this pig's company for a second longer, she'd claw his eyes out. She marched past him and left without saying another word. As she stepped outside, a few tears streamed from her eyes, so she wiped them away.

The suits all watched her leave, and she overheard one of the cocky younger ones say, 'Told you that was no client, mate.'

Vanessa couldn't get away fast enough. She should never have come here. She'd known that all along, yet still she'd forced herself to make the trip. How stupid. She felt so vulnerable. So lost, empty and dispirited. She felt like... *her* again. *Silly Little Essa.* The girl she'd left in Bournemouth was forcing her way back into her life. Vanessa was fading... The strong, optimistic and spirited woman she'd become no longer seemed to be in the driving seat. She needed to see him again. Only he could make this all stop.

Vanessa got back to her car and searched her phone for the nearest garden centre. She'd need to buy a couple of plants to authenticate the lie she'd told her husband.

s he strolled across the yard, the blaring horn blast caused him to jump, spin, and dash aimlessly from the tarmac.

'Stupid prick! Watch where you're going!' came an irate shout from the Volvo's cab.

Curtis peered up at the driver of the rig he'd walked straight out in front of.

A beefy chap in his fifties with a disgruntled look slapped on his face gazed back. He eyed Curtis with a contemptuous glower. Then his jaw dropped, and he mouthed, 'Oh, bollocks!' He jumped from the cab, cheeks blushing, and slapped a hand against his forehead. 'I'm so sorry, Mr Pascall. I didn't know it was you!' he bellowed over the growl of the Volvo's vibrating engine.

Curtis blinked for a few moments, then gazed at the man. It was Albie, one of the mechanics. A known hothead, but a valuable employee who'd been part of the business for a decade.

'I'm really sorry,' Albie added.

Curtis let out a little whistle and smiled. 'My fault, Albie. Head up my backside. I stepped out in front of you.'

'Seriously, if—'

'Don't worry.'

Curtis, dazed and half asleep, ambled across the yard and into the main offices. He grabbed a cup of water from the dispenser and slunk into his office. He undid the top button on his shirt and flicked on the free-standing fan. Not even ten and it was already twenty-six degrees. No sooner had he sat down, Nicole, his PA, waltzed in. 'Hi, Curtis. The sales team are still waiting for a response regarding this McCarthy and Belgrove situation. You said you'd get back to them yesterday about signing off on their request.'

The young PA wore her red hair up in a high ponytail and her tiny designer specs were perched on the end of her button nose.

'Um, so remind me again. What do they want?'

'Two more flatbeds and two Vito crew buses.'

'And how's their account looking?'

'Still twenty thousand due. The payment they promised accounts last week didn't materialise. Sales want to pass the matter on for legal action. They've had the owner on the blower demanding an answer. He says it's a temporary cash flow issue and that they need more vehicles to cover the workload and then can subsequently pay what they owe.'

Curtis sipped the water. He couldn't function properly today. His mind was elsewhere. A jumbled mess.

'Shall I tell them no?' she asked, crinkling her nose in confusion. 'You alright, Curtis?'

Curtis gazed at his phone, desperate to see a reply to the text he'd sent to Hayden last night. Still nothing. Curtis had checked the tides and had decided to row across to Dead-man's Island early on Saturday. He'd asked Hayden to join him. 'Sure. Headache, that's all. Listen, Nicole, M&B needs to pay a minimum of fifteen per cent on what's overdue. If they do that by Friday, we'll sign off on the additional vehicles.'

'I'll pass it on. What happened to the beard?' she asked.

Curtis rubbed his beardless face and grinned. He'd found himself tugging and rubbing his beard incessantly of late. It had driven him mad and so he'd done away with it. But he missed it and now found he looked too soft... too unmanly and characterless. He'd already decided to grow it back. Curtis was about to answer Nicole when his phone beeped. He grabbed it. A text from Hayden.

Sure. Meet you there then.

So that was that. He'd get his one-on-one with the man.

ALBIE STROLLED INTO THE OFFICE, scratching the back of his neck nervously.

'Grab a seat, Albie,' said Curtis.

'Look, Mr Pascall, I'm so sorry about my attitude today.'

'Plonk yourself down. It's nothing to do with that.'

Albie scratched his stubbled neck and slumped into a chair opposite Curtis.

'I heard you got into some trouble a few weeks ago. A mugging, right?'

Albie sniffed, looking agitated by the question. 'Just some cocky idiots trying it on. Walking through Edmonton Green late at night. Guess I was asking for trouble.'

'I heard you single-handedly fought against four assailants, Albie. And one had a knife. You beat the living daylights out of them.'

'Yeah, well, I was having a bad day and so that gang went

and picked the wrong quarry,' said Albie, now with the traces of a superior grin working its way on his face.

Curtis leant closer to the man and said, almost in a whisper. 'You used pepper spray on them, didn't you?'

'Um, yeah. Why?'

'You always carry that?'

Albie swallowed and his eyes twitched. He eyed Curtis as if weighing up if this was all some type of trap. 'I know it's illegal, but there are some rough estates around where I live... Lots of people carry stuff—'

'I need some. Can you get me a can, please?' Then he added, 'For my wife. I'd like her to carry it.'

'I can give you the website I brought it from. They post it.'

'OK, but I could do with some quickly, so if you happen to have some to hand... that sure would be very much appreciated. I'll pay you for it.'

Albie scratched his neck again. 'Alright. I'll grab mine out of my bag for you. You can have it for twenty quid.'

'Perfect.'

Albie watched him with suspicious eyes. As if the man knew Curtis had just fed him a pack of lies.

'And again, what happened earlier was my fault, Albie.'

'You seemed a tad distracted. You having any trouble you need help with?'

'Trouble? No, no.'

'You've moved down the coast, right? Bet that's nice. Those seaside towns can be a bit rough around the edges, though, right? You getting some aggro?'

'God, no. Whitstable is charming. Full of lovely, down-to-earth people.'

'OK. But I know some chaps in Streatham Hill who... let's say... sort out problems... They deal with things. If you catch my meaning.' He gave a conspiratorial wink and stood up.

'Oh, OK. I'll certainly keep that in mind, Albie.'

'I'll pop that spray around later.'

'Thanks. That's great. Mum's the word, right?'

Albie gave a quick thumbs up, and left.

Curtis slunk down in his leather swivel chair and mulled over the conversation. *They deal with things,* he mused, and scolded himself for the sinister thoughts he was having.

25

Curtis slipped into bed. Vanessa lay curled in a ball on top of the covers, her back to him. Still awake, he knew. They would always have a ten-minute chat before bed. Banal chit-chat about everything and nothing. Not anymore. A long, despairing silence seemed to be the new normal these days. Where had his wife gone? Christ, he couldn't handle this any longer. 'Vee, you asleep?'

'No,' she grunted.

Curtis huffed and sighed. 'It's time we talk about this. I mean, properly talk.'

'Go to sleep. You'll be getting up soon.'

'I can't sleep.'

'Because you're yakking.'

Curtis fidgeted about, butted the pillows with the back of his head and grumbled. The morning's boat trip lay heavy on his mind and the idea of being alone with Hayden left him with a worrying feeling that gnawed at the pit of his stomach. It was as though something deep inside of him said, *Your plan, Curtis, is without a doubt one of the worst ideas you've ever had.* Curtis kept seeing that figure on the beach watching him. He knew it was Hayden. He couldn't prove it, but who else could it have been? Who else would have taken his photo?

Plus, he'd lied to his wife, and that didn't sit well with him. When Vanessa had questioned him about why he'd strapped two kayaks onto the roof of the Wrangler, he'd been lost for words. She'd assumed he was taking Jude, but he'd told her that Albie, the mechanic from Finchley, was a super keen kayaker and he'd suggested tagging along as it would be safer. She seemed to buy that.

Curtis lay in silence for ten minutes, then found he was unable to take it any longer. 'Vee... Vee?'

'What?'

'Did he... did you ever get any response from Hayden?'

She didn't answer.

'Well?'

'I got a reply saying it was the wrong number.'

Curtis's mouth went dry. 'Right.' Either his wife had just told him a blatant lie, or Hayden had zero desire to connect with Vanessa. He almost blurted out, *it is his number*, but guessed that would be pointless. If he wanted answers, then he'd need to get them directly from Hayden. He didn't have a clue how he'd even approach the matter, but Curtis knew this – Hayden was not leaving Sheppey tomorrow until he got some bloody straightforward answers from the man.

'I'm worried about you, Vee. I'm worried about *us*.'

No reply.

'You're distracted all the time. We don't talk. You don't eat. You're... you're like a different person. I don't recognise you anymore.'

Curtis let those words sink in. Vanessa's body rose and fell as if she was breathing heavily.

'I just want us to be happy again. That's all I want, Vee.' He wanted more than anything to put his arms around her.

To pull her close, kiss the back of her neck and fall asleep in her embrace. But he didn't. He felt like he wouldn't be able to take the rejection if she rebuffed him.

When Vanessa replied, her words were barely audible. 'One way or another... we need that man out of our lives. Or he'll smash everything to pieces.'

Curtis opened his mouth to respond, only to comprehend he *had* no reply to that. What was she suggesting? He rolled over and closed his eyes. Sleep wouldn't come easily tonight. If at all. Albie's words rolled around in his mind again – 'They deal with things.'

26

Hayden arrived in the small car park behind the Old House at Home pub in a small white Peugeot van. The engine rattled and a grating scraping noise came from the underneath, as though a piece of plastic was being dragged along. The front bumper was cracked and dented, part of it crudely sprayed with grey primer. It looked like a half-hearted attempt had been made to mend the damage. Curtis watched him park at an angle, get out, and slam the door. He appeared dishevelled and grumpy. He wore jeans, flip-flops and a dirty mustard coloured *Ripcurl* T-shirt.

Whilst Curtis unbuckled the kayak straps and unloaded them from the Wrangler's roof rack, Hayden offered no help and instead stood in a vexed silence, sipping on a can of shop brand energy drink.

'So, keeping well, Hayden?' asked Curtis breezily.

'I guess.'

'Right. So, anyway, I'm not sure how much kayaking you've done, but these sit-on-tops are pretty easy to deal with. They're sturdy, but should you spin it, just flip it back over and you'll be fine. They're self-draining.'

Hayden sniffed, as if disinterested.

Curtis clipped the seats into place, the other man's tetchy mood creating an uneasy atmosphere as he undertook the task.

Curtis slid on his buoyancy jacket, zipped it up, and applied the additional clip across his chest. 'This one's a medium. Should fit you OK,' said Curtis, holding out his spare jacket.

Hayden sneered and waved his hand, dismissing the offer.

'Seriously, put it on. It's choppy out there this morning.'

'It's a mile across. I can swim that.'

Curtis shoved the jacket against Hayden's chest. 'Just humour me. Put the jacket on.'

Hayden still didn't accept it. He gave a twisted, unfriendly grin. 'Calm down, Captain Safety.'

'Come on. Jacket on, mate.'

Hayden snatched the jacket, walked to the back of the Wrangler, and flung it inside. 'Self-draining, right? Now stop being a fucking wet blanket, Curtis.'

Curtis shrugged, trying his best to appear unperturbed by Hayden's discourteous and hostile attitude. He ignored the man as he put his keys and phone in separate dry-proof cases. The key case he shoved into a larger dry-bag, which he then fastened under the back netting of his kayak. He put the phone case over his neck and adjusted the toggle.

The sun had yet to rise fully, and it poked up on the horizon, casting a slight, hazy light over the water. Curtis tugged on his wetsuit boots.

They walked down to the boat slipway, set the kayaks in the water, and glided out across the estuary without speaking one word to each other. Like he was, Curtis knew Hayden must be comprehending that they were indeed setting off to engage in some kind of unspoken showdown. They paddled at a leisurely pace alongside a long boat jetty, and headed towards a large cluster of moored motorboats, schooners and yachts.

Curtis spotted an orange container ship heading towards the open area of the estuary. A way off, but still too close for comfort. He called out, 'Hayden, we better wait for that to pass before we head across.'

Hayden, ignoring him, paddled on, weaving in and out of the boats.

'We might not make that! Ease up... Wait.'

'We'll pass it,' shouted Hayden, upping his pace, as the craft rose and dropped down in the rolling waves.

The pair had to row like crazy to cross the estuary and deviate away from the imposing ship's course. With the ship looming behind them, Curtis cursed Hayden for not listening to him. Breathless from the intense rowing, and soaked from the water smashing into the craft, he glared at the back of the other man's head.

Curtis could see their destination to his left, marked by a line of wooden posts set in the water. He didn't know the significance of those marker posts, but he knew that was where the island lay. To their right, the container ship crept by, heading towards Sheerness Harbour and passing four colossal wind turbines.

As the pair neared the posts, Hayden broke the silence. 'You planning to murder me out here?' Hayden spoke in a buoyant tone. Then gazed at him questioningly as if he'd asked Curtis something normal, like what his favourite football team was.

Curtis gazed back at him in astonishment.

Hayden continued to watch him with a nonplussed expression, although as a faint smile crept onto the man's lips, the bad feeling in Curtis's stomach increased tenfold. *This is a foolish game you're playing, Curtis*, he decided as a swarm of white birds swooped over them.

Curtis paddled on, trying his very best to appear unworried. 'If I recall the conversation, you were the one who asked to join me.'

Deadman's Island now lay in their sights. Across the water was the Isle of Grain, an industrial expanse of commercial buildings, huge shipping cranes, and electricity pylons. Another vast ship, black and white with the letters LNG written on its hull, was docked there. It struck Curtis how small and vulnerable their little crafts were on this stretch of water.

Deadman's Island itself appeared no more than an uninspiring stretch of grassy marshland with various inlets and jutting, muddy banks. He decided Jude would probably be disappointed if they came here and didn't spot any ancient bones. The tide had started to ebb and Curtis wondered if the remains would become visible once the tide went right out. Not that he intended to hang around for that.

'Is that why you didn't give me a jacket? Are you planning to make it look like an accident? That's pretty cold, but a good plan.' Hayden glanced at him, his expression serious now as he bobbed about on the waves.

'What... but... oh, leave off! Why would you say that?' asked Curtis, not sure if Hayden was on the windup.

Hayden snorted. 'Oh, do shut up, Curtis. We gonna land and explore the spooky island, or what?'

'We can't land. It's illegal. This is a bird sanctuary.'

'"We can't land. It's illegal,"' mimicked Hayden in a childish voice. 'What's the point of coming, then?'

A massive flock of birds that were huddled on one of the inlets noticed them approach and took flight in a noisy, frantic getaway.

'Is it driving you insane, Curtis? Is that why you're thinking about it?'

'Now you've lost me.'

'Don't lie. Is it driving you insane? The thought that I've fucked your wife. That I've done things with her you could only dream about. I get the sense your love life is about as thrilling as trimming your toenails whilst taking a dump.'

Curtis shook his head. 'You actually want me to respond to that? What's wrong with you? You didn't... screw my wife... You had a relationship with a teenage girl... You don't know Vanessa.'

Hayden laughed. 'Oh, I beg to differ. Little Essa's still in there. I can see it in her eyes.'

'Right. OK. Time to head back. This is insane.'

'Don't have a tantrum, Curtis. We're just chewing the fat. Man talk.'

Curtis ignored him and manoeuvred the kayak through two lopsided wooden posts sticking out from the water. One had some old rope tied around it.

Hayden followed and the tip of his kayak clonked against Curtis's. 'Ah, I see. I get it now, Curtis. You thought we could come out here and have a little heart to heart. Get all close and chummy so I'd open up. You want to worm some intel from me, right? Essa's acting out of character and you want to know what's wrong with her. Come on, sulky pants... admit that I'm right on the ball.'

'Maybe there is some truth to that. I want to know what is going on. But I get the feeling that I won't get any straight answers from you.'

Hayden paddled alongside him. 'I was really beginning to think you'd lured me here to kill me. I wouldn't have held it against you. I'd have respected you for trying.'

'I'm coming to the conclusion that you don't have respect for anyone.'

'Don't presume you know me. You don't!'

'Why did you steal my photo?'

Hayden flashed a surprised smile in response to this.

'Why?' Curtis demanded. 'Why on earth would you take that? And as for burying it on the beach... that's just... weird. Why are you trying to goad me?'

Hayden let out a tired sigh. 'Wow, I think you need to speak to someone. You could genuinely be losing your marbles, fella. Is life hard at the top? Pressure getting too much? People like you are all the same. You want more and more and more. It's never enough and, in the end, you crash and burn trying to reach it.'

'I have no clue what sick game you're playing here, but I'm done.'

Hayden spat out a sarcastic laugh. 'Oh, he's done!' he said in a mocking tone.

'What's this all about, Hayden? Why are you here? Come on, enough with all the bullshit. Are you still in love with her? Is this some odd obsession? Because if you think Vanessa is still interested in you, let me put you straight. You're deluded, man. Not only are you utterly delusional, quite frankly, you are unbalanced. It's not me that needs help... it is you!'

Hayden offered him a snakelike smile. 'Your son looks nothing like you.'

'What?'

'Your son... If I were you, Curtis, I'd be asking myself if a paternity test was worth considering.'

Curtis said nothing, not rising to the bait.

'Bright little chap. Talks like a kid that's much, much older.'

Curtis opened his mouth to respond but stopped himself. Hayden had, to his knowledge, never met his son. He was trying to incite him and he didn't intend to react.

'He's got Essa's eyes. But as for you, Curtis, I dunno, I couldn't see any resemblance.'

Curtis paddled on, biting his lip and ignoring the comments.

'He told me all about his obsession... OK, I technically nudged the conversation in that direction... I might have seen his room, which gave me a tiny inkling that he's pirate mad. Oo, ahh, and a bottle of Caribbean rum!'

Curtis felt his entire body stiffen. He couldn't bring himself to turn and look at the man. He paddled on, splashing the water and clonking the paddles against the side of his kayak with angry, lumbering strokes. Curtis needed to get back to land. Now.

'What kid obsessed with pirates wouldn't be drawn to a place like this, hey?' said Hayden.

Curtis had no intention of exploring the coastline further and spun the kayak so he could return. If he didn't get away from this man, he'd do something foolish.

'You off already?'

Curtis sucked down his anger and paddled in furious strokes, heading alongside more rotten wood. These were sharp pieces, pointing out from the murky water like skeletal fingers. The craft hit against something that scratched and bashed at the underside.

'Man up, Curtis. Show me some rage. Show me you're not a complete coward.' Hayden let out a grating laugh. 'What does it take to get a reaction from the cautious Mr Pascall? Are you dead inside? Fuck me, you boring prick, react, you twat!'

Curtis drew in his lips and took in a huge intake of air. He imagined himself turning, screaming, and smashing the paddle straight against Hayden's face. He thought about the pepper spray he'd hidden in his wetsuit shorts' pocket before he'd got out of his Jeep. Thought about tugging it out and sending a blast into Hayden's soulless eyes and shoving the man into the water. He shook his head. Shook the images away. He would not be provoked into losing control. He *was* better than that.

He paddled away from the island and into deeper territory. But then his world spun in a blurry, wild moment and *he* plunged headfirst into the water.

As he sank into darkness, fear gripped his entire body as he scrambled, desperate in his goal to compose himself so he could return to the surface. He'd gone in so fast he'd swallowed the putrid water and now he flapped aimlessly as he tried to swim. Curtis strove to swim up, but he did not surface. He thrust upwards. He fought, wriggled and pushed, but he could not propel himself up. Nor down. Terrible images formed in his mind. The dead were clawing at his body, trying to drag him down to the prisoners' graves. They sought to claim him as one of their own and stop him from ever rising to the surface.

Full-blown panic threatened to overwhelm him. Curtis swallowed more water in his frantic fight to free himself. He knew he needed to calm down and break free but stopping the racing pictures in his mind seemed impossible. He could kick his legs and flay his arms... so that meant it must be the jacket... It *was* the jacket, he realised... ensnared on some flotsam down here... It *had* to be that.

Becoming hysterical now, he fumbled for the zip and wrenched it down. He dropped out of the jacket, but his head got wedged, as it could not pass the additional safety clip. In a frenzied scuffle with the buoyancy aid, he tugged in a desperate fumble to free the clip, but it didn't seem to want to budge, and it dug into the bridge of his nose and forehead. Like a wild shark caught in a trap, Curtis shook, fought, pulled and wriggled. Finally, he yanked himself free... and with the world turning darker and foggier by the second, Curtis used everything he had to swim up and up.

As he burst through the water he gasped, spluttered, and

cried out in rasping breaths, 'No... No... Jesus... No.' As the fogginess cleared from his eyes, he spun around, eyes hunting for Hayden. He caught sight of him paddling back across the estuary in the slipway's direction.

CURTIS SWAM in clumsy strokes until he could stand and then waded onto the muddy banks of Deadman's Island. He took in the scene as he breathed deeply, then he coughed and vomited salty water. He'd landed on a creek dotted with patches of shells, seaweed, and bits of rotten wood. Curtis scanned around, seeing only a rugged boggy stretch of land covered with long, thick grass, reeds and moss-covered rocks.

Being ashore invoked a deep sensation of unspeakable sorrow and a feeling of abnormal apprehension. It was as though this inhospitable place didn't want him here – didn't want any living soul setting foot upon its unholy ground, and it seemed his very presence stirred the spirits and shadows of those prisoners whose grim fates had landed them on this isolated and bleak spot.

He spotted his craft downshore, upturned in the swirl of the waves and being bashed against a cluster of rocks. The paddle was still attached, the leash stretched and wrapped twice around the nose of the kayak as it danced and jumped with every wave strike.

As he headed along to retrieve the boat, his legs sank deep into the marshy ground. Each step became harder than the next and the moving tide crashed in around him. It seemed like he was walking in quicksand, and again, the images of the dead whirled in his mind. Bony hands reaching up. The undead rising from the filthy ground to claim him. To drag him deep into the plague-ridden depths.

Then he fell, coming down sideways, hard. His shoulder and face slammed down into the sticky mud. He pulled his face free and screamed, 'Christ's sake!' With some effort, he pulled his legs from the boggy mess and lay there for a few moments as the waves slapped over him. He let out a few sobs and cursed himself for being so pathetic. What would his old man have thought of him being such a pitiful wretch? What would his brother have said? *Get up and get your shit together, Curtis!* That's what.

His entire body started to sink into the sludge. He got up and, with pure anger surging through him now, he waded through the gunky muck and went over to the kayak. He washed the worst of the smelly sludge from his face, untangled the paddle, and got the craft back in the water. Curtis floated past what looked like semi-submerged wooden coffins covered in slimy seaweed and littered with shells, then he rowed like a possessed madman back across that estuary.

When he returned to the carpark, he found his other kayak dumped next to his Wrangler. He snatched out his key bag from the net and tossed the crafts up onto the roof bars. He strapped both kayaks down and drove away at such speed, it made his heart thrum like a heavy drumbeat. The phone was still clinging to his neck. A minor miracle that the strap had held.

CURTIS FLOORED the accelerator and drove onto the Sheppey Crossing at such an erratic speed, three vexed drivers flashed their lights at him. As he negotiated the traffic on the towering bridge and raced over the River Swale, he called Hayden. As predicted, the call went to voicemail. 'You listen to me, you stupid bastard! I know people... men from Streatham Hill in London! Do you understand what I'm saying? People that you do not want coming after you... so you stay away from my family!' Curtis ended the call and cursed as he almost sideswiped a grey van.

27

———

V anessa heard screeching tires and raced to the study to check the cameras. It was Curtis. She stepped out the front and found him fighting to remove his wetsuit boots. He was caked in slime and mud and looked infuriated. The kayak straps hung down the sides of the Wrangler and one boat didn't appear to have even been strapped down securely. This, she knew, wasn't a good sign, as her husband was always a stickler when it came to safety. He'd often pull the car over and check the kayak bindings at the tiniest indication of an insecure load.

'You alright?' she asked.

Curtis heaved off the muddy boot and tossed it up the drive. 'Do I look alright?' With wet bare feet slapping on the driveway, he stomped inside.

Vanessa followed him.

He stopped at the foot of the stairs. 'Jude! Jude. Get down here. Get down here now!' he yelled. Before waiting for a response, he hurried to the kitchen and started washing his arms and face. He smashed at the soap dispenser like a maniac, then washed his arms and face with such frantic aggression, Vanessa could only watch in speechless trepidation. Curtis spattered muddy water all over the sink and worktops as he cleaned himself. She wanted to demand that he go straight up for a shower, but the fury radiating from him made her stay silent.

'Jude!' he bellowed, drying his red-raw hands and arms on a tea towel. He spun to Vanessa. 'Your crazy ex-boyfriend just tried to kill me. I've been calling you. Why didn't you pick up?'

Vanessa's chest tightened. 'My phone must be on silent. What happened?'

'He knocked me straight out of my kayak.' Curtis stomped over to the hallway. 'Jude! Down here!'

Vanessa glared at him then. 'You went behind my back. Didn't you?'

'The guy is unhinged. He needs locking up.'

'I told you to stay away from him.'

'If *you* gave me answers, I wouldn't have had to go to him. I'm tired of these games. I got hooked on some wood or something under water! Vee, I nearly didn't come back up. I almost drowned!'

Jude traipsed downstairs and joined them. 'Why are you shouting?'

Curtis crouched down to him, holding him by both shoulders. 'This friend of yours. This Tyler, who is he?' snapped Curtis.

Jude pulled a sullen expression. 'I never said he was my friend. You did!'

'Now isn't the time for smart-arse comments! Where did you speak to him?' asked Curtis.

'He spoke to me. Over the fence. Said you'd told him all about me and that I love pirates. He told me about the island and that his dad used to take him to see it in an old boat.' Jude turned to Vanessa. 'Why is Dad mad at me?'

Vanessa didn't reply. She felt too sick to say anything. Her poisonous past had returned to not only affect her and Curtis, but now her son was being affected, too.

'Look at me, Jude. I need you to tell me everything,' demanded Curtis.

Jude's eyes were moist with tears. 'I didn't do anything. That Tyler just said you'd be too scared to take me. That I should tease you a little... say you'd be too frightened to go. Then maybe you would take me.'

'Why didn't you explain who he was, Jude?' asked Curtis.

Jude shrugged. 'I thought you knew who I was talking about. He spoke like he knew you. I just wanted to go there. It sounded cool.'

'Ooh, is Jude in big trouble?'

Vanessa turned to find Sofia watching the exchange with a wry smile. 'All Jude talks about is that spooky island where the old bones are. He's so weird.'

'Upstairs. Now, Sofia,' ordered Vanessa, ushering her daughter to the stairway.

'Right! This has gone far enough!' said Curtis, steaming past them, cheeks flush with anger. 'Jude, please take your sister up to the lounge. Go. Now!'

Jude appeared as though he wanted to protest, but he could sense that wouldn't be wise. He snatched his sister's hand and led her upstairs.

'Why are they so cross?' Sofia whispered, none too quietly.

'Just hurry,' demanded Jude.

Vanessa followed after Curtis.

Outside, she found him hammering his fist on the neighbour's front door. A riled-looking Mr Gates yanked open the door. His expression soon changed to that of apprehension when he saw the thunderous expression on her husband's face.

'I need to check your CCTV, right now!' said Curtis.

Gates puffed out his fat cheeks. 'Excuse me?'

'There has been a man in your back garden talking to my son!'

Gates pulled an outraged expression. 'What the hell are you suggesting?'

Curtis tried to barge past him. Gates stood in the doorway, belly bulging from his vest as he blocked off the way.

'He's been in your garden! Skulking about in your conifers. Listen to me. Open your bloody ears,' yelled Curtis.

Vanessa pulled her husband back. 'Curtis, you need to calm down. *You* need to stop this.'

Curtis took a few steps back, put his hands on his hips, and peered up into the sky as he took in several deep breaths.

'This is unacceptable! I'll call the police. You can't go around throwing accusations like this,' said Gates in a flustered outburst. His cheeks were glowing purple as he huffed and puffed. 'Unacceptable,' he repeated indignantly.

'No one is accusing you, Mr Gates. My husband is having a terrible morning,' said Vanessa in a placating tone that did little to abate their neighbour's shirty mood.

'Get off my property,' snapped Gates. 'Go on, get away.'

Curtis threw up his arms. 'For God's sake, you must have noticed some random bloke hanging over your own bloody fence. Go check your cameras, man!'

'Sounds to me like *you* need to monitor your own children. And I don't *have* cameras to check,' said Gates. 'Now, if you don't mind, I'm busy.' With that, he stepped back, let out a giant huff, and slammed the door on them.

Vanessa shook her head. 'You handled that so well.'

'Right, I'm calling the police. I want that man locked up.'

'Curtis, you smell like shit. Have a shower. I'll make you a coffee.'

. . .

VANESSA FOUND Curtis sipping on a bottle of beer on the garden steps. He wore his long black bathrobe and a pair of shades, the latter no doubt donned so he didn't have to make eye contact with her. She stood opposite him and he turned away, his face set in a sullen scowl. Curtis didn't fly off the handle. That wasn't who he was, but everyone had their breaking point. *He* had found her husband's easily, and the worst part of it was, he'd probably only just started.

28

Curtis stood in the bedroom and watched his wife on the balcony. She sat with her hands in her lap, frozen and emotionless as she gazed out to the distant fuzzy lights of Whitstable. He felt ridiculous for his outburst yesterday, and he'd have to visit the neighbour with his tail between his legs and apologise for his childish conduct. Yes, he'd been angry, but that didn't excuse his actions. He sucked in some air and walked out to join her. They'd not spoken much all weekend.

'I'm so sorry, Curtis. *This* was never meant to happen.'

'And what do you mean by that, Vee?'

'We need to do something to control the situation,' she said.

'Control?'

Vanessa didn't respond for a while, leaving Curtis time to consider what his wife was suggesting here. She'd said something similar in the week. *Should I mention Albie's offer?*

Vanessa looked him in the eye. 'He wants money. That must be why he's come here.'

'Sorry, what? You are seriously suggesting we give that man money?'

Vanessa nodded. 'We offer him ten grand. That should get rid of him.'

She didn't sound the least bit convincing.

'I see,' said Curtis, followed by a snorting laugh that he couldn't stop slipping out. 'Why on earth would I give that man a single penny? Ten grand.' He slapped the palm of his hand against his forehead. 'Have you lost your mind, Vee?'

Vanessa didn't reply. She didn't even blink or show any signs of emotion. *An unexpressive robot.* It was making his blood boil.

'I want to know *what* he has on you! Tell me *why* we need to pay him.'

Vanessa gazed back across at the lights. 'Let me put this plainly, Curtis. Because it obviously isn't sinking into that brain of yours... That man will destroy our lives. Bit by bit. He'll chip away until he's shattered all that we have. We need him gone.'

'Why would he do that? I don't understand!'

'Because... You just have to trust me. You need to stay away from him. You need to let me deal with him. Is that clear?'

'No! None of this is clear. It's pretty far from clear, Vee. It's the opposite of clear. I need the truth.'

'The truth is simple... We get him out of our lives... or he's going to turn our world upside down.'

Curtis was getting a migraine now. He slumped down in a seat next to his wife. He tried a different approach. 'So, OK, we pay him off. Then what? He comes back in six months, maybe twelve, wanting more. I could set up a regular paycheck for him. Yeah, stick him on the payroll and I'll wedge him out two grand a month. When the accounts team asks, I'll say, it's alright, I'm just paying off my wife's ex-boyfriend from when she was a teenager... Why, you ask? Well, guys, good question... I have *NO* bloody clue! I just have to... *trust* her.'

'There'll be no more payouts. Only one. I'll see to that. I just need you to believe me. And nobody mentioned taking it out of your business. I'll pay him. Out of my own savings.'

'It's not about where the actual money comes from, Vee! I care about the reasons.'

They heard coughing and turned to find Sofia standing on the balcony. She held her rabbit soft toy by one ear and eyed them with a sleepy frown. 'Daddy, why are you mad?'

Vanessa went to Sofia and stroked her cheek. 'Come on, you. Let's make pancakes with oodles of maple syrup.'

'Isn't it a bit late, Mummy?'

'Yep, best time for yummy and scrummy pancakes!' said Vanessa.

'Yay. Can Mrs Milly bunny help? She loves pancakes,' she said, the altercation on the balcony forgotten in an instant.

'Oh, yeah, of course she can, Sweet Pea. You two race off and find that lovely syrupy stuff. And a nice big banana.'

Sofia skipped off. 'Hurry!'

Vanessa made to follow Sofia, turned and said, 'It's hard. I get it. But I need you to trust me. Please, Curtis. Let me deal with this.' She held his gaze and for a moment Curtis felt a tad uneasy by the way his wife was staring at him. Somewhat childlike... yes, that was it... or no, perhaps more comparable to a disgruntled teenager who would stop at nothing to get their own way.

Sofia appeared at Vanessa's side again, grabbing her hand and pulling at her.

Still, Vanessa regarded him, and despite the constant tugging and protesting from their daughter, she did not move her gaze. Then her features softened. She gave him that soft, almost shy smile he adored, and mouthed, 'I'll love you forever.' She succumbed to Sofia's tugging and allowed herself to be dragged away.

And Curtis's heart sank.

29

Vanessa stood naked in the ensuite bathroom and examined herself. For a moment she saw Little Essa gazing back at her, donning a sweet smile and pouting. She rolled her shoulder and saw the small jaguar tattoo. The wild cat climbing up her shoulder blade appeared faded today. Curtis hated it. He disliked tattoos and offered to pay for laser treatment to have it removed, more than once. Vanessa always declined. She liked it.

Their marriage was heading into dangerous, rocky territory. Vanessa understood that. However things panned out, Curtis would struggle to get his head around the situation. He'd find it hard to accept that his wife insisted they give some conniving man money to stay out of their lives, with no proper explanation other than her pleas that their world would be destroyed if they didn't.

If Vanessa had been in Curtis's shoes, she'd have never caved in. She'd have demanded answers, and if not satisfied with the ones she received, she'd have threatened to leave him. Curtis hadn't. She knew he wouldn't. He couldn't endure breaking up the family, and as much as it hurt her, she knew she was using that fact to her advantage. Deep down, he wasn't as tough as her. Thank God.

It would take time, but she would be able to fix things with her husband. But the other man held the key to breaking things that could not be mended. Not now, and not over time. It took a while to convince Curtis not to call the police. How would he prove he'd been purposely knocked out of his kayak? Or convince them someone had been hiding in the neighbour's trees, talking to their son, or staking out their property in a rowboat.

The police getting involved was not an option. That would open up a whole world of trouble. *He* needed to go. Before it was too late.

VANESSA SENT THE MESSAGE.

> We will give you 10k to stay away from us.

The reply came within ten minutes.

> Twenty.

So, not the wrong number after all, she mused. She tapped a fast reply.

> Fifteen. But no more. Then you stay away from me and my family. Come back and I promise you will regret it! You are playing a dangerous game.

Vanessa waited for the reply.
The reply came three hours later.

OK. I'll text where you can meet me –
tomorrow.

Vanessa sat glaring at the phone's screen for a long time. It would be another long night.

30

When Delphine turned up, the atmosphere in the house was, as it had been all day, disquieting and volatile. Earlier, Curtis had returned home, thrown a brown A4 envelope onto the kitchen worktop without uttering a word, then disappeared upstairs. She'd not told him about the additional five thousand that she'd withdrawn from her own savings account today. She'd stashed that in a separate envelope at the bottom of her handbag.

'Thanks so much for having the kids. We'll be three hours max, Delphine.'

'No rush. I've got nowhere to be. Off anywhere nice?'

'We're popping out to see an old friend. Couple of drinks.'

Curtis came into the kitchen. 'Hi, Delphine. The kids are upstairs in the lounge. They'll be pleased to see you,' he said, his tone weary and his face set in an irritable glower.

'Are you OK, lovey? You look a tad washed out, Curtis,' said Delphine.

Curtis's eyes flicked to Vanessa's, then he glanced back to Delphine and forced a half-smile. 'I have come over a bit... groggy.'

'Are you ready, Curtis?' asked Vanessa in a chirpy voice. 'We don't want to be late.'

'Yes, I'm ready,' he replied flatly.

THE PAIR GOT into the Wrangler and Curtis fired up the engine. They sat for a while, not moving, and Curtis gripped the steering wheel and scrunched up his lips.

'OK?' she asked.

'I can't believe we are doing this!'

Vanessa's phone vibrated in her hand. She read the message and turned to her husband. 'He wants me to go alone.'

'No,' spat Curtis. 'No way. Nope.'

'It's a public place. I'll be fine.'

'You really think I'm letting you see that man on your own? Forget it, Vee.'

'If we both go, he'll not show up.'

'Good. Because I'd rather die than give that horrible man a God damn—'

'Curtis! I asked you to trust me... so trust me. I know what I'm doing.'

Curtis growled and pulled at his hair in frustration. 'No... We're not doing this!'

'Let me deal with him. Let me speak with him and end this. This is between us. Please.'

'I need to know what he has on you. You owe me the truth. I'm your bloody husband. I've shared everything with you and you're prepared to just leave me in the dark and treat me like an idiot.'

'Curtis... try to understand that... that...'

'What? Understand what?'

'Promises... were made. Promises I cannot break. I just... can't.'

Curtis switched off the engine and sat breathing heavily. 'Not even for me? Well, nice to know how things are. Who did you make promises to, Vee? Hey? *Him*?'

'Please, just go back inside. I'll text you when I'm at the restaurant and again once I've dealt with this.'

'Fine. Go on then. You go. I'll just sit indoors. Maybe get some popcorn on the go and watch a heart-warming family film with the children. You go off skulking in the shadows with your crazy ex-boyfriend. Give him all that lovely free money!' he hissed.

Vanessa understood this wouldn't be easy for her husband. How could she expect him to sit back and happily accept this outcome? Most men wouldn't have tolerated any of this. She conceded to the fact that Curtis was so desperate to have their old, content life back that he'd reached the point where he'd now do anything to make that happen, even if it included giving a man he detested a chunk of money.

Vanessa would let the dust settle and explain the next part of her plan. They'd need to move. They'd need to stay under the radar so that nobody could track them down. Not a simple task these days. But that would have to be how this ended. They could no longer stay where anyone could easily find them again, because Curtis was right. He'd eventually come back for more. The thought of losing this fabulous home became an unbearable one.

'What do I tell Delphine?' muttered Curtis.

'Tell her you feel sick and I'm going on my own for a bit.'

'I *do* feel sick!' he said, then got out and slammed the door.

Vanessa fished around in her bag for her car keys and got out.

· · ·

Vanessa pulled up outside the Chinese restaurant in Hersden, Canterbury, five minutes before the agreed meeting time. The stark and dreadful reality of the coming confrontation with him hit her and as she removed the key from the ignition, her hand trembled.

It was muggy tonight, but Vanessa started shivering. The anxiety and unease of seeing him, she knew. The weather had been unseasonably warm throughout May and June and the promises of summer heatwaves were being thrown around by weather specialists. This could be the hottest UK summer on record. She wondered if she'd stashed her summer jacket in the boot of the car. She'd been meaning to check, as she'd not been able to find the damn thing anywhere in the house. The car was the only place she'd not yet searched. She could sure do with having it on right now, she decided.

Then a message came through. He'd changed the meeting spot. *Has he sussed out my plan?* 'Shit, shit, shit,' she grumbled to herself as she quickly selected another number on her phone and called it. 'Hey. It's me. You can go now. He's... not coming.'

Her Mini drove up the steep, winding hill, protesting and demanding a new gear change. Vanessa's heart jumped and thudded in her chest. Her head felt fuzzy and her legs were heavy and stiff. She guessed what she was doing would be perceived as insane by most. Going off the grid in such a rural area was reckless, but if she wanted this over with, she'd have to play by his rules. Right now, she'd do anything to get this mess dealt with.

After reaching the top of the hill, Vanessa parked up in an overgrown lay-by and got out, glad to be moving her tense and rigid legs. She walked over a vast scattering of small metallic gas canisters. In London the parks were littered with these little nitrous oxide pellets. Doing balloons, the youths called it. She considered what type of high they produced and guessed it must be good, yet short-lived, going by the amount discarded here. Other rubbish lay littered about the area. Cans, bottles and fast-food wrappers.

She got back inside the car, checked her phone and messaged him.

> I'm here with the cash. I am alone like you said. Time to talk. I am heading to the viewing area.

Vanessa got back out and gazed into the wooded area that led to the viewing spot. The way ahead appeared enclosed and foreboding. Then she headed in.

THE VAST LIGHTS of Canterbury lay several miles in the distance and Vanessa guessed that by day the scenery stretched out ahead of her would be even more marvellous. Her legs, no longer stiff, were instead like jelly now.

She scanned her surroundings, seeing no sign of anybody else. *Where the hell is he?*

31

C urtis took a bite from a slice of marmite on toast and checked his watch. It had been two hours since his wife set off, and if she hadn't messaged him with regular updates, the last informing him she was enroute home, he'd have been going out of his mind with worry. He swallowed down the dry toast.

When he heard the front door open and shut, he tossed down the toast and scurried into the hallway.

Vanessa walked past him and went into the kitchen without even registering him. She filled up the kettle. 'Any toast left for me?' She gestured the slice on the plate and picked it up. 'This going spare?'

Curtis said nothing.

Vanessa shrugged and took a big bite, then set her handbag on the island, yanked out the brown envelope and flung it down as if its very touch disgusted her.

Curtis snatched up the envelope and peered inside. 'What happened?'

Vanessa shrugged again and took another bite of the toast. She chewed it for ages, pulling a face like she'd just bitten on a lemon. She didn't speak until she'd finished off the slice. 'He didn't show. Pop some more toast on, would you? I'll have blackcurrant jam. I need to get changed.' She plonked a flavoured teabag into her *I love Ibiza* mug and poured in the water before the kettle had even finished its boil. 'I spoke to Delphine... She said you took off after I left. Where did you go?'

Curtis cleared his throat. 'For a drive. Ended up at Herne Bay and took a stroll.'

'OK,' she said. 'Would you be a star and bring my toast up, please?'

'Sure.' Aside from the odd bowl of stodgy porridge or the occasional piece of fruit, Curtis hadn't seen his wife eat anything for ages.

Vanessa smiled at him and left.

32

Curtis flopped down on the lounge sofa as another wave of sickness hit him. His abdomen ached, and he kept on getting sporadic chilly spells. Not good considering it was already twenty-five degrees today and not even ten thirty. They'd got so bad in the early hours that his teeth had chattered, and he'd had to wrap up in an additional blanket.

He'd not been himself at all since the kayak trip. His body, especially his limbs, felt heavy, and he seemed to possess no energy to function. When he tried to sleep, the flashbacks of almost drowning came, and a few times when he'd nodded off, a sudden sensation of sinking enveloped him and he'd become wide awake, with his pulse racing and his mouth dry. He'd concluded that he was suffering from some kind of anxiety-induced neuroticism.

Vanessa had told him to see the doctor, but Curtis knew he'd sound like a total hypochondriac if he advised the quack he'd convinced himself he'd gone and caught yellow fever from an out-of-bounds, two-hundred-year-old burial site. Either stress or a severe cold had brought on these symptoms.

He'd ruled out Covid by taking three tests, and the very thought that he'd somehow contracted the damn plague from contaminated mud was laughable. His mind was going into overdrive and playing havoc with his body. That was all this was. Hypersensitivity. He'd researched it online and found loads of information about this kind of thing. Your brain really could convince you of anything.

The kids were despondent that he'd not been able to join them on their visit to the zoo today. He'd kept two days clear from work for day trips to get the school holidays off with a bang. Now he'd likely spend those days moping about the house, overthinking and eating painkillers like sweets. Not what he'd had in mind.

When the doorbell sounded, he sighed and grumbled but decided to ignore it. It rang again and so he dragged himself from the sofa and, taking heedful steps, trotted down the stairs and into the hallway.

As he walked to the door, something told him to check the camera, so he went into the study and scanned the screen. A man in suit trousers and a crisp, short-sleeve shirt. *A damn cold caller.* The man turned and Curtis gasped, 'No way!' He raced to the desk drawer and retrieved the pepper spray he'd hidden at the back, and marched to the door. 'Now he's taking the piss,' he hissed, throwing open the door. Curtis, about to shout, *you have some damn nerve showing up here,* was taken aback and lost for words.

'Hey there. You must be Curtis Pascall. Sorry to turn up unannounced like this,' said the man. The man who *appeared* to be Hayden Knox... but... *but* wasn't.

No, Curtis could see clearly in that moment... it wasn't him, and now he couldn't find his voice to say a single word. He just gaped at the guy.

'You alright there? You seem a tad pale,' said the man. 'Is this a bad time?'

The man's face was similar to Hayden's, but thinner, and his facial features more defined, with fewer frown lines. His skin seemed healthier, and he sported a neat goatee beard. His long, dark hair was slicked back and tied in a small pony-tail. There were odd traces of grey in his temples, but he looked younger than Hayden by several years. And more handsome and affable, too.

'I'm an old friend of Essa's,' said the man.

Curtis continued to gawp at him. *Déjà vu, or what? Was he losing his mind here?*

'You look iffy. Are you alright?' asked the man.

Curtis fingered the pepper spray in his dressing gown pocket. 'What do you want?' he asked tartly.

'Well, bit of a weird one. As I say, I am a friend of Essa's... sorry, Vanessa's... and as lovely as it would be to see her, I'm actually here to find my brother, Russell. My twin. Although I'm guessing that's stating the obvious.'

Curtis couldn't find his tongue for a good ten seconds. 'What?'

'Oh, God, sorry...' The man held out his hand. 'I'm Hayden... Hayden Knox.'

Curtis gawped at the man's hand. Then peered up and met his eyes. 'What?' he repeated dumbly.

'Are you... OK?'

Curtis's mind spun. For a moment, he considered he might pass out in the doorway. The man watched him with a perplexed half-smile, as if *he* was just as confused by this exchange as Curtis was. He must have been gaping at the other man as if he had two heads. He needed to get a grip, because he had to establish what the hell was going on here. 'Um, sorry. Yeah, I'm not well. Ah, so what makes you think we can help?'

Hayden reached inside his trouser pocket and pulled out his phone. 'So, I haven't seen Russell for a few months. But out of the blue, he sends me a random text... He tells me he's gone to find Little Essa. Then I get these snaps.' Hayden flicked through his photo gallery.

The pictures he showed him were taken at their dinner party. Selfie shots of Hayden... Russell, whoever the hell he was. One with Curtis, drunk, drinking a beer. In another, Jonas stood in the shot, grinning. There were more photos of a vexed-looking Vanessa in the background and a concerned Delphine sipping on red wine, her eyebrows raised in a suspicious frown.

Curtis just blinked as the photos flipped by.

'So, he told me he turned up at your house and had a fantastic night.'

Curtis caught another photo. Hayden and Russell, around ten years younger. The pair were clearly identical twins, but with striking differences. The most noticeable being that the years had been much kinder to Hayden. Curtis got the impression he'd lingered on that photo on purpose, before moving on to the next one.

'He said you welcomed him with open arms, even though Essa had the right hump! He was a little embarrassed because he said that he got quite drunk and got a ticking off from your big mate... John was it?'

'Jonas,' corrected Curtis.

'That's the one. He told me you two also enjoyed a night out together. Some rock night in town. Here, he sent me these.' Hayden beamed and showed Curtis more photos on his phone. Drunken snaps taken during the night he'd spent with... with *Russell* Knox.

Curtis glued his eyes on an uncontrived shot of the pair drunk and pulling stupid faces. Hayden showed him another where the pair were laughing and holding up beers.

'Oh, yeah. That night. We bumped into each other and

had a few drinks,' said Curtis, trying to make it sound like it was of no importance.

'I got the impression Russell thought you guys were like... good mates... Honestly, he spoke so highly of you. I mean, it seemed kinda odd to me, under the circumstances.'

'Circumstances?'

'Curtis, when did you last speak with my brother?'

A shiver ran through Curtis and he stiffened. 'Oh, when was it now? Um...' He had no clue what to say.

'I will level with you. Russell is... well, let's say, he has a few issues. And he's meant to be home looking after our mum. He's her primary carer. It's not the best setup, I can tell you. But I don't live in the UK and she has no one else.'

'I see.'

'That photo you saw was us in France. Russell lived there for years. Before her stroke. It's the only time he seemed happy. Probably because he lived like a recluse.'

'Ah, yes, he told me about your mum's stroke.'

'Anyway, Russell's not answered his phone in a few days and we're both getting increasingly concerned about his welfare. It's not the first time he's wandered off like this. And the last time he...' Hayden's face darkened. 'He got himself hurt.'

'Oh, that is a worry.'

'How did Essa react when he walked back into her life like that?'

'She... I guess she seemed a bit... shocked.'

'What has Essa said about Russell?'

Curtis pulled a confused face. 'Nothing!'

Hayden took a deep breath, stepped back a few paces and placed his hands on his hips. He appeared deeply concerned now. His eyes were moist and for a moment Curtis wondered if the man might start crying. Curtis almost asked the man to come in for a drink, but stopped himself.

Hayden took a few more deep gulps as if levelling his breathing, then he turned back to Curtis. 'We need to talk. There are things you need to be aware of. Things that... oh, jeez, I don't even know where to begin with all this.' He rubbed a sheen of sweat from his forehead. 'Have you got time for a bit of a chat? It's pretty important.'

Curtis nodded. He was very keen to learn what the real Hayden had to say. But this man would *not* be setting foot in his house. Not after the fiasco that arose the last time he invited a stranger into their home.

'Pop across the road to the beach. We can take a stroll. I need to clear my head,' said Curtis. 'Give me five minutes to toss on some clothes.'

Hayden nodded. 'Sure, no rush.'

33

'Mummy, why are the animals all hiding from us?' said Sofia, peering into the tiger enclosure, eyes desperately searching for a giant cat.

'It's most likely too hot for the animals today, Sweet Pea,' said Vanessa. One giant paw and a limp tail hanging from a big dead branch being the only evidence the big cats even lived here.

'Aren't tigers from tropical countries like India and Indonesia? How can it be too hot?' asked Jude with a smug expression on his face that irritated Vanessa.

'I don't know, Smarty Pants. Maybe the heat just makes these particular cats really lazy.'

'Mummy, do you like tigers? Is that why you have a tattoo of one?' asked Sofia.

'It's a black panther, stupid,' snapped Jude.

'Don't call your sister stupid, Jude. And yes, I love tigers. They are very... majestic. Graceful, yet powerful and extremely *deadly... roooaarr.*' Vanessa pretend-pounced on Sofia and attacking her with a bout of tickles, causing her daughter to erupt with silly laughter. 'And technically, Jude, it's a jaguar tattoo.'

Jude pulled a sullen face. 'I'm hot and bored. Can we go now?'

'Can we find the adventure area? Please,' pleaded Sofia.

'Yes. Jude can't wait to take you on the big climbing frame!' said Vanessa.

'No, *Jude* can't,' he grumbled, pouting like a teenager.

This boy was maturing fast. By Vanessa's calculations, her son would be the equivalent of a thirty-year-old man by the time he hit adolescence. With any luck, he'd be over his moody teenage years early. She lived in hope, anyway.

They made their way through the park, snaking through the hordes of boiling, agitated parents with their equally hot and irked children. Today was far too warm to be traipsing around a zoo, seeking out exotic animals, most of which showed they were far smarter than the humans and had already taken refuge from the searing heat.

34

Curtis got changed, necked a glass of apple juice and some paracetamol, then washed his face with cold water. He left the house, crossed the road, and made his way down the small steps that led to the beach. He found Hayden tossing pebbles into the water.

The pair walked along the beach toward Whitstable.

'I think I need to explain something here, Hayden. When your brother came to our house... he said *he* was you!'

'He did what?'

'He's been pretending to be you the entire time.'

'Right. OK. I see. That's... unexpected.'

'Why would he do that?'

Hayden puffed out his cheeks. 'So, there is quite a lot we need to talk about. Like I said, I don't quite know where to start. What's Essa told you about us?'

'Not much,' said Curtis guardedly. 'Who went out with Vanessa? You, or Russell?'

'Me. I only got a chance with her because she came from a broken home. *Damaged goods,* as they say. It was the only reason someone like me got with such a stunner like her.

But we fell for each other. We had a rather turbulent relationship. We were young, but it wasn't only that.' Hayden
slipped on a pair of Ray-Ban shades. 'I'll level with you,
Curtis. Essa had some strange tendencies back then. She'd
obsess over silly stuff. She'd get angry if things didn't go her
way. She keyed my car twice after we'd argued over some
trivial matters. And once – you probably won't believe me
because it sounds insane – but once, she even smeared dog
crap all over my bed sheets. At least I assume it was dog
poo.'

'What?'

'Honest to God, you did not piss off Little Essa without
receiving some payback.'

Curtis pondered on this. He found it hard to accept that
his Vee would do something like that. OK, she got a little
obsessed with things. It could be cute if it was a fixation with
making the perfect cake, having the kitchen organised to
perfection, or having wallpaper that appeared completely
unblemished. Even one bubble in the paper would drive her
nuts. Her obsessive behaviour was, at times, a little... disconcerting, but nothing more than that.

'Is she still obsessed with all that fantasy nonsense?'
asked Hayden.

'Fantasy? I'm not sure I—'

'She used to read a lot of garbage about folklore and
myths. She even got it into her head all that sprites and pixies
cobblers might be real.'

'Vanessa? What, like sword and sorcery stuff?'

'More evil fairies and demon worshipping. She'd
convinced herself that some weird creature lurked in her
dad's shed. A troll, she used to call it. Ah, what was it? The
Whisper Troll or some such malarkey. I dunno... something
along those lines. She'd go on about this creature, saying it
shadowed her like some abhorrent entity. I guess... no, I know

it all stemmed from the issues with her mother, Heidi. She ever talk about her to you?'

Curtis shook his head.

'They never rekindled their relationship, then?'

Curtis shook his head again.

'Mm, I guessed as much. Essa told me things about her. The woman sounded like a right vile cow. Treated Essa and Michael so badly. No wonder Essa ended up bananas. How is Michael?'

'Um, yeah, he is doing well,' said Curtis. He wasn't giving this man any information. He was here to listen and learn, nothing more. 'Bananas? What are you saying?'

Hayden stopped and lit up a cigarette. 'We all took acid one night... Not Essa, but me and some other friends.' He offered the packet to Curtis. 'Smoke?'

Curtis shook his head. 'Not Vanessa?'

'No, she declined. Anyway, we drive out to this creepy derelict church. Real sinister old place. Dangerous too. The structure was totally unsafe. The stuff you get up to as a teen, hey? Not one of my better plans, I can tell you. So, we're all out of our brains on this crazy drug, and Essa tries to freak us all out. Going on about some other lad that had come with us. Tells us she thinks it's this troll creature posing as this strange hollow-eyed boy with greyish skin. Then she accuses us of drugging her, and out of nowhere tells me she's sick of me! That she wants us to break up because she hates me and she's now seeing things clearly.'

'We spoke about this. She told me someone spiked her. You're saying she made that up?'

Hayden placed his hand on his chest. 'Hand on heart, we didn't do that. No way would I do that to my worst enemy, let alone my girlfriend!'

'One of the others, then?'

'Dominic and Leanne were both adamant that Essa was

tripping and that she'd taken the tab of her own accord. They thought she'd started having a harrowing experience and so lashed out at me. They would never have spiked her. No way. My honest opinion... she either took the drug herself, or was pretending in order to mess with us.'

'But what's all this got to do with Russell coming here?'

'That was the night everything started to... change. *She* started to change. I mean, *really* change.'

35

S ofia had already found some small children to play
with and skipped around the swings giggling, before
chasing off with two little boys around her age.

Jude joined the queue for the little zip line and almost
seemed to view the other kids like they were inferior to him
as he scanned them with a grumpy scowl. As he stepped up
for his turn, another lad offered him the line and he took it
without thanks, sat on the seat and slid down the line with a
listless expression. After reaching the end, and unimpressed
by the ride, he slipped off the seat and skulked off without
returning the seat to the next child in line.

Vanessa saw Sofia charging about and letting out a gleeful
laugh, so searched for a free picnic bench so she could drink
one of the cold lattes she'd packed. Unable to locate a bench
that wasn't occupied with people, she opted for a spot under
a tree, sat down and cracked open a can, glad she'd packed
the mini cool bag with extra ice packs today. Now, content the
children were occupied, she browsed her messages and
emails. Then found herself back inside *that* file again.

Tuesday 13th June 1995 continued...

My hands were bleeding as I fled the church. I hurried through the ancient graveyard, catapulted myself over a low stone wall and fell into a tangle of shrubbery. I soon found myself walking in this long tunnel of eerie trees. I felt so claustrophobic then. It seemed endless. In my mind, I was walking through those twisted old trees for hours, though I reckon it wasn't longer than twenty minutes in reality. The trees moved and seemed to breathe in and out. The place was alive. I swear it was. Then the tunnel spun. Slow and jerky, like one of those weird tubes you crawl through at a fun house. The fair used to have one, and it made me feel sick. I wobbled about all over the place, struggling to keep in a straight line. Dead weird, that was.

But when the spinning stopped, what I saw waiting at the end of the tunnel was far weirder. There, two giant jaguar cats, jet-black fur glossy and brilliant, were vivid and perceptible in the powerful blue haze of the moonlight that lit up the pair like... I dunno, like a giant spotlight had cast a fantastic glow on that single spot. The smaller of the two beasts serenely cleaned its paw. The larger one – the male, I think – paced the tunnel's entrance with watchful vigilance, each graceful step heightening the huge muscles on its magnificent body. The full moon stood huge behind it, bigger than any moon I'd ever witnessed in my life.

A tree, long ago fallen, lay in the pathway. I sat on it and viewed the cats for ages. But I wasn't even afraid. I dunno if that's because, deep down, I knew what I was seeing in front of me couldn't be real, or if my love of the creatures somehow kept my fear at bay. Either way, I wasn't. The male could sense my presence... I just knew that he didn't mind me being there. These beasts trusted me. Silly thinking about that now, but at the time, it seemed to matter... I cared that they didn't perceive me as a threat. In fact, I wondered if they'd come to save me. To protect me from the sinister shadow that followed from the derelict church. My very own guardian angels.

This gave me hope, because the creature still followed, and I knew it was watching me through the trees and wanted to hurt me. Or worse.

36

They stopped outside the multicoloured beach huts on West Beach. Families were busy setting up gazebos, preparing paddle boards and pitching up wind breaks. The shacks were kitted out like miniature homes, with hanging pictures, tea-making areas and plump beanbags or striped deckchairs. Most carried a nautical or seaside theme with shell decorations, beach-themed cushions and ornaments, and one had three plastic seagulls hanging from the doorway.

Hayden lit up his second cigarette since they'd set off and smiled as he watched a short bald man slathering enough sun cream over his head to cover an entire hippo. 'I think he missed a bit,' said Hayden with a blithe grin.

Curtis didn't acknowledge the comment and started walking alongside the coastline again.

'You alright to keep going, Curtis? You look about fit to drop.'

Curtis wanted nothing more than to curl up into a ball and shut himself away from the world. 'I'm fine. So, what happened after Vanessa dumped you?'

'I missed her. I mean, I really missed her. I thought I'd be OK. I didn't realise the impact our split would have, but I was pining for her like crazy. We told each other we'd be together forever. Yeah, I guess that sounds corny. At sixteen and nineteen... what chance did we have, right? But I loved her.' Hayden took a final pull on the cigarette and flicked it towards the retreating sea. 'That's when Russell took his chance. Of course, I'd sussed he'd had a thing for Essa, but like a fool, I'd not quite understood the extents he'd go to.'

Curtis's legs were becoming stiffer with each step. The beach line stretched in front of him and to his weary eyes, the town seemed a million miles away this morning.

'I tried to rekindle what we had. I arranged to take her out, just the two of us, for a little heart to heart. To explain that she was right. Admit I'd been a total arse, but that would change and I'd be a better boyfriend. Not that I'd done much wrong, but I wanted to appease her.'

'I see.'

'I got showered, spruced up and went out to my car, only to find all my tyres slashed. Even the spare. Then I just knew. I knew what he'd done.'

Curtis received a sudden jabbing pain in his stomach. He winced, but ignored it and carried on.

'I searched my room and my suspicions were confirmed. Russell had stolen some of my clothes. I then find out he'd borrowed Mum's car earlier that evening. Oooh, I was fuming.'

Curtis stopped walking and spun around. 'He met her under the pretence he was... you?'

Hayden screwed up his lips and nodded.

'So then, he has impersonated you before. This isn't the first time!'

'As kids, we swapped identities sometimes to trick family members and friends. A bit of fun, that's all. We were identical back then. Before the ravages of time altered us. But Mum never fell for the ruse. I only prayed that night Essa wouldn't either. The little shit had even used my Jean Paul Gaultier cologne. I found it stashed in his room. *Classique...* Ooh, a divine scent.'

'But surely the car would have been a red flag?'

'No. You see, my old Ford Fiesta was an unreliable heap of junk. I often borrowed her motor because mine didn't always start.'

'So, what happened?'

'I called my mate Dominic, and he drove like lightning over to mine. Dom sped off to the agreed meeting spot, but Essa had gone. We got there way too late. We went to her dad's place, but she wasn't home. So we searched all Russell's haunts. Places I thought he might take a girl... to... get his end away!'

Curtis's jaw tightened. 'What, he just wanted to use her... for sex?' Another stomach pain, this one strong enough to make him flinch. *A knife in the guts.*

'He would leeringly watch Essa sometimes when she'd stayed over at our house. Sometimes he'd barge in my room unannounced, no doubt in the hope he'd catch a glimpse of her arse or whatever. Sorry, that's crass... I apologise, Curtis... that's your wife. Believe me, I had nothing but respect for that girl. I loved her. What we had wasn't sordid... It was... special. I adored her. Shit, you probably don't want to hear this either.'

No, thought Curtis. The more Hayden spoke, the more the imaginary knife twisted in his stomach.

'Russell didn't like it. He was so jealous of our relationship. He stalked us. Spied on us. Stole our things – stole *personal* things. And he wanted to steal Essa from me, too. He knew stuff. About where we'd been and what we'd been up to. So creepy.'

Those words lingered for a moment as an awkward silence engulfed the pair, broken only by gentle waves and seagulls squawking.

'Did you find them?' asked Curtis, unable to take the silence any longer.

Hayden closed his eyes, took a deep breath, and nodded. 'We did. Yes. We checked a few places, but somehow, I knew where I'd find them.' He drew in his lips, clearly reliving the moment in his head as he took a few moments to compose himself. 'There was this beach miles away. Near Burton Bradstock. There'd been some landslides there over the years, and Dorset Council had shut the beach down. The cliffs were crazy high. Sheer drops of yellow sandstone, and there were entire sections collapsing. Russell loved it there, so it wasn't a shock to locate Mum's car in the parking area near the cliff top. You'd get a few daring youths hanging about and messing around on the rocks sometimes, but most people heeded the many warnings to stay away, so the area would usually be deserted.'

Hayden stopped and gazed at the sea, a pained frown on his face. It was a good while before he spoke again. 'The place was a death trap. The steps leading down were built right inside part of the cliff that had subsided and crumbled down onto the beach. You had to watch your footing. They'd put up a barrier, but you could clamber under that. Dominic stayed at the top, and I walked down on my own to search for Russell and Essa.'

Hayden sniffed and shook his head. 'I... I found them... together... on some rocks by the beach. Russell's stereo blasted out rock music so loudly it led me right to them. They were in a rocky alcove, with the sea crashing in around them. They'd not even registered me standing there at first, my jaw practically on the floor as I watched them in horror.'

Curtis wanted to ask what he'd caught them doing but couldn't bring himself to speak.

'Essa saw me first, and she gasped. She pulled away from him and covered herself up, embarrassed by my presence... Then after a few moments, the penny dropped and the reality of the situation must have struck her, because she became angry.'

Curtis blanched.

'Essa was drunk. Seriously smashed. I won't lie... I vented my anger out on her at first. Blamed her for not being able to tell the difference between us. I even considered I'd got it all wrong, and that Essa was playing us off against each other. Sleeping with us both and treating us like idiots. Things got heated. We all started arguing. Essa was bellowing at Russell, calling him a dirty, lying bastard, and the next thing I'm in a full-on scrap with Russell.'

Hayden stopped and lit yet another cigarette. 'We both got a few punches in, then we rolled about on the ground in the waves. We ended up in a twisted heap, and then... Russell starts howling with laughter. He's making jokes and saying, "We're twins. We should never let some slutty girl get between us." I'm not proud of what happened next, Curtis. Believe me.'

Curtis pursed his lips. Sick rose in the top of his stomach and it took a great effort to fight it back down. He didn't want to hear any more, because he knew whatever was coming would haunt him forever. But the morbid curiosity would forever linger inside his mind if he didn't find out. He also knew the answers he'd sought about this entire situation were now tormentingly close.

'He suggested we both have Essa. That we discuss the possibility of sharing her like she was some... some bloody toy for us both to manhandle. Russell wanted to make a deal in order to stop our silly spat. He goes, "No little tart is worth ruining what we have. We need to work out a share plan we can both agree on." I confess, Curtis, we spoke like Essa had not even been standing right there watching our exchange.'

'That's horrible,' said Curtis quietly.

'Russell tells me this, "I want my Essa-days to be Saturday, Tuesday and Thursday. And with today being Saturday, I'd like to finish what I started before your rude intrusion."'

'What?'

Hayden puffed out his cheeks. 'Then things got seriously out of hand.'

37

Vanessa snapped her attention away from the contents of the diary upon hearing a child screaming over the cacophony of the surrounding playground noise. *Sofia*, she knew. She leapt to her feet and raced into the play area, feeling the burning gaze of the entire park on her as she ran over to locate her wailing child, and found her slumped on the floor with a gaggle of children around her. Vanessa saw the nasty gash on her daughter's knee.

A slight man with a pencil-thin moustache and semi-rimless glasses also stood amongst the children, trying to calm her sobbing daughter, to no avail.

Vanessa scooped Sofia into her arms and kissed her forehead. 'Hey, you alright, Sweet Pea? What happened?'

'Jude pushed me really, really hard. I told him to stop, and he didn't!' sobbed Sofia.

'I think they were getting a little overexcited, that's all,' said the man in a posh, calm voice.

Vanessa scanned the many gawping kids' faces and eventually laid eyes on Jude. His face carried an expression of such indifference it rankled her big time.

'It hurts, Mummy! Ooh, it stings. Ouch,' cried Sofia.

'A nice big plaster and you'll be good as gold,' said the man, flashing a big, friendly smile.

Vanessa turned to Jude. 'I think you owe your sister an apology. Don't you?'

Jude offered her a disgruntled grimace by way of an answer.

Vanessa glowered at her son. 'Jude!'

'It's not *my* fault she's too stupid to hold on tight enough! Serves her right,' complained Jude.

Vanessa's blood boiled, but she ignored her son's comments.

'Now, come on, you did push her a bit aggressively. She implored you to slow down, didn't she?' said the man, his voice now carrying a firm edge. The man turned to Vanessa. 'She really flew off that thing. Could have been so much worse.'

Under normal circumstances, Vanessa would have been irked by some stranger sticking their beak into a family matter, but she got the impression this guy was quite shocked by her son's vindictive behaviour, and so held her tongue, instead of telling him to get lost. The deep gash on Sofia's knee suggested she'd been flung off the zip line with some force. Vanessa even noticed grazes on Sofia's hands and elbows too, but wouldn't mention them until she'd calmed down. The blood dripping down Sofia's leg was also doing little to help curb the girl's distress.

Vanessa smiled her thanks at the man and made her way back to the tree where the picnic bags were. Her can of latte lay on its side, its contents long seeped into the ground.

'You need to carry the bags, Jude,' snapped Vanessa. 'We are going.'

Jude stood behind them, making no attempt to pick up their stuff.

Sofia sobbed, sniffed, and lamented.

'Bags, now, Jude.'

'Maybe if you were paying attention to Sofia instead of being glued to your phone she wouldn't have got hurt,' said Jude, a snide grin on his lips.

Vanessa lost it. 'Do as you're told and pick up the bags. Now!'

Jude's lip dropped a bit, but he just glared at her, eyes glowing with defiant anger. 'I *don't* want to.'

'Pick them up... or—'

'Or what, Mummy?' he retorted. 'Will you smack my bottom?'

'No! I'll march you over to the tiger enclosure, pick you up and feed you to the big bastard cats, you rude little shit!'

She'd barked those words with such venom that Jude flinched as though he'd been slapped. Sofia stopped grizzling and everybody in earshot of Vanessa's outburst took notice of her.

As Vanessa struggled to collect the bags, hold Sofia and leave, a sea of startled and outraged faces followed her. Keen-eyed parents scrutinised her with questioning stares as she stomped past the rows of picnic benches. Some even appeared repulsed by her, as if she was a total neurotic bitch that needed to be restrained and arrested. Others looked uncomfortable, and more than one person could be seen hiding a wry grin behind their hands. One older man wearing an orange baseball cap was openly chuckling as he chomped on an apple.

38

'If you want the truth, Curtis, I'll tell you... I went along with what Russell said because I was a coward. I couldn't beat him, not physically, and so I decided that to defuse the volatile situation, I'd pretend to side with him. There wasn't a chance in hell I'd share Essa like a piece of meat!' Hayden shook his head; his neck muscles went taut and an expression of regret and anguish washed over his face.

Curtis said nothing.

'I noticed Essa edging away. I tried to secretly tell her with my eyes that she should slip away whilst Russell was distracted. Then she screamed so loudly it made my ears ring as she clawed Russell across the face and fled.'

Curtis knew by the pained grimace on Hayden's face that he'd only scratched the surface. A fist-like knot churned in Curtis's gut and he wiped beads of sweat that were saturating his forehead.

Hayden lit up a cigarette with an unsteady hand and rested his elbow on a sea groyne. 'What happened next always seems like... I dunno, a hazy dream. Essa sprinting barefoot across that dark, barren beach. Russell shouting

incoherent curses as he pursued her. Me chasing behind...
my legs weighed down like I had lead trousers on. My fear, I
suppose. Essa dashed up those stairs like a rocket, and I think
if she'd not spotted Dominic near the top, she'd have kept
going and outrun Russell. She must have glimpsed a
shadowy shape up by the top steps and this caused her to
falter.' Hayden sucked hard on the cigarette and blew a
plume of smoke up into the sky. 'I bet she thought it was that
stupid Whisper Troll lurking about again.'

The knot in Curtis's gut expanded. A boulder-size
fist now.

'That cliff path was treacherous. Uneven, slippery and
narrow. My brother called Essa a dirty, cock-teasing bitch.
Vanessa screamed, "I'm going to tell the police!" She called
him an evil, lying rapist. I realised at that point... what Russell
had done *was* tantamount to rape. Nigh on impossible to
prove... *but*... still.' Hayden extinguished the cigarette by
thumbing it hard against the top of the groyne. 'I didn't
witness exactly how it happened. There were shouts and
Essa's arms flayed about... I saw Russell skid from the
pathway and... then he... fell over the side. He slid at first.
Going sideways down the rock face... then he dropped. I
swear my heart stopped as he silently plunged down. I jolted
the moment he crashed against a pile of rocks. As I heard that
loud crack when he landed, I gasped in horror and stood
there, watching like a dumb idiot. I was beyond... shocked.'
Hayden rubbed the back of his neck and eyed the waves as
though bewitched.

Curtis, speechless, stood there and tried to process what
he'd just been told.

39

V anessa caught sight of Jude's surly face in the Mini's interior mirror, and her anger once again rose to the surface. Sofia sat in the front. She'd stopped crying but still kept letting out the odd faint whimper as she pressed a hand to her knee.

'I'm telling Dad what you said,' said Jude in a quiet, snarky tone. 'You're horrible.'

'Good for you,' said Vanessa. 'Maybe you should also tell him why you lied to him.'

'I didn't lie.'

'The man over the fence told you to lie. And you did. Why, Jude?'

Jude tutted.

'Why?'

'Because he told me not to say we'd spoken. Because he said Dad wouldn't take me to that place if he knew it was *his* idea.'

'Listen to me, Jude... Don't you dare ever lie like that again. You hear me? If a stranger tells you to lie, you come straight to us. Got it? Dad only went to that island to check if it was safe and he almost...'

'Almost what?' asked Jude.

'Almost... had an accident,' said Vanessa.

'Did he need a big plaster like me?' gasped Sofia, her innocent voice loaded with concern.

Vanessa recalled what she'd witnessed earlier that morning. Curtis moaning and crying out in his sleep. She was certain he'd garbled, 'I can't get out, Vee!' Then hissed, 'Let go of me!' He jolted awake after that, panting and gasping for air.

'Has Daddy really caught the plague?' asked Sofia. 'Will we catch it and need to take pills?'

'No... no one has the plague,' said Vanessa with a long, stressful sigh.

40

'We all thought the fall had killed him. When I plucked up the courage to check... Ahh, the sight of him... the head injury... Oh, man. He'd cracked the top of his head right open. A flap of skin hung there... I was so certain he'd died on impact. I checked for a pulse but didn't find one. Essa peered down, offered no help, but I heard her sobs. I ran up to her. I told her not to worry. Told her I'd fix it and make everything better. That I'd never let anyone hurt her again.'

'Did you not run for help? Or call the emergency services?'

Hayden offered a timid grin and a tiny shake of his head in response.

'But I don't understand... Why not?'

'Part of me felt relief. Sounds heartless, I know it does, but it was like a weight had lifted off me. In those days, Russell was like... He always messed everything up! He... he ruined my childhood. If you want the truth, most of the time I detested him. Plus, it's not like we had a mobile phone to use. The nearest phone box was miles away.'

'So you left him there?'

'Um, no. This is when things get... grim.'

How can it get any grimmer? thought Curtis, but kept quiet.

'I told Essa to go. To take Mum's car back, hide the keys under the wheel, and go home. I told her Dominic and I would make Russell disappear. That we'd make sure no one ever found out what she'd done.'

'You did what?' hissed Curtis.

'After Essa left, Dominic and I carried Russell up the cliff path. Man, real hard work doing that. Took ages and we were sweating our tits off by the time we got him to Dominic's motor. God, thinking back, it's insane... I mean, it wasn't my best plan...'

'Where did you take him?' asked Curtis.

'Dominic said he knew about some abandoned stable blocks right out in the sticks where we'd be able to stash the body. So we could work out what to do. We set off, and I used my jacket to wrap around Russell's head to staunch the blood... so it didn't seep into the car's interior, but the blood still went all over Dominic's seats. Cor, he was super pissed about that. When we got him inside this rickety old place, Dominic blurts out, "He's frigging breathing, Hayden! I don't think he's properly dead!"'

'Oh, shit,' said Curtis.

Hayden let out a snort. 'This sounds atrocious, I know it does... but after what he did to Essa, I didn't want him to wake up. I scanned the stables, and saw signs homeless people had been using the place... It didn't look recent, but we panicked, thinking that if somebody came back there and found us all, we'd be in the right crap. Dominic told me about a storage area underneath the building... He lifted this hatch in the floor and revealed a space... It seemed ideal, so we stashed Russell in there and shut him inside.'

Curtis swooned. 'Oh... that's just... it's...'

'Yeah, I know. It's messed up, Curtis. It really is. I mean, I'm quite claustrophobic myself, so you can only imagine, right?'

'Please don't tell me you left him there.'

'No, no... well, yeah, for the night. I'll admit, I considered *not* going back. I kinda felt the little shit deserved it... but my mum would have flapped, and after all is said and done, he's my brother—'

'Did you not feel guilty?'

'Oh yeah, of course. I didn't sleep a wink that night. The next day Dominic got in touch with his mate, Sparks. This sleazy idiot whose cousin worked in a hospital pharmacy. The lad was always getting stuff from the dispensary for Dominic and some of his other cronies. God knows how he did it, but if Dominic wanted temazepam, or other drugs, Sparks stole the meds that same day. Dominic tells Sparks he wants medication to help with a severe head injury. Then he was supplied with enough pills to choke a pony. There was even liquid morphine.'

'Are you saying you treated your brother's injuries yourself? That's just... madness!'

'I didn't think he'd even survive the night, if I'm truly honest. I guess I wanted to make the effort. Just to tell myself, *I tried.*'

Curtis could not comprehend what he was being told. He only wished he didn't feel so rough and that his mind didn't seem so foggy. Perhaps he'd be able to digest all the information a little better. Or perhaps not even then.

'We cleaned the wound. Or, I did, because Dominic lost his breakfast when we inspected the damage up close. I'd never been much cop with a needle and thread, so we used modelling resin glue. Super strength stuff. That did a decent job. I say decent... it helped. By the time I'd finished wrapping him in bandages, he resembled something out of an old horror film.'

'Why didn't you just take him to hospital, Hayden?'

Hayden snapped his sunglasses away from his face. 'Because then Essa would have learnt that he survived... and she'd have told everyone he raped her.'

'But you said yourself he all but did! Why would you care if she hated him? What you did makes no sense!'

'I didn't do it for Russell! I did it for Mum,' snapped Hayden with venom. His eyes clouded over and Curtis took a step back from him.

'So *I* nursed him. *I* tended to his wounds. *I* kept him alive. *Not* for him. His horrid deception sickened me. I'm not proud of what I did, but I'm trying to explain so you can better understand what's going on now!'

Curtis nodded. 'OK.'

'After I calmed down, I realised some things. Yes, I hated him, but I couldn't face giving Russell up, and of course I didn't want him to die. But I couldn't let him hurt Essa again, either.'

'How long before he woke up?'

Hayden took a deep breath. 'A few days. He came in and out of consciousness for a while. I changed his dressings twice a day and forced some liquids and crushed pills down him. On day three, Dom and I were both convinced he'd not see the night through. We arrived on day four expecting to find a corpse, but we found him bumbling about in the stables like some bloody drunk zombie, before he flaked out again.'

Hayden lit up another cigarette and took three hard puffs before continuing. 'When Russell became coherent enough to hold a brief conversation, he told me he couldn't recall the fight on the beach, the chase up the cliff path, or... the fall. I told him that if he ever showed his face in town again, Essa would call the police and tell them he'd attacked her. I made it clear that I'd not be able to protect him from the repercussions of his actions.'

41

Vanessa found Jude at his Lego table, where an assortment of pirate ships, castles, and buildings were under construction in varying stages of assembly. Jude, ignoring her entrance, keenly erected a ship's mast, an expression of concentration set on his face. Much of his beloved collection hadn't stayed intact after being transported from London, and there'd been some serious bleating when he'd started unboxing his sets to find entire pieces in ruin. Vanessa had seen this as a blessing in disguise, as he'd been so preoccupied with rebuilding his old collection that he hadn't been on her case to buy any new kits. His room was already brimming with Lego.

'OK?' she asked, squatting down to his level. 'Looks like you nearly have all your ships fixed up, at least.'

Jude jutted his bottom lip and shrugged. 'Where's Dad?'

'I don't know. Maybe he popped out to get some medicine.'

'Oh.'

'Look, I apologise for being mean, Jude. Alright?'

Jude rooted around a big pile of multicoloured bricks,

tree tops, anchors and nets, spreading them out in his hunt for the correct piece.

'You know, it wouldn't hurt you to say sorry as well, Jude.'

He selected a small brown tube, examined it, then tossed it aside. 'To who?'

'Um, your sister, for a start. To your dad, for holding back the truth about that man.'

Jude eyed her for a moment, scowled, then continued his search.

'No?'

'What will you do if I *don't* say sorry? Toss me head first off the bedroom balcony?' he asked in a sneering tone.

'Fine,' she snapped, standing up. It took all her willpower to leave the room without backhanding his ship and undoing the arrogant sod's work.

42

'What did you tell everyone?' asked Curtis.

'Once we reported Russell missing, it all got out of hand. The lie spiralled, and I felt like I couldn't stop it. It sounds bonkers, but at the time, I thought I was doing the right thing. I was trying to protect all the people in my life I cared about.'

'And Russell?'

Hayden took in an intake of breath and let out a long exhalation. 'He got it. Yeah, he was pissed off. But he didn't want to be branded as a pervert or rapist. He took some convincing, but he agreed I was right. He needed to stay in the shadows and move away. A fresh start seemed like the sensible option.'

'And your mum? I take it she knew.'

Hayden shook his head. 'Not about what happened with Essa. No way. That would have ripped her heart out. No, I made up some story about him running up a debt with some unsavoury characters in the area, and they'd beaten him up. I explained that we were faking his disappearance so they'd back off. Mum got on board straight away. It was her nature to protect us boys with a ferocity that knew no bounds. Especially where Russell was concerned.' Hayden smiled and shook his head as if remembering something. 'She even printed up posters and did an interview with the local paper. God, thinking back, it was so mad. I still can't get my head around it myself.'

Curtis tried to imagine things from their mother's perspective. Yes, she'd lied too, but under the pretence she was saving her son from undesirables that wanted to hurt him. Would he protect his own children in such a way? *Yes,* if that's what it took, he probably would.

'How long did you keep him hidden?'

'His injuries took a while to heal. Over six weeks, and he lived in squalor during that period. Once he was fit enough, we arranged for him to stay with our cousin in Reading. I drove him there myself.'

Curtis struggled to get his head around this. Hayden had weaved an elaborate plot and bent over backwards to get Russell out of the picture. Out of Vanessa's life.

'Whilst Russell was on the missing list, Essa told Michael how unhappy she was. She even said she was considering, you know... ending it all. Her dad told her he'd received some job offer near London. He'd intended to turn it down because he assumed Essa wouldn't want to move away. After he found out she'd go, he said they could leave whenever. That was that. Within a few weeks, he'd made all the arrangements. I begged her not to leave me. I said I'd do anything. But she told me it was all over.'

Curtis saw the sadness wash over Hayden's face. He rubbed the ridge of his nose and sighed. 'I tried telling her things would be different. That with Russell out of the picture, we could finally be happy.' He gave Curtis a sad smile. 'She was so cold. Told me she never wanted to see me again! I'd done all that. Made my twin brother become a... a ghost... and she still went. Still left me alone. I was heart-broken by it all. I can tell you that, Curtis. Stupid, right? We were only kids, really. But even so... it tore me up.' Hayden gazed past Curtis and stared into the distance.

He expected Hayden to continue unloading, but he now looked drained and confounded by his disburdening of the past. As if releasing all this had wiped him out, both physically and mentally.

'Hayden... Did Vanessa... Did you ever tell Vanessa the truth? Did you ever let her know that Russell... that he survived that fall? You must have told her before she left.'

Hayden swallowed hard and took in a big intake of air. Then he recoiled as he let out the air as though he was expelling a demon trapped inside of him. He shook his head, all the time keeping his eyes anywhere but on Curtis.

'Hayden, you mean to tell me that for all these years she's been living with this?'

'I guess so, yes.'

'So she's spent her life believing Russell was out there somewhere in some unmarked grave? Jesus. Oh, Jesus! This is... it's just insane.'

'I wasn't thinking straight. I was so obsessed with keeping her... I... I didn't think she would go. Actually leave me. I needed her, and she bailed.'

'You were nineteen. You should have known better. That's so appalling. How could you do that?'

'Look, Curtis, at nineteen you might have had your head screwed on, mate. But me... I was a nightmare. I didn't know my head from my arse. I was so screwed up on drugs and booze I didn't have a clue how serious this all was.'

Hayden shook his head and sighed again, a tormented expression fixed on his face. He closed his eyes and rubbed his forehead, making a hissing noise through gritted teeth. 'I ended up losing everything. I'd got it into my head that

Russell would go to prison. My mum would've had a break-down, and I'd have been responsible because I didn't stop it all from happening. It sounds crazy now, I can grasp that... but that's what I believed back then.'

'I just... I'm not sure what to say. I mean... Shit.'

'After a few years, Russell came forward and informed the authorities he was alive and well and that they could remove him from the missing persons' register. But he stayed under the radar. No credit cards, voting or social media. He got a bank account and passport, but he tried to make himself as untraceable as possible.'

'You said Russell didn't remember the fight on the beach... but did he blame Vanessa?'

Hayden nodded. 'Yes. Instead of fading, that hatred magnified and festered. He'd often bring it up. It made him bitter. I tried to tell him to forget the past, but he'd never let it go. He was adamant that one day Essa would regret causing his injury. Causing him to lose his memory. And his... life.'

The pain in Curtis's abdomen returned, accompanied by an icy dread that chilled his very bones.

'Before Essa left, she said, "I'm glad he died, Hayden. I hope he rots in the darkest pits of hell."'

CURTIS AND HAYDEN headed back along the beach, and by the time they'd made it back to the house, Curtis's legs struggled to hold him upright.

'So, what now? Do we call the police?' asked Curtis.

'God, no. We can deal with this ourselves. We'll play the mediators here, Curtis. I'll deal with Russell. I just need to find him. Get him back on his meds. You tell Essa not to worry. That I'll sort this out.'

'He's on meds?'

'Some anti-depressants. He goes off the rails a bit without them.'

'If he's a danger to my wife and kids, I'm taking no risks.'

'I promise you he's unstable, but not violent. He'd be far more likely to harm himself than anyone else.'

A flashback hit Curtis. He recalled going under water and fighting to free himself from that debris. 'Mm, I dunno.'

'I'll handle Russ. You speak to Essa and explain the situation. Maybe she'll speak about everything now it's out in the open. Tell her we can sort all this mess out.'

43

Vanessa poured herself a glass of White Zinfandel and downed it in one. Sofia busied herself at the dining table, scribbling in her colouring books. Pens and paper lay scattered everywhere, and Curtis would no doubt have a meltdown if he came home to find the table being used as a drawing station without the easy-wipe tablecloth to protect its precious surface, but right now Vanessa couldn't care less.

She poured another glass, untied her velvet, leopard-print scrunchie selected especially for the day trip to the zoo, and let her hair fall loose. As she raised the glass to her lips, she closed her eyes and her mind swam. She tried not to drink during the weekdays unless it was warranted – a special occasion or night out – but today she needed to take the edge off. She made her way out into the garden and collapsed down onto the long rattan sofa, enjoying the sun's rays on her face. Then she took out her phone.

Tuesday 13th June 1995 continued...

I found my way into a vast orchard and I walked for a long time through endless rows of apple trees until I came to a white van. This old Ford must have stood here for an age, because all of its tyres had sunk about three inches into the ground. It had no windows; they'd all been smashed. Moss blotches and patches of rust smeared the weather-faded paintwork. I approached, but I got the sense I was no longer alone. I peered in through the back window, and the smell of damp and mouldy apples hit me. My torch beam flickered across the inside – I saw two plastic garden chairs, an overturned crate and a foil cake tin that had been used as a makeshift ashtray. I assumed the fruit pickers used this smelly van as some kind of shelter or smoking den.

As I pulled the torch away, movement inside caught my eye. I stared for a few moments until my eyes adjusted to the darkness, and I gasped when I caught sight of a set of white, glassy eyes that seemed to follow me with malevolent intent. That dammed creature from the church had tracked me down. But then a sudden thought occurred to me... The troll had trapped itself, and now the upper hand belonged to me. I hissed and swore at it. Told it that tonight Little Essa, the big pushover, was changing. I'd no longer be taking his, or anyone else's, shit. I got so mad. Like crazy mad. I called it a dirty, grey-faced fuck-head. I said I'd send that skinny wretch to hell where it belonged.

The door wouldn't budge, so I yanked and wrenched it until finally it swung open, showering tiny pieces of glass on the ground and over my sandals. 'I'm done being scared of you,' I growled then. It's weird, because I felt their presence before I saw them, and as the cats approached, one on either side of me, I gave the creature a sly grin. A grin that said, yeah, mate, you're done for now, aren't you?

Skulking, low and hunched, ready to spring an attack, the cats moved forward.

The creature's eyes went wide with fear and I laughed. It was good to know the tables had turned and that thing would experience my anxieties.

The jaguars were silent as they crouched lower, and ignored me as they inched towards the open door. To my surprise, after sharing a quick look with the larger cat, the smaller one – the female, I suspected – pounced. In an action so fast, it appeared no more than a blurry flash of glossy black fur, the cat flew into the back of the van, latched onto the creature's skinny torso and shook the thing ferociously. Calm and quiet, the male watched the attack. I could sense its pride as he relished in the female's skill. Bones crunched and flesh tore.

I couldn't see clearly, so I dared to dance the light of the torch inside in time to witness an enormous paw slamming down on the woeful creature's pummelled head, followed by the cat ripping and rending at its scrawny neck. This caused the head to almost fall away. Ew. I sat down, crossed my legs, and cheered. Tonight was all about taking out the trash. Cleansing my soul. Moving on to pastures new. I turned to my left and the male jaguar stared at me with sparkling eyes. I nodded, and he too leapt forwards to join the slaughter.

Within seconds, the creature was nothing more than shredded flesh, erupting pulpy organs and splintering

bones. The van rocked around as the cats played tug of war
with a spindly leg drenched in gore, and I clapped my
hands with a gleeful chuckle, like I'd just watched some
wonderful piece of theatre or amazing play. I even shouted
out, 'Bravo, bravo.'

But then the tap on my shoulder scared the absolute crap
out of me.

VANESSA STOPPED READING and gazed down at her phone
nestled in her palm. She did this for a very long time, before
setting the phone down on the glass table top and slugging
the Zinfandel. She couldn't even recall writing this part of the
experience. Not in so much detail, anyway. Was that how
she'd remembered events taking place? Had she truly
conjured up this little fantasy and imagined it playing out in
front of her in such visual and ghastly reality? Unnatural
things stalking her in the night. Guardian angels in the form
of giant, monster-destroying cats. Where had her head been
at back then?

Maybe those things her mum used to tell her were true...
'You're a weird little girl, Vanessa – you'll always be an
oddball. Sometimes I swear those midwives swapped you at
birth, because no daughter of mine could ever be so abnormal.' Her mum's face when she'd picked up that tatty copy of
The Little Grey Men would always stay with Vanessa. The
expression of disgruntled distaste, as she'd said, 'Proper little
girls shouldn't be obsessed with goblins and fairy-tale
monsters.'

'It's about gnomes, Mummy. They have a little boat and go
in search of their brother, Cloudberry. They have an amazing
adventure in the countryside. It's my favourite.'

'Dear God, your dad has a lot to answer for. Why is he
letting you read this stuff?'

'It's just an old library book. I could read you a page. You'd like it. I love it.'

'No wonder your head is stuck in the bloody clouds, girl.'

'It's not a silly story, Mummy. The gnomes even kill a giant! Well, he's really a man... One stuffs oak leaves inside the barrel of his gun, and—'

'Vanessa, I don't care if these idiotic, pitiful gnomes murder a golden unicorn with a magic sabre, eat its eyeballs for breakfast, and fly to Jupiter on a rocket made of tiny pixies' wings and jagged gremlins' toenails!'

Vanessa had chuckled at that, but received a whack over the head with the novel in response.

'Bloody gnomes on boats! Do you even have any friends at school? I mean really, do you, Vanessa?'

'Yes, I have a few.'

'Come on, get to sleep now, silly old Billy.'

Now Vanessa tried to picture the scene in the van. Tried to recall the creature getting butchered by the black cats. It wouldn't materialise. What seemed odd was that she could recall the wrinkly-faced lady in the beanie hat and threadbare dressing gown who'd pointed out that Vanessa was trespassing. The lady had seemed more concerned about her welfare than angry. 'Did something bad happen to you, sweetheart? Are you hurt?'

Vanessa explained that she'd had a barney with her boyfriend and she'd tried to find a phone, got lost and ended up stranded in the maze-like farm orchards. The kind lady took her into some secret garden – a little area enclosed with tall trees. Wind chimes and dream catchers, of all shapes and sizes, hung from every branch and the lady told her she'd made the special area for her grandchildren, all of whom had moved far away now. The garden had made her feel safe but strangely sad, and she'd talked with the lady for a long time about their respective lives. The sun had risen, and she'd been amazed to learn a new day had arrived. All night, she'd spent exploring the woods and orchards.

'Would you like to go inside and phone somebody to come and collect you?' the old lady had asked.

Vanessa snapped out of the past, finished her drink and realised she was no longer alone outside.

'Hey, Vee,' said Curtis.

'Hey, you,' replied Vanessa lazily.

'Good day at the zoo?'

'You look terrible, Curtis.'

Sofia appeared at Curtis's side. 'Daddy, Jude was naughty and Mummy threatened to throw him to the tigers!' She chuckled. 'And everyone gave us funny looks, so we left early.'

Curtis flashed Vanessa a questioning look but carried a faraway expression that made him appear odd and disorientated.

Vanessa was quite surprised her daughter hadn't spilled the beans on her little accident, too. She'd no doubt remember in a few minutes.

'We need a chat, Vee,' said Curtis. 'It's about Hayden. And... Russell. I have just found out about what happened on the beach.'

Vanessa, mid-sip during this dropped bombshell, felt her arm go numb and let the glass fall from her grip.

44

Vanessa stepped out onto the lounge balcony and tried to process everything her husband had told her about his encounter earlier that day. Vanessa had listened patiently, not reacting, or saying a single word, as he relayed everything in a quiet, trembling tone.

Russell is alive... he survived that terrible head injury...

'Aren't you going to say anything?' asked Curtis.

Hayden kept Russell hidden... He nursed his twin back to health...

'I think you owe me some answers... Don't you, Vee?'

Russell holds you responsible, Vanessa.

'I understand this must have been traumatic for you, Vee... but...'

Vanessa's limbs became numb and devoid of strength. 'You should never have spoken to him, Curtis. This is what I've been warning you about.'

'No. No, I think that finally I'm getting to the bottom of all this. You've had the opportunity to tell me the truth. But instead, you've kept me in the dark, and quite frankly, I'm starting to believe all sorts.' Curtis slumped into a chair. He didn't seem angry; just drained, bewildered, and lost.

'You have no clue what you're doing here,' croaked Vanessa.

'But... How could you keep this from me? We've been married for ten years and together for almost twenty. You'd think at some point you might have mentioned that you were mixed up in a plot to cover up some lad's death!'

Vanessa stayed silent. She'd mentally prepared herself in case this day ever came... or so she'd supposed.

'You've never trusted me enough? Is that it? Never felt you could confide in me?'

Vanessa took some deep breaths to stay calm and focussed. Losing her cool wouldn't solve anything. A sudden vision flashed in her mind – a head cracking against a rock – making her jolt and bite down on her lower lip.

'So, what is this? Is this you keeping your promise to *him* and staying silent? I can't get on board with that. I'm your husband.'

Tell him everything, she urged herself. *Now is the time.*

The blood... all that blood. No one could have ever survived *that* much blood loss...

'Vee! Please. Stop shutting me out!'

Vanessa closed her eyes. Her mind felt like it was spinning at the speed of an erratic washing machine that had almost reached the end of its turbulent cycle.

Not your future husband. Tell... no... one.

Crack, crack, crack. His head smacking down, again and again and again, as though someone kept rewinding and playing the same spot in a movie.

I won't. I swear it... Not anyone. Never.

Only this movie was stuck inside her head and couldn't be switched off.

Crack... crack.

The sound of the distant waves was stuck in her head now, too. But still with it the awful noise... *crack... crack... crack.*

Wasn't his skull pulverised?

Vanessa conjured up an image of herself running – heard that song in the background... saw the giant cats tearing at grey flesh and play-fighting over body parts...

'Vee? What's wrong?' asked Curtis.

It sounded like she'd gone deep under water.

'Vanessa?'

Was she drowning in her own mind?

Why did Delphine draw away from her? She'd *seen* something. But... what?

Vanessa wanted to scream... Her heart smashed inside her chest...

Tell... NO... one.

She pictured the male jaguar as it hauled the body up onto a lumpy, dead tree trunk.

Vanessa heard Sofia's voice inside her head saying, 'Mummy, are the big cats going to eat Jude all up for their dinner? I bet he tastes yummy and scrummy.'

Curtis was calling out, 'Vanessa! Vanessa!'... but that faded and all she could hear were heavy waves crashing and another voice shouting, 'Essa! Essa!'

Her worlds were colliding, past and present crashing into one another. Paths that never should have crossed were becoming entangled.

The limp, mauled body slumped from the trunk, dangling head first. Vanessa viewed the corpse's face... *Jude*... His chest had been gouged open... His ribs... the cats were pulling and champing down on his ribs.

No, no, no, no. *What have I done?*

Sofia sang, 'Mummy fed Jude to the big cats... the big cats, the big cats... Mummy fed Jude to the big cats... the big cats, the big cats.'

'Vee, speak to me! Oh, God, Vee!'

Abnormal little girl.

'Ambulance, please!' gasped Curtis. 'My wife is having a stroke!'

She does love you, Jellybean. In her own way.

'Yes! She's just collapsed!'

He'll come and snatch you away, Vanessa...

I'm nothing like you. Nothing.

Then everything went silent... and black.

45

Delphine took in the cottage's interior and pulled a face. It all seemed a bit ordinary. Yes, it looked nicely decorated, and the furniture was fine, but she just couldn't see the South African inside this plain house. The decor and, in particular, the wall art, could only be described as uninspiring, the most interesting piece being an abstract image of a white coffee mug, closely followed by a large black and white canvas featuring a stack of five zen stones.

'What do you think of the place?' asked Jonas, waltzing in from the kitchen with two glasses of red wine. Today he wore a funky dark blue short-sleeve shirt, printed with flamingos and pink flowers.

'My first impression is that it's spotless, and unlike your jazzy shirts, a bit...'

'Go on, you can say it.'

Delphine scrunched up her nose. 'Vanilla.'

Jonas chuckled. 'What? You mean to tell me you don't like those mole ornaments? I'm crushed.'

Delphine hadn't even noticed those sitting on the windowsill. 'Who doesn't love a wicker mole?'

'When I said this was *my* place... I meant temporarily. I only rented short term. Fully furnished, as I'm sure you've already guessed. Doesn't feel like home to me. Far too beige and unimaginative for my taste. I like strong, vibrant colours. But I won't be staying long enough to add my unconventional touch to the place. Not without losing my massive deposit, anyway.'

Delphine accepted the wine and smiled her thanks. 'How long?'

'I've seen a place in the city. Same price range as here. Bit of a rabbit hole, but I'm gonna need to be closer to the action. I don't enjoy the commute.'

Delphine tried to hide her disappointment behind her wine glass.

'Be a shame, because I have really enjoyed my time here. Love the area. Plus, I have the riding club... I've got real friendly with my man, Curtis, and...' Jonas flashed an embarrassed grin, making the gap in his teeth appear bigger than ever. He chuckled, his huge shoulders bobbing up and down. 'Plus, I guess a few other things are holding me back.'

'Interesting.'

'I bought a replacement picture online. Sooo, maybe a little part of me *wants* to hang around.' He placed his wine on the windowsill. He then scurried into the kitchen and returned after a few moments with a thin, square box. 'What about this, hey? It's both quirky and happens to be my all-time favourite movie.'

As Jonas removed the piece from its packaging, Delphine smiled as she studied the illustration of an open-mouthed Jaws popping out of the sea behind the Orca fishing rig, with Quint pouring a can of beer into the great white's gaping mouth.

Jonas placed the picture up against the coffee mug illustration. 'Saw one of these in a local bar and decided I needed one for this spot.'

Delphine laughed, thinking that not only did that seem a lot more like Jonas's style, but it would be a delightful addition to the boat house. She raised her glass. 'To Jaws getting tanked!'

Jonas put down the picture, grabbed his wine and clinked glasses with Delphine. 'Nice. I'll drink to that.'

46

V anessa opened her eyes and yawned, glad to see she was back in her own bed. Had she slept? She must have. The previous events flooded back to her, and she shuddered. *Dear Lord, I went and pissed myself,* was her first thought. Vanessa recalled being more mortified by learning that in the hospital than anything else.

'Vanessa, I believe you have had what is known as a psychogenic, non-epileptic seizure,' the tall male doctor had said. 'Your husband has explained that not only have you been under a severe amount of acute stress, but you've not been eating or sleeping properly for some weeks, which would likely have exacerbated your issues and led to the attack you experienced.'

Vanessa heard someone come into the bedroom, considered pretending to be asleep, but decided it was time to face the world.

Curtis winked at her. 'Hey, sleepy girl. Here, a nice, strong, sweet tea. Did you sleep OK?'

Vanessa sat up and accepted the hot drink. 'Weird

dreams, but the best night's sleep I've had in a while. How much diazepam did they prescribe?'

'A week's worth.' Curtis sat on the end of the bed and rubbed his forehead. 'I'm so sorry, Vee. I made this all about me. I was untactful and insensitive.' He wiped tears from his eyes. 'Never scare me like that again, you hear me?'

Vanessa's breath caught in her chest, and she fought down the urge to start panic-breathing again. One tiny sign that all was not well, and Curtis would chase her off to A&E again within seconds. He'd been adamant she'd suffered a stroke. 'I'm fine now. You? Has the yellow fever lifted yet?'

Curtis smiled wryly. 'I think it was a forty-eight-hour bug. The kids are all packed and super excited,' said Curtis. 'I'll drop them off to my folks in the morning, then I need to head to the office for most of the day to play catch-up. Will you be OK on your own, or shall I ask Delphine to pop in?'

'I'll be fine.'

'How would you feel about a weekend away? Just us?'

'I'm not sure—'

'Hear me out, Vee... You remember that cottage in Symonds Yat? I should hope you do.'

Vanessa nodded.

'I called on the off chance they might have some spots, and I got lucky, because they've just had a cancellation for Saturday. Two nights. So I booked it.'

Vanessa forced a thin smile. The cottage was a truly magical place, and they'd had the most amazing weekend there. Curtis had proposed to her in the stunning riverside garden, but revisiting that cottage now, with everything going on, might taint the memory.

'Take as much time as you need, Vee. You can tell me about everything that happened in your own time. I promise, I won't push you anymore on this... I just...' Curtis wiped more tears and sniffed. 'I just want *you* back. And I want to help you work through all this mess. OK? I'll do whatever it takes to make that happen.'

Vanessa opened her mouth to speak, but the kids rushing in stopped her.

'Mummy, I've drawn you some pictures,' said Sofia, waving two pieces of paper with colourful drawings on them above her head.

Vanessa smiled and accepted the pictures. 'Aw, thanks, Sweet Pea.'

'That one's you and Daddy at a posh restaurant. And that's me and Jude eating yummy hotdogs in Nanny and Grandad's camper van. We're going to Bude. That's in Cornwall.'

Vanessa examined the pictures and threw her a quick wink. 'I'll put these up on the fridge. I bet you'll have an amazing adventure.'

Sofia clapped her hands, an exuberant smile on her face.

'Ten days! That'll seem like forever. You make sure you phone us every night!' demanded Vanessa.

'Every night. I promise, Mummy.'

Vanessa turned her attention to Jude, who stood at the bottom of the bed, a thin, sheepish grin working its way onto his face. 'You take care of your sister, Jude.'

Jude nodded, and it seemed obvious to Vanessa that he wanted to say something. He looked like he'd been crying by the red circles around his puffy eyes.

Curtis put his arm around Jude and said, 'Now, someone is a bit upset and thinks his actions might've contributed to your funny turn.'

'Come here, Jude. It wasn't your fault,' said Vanessa.

Jude shuffled over and allowed Vanessa to hug him. He leant in, stiff and awkward, but didn't hug her back.

Curtis scooped up Sofia and planted a kiss on her cheek.

'Right, guys, let's double-check you've packed everything you need and let your mum rest in peace now, yes?'

Vanessa shared a warm grin with her husband. Her episode had brought it all home to her just how lucky she was to have Curtis in her life. Soon, when they were alone and away from here, she'd take the opportunity to explain everything to him, not only because there could be no other path to take now, but because he deserved to know. Promises would be broken, and there were tremendous risks involved. Perhaps he wouldn't be able to understand why she'd done the things she'd done back then. Only time would tell if he could handle the truth.

At the cottage in Herefordshire, she'd considered the best way would be to lay all her cards on the table and suffer the consequences, whatever they may be. That way, she would find out how much her husband truly loved her.

47

A fter Curtis and the kids set off for London, Vanessa showered and prepared for the day ahead. As she tied her hair up using a black clasp, she tried not to contemplate too much what she'd planned to do. She'd already made a quick Facebook profile the night before, but decided she'd wait until she was close to Portsmouth before sending the message. As she munched on a rather unripe and tasteless banana, she went over the CCTV footage from the day of her seizure.

VANESSA STOPPED at Cobham services on the M25, opened the Facebook app and typed the message:

> I want to meet you at 12 o'clock in Portsmouth. Say where, or I'll wait for you at your house, or come to your workplace.

Vanessa had set the profile name as Russell Knox and used a picture of a decaying zombie. This was in very poor taste, she decided, but she wanted to capture the recipient's attention. She decided to grab a coffee and wait for a response, but to her surprise, a message came back straight away.

Who is this???

Vanessa typed back:

Name a place, or I go knocking on your front door.

She guessed the blag would work. Dominic wouldn't play hard to get for long. He couldn't risk it. Or so she hoped.

Whatever. I'm not falling for it. I'm BLOCKING this account, you total dick-head.

Vanessa thumbed a rapid response:

Then I guess you'll find me having a cuppa with your wife, Yoselin, when you get home from work later.

Five minutes passed with no comeback. She eyed that screen with a furious intensity.

Ten minutes passed... no reply.

Fifteen... still nothing.

Vanessa started the engine and admitted defeat. But then the reply came.

Gunwharf Shopping Mall, outside The Ghost at 1300. I'll give you five minutes. Not a second more. See you later... Little Essa.

VANESSA ARRIVED at the waterfront outlet and headed to the agreed meeting spot five minutes early. The clothing shop, The Ghost London, a trendy woman's fashion clothing store, was situated along the North Promenade building in the Gunwharf Quays mall.

She found Dominic already waiting there, standing outside the shopfront that displayed several headless mannequins fitted out in long, striking dresses and positioned in front of the floor-to-ceiling windows. She wondered if he'd picked this shop as a way of exhibiting some kind of ironic mockery, but she didn't reckon he was savvy enough to have come up with that.

Dominic's arms were folded, and his slim face fixed in a sullen pout. He wore a pinstriped suit, his light-blue tie askew. As Vanessa approached, he clocked her, raised one eyebrow and offered her his signature vile sneer. He checked his chunky gold watch. 'Five minutes. Not a second more. I'm a busy man. And just for the record, I don't believe you know where I live.'

Pretentious wanker. 'This won't take long, Dominic.'

'It better—'

'What did you mean by, "mind fuck of my life?"' asked Vanessa sharply, cutting him off.

They stepped aside to allow shoppers to meander past them.

Dominic rolled his tongue around the bottom of his mouth, causing his lower lip to bulge as he appeared to be considering how best to play this.

'Come on, you're wasting my five minutes here, Dominic.'

'I don't want to be dragged back into all this mess, Essa!'

'Did he survive?' snapped Vanessa.

The tongue rolling continued, and now Dominic's eyes darted around the place.

'Well?' she asked.

Dominic's face contorted, and he ground his teeth. 'I want you to stay away from me! I'm nothing to do with all this anymore. Stop pestering me.'

'Did you help take Russell to some abandoned stable block, then secretly treat his wounds with stolen medication?'

Dominic glowered and spoke in a low, irritated voice. 'Who told you *that*?'

'He told my husband.'

Dominic raised his eyebrow again. 'Hayden?'

Vanessa nodded.

'Why the hell would he do that?'

Vanessa shrugged. 'It is true, then? He survived?'

Dominic let out an irritated sigh, waited for several shoppers to wander by, and gave a curt nod.

Vanessa's stomach lurched, and she fought back the tears pricking at her eyes.

Dominic checked his watch, gave Vanessa one final sneer, and trudged away.

'I have spent most of my life thinking he was dead,' Vanessa exclaimed.

Without even turning to face her, he said, 'Never contact me again, Essa.'

So that was that. Even though the side-by-side CCTV printouts of the twins had confirmed it, she still needed that additional confirmation to be sure that she wasn't being duped. Now she knew – Russell lived. It took every fibre of Vanessa's being not to scream until her lungs exploded.

48

C urtis left the office and made his way to the Wrangler. The Jeep would be sold in a week, so Herefordshire would be its final outing. A fresh batch of vehicles were arriving on Monday, and he'd already selected his new, temporary wheels: a top-of-the-range Range Rover Sport in Firenze red.

He'd not received any reply to the messages he'd sent Vanessa earlier, so he slid into the Jeep, cradled his phone and made to select her number. A figure appearing at the front of the car stopped him from making the call. Curtis's mouth went bone dry. At a quick glance he couldn't fathom which of the twins stood there, but he surmised, mainly by the sharp clothing, that it was Hayden. The man appeared distraught and disoriented.

Curtis got out. 'What are you doing here? Are you following me?'

'I have been calling you and leaving messages. Why are you ignoring me?'

'I've been really busy today.'

'It's Russell... He's... Something bad has happened. Something terrible!'

Curtis scanned the yard, spotting two office staff nattering outside one of the mobile office units. The women were watching something on a phone and sharing an embarrassed chuckle. But even though he didn't see anyone, he guessed someone would be snooping. The gossip gang would have a field day speculating on why *the boss* was having a clandestine meeting in his car with a stranger. Either he needed to whisk Hayden inside and treat him as a potential client, or remove him from the site. He opted for the latter. 'Jump in. I'll buy you a coffee.'

As they drove away, Curtis caught Albie's eye as he stood inspecting a silver VW Caddy with a clipboard and pen in hand. The mechanic followed his car with a suspicious glower. Curtis saw in the interior mirror that Albie continued to view them until they'd pulled out of the yard, sped up the road and headed into the industrial site.

HAYDEN DECLINED the coffee Curtis had offered and sat in the passenger seat with his hands on his knees.

They'd parked up on the outskirts of the industrial sector. A hidden, dead-end lane that was distastefully dubbed *Shaggers' Corner* because of the amount of extramarital sex that was said to take place here. Curtis wondered if he should have stayed in the yard or ventured further afield, but his desperate desire to learn what Hayden wanted to divulge overrode the worry that people might conclude he was getting jiggy with another man.

They parked opposite a bin, which bulged with rubbish from the nearby takeaway hut. Some items were just left scattered around its base, as though the owners of the litter decided that it wasn't their problem that the bin could not accommodate their crap. Heaven forbid they find an alternative place to dump it. Towering, bottle-green coloured panels, marked in several places with crude, unreadable graffiti, sectioned off the area, so the factory units behind were cut off from the road. The place was merely a turning point for lorries, as no businesses were accessible via this route. Curtis decided that the idea of anyone choosing this as a destination to copulate within sniffing distance of yesterday's greasy sandwich wraps was a bleak one.

No worse than a filthy nightclub toilet cubicle.

Does that even happen? Curtis wondered.

Hayden's previous words rattled around his head – 'He used to steal things – personal things.'

Curtis shook the smutty images out of his head. They sickened him to his very core.

'I've located Russell's vehicle, Curtis.'

At Hayden's sorrowful tone and stiff body language, Curtis's first thought was that Russell had taken his own life. Had Hayden found his twin's body hanging from a tree?

'Mum came across his phone passwords and codes, so we did a find-a-device tracking thing. I logged in on my phone and it pinpointed the location. I drove there yesterday.'

Hayden gazed straight forward as he spoke and his right eye twitched.

'Did you find him?'

'Found his van. Unlocked. Found his phone. Didn't find Russell.'

Hayden took out his lighter and thumbed the roller. Curtis knew he needed a smoke. He wouldn't be having one in here.

'So, why didn't you mention the money you offered Russell?'

Curtis cleared his throat. 'The money?'

'Come on, Curtis, don't play dumb. I've got his phone. I know. I mean, I don't know why. Care to explain about that?'

'He didn't take the money. Vee took it to him, but he didn't show,' said Curtis, his voice sounding broken and strained to his own ears. He shifted uncomfortably, sat up straight, and spoke in a firmer, more pertinent tone. 'Get to the point, will you?' He glimpsed his own face in the interior mirror. An ashen face, oozing nervousness, peered back at him.

'Money for what? Why offer him fifteen big ones?'

'We offered him ten... to stay away. To leave... to leave us alone,' stammered Curtis.

'Essa's idea, I take it. For the record, and I have text messages to confirm this, Essa was taking him fifteen, not ten.'

Curtis fidgeted in his seat, cleared his throat again, but made no response.

'I'm finding it hard to believe you let Essa go alone.'

'It was a busy restaurant. She insisted—'

'Stop insulting my intelligence. We both know the meeting place changed.'

'But I—'

'Don't deny it, Curtis. You must have known!' Hayden snatched out his phone, thumbed the screen and then spun it so Curtis could view it.

Footage played. Dash-cam footage that had been ominously slowed – headlights on a twisty lane. Curtis stared hard at the slow-moving footage, until a vehicle came into the shot – Vanessa's Mini, the number plate clear and readable, parked in a lay-by. Vanessa stood on the other side of the car, by the bonnet, gazing into an opening in the woods. A foot-path perhaps. She didn't turn to acknowledge the passing vehicle. She just stood frozen, hands at her side, her hair draped down over her waist-length, distinctive, floral summer jacket.

The dash-cam journey continued, passing by Russell's old van, parked haphazardly so half of the vehicle lay in a bush, the other at an angle on the road, before finishing its course outside a set of fortified gates with a big, bold sign stating: *24 Hour Security Patrols Operating.*

'There's more,' said Hayden, selecting another clip.

Compelled by where this was leading, Curtis continued to stare at the screen. More footage began. Curtis noted the fifteen-minute time jump and that the speed was running in actual time. He heard the grumble of the vehicle's diesel engine and a gravelly cough in the background. The same lane as the first film, but this time the vehicle headed in the opposite direction. Back past Russell's van and then, with the Mini in view and drenched in its headlights, it stopped, the engine growling. More coughing and a big sniff were audible. It sounded like a man, and the gruff clearing of a throat confirmed this.

Several minutes dragged past. Then movement from the woods. *Someone* came out of the cut-through. *Vanessa again?* Yes, definitely her. As she walked with urgent steps to the driver's side door, she froze and her eyes flicked to the watching vehicle. For a few seconds, it almost appeared as if she was considering heading over, but decided against this and got into the Mini. Her car's headlights burst on. *She no longer wore her jacket,* Curtis noticed.

The vehicle moved on, the camera passing Vanessa, who gave it a furtive glance as it passed by. Then Hayden snatched the phone away.

'That's footage from the security patrol car. The owners of the big house at the end of the lane have the guards scout the lane at regular intervals. I had a chat with the security chap after I located Russell's van. Once I explained I was looking for my missing brother and was concerned for his safety, he scanned through his footage for the timeframe in which he first noticed the van. He'd remembered it because he assumed it was someone fly-tipping or smoking drugs. Then, after returning and spotting a lone woman in the Mini, he concluded that perhaps the owner of the van had met the woman for a touch of hanky panky, so he'd left them be.' Hayden flashed him a contemptuous scowl. 'I searched the area. Do you want to know what I found?'

'What?' asked Curtis meekly. He didn't like the way Hayden's demeanour had changed from dismayed to threatening. His eyes, in particular, seemed to have gained a dark, foreboding glint. He now felt unsafe, and it made him cast his mind back to the kayaking trip. He cursed his stupidity for once again putting himself in a situation where he was alone with an untrustworthy stranger. Another Knox brother. The quick change in the man's manner put him in mind of Russell's rapid mood changes.

'I strung the timeline together from their text messages. Russell had been the one who changed the meeting spot. He'd asked Essa to meet her at the viewpoint and text her a map location. So, I took a gander for myself this morning,' said Hayden, selecting another clip on his phone. 'Here, why don't *you* take a peek?'

At first, all Curtis could see was a carpet of silver laughing gas capsules all over the ground. Then the camera panned up and moved onto a skinny footpath lined with bluebells and stinging nettles. The path snaked through a wooded area for a short while, then opened up into a small viewing spot where two wooden benches sat facing in the direction of the scenery ahead. The camera scanned the panoramic display of sloping hills, miles of variegated farmers' fields, and a huge stretch of urban area that dominated the land in the far distance.

A pair of Merrell walking shoes came into shot as the camera footage shook and then descended through a thicket of trees, before moving off track onto a steep, unlit thicket. The footage became jarring to watch as the camera holder fought to stay upright, as the hill became almost vertical and was overrun with nettles and ropey brambles.

As the camera moved forward into an open track of land, the footage became clearer. The little sun-soaked area, that was dotted with boulders and surrounded by white birch trees, seemed to Curtis like a hidden glade where teenage lovers would meet. Then he noticed what looked very much like splashes of blood streaked across one of the trees, and he recoiled. An icy chill passed over him. As more and more blood splatters became apparent, his heart rate quickened.

The camera scanned across the broken ground where more thick blood patches lay. Dark red droplets spotted a tree stump. Then he saw a piece of clothing strewn on the ground, stained with more thick gore. He choked down a gasp once it sank in... once he registered what he was gazing at. *Vanessa's floral jacket.*

The scene transported Curtis back to a time after Steve had passed. His dad, preoccupied in his sad thoughts, had slipped using a bandsaw whilst working on some pointless carpentry project. He'd been rushed to the hospital to have the horrendous gash on his arm stitched back together. Several days later, Curtis's mum had asked him to clean up the garage.

Now, the camera continued to move... It left the grove and continued downward onto a track that gave a brief glimpse of vast fields and dense woodlands ahead, before dipping down into more bracken and thick vegetation. Curtis wanted to tell Hayden to stop the film. He wanted to turn away, tell him to piss off and stay out of his life... but he couldn't. His morbid curiosity kept his eyes stuck to that little screen.

He almost felt like he was there, stepping amongst the thorny undergrowth and... *he* shuddered when he caught sight of something on the ground. *A knife*... a kitchen knife... lying in the bushes, blade smeared with thick, dark blood. It looked like one of theirs, but he couldn't be certain. The camera moved again, stopping and scanning another tree... yet more gore.

Hayden turned off the clip.

Curtis tried to process what he'd seen. His mind drifted back to the garage – remembering the same reddish-brown spatters and smears over the workbench, floors and walls. Much the same as he'd just seen in the clip. That grey, mangled cardigan caked in blood, torn and abandoned on the floor, where his dad had ripped it off in an attempt to locate and patch up the deep wound before stumbling into the house and bellowing for help. Curtis's weak legs buckling as he tried to mop up the grim mess. Dry-heaving with each wipe of that blood-soaked cloth. His mum coming in to assist him and saying, 'It's just a bit of blood, Curtis... Don't be so squeamish.'

Hayden's voice snapped Curtis back to the present. 'I can take you there now. You can see all this for yourself. It took me a while to find the spot. I left my phone in my car, so after I retrieved it, I took a moment to process what I'd found, then walked back down and filmed it.'

Curtis kept replaying the footage in his head... and a sickening sensation jabbed and spun in his belly.

'My guess would be they spoke... they fought... one, or both of them, slipped over the edge... I dunno.' Hayden narrowed his eyes and waggled a finger at Curtis. 'Or maybe you know more about this than you're letting on. Maybe you were there. Perhaps... she told you all about what happened.'

Curtis was trembling all over.

'I couldn't find Russell. I'm guessing he got hurt really badly and stumbled away down that track... But by the look of all that carnage...' Hayden frowned and shook his head.

Curtis was no expert, but knew that anyone losing that much blood without getting urgent medical assistance would be in serious trouble.

'I've searched every spot... every direction in which that track leads, but I can find no more trace... no more *evidence* to suggest where he ended up. But there are miles of fields, woods and pathways... I just don't know.'

'Have you checked hospitals?' asked Curtis.

Hayden nodded and gave him a barbed *do you think I'm stupid* look. 'I guess we'll hear something. Eventually. When... he's found.'

'Why show me this? Why haven't you contacted the police?'

Hayden drew in a long breath. 'I need a cigarette.'

'That footage is fake. This is some kind of trap,' said Curtis, realising how unconvincing he sounded. 'My wife would never have done what you are suggesting. No way!'

'Drive then. Come on, see for yourself. I didn't move anything. You can chat with the security bloke, too.'

'You didn't say why.'

'I'm a little concerned about my safety. Which is why I have saved copies of these files. If anything happens to me...' Hayden tapped on his phone.

Curtis grimaced when he heard his own voice coming from the device. 'You listen to me, you stupid bastard! I know people... men from Streatham Hill in London! Do you understand what I'm saying? People that you do not want coming after you... so you stay away from my family!'

Curtis bit down hard on his lower lip as he recalled speeding across the Sheppey Crossing and leaving the angry voicemail.

'You have money and the means to get *things* done, Curtis.'

'He nearly drowned me. He'd been trespassing in our neighbour's garden and—'

'And you threatened him. I get it.'

'It was an empty threat. That's all.'

Hayden spun his phone and showed him a photo. A photo of Jonas in the driver's seat of a car, an expression of deep concentration etched on his face.

'What's he got to do with this?' asked Curtis.

49

'Hey, JB, everything alright? You didn't say you'd be calling.'

'Hi, Dad,' said Vanessa, eyes streaming with tears as she joined the busy M25 homebound.

'You sound upset. What's going on?'

Vanessa fought to hold back the choking sobs that desperately tried to escape her. 'My past is about to come back and ruin everything.'

'Honey, tell me what's going on. Where are you?'

'Heading home from Portsmouth. I have just spoken with Dominic Brookes.'

'Why would you go and see that scumbag?' he asked.

'Dad... it's Russell Knox... He... he's not dead.'

It took a long time for a response to come, and Vanessa wondered if the connection had been cut, when he said, 'Are you sure about this?'

'Russell came to the house. He pretended to be his brother... I assumed he'd come to stir things up... to see what he could get out of us... Now I have no clue what's going on.'

'But... we kept checking. He was registered missing... He'd vanished.'

Vanessa wiped some tears from her eyes and sniffed. 'They hid him away. Moved him out of Bournemouth. He started a new life. He lived in France for years, but now he lives in Bristol with his mum. I'm sure he's not... right.'

'How do you know all this?'

'Because *he* has been talking to Curtis.'

'Hayden has?'

'Yes!'

'So... why? What is this? What's his end game?'

Tears obscured her vision. She sniffed and wiped her eyes. 'I'm losing the plot here... Curtis doesn't have the mindset to deal with this... He'll never grasp how manipulative and conniving *that* man is.'

'Calm down. Please, can you pull over and take a moment? Would you please do that for me?'

'Dad, what if it all comes out? What will we do?'

'Listen to me... You need to calm down and hear me out. Understand? Now stop that car. Stop and take a moment. Would you, please, love?'

'OK. But please tell me what to do.'

'You can ride this out. You did it before... You can do it again. Trust me.'

'It will be hard for Curtis to accept everything that happened.'

'Listen, love... Just think carefully before—'

'Dad! I can't go on like this... I really... can't.'

50

'That's the guy from your house, right? Jonas?' asked Hayden. 'According to the messages on his phone, Russell said he'd sussed this guy had gone to the agreed meeting place at that Chinese restaurant. He was skulking about in a separate car. Did you tell him to go, Curtis? To make sure your wife stayed safe? Were your London thugs lurking around, too?'

Curtis kept his eyes on the photo of the South African and said nothing.

'When Russell contacted me about that night he showed up at your house, he explained that Jonas dropped a few things about his past into conversation. Once he'd had a few stiff ones, he mentioned being part of a security unit called Koevoet. He also escorted him out of your house and told him it wouldn't be wise to upset his friends. Said he'd be observing him.'

'Your brother was disrespectful and rude,' said Curtis.

'It's just the way he is. He's always been the same,' said Hayden flippantly.

'Wait up. What? So he told you Jonas threatened him in

one of his messages? Why then didn't you mention this when we first met, Hayden?'

'I didn't think it was relevant then. But now... I do. Anyway, I researched this Koevoet group.' Hayden sucked in air through his teeth. 'They were a police counter-insurgency unit made up of the local population. Long disbanded now. So, in the height of the war... the border war, I think they called it, these guys were trained as a mobile unit to gather intelligence, track guerrillas and kill them.... Back in the early eighties, the Koevoet had a heavy-handed presence and soon gained a grisly reputation for their brutal methods. Did your *friend* ever speak to you about his past?'

Curtis glared at Hayden. 'I know what you're doing here.'

'The Koevoet – that's Afrikaans for crowbar, by the way – were feared because when it came to interrogation and torture, these guys did not screw about. We're talking about strapping people to the front of trucks and driving them at high speed... shredding them to bits until the victim's comrades, forced to witness the ordeal, spilled the beans. They even got paid a bounty per corpse.'

'You haven't answered my question... Why are you telling *me* all this and not the police? Don't tell me it's because you're frightened for your own safety. You'd hardly be sitting here with me if that were the case.'

Hayden opened the window and lit up a cigarette. Curtis didn't bother contesting the action.

'I don't have a clue what happened below that viewing area. I don't know if you're involved, your heavies from London, or this Jonas. But my theory is that Essa met Russell and things went south. She also sent him threatening text messages. Not sure if you knew about that.'

Curtis dug his fingers into the steering wheel as the odious cigarette fumes filled the car. Curtis visualised all that blood... Even if Russell survived, those injuries would've been terrible... enough to suggest attempted murder.

'In answer to your question... I want to suggest another solution... I propose we work together and help each other.'

What a surprise, thought Curtis.

Hayden, cigarette in his mouth, scratched the nape of his neck. 'As you know, I've no real love for my twin. I've tried, for my mum's sake, but... the guy has always been intolerable. Toxic. Detestable. You want to know the truth? I don't give a flying monkey's cock if he's lying dead in a cornfield or a ditch somewhere,' he said, his face screwed up in a vexed snarl. 'He chose to come here and poke the wasp's nest, so that's his own doing. But I do care about my mum. I care about getting her the care she needs. You care about keeping your family together. So, I suggest we make a deal to accommodate each other's predicament.'

'Call this what it is, Hayden... blackmail.'

Hayden took three quick puffs on his cigarette, tossed it out the window and shrugged. 'I have business elsewhere. I can't stay in the UK and look after her. Russell, total unpredictable prick that he is – or *was*, as may be the case – did a good job in that respect. But it's complete care she needs now. That won't come cheap.' He took out a piece of paper and waved it in front of Curtis. 'You pay that amount into the listed crypto account by nine am tomorrow, and I'll clean up all the mess. Essa's jacket, the knife, Russell's phone, van... all of it will be dealt with.'

'What?'

'Oh, you heard me, Curtis.'

'Yes. I did... What... what about the security guy?'

'I paid him a hundred quid for that memory card. I have the only footage of Essa heading in and out of that viewpoint. The guy was a total fat moron. The only thing he'd ever remember was where he'd stashed his supply of custard doughnuts.'

'Why leave the knife behind?' asked Curtis.

'The same reason the jacket got left. Panic took over. It would have been dark, and with all the commotion... Who knows?'

Curtis closed his eyes and massaged his throbbing temples.

You did not piss off Little Essa without receiving some payback.

Curtis opened his eyes and read the tatty note.

Hayden watched him with unfriendly eyes. 'By nine, or I involve the police. I'll give them the entire sorry tale. From what happened on the beach all those years ago, to your threats, Jonas's history... and everything in between. Let them do what they will with all that knowledge. The papers would love a scandal like this. The impact on your personal life, not to mention your business, would be catastrophic.'

Curtis glared at him, wishing he had it in him to lunge at the man and throttle the very life out of him. If he'd have purchased that coffee, Hayden would be wearing it. What would his father have done? How would *his* brother have dealt with a shakedown like this if he'd been alive?

'You got any siblings, Curtis?' asked Hayden.

Curtis gazed incredulously at him, horrified by the question. He felt violated, like Hayden had intruded on his thoughts somehow. 'I lost my brother. Car accident. A long time ago.'

'Oh. Sorry. Did you get on with him?'

Curtis nodded. 'We had our moments. But yes, I did.'

Hayden laughed without humour. 'I'm guessing you find it hard to understand how I've always carried this hatred for Russell.'

'You can't choose your family. Just because you're related to someone, it doesn't mean you are obliged to like them.'

Hayden nodded thoughtfully, then said, 'I like you, Curtis. Hand on heart, I don't want to ruin your life or hurt your family. I no longer resent Essa, or hold any enmity towards her. My bitterness lifted many years ago. I moved on. But this is an opportunity I just cannot pass up. We can both move on from this unfortunate mess. Then we never have to cross each other's paths again.'

Curtis's throat felt like it was constricting. He tried to swallow, but struggled. 'I can't just get that sort of money at short notice—'

'Curtis!' interrupted Hayden. 'Your company makes millions. This amount will not sink you, and in the grand scheme of things, it'll barely make a dent!'

'I can't just take funds—'

Hayden slapped the palm of his hand on the dashboard. 'Find a way. Do it now, or tomorrow you can expect the world as you know it to turn into a very dark and unforgiving place. Once this ball gets rolling, irreversible damage will begin. Do you grasp that? Irreversible. Listen to me! Don't make me ruin your life. I don't want that.'

Curtis again saw himself snapping – lunging over and grabbing Hayden's scrawny neck and shaking the life out of him. Imagined whacking his head against the glass until his face smashed through it. He envisioned Hayden screwing a teenage Vanessa in that nightclub toilet... he could hear her urgent panting and screams of elation as this arsehole brought her to orgasm. Saw Vanessa's hands slapping against the side of the cubicle as she rode him... faster and faster...

Fuck you, fuck you... FUUUUCCKKK YOU!

Hayden interlocked his fingers and bent them back until they clicked. 'Guess this will be testament to how much you love Essa.'

'Stop calling her that!'

Hayden gave him a sly wink and opened the door. 'Give *Vanessa* my best.'

'I want the jacket, knife, dash-cam card and Russell's phone. All of those things. I want them all. Are you hearing me?' demanded Curtis, desperate to stamp some of his own authority on the situation.

Hayden nodded. 'OK. Sure. I'll bring them to your house the moment that money drops.'

'Not the house... By the painted beach huts where we spoke before. Then this ends, Hayden. Because you're right, I do have contacts. That family in Streatham... they do deal with problems. One phone call! Understand what I'm saying? One phone call and you'll regret doing this.'

'There is no need for any more threats. I'm doing this for my mum. That's all.' Hayden got out of the vehicle and popped another cigarette between his lips. 'This doesn't need to get any messier than it already has. Just don't do anything you'll regret.' With that, he slammed the door, lit his smoke and walked away.

Curtis started the Wrangler, revved the engine and watched the man walking off, puffing away as though he didn't have a single care in the world. Curtis whacked down the handbrake and scanned around for signs of life. He raced the car forward towards Hayden, flooring the accelerator, gritting his teeth and snarling. All he had to do was turn that wheel... turn it just a fraction and veer the beefy Wrangler up onto the path and ram straight into the bastard's back. He could mow him down and crush him under the weight of the hulking tires. *Turn the wheel and mount the path*, he urged himself... *Take that creep down... now... now...*

Hayden strutted on with confidence, unperturbed that Curtis might snap and run him down... Was he so sure Curtis didn't have it in him?

Now... It has to be now... Don't hesitate... but he passed, catching Hayden's self-assured grin as the motor whizzed by and raced into the industrial estate proper.

With the opportunity missed, Curtis slapped the side of his head in frustration and let out a roaring cry of fury. He did doubt for a few moments that the scene he'd witnessed was real – that Hayden had manufactured everything to resemble a bloodbath... But somehow, he knew that what he'd seen *was* real. Russell had been badly attacked... Injured and left for dead. But he refused to believe his Vee would ever be capable of such viciousness.

Then another idea popped into his head... Could Hayden have attacked his own twin in order to stitch them up?

He raced along for a few miles and skidded to a halt at a bus stop. *The police.* That was his only route now. He snatched up his phone and considered what number to call. What would he even say? Where would he start? He didn't even have a clue where that viewing point was. He'd not asked.

His mind spun and his vision blurred. Now hundreds of scenarios, thoughts and outcomes raced around his brain until he seemed unable to hold a single rational thought... He needed to calm down and think things over... Time was ticking, and if he made the wrong move... life as he knew it would shatter around him.

That photo of Jonas popped into his head. He couldn't picture the big, friendly guy torturing and interrogating people... not even during a war.

Curtis leapt from the vehicle and spewed up his guts for several minutes. It wasn't until he'd finished being sick, and sat back down in the Wrangler, when he noticed a congregation of people standing at the bus stop gaping at him. At this rate, he was likely to lose his mind.

More questions rattled around his aching mind.

Did Vanessa decide to take action, fearing her family and

her *secret* weren't safe? Did she instruct Jonas to take care of the situation? Maybe it was never meant to go this far...

Another thought occurred to him. What if the money she'd taken hadn't been for Russell? Could it have been for Jonas? But then... why bring it back? And the question that was driving him totally insane – Did she realise it was Russell from the moment he'd arrived at their house?

51

'Bruh, slow down,' said Jonas calmly.

Curtis, almost hyperventilating, stood in Jonas's lounge. He'd barged his way in, shouting and accusing the big man in a blabbering rant, and Jonas was watching him with a miffed grimace slapped on his face.

'Just answer me. Why were you there? Tell me!' demanded Curtis.

'OK, listen. Vee was concerned about meeting that guy on her own, so she called me and asked if I'd drive to that Chinese restaurant and stake the place out. That's all.'

Curtis paced the lounge, his mind racing like the fast lane of a hectic motorway.

'Vee said she'd feel better if I was there, so I'd intended to wait around on the far side of the carpark whilst she ironed out her business with him.'

'Yeah, big, bad mercenary that you are, hey? Why wouldn't my wife go running to you?'

'Get lost, man. The fuck you talking about?'

'The Koevoet.'

'Agh, man, who the hell have you been talking to?'

Curtis stopped pacing and jabbed a finger at the big man. 'Why go bragging to that idiot about your past?'

Jonas let out a heavy, annoyed sigh. 'What does it matter? I was drunk and chatting shit, man.'

'You didn't tell me.'

'Look, I guess it was *my* way of warning that obnoxious bastard to rein it in. That bastard who you seemed happy to let sit there drinking your booze and disrespecting you in your own home. What's wrong with you?'

'You threatened him, too?'

Jonas shrugged. 'Not exactly. I may have had a few words with him on the quiet once we got outside. So what? I'm your friend, Curtis. I didn't react in your house because of the ladies, but I didn't like the way that guy acted. Truth be told, I didn't trust a single word that came outta his trap.'

'What happened at the restaurant?'

Jonas crossed his arms. 'Nothing. He didn't show up and Vee called me to say I should go home.'

'So, where did she go?'

'Home, too, I guess.'

Curtis took some calming breaths and sat on the arm of the sofa. 'Jesus!'

'And just for the record, I was never a mercenary. Once my unit was disbanded, I took a different path to many of my comrades. But that business is old news. I was a young man. Barely a teenager.'

'You chased insurgents? You were actually... in a war?'

'Yeah. The Bush War. Up against the SWAPO... Believe me, Curtis, I was one of the lucky ones... I escaped that world, but many of my comrades... my friends... They didn't.'

Curtis wanted to ask the man how many people he'd massacred, maimed or executed in his younger days, but stayed himself.

Jonas ran a hand over his head. 'After the disbandment of

the unit, most Koevoet members used their expertise in other areas. Doing what they knew. Some moved into contract work like protecting oil tankers against Somalian pirates... Others worked in areas of high conflict like Bosnia and Iraq... using their explosive expertise and military proficiency to get by... I got given an opportunity to work in another area... and I took it. Which led me on a very different path. A much... safer path.'

It now occurred to Curtis that someone with military training would not have been incompetent enough to have left evidence behind. If Jonas had been involved in the attack against Russell, surely things would have been much... cleaner... The grim scene flashed in Curtis's mind again and he swooned. Should he confide in the South African? Could he help?

No... He'd already kept *this* from him, so he couldn't be trusted. Neither, it seemed, could Vanessa.

VANESSA RETURNED HOME and had a shower. Just being in the same space as Dominic made her feel grubby. She needed to wash the entire day from her. Erase the stink of that rank pig. She grabbed a glass and a bottle of Zinfandel from the fridge and headed upstairs.

Vanessa powered up the shower and stripped off her clothes. She caught sight of her naked self in the mirror and for a moment she didn't see herself standing there... she saw Little Essa. Vanessa blinked away the vision and flinched as though she'd been punched. She gripped the sink and gazed hard. She studied that white scar just above her right eyebrow. A tiny, raised lump. Vanessa held two fingers against the tiny bump and stroked it. That wound was barely notice-able. It's amazing how the human body can heal itself.

Vanessa would never forget *his* stunned expression when

she'd held onto that metal roundabout and slammed her face against the outer steel safety bar. Her legs had gone wobbly, and she'd come close to throwing up as the pain burned into her face and the back of her eyeball. But the gash had created the desired result: a waterfall of thick blood spilling down her face.

Vanessa heard her phone ringing. She slipped on her dressing gown and padded into the bedroom to retrieve her mobile from the bed. *Jonas.*

'Hey, you OK?' she asked.

'Vee, your hubby has just been here. He's pissed off, I can tell you. He somehow found out that I came with you to that restaurant. He's fuming that I didn't tell him.'

'OK, tell me everything he said.'

52

C urtis headed straight into his study and switched on the computer. It took him less than a minute to find deeply worrying news on the *KentOnline* website. A recent post with an accompanying photo of two police cars and an ambulance parked outside a train station grabbed his attention. He read the article.

Injured man spotted by residents of Chartham, near Canterbury.

Officers are currently looking in the Chartham and surrounding areas after a man was spotted with multiple injuries. Inspector Jim Trenton, of the local policing team, tweeted at about 23.30 yesterday:

"Team out searching the area for a seriously injured male. No risk to the public at this time. We're asking locals to check camera footage."

Police officers and paramedics descended on Chartham,

*near Canterbury, on Monday night, following several
reports of a man with serious injuries staggering through
the village in a disoriented state. One resident explained
that he'd noticed this individual whilst retrieving his glasses
from his car, describing the person as a white male in his
mid-forties, with long, messy hair. The individual had
several deep slashes on his arms, and blood on his chest and
face. The man was last seen clambering across the railway
line before making off into the fields behind Parish Road,
then heading off along the banks of the River Stour. It is
thought that he then crossed the Stour near the cemetery.*

*One witness stated, "I called out to the man, but he looked
lost and confused and didn't seem to hear my voice. I
rushed inside and told my wife to phone for help. I dashed
back out to follow him, but I have bad knees, so I couldn't
chase him. I'd hazard a guess that somebody attacked him
with a knife."*

*Police are getting increasingly concerned for the individ-
ual's wellbeing and are appealing to any witnesses who
may have seen this person in the local area, or anyone who
may be able to identify him. They believe that he is the
victim of a very serious assault, and it's imperative he is
located so he can receive urgent medical care.*

Curtis pushed back from the desk as if the monitor was
about to blow up. Shit, this was bad. So bad. He slapped a
hand over his mouth and raced to the kitchen. Went to the
knife block. Run his hand over the space where that knife
should have been... the knife Vanessa had used to cut her
homemade cake...

It was as sweet as that raspberry cake over there.

'Oh, no,' groaned Curtis. He raced back into the study, logged into his personal banking page, and checked all of his accounts. With a deep, choking breath, he transferred what funds he could from his savings. Next, he emailed Jodie at the accounts department and informed her he required her to arrange an urgent, large transfer to his own account. Sweat dripped from his face as he sent that email. He'd worry about how to deal with unusually large deposits at a later date. He'd think of a way of managing that when he had a clearer head... a business opportunity gone awry, or some scam he'd fallen for, perhaps.

All he knew right now was that he needed to act fast, because if the police located Russell before Hayden cleared up the grove, or heaven forbid the officers stumbled upon that place themselves... what then?

Curtis went numb all over as clear images played in his mind.

Russell's back covered in blood as he moved through the thicket in a clumsy stumble.

He even imagined seeing the absolute terror in Russell's eyes.

The blood on the knife.

Curtis imagined Russell collapsing on the river bank, covered in blood and taking his last dying breaths.

Go through the facts here, Curtis told himself.

Vanessa had a motive.

There was evidence Russell had been back in contact with her... been to *their* house.

Her threatening texts...

The ties to Jonas... Could they trace his past?

His own threat left on a voicemail... The Streatham Hill men...

Would he be implicated? Would they link him to Albie

and the people he'd spoken of? What if they both got plunged into this mess?

The kids... How would his parents react? Oh, God, they'd be so disappointed in him.

Curtis's heart was thrashing in his chest as he tried to take all this in...

Hayden said Vanessa had tried to kill Russell before. This notion spun over and over in his mind until his brain felt like it was about to implode. Whoever attacked Russell would be looking at a severe sentence. GBH? Attempted murder? Or, God forbid, something worse? Then he saw Vanessa, just a teenager, shoving a younger Russell from that cliff path, a contorted sneer fixed on her face as he plunged.

'We need to do something to control the situation,' were his wife's exact words...

This stunning house... their wonderful kids... their idyllic life... Who *wouldn't* kill to keep everything they had?

CURTIS WALKED into the bedroom and found Vanessa sprawled on the bed, sipping a glass of Zinfandel. He composed himself, smiled and said, 'How you feeling? Is it wise to be drinking, Vee?'

'I'm fine. But are you? You look grey.'

'Tired. That's all. We should pack some things. For Herefordshire. If you still want to go?'

Vanessa nodded. 'Yes, we—'

A text pinged through. Vanessa's phone.

Curtis watched, apprehension growing by the second, as his wife studied her message. His heart rate had decreased, but now he kept getting disconcerting heart palpitations and his back was drenched in sticky sweat.

'Delphine is going to pop in shortly,' she said.

'That's nice,' he said, trying hard not to puke again.

53

Delphine smiled her thanks as she accepted the coffee Vanessa offered her.

'You sure you don't want wine?' asked Vanessa.

Delphine took off her large sun hat and shook her head. The pair sat in the garden. Vanessa had erected the parasol for them to relax under as the temperature this afternoon was becoming unbearable.

'Where has this heat come from?' said Delphine.

'We could be looking at record-breaking temperatures this year,' confirmed Vanessa. 'But they say that every year, right?'

'Ah, I hope not. So, what's this place you're heading to like, Vee?'

'It's called Daisy's Lookout. A spectacular seventeenth-century cottage on the Wye River. I hope it's as charming as I remember.'

'I bet you will both have a wonderful time.'

'Yes. We need to smooth over a few things whilst we are away.'

'Vee... you can always confide in me. With anything. I'd never judge you.'

Vanessa sipped her drink, forced a polite smile and said, 'I know that.'

'Whatever happened between you and that lad when you were youngsters... I'm sure your husband will understand. He's a compassionate soul. He's such a good man,' said Delphine emphatically.

Vanessa nodded, unsure what to say to that.

'Make sure you tell him everything!' said Delphine with such forceful authority that it made Vanessa jump.

'I...'

Delphine put her hand on Vanessa's. 'If you don't, your life will fall apart before your eyes. You risk losing everything. Do you hear what I'm saying?'

Vanessa nodded dumbly, taken aback by the sudden change in her friend.

'Keeping quiet is what you've always done. It's always been *your* way... right? But it's time to start talking. It's time to seek help and stop hiding from what happened. Please, please trust me, lovey. I'm trying to save you from yourself. You need to stop history from repeating itself.'

Delphine's voice sounded broken and desperate. It made Vanessa feel terribly uncomfortable.

Hayden's voice echoed in her mind – *The Whisper Troll will no longer be whispering.*

'It's not that simple,' Vanessa murmured. 'It's really not. This doesn't just affect me!'

'Vanessa, there is a dark energy clinging to you. You'll never be rid of it without help. Do you understand me? It's never going to lift! Not until you decide to break free. You must help yourself.'

Vanessa snorted and snatched her hand away. 'I need you to stop this. Stop this now.'

'Why? So you can stay quiet and live the rest of your life, with this... this unhealthy darkness clawing at your soul?'

'I think you should leave.'

'And then you'll continue to suffer in silence, whilst you keep protecting... Who exactly are you protecting?'

'Get out. Get away from me,' spat Vanessa.

Delphine, shaking now, put her sun hat on and stood up. She looked mortified.

Vanessa winced. 'Please, leave. I can't deal with—'

'I'm sorry... I'm so sorry... But people are going to get hurt, Vanessa. Don't you see that?'

Vanessa stood up so fast she became lightheaded and unsteady on her feet.

Crack... crack... crack... his head smashing against those rocks...

I have spent most of my life thinking he was dead... She closed her eyes, worried another blackout was coming for her.

Delphine headed for the back gate, turned and said, 'People *will* get hurt because you did nothing!' Then she left.

54

Curtis lay awake as he tried to make sense of everything. Vanessa hadn't moved for a few hours, but he sensed she, too, had not gone to sleep. He couldn't recall the last time he heard her cute, soft, whistling snore.

Did he know her at all? Did he do the right thing in paying that money? Yes... yes, yes, he told himself over and over. He'd do everything in his power to make sure his wife was protected. He felt like his heart would stop beating if he lost her. *Go to sleep*, he urged himself, over and over.

THE IDEA of driving to Symonds Yat filled him with dread as he sipped his third coffee of the morning and let out a gaping yawn. He didn't like getting behind the wheel this drowsy.

He checked his watch. One hour to go. But what if Hayden didn't show and decided to double-cross him? He'd transferred the crypto now. Curtis shook that idea from his head. He walked outside and loaded the bags in the car so they could get away as soon as he'd made the exchange. As he stuck their suitcases into the Wrangler, he glimpsed Mr Gates strolling past the house, brow knitted and bottom lip curled. Curtis flashed him a warm smile and nodded, but received a frosty glare in response. Then his phone vibrated in his shorts. He retrieved the device. *Unknown caller.*

'Hello?' said Curtis in a cagey voice.

'Morning, Curtis. It's me. I have a delivery for you.'

'What? Where are you?'

'I'm close by. Shall I pop to your house?'

'No! We agreed to meet by the huts, Hayden! Why have you come here?'

'Places to go, Curtis. You want this stuff, or not? I'm standing at the end of Bowyer Road. Between two small trees. Oh, palm trees. How nice. Why don't you have palm trees, Curtis? They'd look fantastic outside your house.'

Curtis started running, keeping the phone to his ear. 'I'm coming. Any news on Russell?'

'Nope. But some witnesses clocked him staggering through some village. The police are looking for him.'

'I saw.' Curtis lowered his voice. 'What are we supposed to do if he comes back here?'

'Hey, I see you.'

Curtis saw Hayden slouched against a taxi, dressed in a pressed shirt and black trousers. He smiled, put away his phone, and held out a tatty canvas bag. 'It's all in here.'

'The phone too?' asked Curtis, grabbing the bag as he surreptitiously scanned the area. He recognised the bag from the night Russell had first come to the house.

'Forget about Russell. You'll never have to worry yourself about him again. Trust me. This is all over now, Curtis.'

'What exactly does that mean?'

Hayden stood bolt upright as if he'd received an electric shock. His cocky visage lifted as he gazed past Curtis and said in a nervous tone, 'Hey, Essa... Wow, you are looking well.'

Curtis spun to see his wife standing in the middle of the road, hard eyes locked on Hayden and her lips drawn in.

Hayden reached behind and opened the passenger door, keeping his eyes fixed on Vanessa. Then he flashed a slimy smile and said, 'Looks like I get to win this time, Essa!' With that he got in the taxi, slammed the door and started jabbing his finger and gesturing the driver to go.

Curtis hugged the bag to his chest, unsure what to do as the taxi drove off, and his wife ran back towards the house, kicking her flip-flops from her feet as she went. He walked back to the house, seeing Vanessa sprint up the driveway and dash through the front door. Before he even made it to the drive, she came charging back out of the house, got into her Mini, and sped off down the driveway. He had to leap from the road as she floored it and raced off in the same direction as the taxi.

VANESSA, rage annihilating any rational judgment, floored the accelerator with her bare foot and hared along Preston Parade, hitting forty in the strict twelve-mile-per-hour zone. The Mini bumped and thudded over the small speed humps as she trained her eyes on the slow-moving taxi ahead. A dog walker, oblivious to her speeding presence, stepped onto the road ahead, forcing Vanessa to hit the brakes. The middle-aged woman in a pink baseball cap gave her an incredulous pout as she passed, but Vanessa sped up again.

Vanessa caught up with the taxi as it took the bridge over the railway line and indicated left, suggesting the car was heading town-bound. She had to wait for a bus and three cars before she could pull out onto Joy Lane and give chase through the residential area. Vanessa only hoped the traffic would be snarled up and she could somehow intercept the other car. A Saturday with the promise of soaring temperatures would get busy, even before ten am, but first she had to pass these vehicles. She tried to overtake the first car, but was thwarted by several oncoming motors.

Her phone vibrated in her shorts. She ignored it, knowing it would be Curtis. She applied the brakes, almost rear-ending the car in front, which then turned off up a side street. Vanessa took the opportunity of a clear stretch to tear past the next car and continued at speed to overtake the bus, too. An oncoming cyclist shouted something as she zipped by, but she didn't catch what.

Vanessa soon found herself behind the taxi, a silver Toyota Prius, as it slowed to let a couple of kids across a zebra crossing. Not even sure if he'd grasped that she'd caught up, Vanessa followed right behind the taxi as it left the town's peripheral streets and headed under the railway line and into the town centre, where, as predicted, the traffic became heavier and the taxi slowed to a halt. Vanessa put on her hazards and leapt out of the Mini. She stomped to the front of the taxi and yanked open the passenger door.

Hayden jumped in his seat and then smiled, his mouth like a slash. 'Hello again, Essa. Where did you pop up from?'

'I swear I'll follow you all around town if I have to. We need to talk...' she growled, almost letting his name slip out but stopping herself.

Loud beeps came from behind. The pair locked eyes, and she imagined that inside his devious brain, the cogs turned as he deliberated on a way to slip away from her. More beeps echoed around the street, and someone boomed, 'Move out of the way!'

A lorry had stopped in front, and it was slow going, but there was space to drive ahead now.

'Can you please shut my door?' said the driver, a guy in

his sixties with pockmarked skin, thinning grey hair and tufts of thick hair popping out of his large ears.

'It's essential I have a chat with this man. So, no, sorry,' she said, flashing a cruel smile at the passenger. 'Get out!'

Hayden turned to the driver. 'Pull over up here, fella. This won't take long. I'll see you're alright.'

CURTIS TIPPED out the contents of the canvas bag onto a bin liner he'd placed on the kitchen floor. The jacket was caked in dry mud and stained with gore. It stunk of blood and made him gag more than once. The phone had a cracked screen and wouldn't turn on, and the knife, still stained, lay in a clear plastic bag. The dash-cam footage he located after shaking the bag until it dropped out.

It dawned on him that he didn't have a clue what he should do with the items now that he had them. Burn the jacket? Toss the knife in a river? Did it seem more sensible to clean the knife and put it back in its housing? Would it be more suspect to have a single missing kitchen knife? No, the entire knife block needed to go, he concluded, chucking that down with the rest of the stuff.

He tried to call Vanessa again... No reply.

THE TAXI PULLED up the next street by an antiques store and Hayden got out and walked in front of the taxi. Vanessa parked the Mini behind it and approached.

Hayden held up both hands and grinned. 'Just remember, Essa, you're on camera.' He jabbed a thumb at the taxi.

'We had an agreement...' She lowered her voice. 'We made a pact.'

'I didn't break it. Did you?'

'No, I didn't break it! But mine was based on a sham...

Because Russell... *survived*... Why? Why would you let me believe that he'd died? Do you have any idea what that did to me? Twenty-seven years I have lived with this! Even by your limited standards, that's messed up.'

'I am sorry for that, Essa,' he said, but in a tone belying his words.

'My name is Vanessa. Little Essa is gone. We were just kids! Stupid kids with no grasp on reality. Why have you come crashing into my life to ruin everything?'

Hayden granted her a cocky smile. 'I think a bit of Essa is still in there. Because clearly, you are still a bit crazy. I mean, look at you... tearing around town with no shoes on. Do you realise how mental you look? I reckon you hate me because *I* know you... I know you like nobody else ever did, or ever will.'

'You're broken and poisonous. You were then, and you still are now.'

'Fifteen thousand? Essa, I'm so disappointed in you. Rather patronising, don't you think?'

'Why risk sending Russell to our house? Why not come yourself? Were you too scared to face me?'

'No, of course not. Bad timing. I'd have loved to have been there to see you squirm. But it needed to be Russell for things to work out the way they did. I was busy anyway. New business dealings. Which reminds me, would you let your gullible hubby know his money will go to excellent use? I'm set to make millions with that seed money.'

'Oh, I'm sure he'll be so thrilled to hear that.'

'I bet. Tell me, Essa. I'm intrigued... What did the South African have planned?'

'He just said he'd deliver a stark message. And that it would put an end to the matter.'

'Ooh, I'd love to know what that entailed.'

'Stick around. You'll find out.'

'Promises, promises, you tease.'

'You were there? Outside the restaurant?'

'Yep. I arrived that morning. Tell your big friend he really should brush up on his old espionage skills. He parked directly under a glaring light and gave his position away.'

'I'll tell him to be more careful next time.'

'I was watching you every step of the way, Essa. A bit of precise planning was needed, but it all worked out rather well.'

Vanessa did not like the sound of this. 'You were in that car watching me on the lane,' she said flatly.

'I sure was.'

Vanessa scowled at him. 'What did you do?'

'I think the right question is – what did *you* do, Essa? Speak to Curtis.'

'Oh, I will,' growled Vanessa.

'I'm going now, Essa... You'll never see me again... I've had my fun... played the game and got what I wanted.'

'You won, did you? And Russell helped you?'

'Yes, he did. Didn't see that coming, did you? Fancy thinking he was me. Tut, tut, Essa. I mean, I know it's been a long time, but I'm surprised you fell for that one... How's your dad doing, by the way? I hear he's sunning it up in Spain. Did he come out yet?'

Vanessa glared at him. 'Don't... *don't* go there.'

'Still ready to protect him with such a vehement devotion.'

'Don't!' she warned. 'Don't you dare!'

Hayden placed his hand on his heart and whispered in an aristocratic voice, 'I know, I know... Let's not stir the dreaded demons... I, Hayden Knox, am bound by the blood pact. Hence, I shall never utter the truth. Said truth will die with me once I take my last gasp of air upon this weary earth.'

Vanessa marched back to her car and yanked open the

door. 'You better stay away from here! I mean it. Don't you push me!'

'I guessed right though, didn't I, Essa?' He grinned. 'Yeah, I guessed right.'

She scowled at him for a few heartbeats, then jumped in the car and raced away.

55

Vanessa drove for a long time, her mind in a muddle. She'd ended up stopping at a deer park in the middle of nowhere and tried to get her head around the messed-up situation. After taking some time to calm herself, she phoned Curtis, and after a long, painful conversation, she extracted all the information about his recent negotiations with her ex-boyfriend.

'You gave him sixty thousand, Curtis!'

'That's what I said. You were prepared to give him fifteen just to be rid of Russell.'

'I didn't know it was Russell!'

'Well, I took control of the situation. Like you said, we needed to. I dealt with it.'

Trust me, you never had any control over this, she thought.

'Vee, I can't fathom why you chose to go alone to that viewing point. Or did Jonas go with you? What happened?'

'I asked Jonas to go to the restaurant. If you want the truth... Once I'd handed over the cash inside, Jonas was going to collar him as he approached his car and put the frighteners on him. Nothing serious, just rough him up a bit and make sure he took that money and didn't come back. But he sussed my plan and changed the meeting spot. I went there alone. I didn't want to risk spooking him again. I wanted to put an end to the matter. I didn't tell you, because I knew you'd have been worried and upset.'

'Yes, I saw you in the footage, Vee. In the first clip you were wearing your floral jacket... in the second one you'd taken it off. I don't understand why you left it behind.'

'Let me be clear here, Curtis... I haven't worn my summer jacket for ages. Because I can't find it. Whoever you saw in that clip was not me.'

'OK. But going alone was irresponsible and dangerous.'

'Yeah, maybe. But I needed to face him. I had things to... straighten out.'

'Did you seriously have no inclination that it was Russell?'

'For Christ's sake, Curtis,' she said tersely.

'Did you?'

'No!' she spat. 'It also concerns me that you'd think I'd be foolish enough to leave a knife and my jacket at the scene of an attack. I mean, how stupid do you reckon I am, exactly?'

Vanessa waited for a reply... It didn't come.

'Evidently, not as bloody stupid as you, Curtis, who just got scammed out of sixty big ones! If you'd have confided in me first, all of this would have been avoided!' With that, she ended the call and switched off her phone, wondering how there was footage of her in the damn jacket that night... That made zero sense.

After thanking her lucky stars there was a pair of old wellies in the boot, she popped them on and booked herself in a room at the nearest Travelodge ten miles away.

After checking into her room and receiving some intrigued stares from the man sat at reception who glanced twice at her attire, she shut herself away from the world and brooded over the situation and how she would deal with it.

Later, after four cups of sugary coffee, she messaged Curtis and advised him to meet her at the cottage in Herefordshire tomorrow afternoon.

They'd already forfeited the first night. Why waste another?

Then she sent a text to Delphine.

> I'm so sorry. Can we talk soon? xx

A text pinged back within seconds.

> Of course, lovey... Send me some snaps of Symonds Yat. Can't wait to see this magical place. xx

56

Hayden tried to connect with Poppy via a Skype call, but got no reply. He'd already messaged her, but she'd not responded yet. Stupid time difference.

He tossed a handful of salt and vinegar peanuts into his gob and chuckled as he chewed, recalling that naïve idiot's face once he'd presented him with the incriminating evidence. Hayden had enjoyed himself... he had to admit that. This was something a little different to his usual score, but he'd made it work, and with the bonus of finally screwing over that little bitch, Essa. It ended up being a touch more macabre than his normal projects, and although it had been rather stressful, he could relax knowing the Bitcoins were in the bag.

He consumed more nuts and decided that Curtis reminded him a bit of Kevin Jules. Curtis didn't resemble Kev, who had the look of a frightened ferret with a dodgy comb-over and cheap prescription spectacles, but they carried themselves in the same way. Both were as clueless as a goldfish. Kev's wife was hot, too, so they had that in common.

Hayden got to know Kevin quite well. They'd gone to the gym, played tennis and often enjoyed a few drinks. Kevin, once he'd had a few nice beers, liked to natter... a lot. He'd married young, had two kids, with another on the way, but he'd become infatuated with one of the drivers at the courier firm he worked. Hayden, great friend he was, egged him on. 'Go on. You only live once, Kev. Bang her. Just keep it hush-hush.' So, Kev did. After his sordid liaisons, he'd brag to Hayden about his escapades in grubby detail, the dirty, four-eyed dummy. Hayden had encouraged him, of course. Pretended to be captivated by his naughty behaviour. He'd also recorded every single conversation on a second-hand Dictaphone he'd purchased from a Cash Converters for a tenner.

That's how it started... It just happened. Hayden had been drunk and thought, wow, how would his poor wife react if she heard this seedy little loser talking about screwing some skanky bird doggy-style in the back of a delivery van... And *PING*... major eureka moment. After a month of gathering a ton of recordings, Hayden blackmailed a flabbergasted Kevin Jules for five thousand quid, and used that money to travel to the States. He'd been in his early twenties and eager for adventures. The scamming, in a way, became his career, between a few other tedious jobs he'd been forced to take. He'd also tried to break into acting, but that pursuit didn't take off.

Now, what were his initial rules he'd set for his man-scams? He could still remember them all now. Rub their egos to make them feel special... that was the first basic rule. Talk about shit they like, and never dispute anything *they* say. Become the friend that the sad, friendship-deprived shit-stain of an individual never had. Never had, because any of their previous friends soon sussed that they were a lonely fucking loser with serious narcissistic tendencies. But now here *he* was – the perfect friend – and once they comprehended he liked the same things, the same warped, sinful stuff, *they* believed they'd hit the new buddy jackpot. And that was when he reeled in the big, dirty fish. That was when he gathered up all the dirt, slowly and diligently, ready to present it in a nice package that would blow their little socks off. But he vowed never to get too greedy. The sum always needed to be a realistic figure that they could get their mitts on.

Yeah, the situation did sometimes go sideways. He'd had his nose broken more than once, and his arm... but he'd also made a lot of dough over the years. But he wasn't good at keeping said money, a fondness for gambling, partying and drugs always being his downfall.

The call connected. Poppy's face filled the screen. 'Hayden. What's up?' she asked in her honeyed South American lilt. She appeared so young and pale without makeup. Was it the lighting on the screen? He hoped so, because she only looked about sixteen instead of twenty-five. Her strawberry-blond hair was swept over one shoulder and she squinted like she'd either just woken up or smoked some super strong weed.

'My little cherry popsicle. I have missed you so much!'

'Hayden, don't call me that. We talked about this,' she whined. 'Where are you now? You still in Hong Kong?'

'No, I had to come over to the UK. Great news. I've accumulated the investment money for Mr Mahtani. I'm so close to tying up this deal I can taste the lavish celebratory champagne.'

'Yeah, about that, Hayden... About the whole moving to Hong Kong thing?'

'You're packed, right? I have sent you all the flight details. You get all that?'

Poppy scrunched up her face, puckered her lips, and moved them from side to side. She did that subconsciously when nervous. This didn't look good.

'Popsicle?'

'Hayden, look, it's me, not you, OK... No, actually... it's you. I can't live with somebody that defrauds people. It's unethical.'

'What? But you've helped me find some of these sick freaks! Some of the best scores have been down to your researching.'

'But it won't ever stop, will it? I'm not sure you'll ever be happy unless you're playing the game. I think it's like a drug to you. And what about Russell?'

'Um, what about him?'

'Did you put him straight? Or does he still think he'll be getting a set of keys to a new flat for your poor mom? Mm, well?'

'I intend to come through with my promises. My mum will get her new flat and live-in care help.'

'But not straight away. You deluded Russell. I think you should be ashamed of yourself! You said he's unwell, Hayden. Why screw with him like this?'

'My brother wouldn't have understood. If I'd have told him they'd have to wait for a year or more for my investment to produce real money, he'd never have agreed to help me.'

Poppy's eyes narrowed. 'You lied to your own twin? Have you lied to me?'

'No! Plus, it's only a white lie. For the greater good, Pops. I needed his help. I couldn't be in two places at the same time.'

'You use people, Hayden.'

'I promise all that's over now. Hand on heart. Once I invest this money, I'm on a different path. In five years, the return on my investment will be so substantial we'll be set for life.'

'So those Chinese men tell you. I don't even get why they need you.'

'Pops, I told you, once I invest, I become a partner. I am going to be their primary contact in Singapore, dealing with all the shipping arrangements.'

'Why are they so keen to have a Westerner arrange this trade deal, Hayden? It also seems strange that you need to ship to Malaysia first, and not directly to China. You sure they're not using you for something illegitimate?'

'No. It's components... innovative machine parts. This partnership is a big deal.'

'Like that Cash-Swift-One was gonna be huge... Bigger than PayPal, right?'

'And it will. Once crypto hits the mainstream, Cash-Swift-One will be as synonymous with crypto card payments as KFC is with chick—'

Poppy cut him off. 'I don't use crypto, and... I don't wanna live in Hong Kong. So, I've decided I'm not coming, Hayden. I'm sorry. I really am. I hope you make an enormous success of this new enterprise. But I'm not gonna be part of it.'

Hayden coughed, salty nuts choking his throat. 'What? No. No, don't say that. It's not long term. Six months max. Then we can go anywhere you want.'

'My folks are moving back to Montgomery soon. I think I will go with them. They want me to go, so... It's for the best. They aren't exactly happy with our relationship, Hayden... The big age gap especially... Plus, you always swear in front of them, and my parents don't like that. My folks also think you are quite... imperious.'

Hayden turned away from the screen. How could this be happening? He was regretting not taking that escort girl up on her proposal when she'd offered to nosh him off. Hayden's mind drifted, and he pictured the sexy floozy. He had searched several seedy online databases to find the perfect lookalike. He found a pretty close match to Essa in the form of a Bulgarian beauty called Gloria. She'd been miffed when he'd explained that all he wanted her to do was slip on a jacket, stand by a car and gaze into the trees, then meet him further up the lane. He'd been very strict in his timings, and she'd seemed to grasp the importance of this. If Vanessa had come back from the viewing area and bumped into the escort, that would have screwed his plan right up.

'Is this some kind of weird sex game, yes?' Gloria had asked with a perplexed frown when he'd returned to collect her in the rental car. 'And who was that other lady? Is that your wife? Is she in the bushes watching? I am confused. Shall I suck you good now? Make you cum lots in my hot mouth. Mmm, is that what you want me to do? We making a filthy movie together?'

'Um, no, that's fine. Just take off that jacket,' he'd ordered, shaking the garment free of any stray hairs. 'And please, no talking in the car. We need to drive back down here and you need to stay utterly silent.'

'For the movie, yes?'

'Yes, Gloria, for the movie.'

He should've screwed her senseless and pretended she was Essa, he now considered. Would have been amazing so long as she'd kept her trap shut.

'Hayden, are you even listening to me?' said Poppy.

Hayden snapped out of his reverie and focussed on Poppy's youthful face. 'Don't leave me, Pops.'

'Please don't hate me, Hayden. I know deep down you must understand. And I care about you. I will miss you, but it's time to move on... Sorry, I gotta go.' She kissed her hand and placed it on the screen's camera. 'You take care.'

The screen went black and Hayden sat frozen to the spot.

'No... For crying out loud... Noooo!' he bellowed, slamming down the laptop's screen. He stood up and roamed around the cramped, fusty guesthouse room, scratching his chin like a madman. Then he flipped up the laptop's screen and searched Expedia for the next available direct flight to Miami.

57

As Vanessa drove, she sought to blank out the current situation by checking out the verdant scenery. The Wye Valley, which lay close to the England-Wales border, was even more lovely than she'd remembered it. Impressive natural landscapes, elevated views and charming woodland stretches. With sweeping views of Gloucestershire and Herefordshire, the area was a magnet for ramblers, sightseers and cyclists. The miles of meandering waters had cut deep gorges through limestone rocks, creating soaring rock faces and captivating valleys, which also made the location very popular for water-sports enthusiasts and rock climbers.

Vanessa travelled past signs for Symonds Yat, a picturesque village that straddled the River Wye, and checked her GPS, realising she was close to her destination. The cottage lay a few miles away in a remote woodland area.

VANESSA GOT out of the Mini and drank in the surroundings. A beautiful old stone cottage, with elegantly carved wooden fascias and a garden bursting with pink rose bushes, apple trees, and creamy white magnolias. Vanessa caught the lush, lemony fragrance as she walked, still aware of how silly she looked in her shorts, Cornwall T-shirt, and low wellington boots with no socks.

Curtis opened the door and came out to greet her. He offered her a relieved grin, but his body language made him appear vulnerable and ashamed. 'I have been worried sick, Vee.'

'I needed some time to... go over everything.'

Curtis granted her a timid nod. 'I packed your flip-flops in your bag. It's in the room.'

Vanessa stepped closer to him. 'I don't know whether to kiss you... or slap you!'

'Vee, I...'

Vanessa stepped closer until they were almost touching. She spoke in a smooth, level tone. 'You truly suspected I'd taken one of our knifes, hacked a man to ribbons, left the evidence in a bush, driven home and acted like nothing had happened?'

Curtis opened his mouth, frowned, and closed it again.

'Then you paid thousands of pounds to cover up my mess?'

Curtis swallowed. 'I... I panicked.'

Vanessa shook her head, still unable to accept what her husband had done. 'Curtis, you are stupid and totally naïve—'

'After your funny turn, I didn't want to upset you! I was worried, Vee. The stress you've been under...'

'Curtis... I'm—'

'I saw it on the news, Vee,' Curtis blurted, cutting her off. 'There were witnesses, too... You were caught on camera standing on that lane... Your bloodstained jacket was left at the scene!'

'Yes, Curtis, you explained yesterday.'

Vanessa took several deep breaths. Curtis had been out of his league... On reflection, she'd of course taken all that on board and decided scolding her husband would be unfair. Curtis, a mere minnow, had been swimming in treacherous waters with a great white shark.

'With everything going on, Vee, I admit that for a moment a tiny part of me did believe it. Just for a moment... only a moment.'

'What, until you realised it was all a bit... convenient?'

'No, because in the end I refused to believe it, Vee. I know you... and I know that you would never have done such a terrible thing. But the truth is... it wouldn't have mattered what I believed in the end.'

'Why?'

'Because I'd have still acted in the same way. I'd have still done those things, and more, to protect you.'

Vanessa hugged Curtis and kissed his neck. She felt her husband tense under her tight embrace.

'You're not angry, Vee?'

'What, that you even considered me capable of knifing someone? Or that you made yourself complicit in a serious crime?'

Curtis pulled back from her, unable to grasp the situation. He seemed fearful of her, and did he not understand that he'd committed multiple crimes in order to cover this up?

'Vee, I had no choice but to pay. Your prints would have been on that knife... You'd sent threatening texts. You'd have been implicated and drawn into this mess. I couldn't take any chances. That's why I paid him.'

'Take me upstairs,' she commanded, enjoying his expression of complete confusion and disbelief at the turn of events.

'Hey?'

'I want you, Curtis!' she whispered in a deliberately sultry

voice. Oh, she meant it too. Her husband had done everything he could to salvage the situation. *Until death do us part...*
and Curtis meant it. At least now she knew for certain she
could trust this man with *anything...* and that meant everything to her... Vanessa could finally be free of all her secrets.
But not tonight. Because tonight she needed to recreate the
passion that they'd experienced the last time they'd stayed
here. When Curtis proposed and she'd made the best decision of her life.

'Vee... the money?' he murmured.

But she kissed him forcefully, and he kissed her back. The
pair raced inside the cottage, not making it further than the
stairs before she kicked off those uncomfortable boots and
they started ripping off each other's clothes.

58

Hayden fell backwards onto the huge, exquisite hotel bed and slid off his Merrells, letting them fall onto the white marble floor. This place was a far cry from the drab, cramped guest house he'd stayed in back in the UK. This classy boutique hotel, lit an eye-catching neon blue from the outside and situated in Miami's iconic Art Deco District, was where he'd first made love to Poppy.

She'd be blown away by the fact he'd raced back here to save their relationship, instead of heading straight for Hong Kong as he'd planned to. Once he spoke to her in person, he knew she'd be knocked for six by his romantic gesture. He would have no trouble talking her round and making her see sense. This last-minute direct flight had cost him a small fortune, and he could do without the detour, but the idea of losing her filled him with a forlorn, unbearable angst that made his heart ache.

Hayden checked his phone again, discouraged that she'd yet to reply to his request to meet him here. There were missed calls and messages to respond to, but he couldn't face that now. He needed to get a couple of hours' shut-eye first. He'd left the UK at nine pm last night and he felt like total crap.

Hayden dreamt about Russell during one of his fleeting snoozes on the flight. A tenacious guilt had beleaguered his thoughts after that dream, and even now, another stab of guilt hit as the enormity of what happened with Russell and the Pascalls slapped him in the face.

He blamed that tight wanker Ericsson for all this. When that Hong Kong investment offer had been presented to him by his new acquaintance Li Mahtani, he'd finally got a chance to go straight... Of course, that just had to be the time when his current scam would go tits up on him. *Bloody typical.* One last job... that was all he needed. It wasn't asking for much. He intended to use the funds from his final operation to invest in the new business. A chance-of-a-lifetime deal set to make him millions. Hayden still couldn't believe that slimy arsehole's reaction when he'd shown him all that condemning footage.

'You'll get my money when hell freezes over, you God damn unscrupulous fuck!' Todd had screamed at him, his cheeks flushing scarlet with fury. They'd been sitting in Todd's car out the back of some fancy-pants restaurant on South Beach, with the man's bloated and vexed face drenched in sweat as Hayden played him clip after clip.

'Todd, your wife sees just one of these... you're done,' Hayden had said, using his superb Californian accent and continuing under the guise of Ritchie.

'I trusted you, boy! I thought we had a connection. What the hell is wrong with me? My bullshit detector has been top notch since I was a nipper. How did I not sense you were screwing me over?'

'Testament to my skills, I guess. Don't beat yourself up about it. I've been a prolific blackmailer for years.'

'I told you... things... private things.'

'Yeah, I know that alright... Ick. And so will your poor wife if I don't get that crypto currency by the end of today.'

'I'm warning you, son... you are out of your depth here. The people I know—'

'Please, don't bore me with all that intimidatory crap. I have heard it *all* before,' he'd said in an indifferent tone.

'Is that a fact? Right, fine. But you will be sorry. I am strongly suggesting you rethink this.'

'Um...' He'd feigned contemplating. 'Nope.'

'Show her. Go on, I don't care. I've wanted to leave that musty old crow for years, anyway. You'll be doing me a fucking favour,' Todd had spat.

'Maybe I'll show the police. You want your reputation besmirched by this?'

'I like a little variation. I like to treat myself now and again. That such a crime? I work my arse off!'

'Todd, most people treat themselves to a bottle of wine and a takeout. They don't go out boning teenage boys up the rusty dusty.'

'Screw you. I like women too!'

'Yeah, but you like young boys more, don't you? I emphasise the word young.'

'You'd better go whilst you are still able! You have no evidence they were minors... and you won't find any!'

Hayden decided it would be best to just erase the lousy six months he'd spent with that horrendous turd. Six months that were totally unfruitful. He'd seen and heard things that would haunt him till his dying days.

It didn't matter now... But back then, with that job not producing results, he had to think of another subject to swindle and pronto. Usually, he'd take his time and do his homework... have internet accounts searched, make sure he was onto a sure thing, but there wasn't the luxury of time for such preparation and discretion. He'd *needed* that money. Time was ticking quickly and if didn't have the funds ready by the set deadline, then the entire venture would have been a nonstarter. Li had informed him that there would be no extension given. No capital – no business... No future.

Hayden had racked his brains for an idea... *Little Essa and the beach...* A few ideas soon formed, and when he did a little research on Essa... saw the lifestyle she now had, he knew he could be onto a winner. He'd considered just getting a message to Essa and telling her that if she didn't cough up, his loose lips would start flapping about her past. But if she'd called his bluff like that silly prick Todd had, he'd have been left with no more options. So he needed an infallible and intricate plan that involved her husband, and if need be, her children. But he needed to be in Hong Kong to meet Li and deal with his potential business associates, so he couldn't race over to the UK to get the ball rolling on the new scam. That's when it hit him. Russell could help. His twin could play an integral role in the setup. In fact, he decided Russell's role would be essential, because there was going to be a good old-fashioned revenge plot that would lead to bloodshed, and he couldn't execute the scheme alone. He'd had to promise his brother the earth in order to talk him around. A new house, for starters. Plus a live-in care worker for their mum. A chance to get out of the dirty, cramped flat the pair had been shacked up in. And a shot at revenge against Essa.

'Just think about how she used you, Russell... Remember how she played us off against each other...' Hayden had said. 'She pushed you and never paid the price! We always said one day she'd pay. That day is coming soon.'

His twin hadn't been so keen. 'Is this a wise move? Do we really want to start digging up the past and bringing this all back to light?'

'Fuck, yeah. We do when there is a fat wedge to be made,

Russ.'

OK, he'd made it sound like he'd buy Russell and his mum a house outright. He might have misguided his twin a bit there. He'd intended to come through for them, but he'd not made it clear they'd have to wait around a year, maybe two, before he'd have the deposit together. Once his investment generated a good return, then he'd arrange for regular mortgage payments. Yes, Poppy was right. He did delude his brother by making it sound like this would all be happening immediately. But he'd been desperate to get his twin on board and he was sure that Russell would have said no if he'd explained they'd need to wait ages for the payout.

With Russell onboard, Hayden laid out the plan. First, Russell needed to drive a wedge between the happy couple, and as soon as he'd dealt with his business, Hayden would fly over to help wrap up his project. As he'd predicted, there'd been the odd blip, but overall, Russell did an amazing job, considering his brother's unstableness.

Hayden prepped Russell on all the things he should mention, and the stories to use. He called him every day, getting updates and coaching him on how he should proceed. There were risks, but those risks made the entire thing even more exhilarating. Curtis, he quickly decided, would be the primary target, thus keeping Russell away from Essa, so he could concentrate on his efforts at breaking the guileless husband. He'd orchestrated everything from Hong Kong. He'd even drawn up scripts for Russell to keep on his phone.

Hayden removed his clothes and closed his eyes, willing his racing mind to shut down, because he needed to grab some zeds. He wished he'd eaten now. Why hadn't he grabbed a giant burrito from that Mexican place near the hotel? The aroma when he'd passed smelt so delicious. Although what he craved more than anything was some nice Ambien... just to send him off...

As he elbowed the pillows into a comfortable shape, Russell's face flashed in his mind once again and he couldn't shake the images of him in that glade.

'You look a right state, Hayden,' Russell had said, pointing at his blue plastic overshoes, matching gloves, decorating overalls and a lady's floral jacket. *Vanessa's jacket.*

'Yeah, yeah, hilarious. Come on, hold your arms up. Like you're defending an attack.'

'I don't think I want to do this,' Russell had replied in a pathetic whine. 'You kept this part quiet, you bastard.'

'Let me spray some more of this numbing stuff. It's good. They use this one in the States for tattoo work.'

Russell had pinched his left arm. 'My arms are already numb.'

'Then what are you complaining about? You need another Lidocaine injection? Or pop another Fentanyl if you're not sure.'

'No, Hayden!'

'That's morphine. Another dose will zone you right out.'

'No more drugs. Let's cut you to ribbons instead!'

Hayden had shaken his head and sighed theatrically. 'We both know you have a high pain threshold. You're tough... I'm a total wimp with injuries. Do you want this to work? Do you want revenge?'

'Can't we just fake it... like they do in the movies? That looks real, right?'

'Oh, and you know some special effects expert we can call upon to do a quick job on you? Come on, Russ, we've put in all this work. Last push and your part is over... It has to be the real deal. Let me do one slash, see how it goes. I promise you'll not feel a thing. Think of Mum's face when you give her the keys to her new house. Think of that!'

'I'm so nervous.'

'Bro, you did so well stealing all the stuff. A real pro, mate.

Honest to God, you have impressed me so much. The way you've handled that muppet, Curtis. Class. Pure class. I couldn't have done it better myself. Straight up. I wish I had been there to see you shove that dipshit out of his kayak. I didn't think you'd actually have the bottle to go through with that, Russ.'

'I felt a bit mean... but I guess I did enjoy that a little bit more than I expected to.'

'Of course you did, because he is a total sap. But what's the point in going through all this if we don't follow through with the main event? I promise this will all be worth the effort.'

'We shouldn't have involved the kid, Hayden. I didn't like snooping in his room and skulking over fences like some peeping pervert!'

'Stop being such a drama queen. We needed to make an impact and it worked, so stop with all the bellyaching, Russ.'

There'd been a tiny crackle in the bushes, and as Russell turned to investigate the noise, Hayden took the opportunity to whip the knife across Russell's left arm. The look of flummoxed horror on his brother's face caused Hayden to spit out a snigger.

'Owww! Hayden. I wasn't ready.'

'Did it hurt?'

'Not really. I mean, I felt it.'

'So what you moaning for, then, Russ?' He'd slashed the knife again, deliberately harder because he'd decided the first gash didn't produce enough spill.

'Jesus, stop,' Russell had moaned. The blood started flowing well, and his brother, clearly baffled that the injuries were not causing him a great deal of pain, eyed the second slice as though a two-headed alien had popped through his torn skin.

Hayden had known the medication would stop the pain

nerves from sending signals to the brain, but this would only last so long. Russell still needed to move through the woods, backtrack to the village and get to the agreed meeting spot on the other side of the river so Hayden could patch him up and get him into hiding.

When Hayden had readied the blade for a third swipe, Russell started backing away, hands up in surrender. 'Leave off. A couple, you said.'

'A couple of good ones, yeah. They were only little practice cuts to see how you felt.' With that, he'd attacked again, harder and more viciously, catching Russell's left palm, and then right knuckles.

Russell had howled in agony, fell to his knees, and started sobbing.

'Were you clenching your fist? You gonna hit me? What the hell, Russ?'

Russell had whimpered. 'I wasn't!'

'Oh, what, Russell... leave off. Are you bloody crying now? Have a word with yourself. You know I have medical training and can patch you up. You'll be good as new in an hour or so. And make sure somebody spots you in that village. Understand? This is all pointless otherwise!'

'That seriously hurt!' he'd cried out. 'Are you enjoying this, you horrible prick?'

'Shh. Keep it down. Anyone sees us down here, the plan is screwed. Now, get up and stop wasting all that lovely blood. Come on, grab the jacket. Get a good firm grip and shake me.'

Reluctantly, Russell had got up, grabbed him by the lapels, and shook him with such frantic aggression it caused the blood to splash all over the place.

'Oooh yeah, that's it, go on. Pretend that bitch is standing here, Russ! Go on,' he'd said nastily as he'd shoved him backwards and prepared to strike him again.

Then he'd got carried away.

59

C urtis made the coffee and let out a gaping yawn. He felt great after a decent sleep, but as he stirred in a big, heaped spoonful of demerara sugar, he reflected on the past day's events and a gloomy torment fell over him. He'd abandoned those bloodied items in a shrouded section of the River Wye the moment he'd arrived in the area, but he still felt paranoid about the entire affair. He'd stuck the jacket into a thick plastic bag with a collection of rocks and tossed it right into the middle of the river. Even though the phone wouldn't switch on, he still battered it into tiny bits before he'd flung the device into the water.

Curtis kept thinking about yesterday afternoon... Who the hell had arrived at the cottage? Because he'd never experienced such a fierce and fervid night of passion with his wife... They'd both been left in a shaking, burning mess after their long stint of lovemaking. Did she actually get off on the fact he'd committed a crime on her behalf? This idea made him extremely uncomfortable. No, more than that, it totally freaked him out. Before he'd slipped downstairs, he'd viewed his sleeping wife as though a complete stranger lay in that bed.

He also felt rather perturbed abou" wha' had really become of Russell Knox... Surely to God Hayden hadn't murdered his own twin brother... had he?

60

Hayden opened his eyes and knew he was no longer in the hotel room. He tried to get up as a wave of sickness rumbled up from inside his churning guts and his mind whirled like his eyeballs were spinning in their sockets... His arms were stuck firm behind his back. *Calm down and breathe*, he said to himself over and over, as he tried to adjust his focus to adapt to the darkness. He heard a clunk and squinted as streaming light burnt his eyes.

'Rise and shine. Open them peepers,' said a deep voice. American... Alabamian perhaps? Was this something to do with Poppy? He could smell cigarette smoke, but not his brand. This was a pungent, choking stench he didn't like. His eyes focussed, but all he could see was a grey, concrete wall with big white lettering stating: Do Not Park Here.

'Tell me what you want,' he croaked. His throat was red raw, and he needed water pronto. He'd fast established he lay in the boot of a vehicle, and that his hands were bound so tight his fingers were numb and throbbing.

A tall figure walked over to him. The gangly, hook-nosed man with a shock of reddish fuzz under his bottom lip bent over and gazed into the trunk as though he were a farmer inspecting a sow he was considering purchasing. Then he gazed into Hayden's eyes and checked his pulse. 'Mmmm, he's fully conscious now, Mr Ericsson,' he said. 'Can't believe he's awake already. Impressive.'

Todd Ericsson... Jesus, no... The Texan.

Todd, clad in jeans, a brilliant white shirt and big burly boots, stood in front of the wall. He stepped closer, peered down at Hayden and grinned from ear to ear. A grin that said, *Well, I warned you, dipshit.*

'OK, Jeff... Gag him, break his ankles, and we will get going,' said Todd in a breezy tone.

Jeff nodded and gave him the thumbs up, and stepped out of view.

'Now wait... hold up. Come on, guys. Stop, just stop,' begged Hayden. 'Don't break anything!'

Todd stepped away as Jeff returned, brandishing a large wrench.

61

Delphine spread out a selection of outfits on her bed and deliberated on what she'd wear on her date to the Lobster Shack with Jonas that evening. She settled on a flowy, oriental style dress, which she'd worn to a psychic and holistic festival in Brighton. She had received plenty of complimentary comments on how stunning she looked. The soft, breathable material would also suit this evening's predicted humid heat. She smoothed some creases out and mulled over what beads would work well with it, and if she should wear any headwear.

Delphine slipped out her wicker box from under the bed and rummaged through her accessories, but a knocking sound, like something clanking down on the floor, drew her attention. She listened for a moment, but heard no further noise so picked up one of her wide vintage headbands. She soon dismissed this one and selected a thinner, more vibrant band that caught her eye.

Delphine froze when another noise, a thudding sound, came from the next room. Someone was in here. Nobody ever just waltzed in without first knocking or announcing their presence. A deep, foreboding dread rose in her. She spoke in the most strident voice she could muster and said, 'Hello? Hello? Who is there?'

No reply.

'Who is it?' she repeated, using a more forceful tone this time.

Delphine, tightening her silk robe by the front toggles as she went, crept into the lounge area. Her breath caught in her throat and she gasped aloud when she saw the man standing in her lounge.

The intruder fiddled with a mobile phone, his face set in grave confusion. Then she noticed the cartoon duck case confirming it was her phone he was inspecting. He acknowledged Delphine, fixed his stare on her. Blue, flinty orbs absent of emotion, set in a ghostly white face, watched her.

Delphine struggled to find her voice. The cramped lounge area appeared smaller than ever and seemed to shrink around her as the man stepped closer and, in a confrontational snarl, said, 'Where are they?'

Then she registered who the man was. Vanessa's ex-boyfriend. The unpleasant man who had gate-crashed their dinner party. The man who'd been causing her friend's anguish of late.

'Answer me! Where are they?' he repeated more vehemently as he took a step closer.

Delphine shrank away, stepping back into the bedroom 'Who?' she asked, her voice sounding feeble and broken. The shock of seeing the prowler in her home was one thing, but it had been the physical state of him that made her falter. His hands and arms were heavily wrapped in tight, blood-soaked bandages. His grey T-shirt shredded and stained with blood blots. The small open gash under his left eye, the reddish slice vivid in contrast against his waxen complexion.

'Where are Essa and Curtis?' he barked.

'Gone away,' she said. Then added, 'Spain.'

Delphine noticed the man's jacket strewn across her armchair. *That had better not stain my new chair,* part of her brain thought... Another part desperately sought to recall the man's name. But her numb fear had rendered her mind into scrambled eggs.

'Unlock your phone. And I need you to get me more bandages,' he demanded.

'You need to leave... right now,' she retorted in a quiet yet erratic voice.

Delphine prayed someone had spotted this bloodied stranger head into the private community. How did he even know where she lived? Had he been here before? she wondered grimly.

He stepped closer and Delphine could smell the metallic blood and some type of sharp antiseptic cream or disinfectant spray rising from him.

Vanessa's words came to her – 'Is this who you saw in your vision?' Then the name materialised – *Hayden.*

'You need medical attention. Hay... Hayden, isn't it?'

He shook his head and curled his top lip, a feral glint in his eyes.

'Who attacked you? Because you've lost a lot of blood, lovey... I can help you. Please, let me examine those injuries.' Delphine held up her hands. 'You have to trust me. You need help,' she whispered, wondering if his injuries were causing some severe confusion and disorientation.

'I need to find Hayden... I need to find my brother! I want your phone. Open it. Now!' he screamed so frenziedly Delphine flinched.

Then she tried to dash past him, and he bolted after her.

62

V anessa joined Curtis on the bank of the River Wye and sat next to him, resting her head on his shoulder as they sipped glasses of chilled Pinot Gris. After their night of amazing lovemaking that left them both trembling in a euphoric languor, they'd both fallen asleep, entwined in a tangled embrace, and slept until gone lunchtime today. She'd not experienced a deep slumber like that in a long time and suspected Curtis hadn't either.

She almost didn't want to sully the moment by dredging up the past, but she was as ready to talk now as she'd perhaps ever be. 'I told him things about my childhood... things I'd never spoken about before. I believed I'd found someone that I could open up to. Of course, there was my dad, but back then, I needed somebody uninvolved in my messy home life. I'd been so certain he was compassionate and trustworthy, but that had all been an act. By the time I came to comprehend the type of person he was, there could be no going back. I'd opened a door to a terrible place. I'd stepped inside a nightmare of my making. My stupidity—'

'Hey, listen, Vee... You were sixteen. Aren't you being a bit hard on yourself?'

Vanessa sipped the drink. 'He had this way of making people believe whatever *he* wanted them to. He made people do things they'd never normally do...'

Curtis drew in his lips, his cheeks flushing as he muttered, 'You don't say.'

'He enjoyed befriending weaker people. Not necessarily weaker in a physical sense... weaker minded, so he'd be able to mould and condition them to suit his needs.'

She felt Curtis tense up.

She'd tried to warn him...

'I'm not trying to make you feel worse, Curtis. He liked to play sick games. He was always daring others to do dangerous deeds. Because he enjoyed putting vulnerable people in harm's way... He also bullied, belittled, and wrecked most of those unfortunate to come into his orbit... On the surface, he seemed charming... gentle... likeable. But scratch that surface and you'd find something else. A bitter boy that thrived on seeing others suffer. Trust me, I know, because I experienced it first-hand. I was a stupid, impressionable girl that didn't grasp the trap I'd led myself in... I... I told him things... things that should never, ever have been spoken of...' She shuddered and a chill rippled over her.

The Whisper Troll will be shouting your secrets.

'Things that might destroy our very existence,' she said.

No more, she decided. Curtis wasn't Hayden... He was nothing like him. He needed to hear the truth.

'*Our* existence? What did you tell him?'

'I scolded you yesterday. Blamed you for not coming clean about your dealings with that man... but that makes me the biggest hypocrite ever. Truth is, if I'd have been straight with you from the start... if I'd explained how fragile the situation was... how my past could jeopardise everything... we might've controlled this... God, this mess is my fault.'

'Tell me... I can take it.'

63

Todd had followed the Hyundai Elantra along Interstate 75, the stretch known as Alligator Alley, Naples-bound, for two hours before the car had taken a side road and ventured into a spread of grassland so lonely and characterless that even the gators didn't seem to bother to loiter around it.

After another hour of driving, Jeff pulled over to open a swing barrier gate with black and yellow markers on it, and they both drove their vehicles onto a long, straight access road that, to Todd's eyes, seemed to stretch out endlessly alongside a murky brown canal.

On they drove, and Todd got so pissed off he ended up doing some nature spotting. He wanted to see some gators. Not those scrawny little beasts that didn't look tough enough to chew off a boot heel, but one of those giant bastards. The type which would be brazen enough to waddle out in front of his pickup truck and dare him to approach to shift its stubborn arse. He clicked his jaw, getting irritated with Jeff for all this messing about. Where was he heading? This place wasn't on any tourist route. He knew that much.

Another thirty minutes drifted by, and Todd blew a relieved sigh when the Hyundai left the road and drove onto a white-gravelled track. The skinny trail, surrounded by thick grass and coarse bracken, was like driving into a tunnel of dense undergrowth. Todd checked his GPS. They were still in the Everglades, and in the back of beyond. Jeff parked up under a canopy of overhanging maples and thick mangroves near an area of swampy wetlands. Some red-beaked ibis birds were skulking in the spot, but the tall white birds soon departed as they arrived.

Todd brought his Nissan Titan to a stop, jumped out, and stretched his legs. 'The hell is this place?' He checked his watch: three thirty.

'You said middle of nowhere,' said Jeff evenly, as he handed Todd a phone. 'He's had a lot of missed calls. I have reset the pin code. It's six zeros. Location services are off.'

Todd popped the trunk. Hayden, butt naked, bound and gagged, gazed back at him, eyes glazed in terror. Todd noticed the man's ankles were twisted, swollen and definitely busted. He'd not stayed to witness Jeff's work, but the guy had done a top-class job. He hoped that hurt like a real bitch.

Todd removed Hayden's gag. 'Who's this Russell guy? He's phoned you like a hundred times since yesterday,' asked Todd, holding up Hayden's phone. He wondered why Jeff hadn't already disposed of the device. That seemed an amateur mistake, even with the GPS off. Not that it mattered in the long run.

Hayden tried to sit up, but hit his head on the trunk and winced. 'My brother. He's mentally unwell. Please, just let me talk to him. Just for a minute.'

'I dunno about that.'

'Please, Todd. Let me say goodbye to him. He's nothing to do with this.'

Todd tutted and let out a long, whistling sigh. He put the

phone to Hayden's ear. 'Jeez, I must be going soft. One minute. That's all you get. Just to say goodbye. No funny business.'

'Thank you, Todd... Wait, I don't think it's ringing... Todd?'

Todd snatched the phone away.

Hayden groaned and wailed. 'I... I only wanted to tell him I've not forgotten him. I wanted to say goodbye.'

'I'll fuck your goodbye with a rusty pickaxe.'

'Please, don't do this. I'll get you money... I can get you as much as you want... I have a big deal—'

'Shut it. I don't want your God damn money!'

'I'll do anything.'

Todd leant in close to Hayden. 'Boy, you know, I wouldn't give you a single squirt of my piss if you were on fire and rolling around the ground, hugging my motherfuckin' granny right now.'

'Pleeeeese,' cried Hayden.

'You pathetic little toad. Ooooh, you just wait to see what I have for you.'

'Todd,' mewled Hayden. 'Mr Ericsson! Please...'

Todd took in a deep breath and shook his head. This guy was a worthless, gutless deadbeat.

'I'm sorry, Todd. I took it too far... I'll—'

'Shut your mouth! I don't wanna hear it. You involved my little girls, and that was a huge mistake.'

'Surely your wife would've told them anyway, Todd. Come on, you know this is going too far.'

'No! She wouldn't have. You don't know shit, so zip it.'

'Why didn't you just pay?' cried Hayden, shoulders bobbing as he let out deep sobs.

Todd spat on the ground. 'Outta principle! That's why.' He turned to Jeff, who leant against a metal gate, watching with an aloof expression. 'Jeff, can you shut this no-good bum up?'

'Sure,' said Jeff, approaching the trunk with industrial strength duct tape.

Hayden jolted around and tried to move his head away from the man. 'No, no, no, wait—'

Jeff grabbed Hayden's face and applied the tape to his mouth. He wrapped it around his head five times, ripped the roll away and shoved Hayden back. 'Chitchat is over, pal.'

'Get the bag, Jeff,' said Todd, feeling a big grin spreading across his face. He knew the act he was about to carry out was indeed wicked and warped, but in this moment, the thought of doing it filled him with utter joy.

'Here,' said Jeff, offering Todd a tatty beige canvas sack. 'Hold it from the top. In case he shoots out of there.'

64

'I told him about my mum,' said Vanessa. 'I... I told him all about the way she treated me when I was a child and the things—' Vanessa's phone ringing stopped her mid-sentence. She checked the caller ID. *Jonas.* She answered, hearing the hesitation in her voice as she said, 'Hey, what's up?'

'Vee, listen to me... It's Delphine. She's been rushed to hospital. She's taken a blow to the head, and she's being treated for a severe head trauma.'

'Christ! What happened?' she asked.

'It looks like somebody broke into her place and attacked her! She was meant to meet me at a restaurant in the Harbour. When she didn't show or answer the phone, I got concerned and went to her place. I found her out cold. I couldn't wake her up, Vee... I think she's in a real bad way. The paramedics have taken her and I'm hanging around here for the police.'

Vanessa's chest tightened.

'Was it him? That shit-bag, Knox. He do this?' growled Jonas. 'I'll rip his bloody head off!'

'Jonas, I—'

'It's all your fault, you know that, right?' snapped Jonas.

'I'm coming back to see her now.'

'Listen to me, Vee... I can't find her phone anywhere. Is there anything on that device that might expose your current location?'

Vanessa caught Curtis's eye, who watched her tentatively as he chewed his lower lip.

'I... I sent her pictures of the cottage... Oh, no... I think...' Vanessa's heart sank. 'I need to check my photos.'

'I reckon she's been out for hours, Vee. You understand what I'm getting at?' said Jonas, his tone now carrying a softer, more composed edge.

'Yes. I do... Will he have been able to unlock it?'

'Her phone has the old fingerprint sensor. So easily.'

'Right. Keep me posted, Jonas.'

'Will do. Keep yourselves safe.'

The call ended. Vanessa checked her messages to Delphine. Over three hours ago, she'd sent some photos of the cottage's exterior. She zoomed into the one she'd taken from the front and there it was – the wooden plaque with the name Daisy's Lookout in clear black letters.

Vanessa checked the response:

> Delightful pics. Only wish I could be there too xx

Vanessa wondered who'd sent the message.

'Vee, talk to me,' said Curtis.

'We need to pack up and leave. Right now!'

65

Todd watched on with a wide grin. Hayden's eyes bulged and he gazed at the sack in horror.

Todd winked at Hayden. 'Now, I bet you're literally *dying* to see what's in here.'

Hayden shook his head frantically. His nostrils were wide as his breathing went crazy.

'I did ask my colleagues to retrieve a Mojave rattlesnake, but then I thought of something even better.' Todd placed the bag between Hayden's legs. 'We have a little rhyme in Texas... If red touches yellow, it'll kill a fellow. That means you're dealing with a coral snake. The most venomous snake in the state, and believe me, we have a lot of snakes, boy.'

Hayden was pushing himself away from the bag. His neck veins were like taut wires, and sweat poured down his face as he desperately tried to speak through his bindings.

'There are around four types of snakes in the state that look similar. The milk snake, for example, is often mistaken for the coral. But that's an imposter. Non-venomous. Now, I dunno where they got this fella from... Who knows, perhaps they messed up... perhaps you'll get lucky. *Perhaps...* but, unlikely. Hell, I sure as shit ain't opening the sack to check.' Todd laughed and turned to Jeff. 'Hey, there's a snake in my boot! That's what the Brits call a trunk, right?'

Jeff sniggered. 'Yeah, I get it. Good one.'

'I am one funny son-bitch.'

Hayden was shaking his head like a madman.

'The coral snakes are pretty reclusive critters. They only attack if threatened. So best not upset the little guy. He only has small fangs, so if it latches on, it'll likely hang on and chew for a while. Untreated, the bites can cause paralysis and, in severe cases, respiratory failure. Oooh, imagine that! Stuck in that enclosed spot with your throat closing up and your breathing going to shit. This takes a while. You'll have around twelve, maybe thirteen hours, before *bad* things will happen.' Todd put his boot on the bumper, rested his elbow on his knee and his chin on his knuckle. 'Most people unlucky enough to get a nip by a coral can easily get medical treatment to deal with the venom. So, deaths associated with these guys are extremely rare... but then, most people are not stuck in the trunk of a stolen Hyundai and left in the middle of the Everglades.'

Todd let out a booming laugh. God, he was enjoying this way too much. What a sick bastard he was, but this arsehole did not deserve the luxury of a quick end. He'd have plenty of time to mull over all the people he'd screwed over in his life. Todd felt quite proud. Like he'd dispensed some much-needed justice.

Hayden had tears in his eyes now. Eyes that pleaded for help. Pleaded for this nightmare to end. It had only just started.

'Well, Hayden, Ritchie, or whatever the hell you prefer to be called... it's time for lights out. We'll leave you two little snakes to get properly acquainted,' said Todd, standing up ramrod straight and dusting off his hands.

Jeff leant in and flicked a switch on a small fan that was stuck to the trunk. 'Battery will last three to four hours. Generate some airflow. For a while, anyhow.'

Todd stuck his hand under the fan, which only seemed to produce a meagre blast of air.

The sack moved, and the top fell open. Hayden's eyes opened even wider, and he screamed through his bindings.

'So, Hayden Knox, it looks to me like someone's awake and wants to pop out and say hi. If I were you, I'd stay as still as a dead, black-tailed prairie dog,' said Todd, then slammed the boot shut. He walked back to his Nissan. Jeff followed.

Todd heard a muffled, 'Mmmmhhhhhh.'

Jeff popped a cigarette in his mouth. 'How long you wanna leave him?'

Todd tapped his right index finger against his chin. 'You sure no one will find him up here?'

Jeff lit the cigarette and blew a long plume of smoke from his nostrils. 'Nope. There ain't nobody coming up here. Once we leave, I'll chain up the gate. The only thing down this track is an unused ranger station.'

'OK. Leave him for two or three days. If the coral doesn't snuff him out, the heat will. Even in the shade, it'll be stifling in that trunk. Then submerge the vehicle in the swamp.'

'As good as done.'

Todd gazed back at the car. It wasn't bouncing around yet. Hayden had a long couple of terrible days to endure. Every minute would seem like an eternity, and his mind would go into overdrive and slowly drive him to pure insanity.

'You removed the emergency release hatch, right, Jeff?'

'He ain't opening that trunk. Trust me.'

Todd smiled. 'Good to know.'

Hayden's phone pinged again, and he read it. 'Oh, nice. Pop that trunk, Jeff.'

Jeff shrugged and re-opened the trunk.

Todd leant over Hayden and, in a gleeful tone, said. 'Text from Poppy.' He then spoke in a feminine voice as he conveyed the message. 'No, Hayden. It's a sweet gesture – you coming here like this – but I have decided. I'm not coming. Sorry it has to be this way.' Todd let out a long, sad sigh and reverted to his own voice. 'Ahh, not even a single kiss. I've seen a picture of this Poppy. Don't you worry about her, boy, I'll make sure that little cutie gets what she needs.'

With that, he closed the trunk again and muttered, 'See you in hell!' Todd dropped the phone onto the ground and stamped his chunky Stetson boot onto the screen.

Jeff struggled over with a bag of gravel he'd removed from the Nissan, his legs bowing under the weight, and thrust it up onto the trunk, expelling a loud grunt as he did.

66

Vanessa piled the last of the bags onto the backseat of the Wrangler, racking her brains for what she'd left behind.

'That's the last of it,' confirmed Curtis, carrying a small rucksack. He pulled the door shut. 'Pop the keys inside that box on the wall and we are good to—'

'Wait. What's that?' asked Vanessa.

The pair stood in silence and listened. The only sound here at night was the serene gush of the nearby river, the hoot from owls, or subtle sounds from other wildlife in the surrounding woodlands. But now another sound rumbled in the darkness – an approaching diesel engine. *Fast* approaching, too.

'In my car. Go, Vee.'

They got into the Wrangler. Curtis started the engine and sped for the gated entrance, churning up gravel that clattered against Vanessa's Mini in his haste to exit. Vanessa, pleased they'd not closed the gate, gasped as Curtis bolted through the entrance and braked hard.

Headlights were streaming down the narrow lane that led

back out onto the main road. The vehicle heading down wasn't hanging about. The lights danced, and the beam intensified as it closed in on them.

Curtis floored it and raced in the opposite direction, sending the Wrangler bouncing along an uneven farm track. The pair slid on their seatbelts.

'Where does this lead?' Vanessa asked.

Curtis shook his head, scanning his mirrors, but didn't reply.

Vanessa spun around to check and shuddered when she saw the glaring lights hurtling towards them. She recalled they'd ventured down this track when they'd visited years ago and she tried to remember where it led to.

'Glove box... open the glove box,' demanded Curtis. 'There's pepper spray. Get it ready.'

She did as he requested. The headlights were right on them now and flooded the vehicle, momentarily dazzling Vanessa's eyesight. 'Careful, Curtis...'

Curtis, an expression of furious focus fixed on his face as he scrutinised the twisty route ahead, cried out, 'We'll lose it in a minute... He won't keep up!'

'Pull over. Let me talk to him! This is getting out of hand.'

Curtis shook his head sternly.

They raced on, and with the vehicle hitting sixty, Vanessa started applying her imaginary brakes as her heart rate soared. 'Stop! I think you should stop now.'

'I'm losing him. He's backing off. He can't keep up with this, Vee.'

Vanessa checked again and, sure enough, the gap between them had grown. As they sped along more snaking bends that soon changed into a track only just wide enough for a standard vehicle, let alone their stout Jeep, the lights disappeared from sight.

'I can't see it,' she said.

But as the Wrangler raced into an area with coiled trees and crooked overhanging branches, Curtis did not slow.

'I'm sure this lane is a dead end, Curtis. Slow down before you kill us both.'

Vanessa, about to plead again that he ease up, was thrust forward as he slammed on the brakes. He dimmed the lights, and in one swift manoeuvre, expertly reversed backwards and took the vehicle off the lane and into a field. He kept reversing back until the crop semi covered the vehicle, although, Vanessa suspected, not quite enough to immerse the motor entirely.

Curtis cut the engine and lights. The pair held hands as they waited in total silence. She could feel her husband shivering all over and taking in sharp breaths.

Vanessa tensed as the noise of the other engine broke the silence. She noticed Curtis readying the ignition, beads of perspiration collecting on his forehead. She cursed the full moon tonight. It cast a bright shimmer overhead that almost felt like a search light exposing their position as they waited in an anxious stillness.

Then they saw the small van speed past and Curtis roared the Wrangler to life.

As he made for the field's exit, Vanessa heard the van's screeching brakes and cursed when the sound of a vehicle rapidly reversing filled her ears.

'He saw us!' she bellowed.

The Jeep charged forward, but the van filled the exit and shuddered to a stop.

Curtis stopped the vehicle, slammed it into reverse and steamed backwards, but then stopped again. For a few seconds Vanessa was certain her husband intended to charge forward and ram straight into the side of the van, but if that had been his initial intention, he changed his mind. He faltered, reversed once again, and spun the vehicle right around to change direction.

The next thing she knew, they were hurtling through the field proper, crushing the crop under the hefty tyres on its bumpy stampede into the unknown. The undulating field sent them on a rollercoaster journey that had the pair bouncing and juddering in their seats as Curtis tore the four-wheeled motor forward.

With the course obstructed by crops that appeared to be getting higher and denser the further they drove in, Vanessa prepared herself for a sudden, violent impact. Then it seemed like the Wrangler left the ground altogether for a moment before it smashed down with such ferocity, Vanessa envisaged the entire underneath of the vehicle crumpling in on itself, but the sturdy Jeep hurtled on. They found themselves crashing out of the cropland and darting across a churned-up section of land, before battering straight through a line of shrubbery and bushes that collapsed under the machine with zero resistance.

They emerged just in time to sight a line of trees and compact vegetation which they were fast drawing near to. Curtis gripped the wheel, slammed on the brakes and sent the Jeep skidding into the thicket. And in one sudden, frightful moment, everything became a reeling blur as the vehicle descended.

Now, with no control over their passage, total fear gripped her as branches and bracken swatted and thudded against the Jeep. Vanessa yelled hoarsely when she perceived they were hurtling towards a sheer drop.

A drop that would send them straight into the river.

67

Todd stepped into a ring of cypress trees where a multitude of sun rays streaked his face and decided this would be as good a place as any. The clearing, thick with lush sawgrass and thick shrubs, evoked a sense of warm tranquillity that made him feel oddly content and, most importantly, ready. Birdsongs and the chirp of a plethora of insects surrounded him. He'd left his lawyer in charge of dealing with his affairs, including distributing a set of letters to all those deemed important to him.

He held a photo of his daughters to his chest and closed his eyes. 'Sasha and Crystal,' he moaned. 'Sorry your daddy is such a monster, my angels! Sorry I brought all my...' He became aware of a presence behind him. 'Um, hey, Jeff. I have made payment via the investigator for services rendered.'

'Appreciated, sir,' said Jeff.

Todd heard a click and tensed. But he wasn't scared, despite knowing that the man had prepared his very own Smith and Wesson.

'Ready, Mr Ericsson? No last-minute change of heart?'

'Nope. I'm all done. I'm... I'm ready now. Yeah...'

'Bet a small part of you wishes you'd caved in and paid that reprobate.'

'Yeah. But I'm a stubborn bastard. Always have been.'

'Well, OK then.'

'Wait... Jeff, have you... have you done this kinda thing before?'

'I did once. For a terminally ill lady. But you know, your girls will surely come around and forgive you. In time.'

'Jeff, I didn't hire you to be my blasted shrink. And trust me, after the sordid footage they saw... they'll never look at me in a good light again.'

'Sounds like you've just got diverse taste. Not so bad, is it? Maybe counselling or therapy might be another option for you to consider.'

Todd let out a deep, gravelly chuckle. 'Jeff, there is no therapy in the world that can fix my fucked up—'

The final words didn't leave his lips as complete darkness swallowed him up.

68

'Vee? Vee? You alright?'

Vanessa, taking in shallow gasps of air, nodded. 'I think so.' She saw a large crack in the centre of the windscreen. They sat there for a while, silently contemplating the situation as the adrenaline of the crash ebbed away. Both of her hands were trembling.

'We're close to the edge, so no sudden movements,' said Curtis in a cracked voice. 'You get out first. Nice and easy now.'

Vanessa opened the door in a gentle movement and, as gingerly as possible, stepped outside, where she heard the unmistakable sounds of fast-flowing water. Twisty, protruding tree roots had been their saviour, because nothing else lay between their vehicle and a twenty-foot drop into the foamy, shallow rapids of the river below. The Wrangler's front wheels were precariously close to the edge.

Curtis stood beside her and they both peered over the side, sharing a bewildered look as he too absorbed the fact that if the vehicle had gone another couple of feet, or the roots hadn't been there to act as a crash barrier, they'd have both plunged to their doom.

Vanessa sensed the other presence a few seconds before seeing the dark shape appear on the hillside. So had Curtis, because he seized the small can of pepper spray from Vanessa's vice-like grip and popped the lid off, then stood in front of Vanessa as their pursuer came into view.

Vanessa felt a cold stab to her heart as Russell drew closer.

Curtis raised the spray. 'You don't want to come down here!'

'Tell me where Hayden is,' Russell demanded.

'He's gone, Russell,' said Curtis. 'You need to back off!'

'Liar! What have you done to him? It's that South African, isn't it? He's involved in this. What did you have that nutter do with Hayden?'

Vanessa took a step forward and raised her palms. 'Russell, we need to talk. There are things *we* need to discuss. You and me.'

Russell took a step closer. 'Did you get your London hitmen to deal with him? Is that what happened?'

'No,' said Vanessa. 'There are no hitmen!'

'*You*... he told me all about you, Essa,' Russell spat. 'I know what you're capable of!'

Curtis cut in. 'Hayden has taken the money... Looks like he's swindled you out of your cut. How much did he promise you? What were you meant to get out of all this deceitful plotting?'

Russell edged closer and Vanessa could make out the bloodied bandages hanging from his arms and saw his ashen face... Saw his contorted, menacing features.

'He's been using you, Russell,' she said in a placating tone. 'This is just some twisted game of revenge and he never intended to pay you anything.'

Russell gaped at Vanessa for a quick moment, seeming lost and confused, then he snapped his teeth together and growled, 'I won't let you trick me. Do you hear me? I won't let you trick me! He told me you'd do this. He warned me that you'd twist everything and lie.'

'Russell, who did that to you? Did you hurt yourself? Or... did your brother hurt you?' she asked.

'Where is he? I have been calling him constantly... Something bad has happened to him, and I know you're involved,' hissed Russell, stepping towards her.

Curtis aimed the spray, but before he could let out a blast, Russell barged into him with brute force and sent him sprawling into the undergrowth.

Russell made to aim a kick at Curtis, but Vanessa grabbed him by the T-shirt and yanked him back. 'Stop! Just stop and talk to me. Stop, Russell!'

Then Curtis found his feet and barrelled into the other man, sending them both crashing down. A messy fight broke out. A tumbling scuffle of entangled arms, elbows and furious grappling. The pair crashed down in a heap.

'Stop fighting,' Vanessa yelled. 'Please stop!'

Curtis fought his way on top of Russell and rained down a flurry of clumsy hammer-like blows.

Vanessa continued screaming at the pair, but the men's minds were lost in a sea of wanton aggression as they both tried to obliterate the other.

A flashback of the twins battling on the beach came to her then... *It's happening again*.... 'Stop! You have to stop this!'

The pair wrestled and rolled down towards the drop. They were locked in a deep, murderous frenzy and seemed oblivious to the hazard.

Then they were on their feet, throwing erratic punches and viciously going at each other.

A vision resonated in Vanessa's head... of a younger Russell falling from that cliff path...

Curtis and Russell fought on.

She saw Russell's head cracking on that rock... 'Stop!'

The fight moved dangerously close to the edge... One, or both of them, would go over the side... She had to stop them.

She remembered all that blood... that horrific head wound.

Vanessa heard a nasty thud as Curtis swung a clumsy but powerful blow that hit the side of Russell's head.

'You weren't always like this!' she cried.

Curtis, overpowering a stunned Russell now down on his knees, gripped him by the back of the neck. 'Let's see if you enjoy going for a dip, you psycho!'

Curtis seemed unrecognisable now. Fuelled by some maniacal fury that had transformed him entirely, he now wanted to execute his own grim justice.

Vanessa moved to the edge and barred his way. 'Curtis!' she bellowed. She fixed him with a firm, confrontational stare. 'Enough now. Just... stop.'

With his chest heaving and face set in a twisted, hateful sneer, he growled, 'This pig tricked you! He could've drowned me. He tried to ruin us!'

Vanessa shook her head. 'No... that's not true,' she said warily. 'This is all... Hayden.' Saying his name was like pouring a noxious poison into her mouth. 'He's been lying to you, Russell.'

The fight drained from Curtis and he slumped back against a tree, coughed, and held his ribs. 'Get back from the edge, Vee!'

'That's what he does... what he's always done. He lies,' said Vanessa. She stepped away from the edge and knelt down to a battered and exhausted Russell. He sat up and gazed around in a dazed stupor.

'You don't remember the beach, do you, Russell?' she asked.

Russell held the side of his face, flinched and shook his head.

'What do you remember? Before the... fall?'

Russell stared at her, and his woeful expression told her what she needed to know. A lugubrious shadow cloaked him. The fall had caused life-changing damage. It must have. As she'd already guessed, his memories were gone. Or at the very least, they'd become disjointed and obscure. Could he not recall one tiny piece of what they'd shared?

'I have spent my entire life tormented by the knowledge that I'd been responsible for your death, Russell. It's been a heavy burden I have carried.'

'Vee, let's go. We'll walk back and get your car. Leave that wretched man for the police to deal with. Come on. Get away from him. He's dangerous,' said Curtis.

'I didn't mean to hurt her,' Russell lamented. 'That Delphine lady... I... I tried to stop her running, and she fell over and bashed her head. I really hope she's OK. Do you know if she is alright?' The anger from the man had completely abated and he appeared lost and muddled, like he'd snapped into a different character now.

Curtis flashed him a contemptuous glare. 'She ended up out cold for hours. God knows what damage you did to that poor woman.'

Russell grimaced. 'Jesus... I'm such a stupid idiot,' he said, his tone almost childlike now. He slapped the side of his head. 'Essa, I... I do sometimes get these flashbacks. They are like little memory bubbles that show a tiny glimpse of some event inside it.' He took a deep, wheezing breath. 'They float around inside my head, then pop and vanish from my thoughts. Then I'm left wondering if what I'd seen was in my past... or just something that I'd imagined.'

'Do you remember driving out to that farm to pick me up early in the morning?' asked Vanessa. 'When the crazy old farm lady insisted you came in for breakfast? She cooked us both the biggest fry-ups! Enough to have fed ten people. I couldn't eat mine because I felt like crap. You ate yours and forced down some of mine, too.'

Russell shook his head. 'Why did I pick you up?'

'Because Hayden and Dominic spiked my drink. I got lost in the woods and you came to rescue me. Took me home to your makeshift studio room in the garage and brought me sweet tea and cookies. Then you played for me on that old acoustic guitar with all the stickers on. It had a faded rainbow strap. Do you remember that guitar? You loved that old thing.'

Russell sighed. 'I... I don't know... maybe... maybe I kinda do.'

'You played Nirvana, Pearl Jam and The Smashing Pumpkins. You used a ten pence, because you said you were always misplacing your plectrums. You helped me through the comedown of the drugs they gave me. You saved me that day.'

'I can't play the guitar now. Hayden told me I never could... not very well.' Russell's voice trailed off, and he sniffed.

'You could. I swear it,' said Vanessa. 'Russell, you were fantastic.'

Russell clenched both his fists. 'He said I was too slow... Lame-brained was his favourite nickname for me. My forgetfulness often narked him. He'd shout at me and call me useless.'

'Well, trust me, you rocked. You loved grunge and metal.'

Russell gave a self-deprecating shrug. 'But... how do I even know you're not making all this up?'

'I'm not. I promise, it's true. Russell, you were such an unassuming boy... and you were good-natured and dependable. Nothing like Hayden. He didn't like the clothes you wore, or the music you listened to... or the fact you were far more intelligent than him. So he ridiculed you. He'd often belittle and bully you in front of his boisterous friends... He treated you much the same way he treated me... and that's what ended up bringing us together... We... we found solace in each other. Sort of... a shared grief, I guess. Because both of us were misfortunate enough to have come into Hayden's world.'

Russell studied her with wide, confused eyes.

Vanessa continued. 'We kept our friendship a secret. You told me you'd always hated the way Hayden treated me. How it broke your heart every time he used me... demeaned me... and boasted to everyone about our exploits. You told me I deserved better. You were gentle and sweet.'

Russell climbed to his feet and stepped over to the drop, gazing down into the water below. 'Hayden has always been there for me. You know nothing about me... Whatever did or didn't happen between us... you...' He tapped the side of his head. 'You still caused this.'

'I saw sense and walked away from him... but he wasn't prepared to just sit back and watch our friendship flourish into something more. When he got wind that we had been spending time together, he hated it.' Vanessa gazed back at Curtis, seeing his face twisted into a baffled scowl. She inhaled deeply and let out a long exhale. 'We went miles away so we could be alone. So we could be far away from him. We were lost in the moment. A small fire on the beach, some cans of cider and your boombox blasting out music... I loved to dance. House and trance, but you wanted to convert me into a lover of rock and metal. You made me a compilation of all your favourite tracks.'

'I don't... I can't remember... not one moment of it,' exclaimed Russell.

'Metallica's "Nothing Else Matters" echoed around that beach,' said Vanessa. 'And nothing else did matter in those moments. But that music had drawn Hayden to our location. He'd arrived the very moment we kissed for the first time. He'd tracked us down to wreck our first proper intimate moment.'

Vanessa could picture Hayden's frenzied and disgusted expression as he gnashed his teeth together.

'He'd yelled, "You think I'll ever share my girl with you, Russell? Essa's *my* first love. You won't have her! Not ever."'

She saw that silver flick-knife... that ominous blade darting out.

The twins fighting as the powerful waves crashed in around them.

That poignant song playing in the background.

Hayden thrusting that knife at Russell – almost catching his face.

Russell shoving Hayden down into the water and bellowing, 'Run, Essa! Get away from here!'

'Hayden came at us with a knife... But you still fought him off... You got in front of me... and shielded me. Told me to run.'

Vanessa recalled her ears ringing and buzzing as she'd turned and run, her bare feet pounding across that sandy beach... daring a look behind, seeing Russell sprinting up behind her, shouting her name.

Then an enraged Hayden giving chase and shouting incoherent curses as he pursued them with that knife.

They'd fled up those steps... seen Dominic obstructing their path.

'As we bolted up those steps, I spotted Dominic Brookes blocking the way up. You remember him? Hayden was screaming at him to stop us and to shove us back down the steps.'

Now, Russell averted his eyes from the drop and gazed at her, and with the blue of the moon behind him, he appeared almost spectral – *a mere ghost.*

'Then I lost my footing and fell... You grabbed my arm and stopped me from going over the edge...' Vanessa rubbed her palm against her eyes to staunch the tears filling them. 'I've replayed what happened next over and over in my head a million times... imagined it happening differently... That when Hayden shoved you and caused you to skid from that path... I imagine that as I grabbed your hand... I *did* have the strength to hold on... that I *was* able to pull you to safety... I have pictured that moment... so many times... I should have held on.' She closed her eyes. They were now soaking wet with tears.

She'd always blamed herself. For falling for Russell... for losing her footing... for not being strong enough to *just*... hold on... for a while longer. The look of horror on Russell's face as he dropped had never left her... nor had the paralysing terror upon seeing his body skimming the cliff-side... and the horrific sound of the almighty *CRACK* as his head had thudded against those rocks.

She'd always seen him falling... every time she'd closed her eyes.

'I thought I'd lost you,' she whispered. 'I was certain of it.'

Russell's face dropped. 'He... pushed me.' A deep sadness darkened his face.

Vanessa remembered the shuddering sobs pulsating through her as she sat on those uneven steps on the cliff path, as Hayden reluctantly went down to investigate the aftermath of the fall.

Dominic shaking her and telling her to calm down.

Hayden screaming obscenities from below.

Her own screams as she protested that they needed to run for help.

Dominic grabbing hold of her... getting in her face and yelling that she needed to stay down and shut up.

'When Hayden came back up those steps, he had murder in his eyes. I thought he was going to push me over the edge, too. But he'd said, "Shush. No tears. I'm going to clean up your mess, Essa. No one needs to know what *you* did."'

Vanessa, shaking all over, flinched as Curtis took hold of her hand and gripped it. She'd been so lost in reliving the moment, she'd almost forgotten about her husband's presence. 'Hayden made it clear that if I ever spoke about what happened on the beach, they'd turn it around on me. The pair would tell everyone that they'd caught me cheating with you, Russell. Then everyone would know that Essa was acting like a dirty whore. That I'd been so ashamed about getting caught out, I tried to flee the beach and you'd chased me. That he and Dominic witnessed me pushing you from the pathway, screaming that I wanted you to die. They outnumbered me.'

Russell wiped his own tears away. He looked like he was about to speak, but clamped his mouth shut.

'I guess, being so young and naïve, I believed every single word that day. Hayden had the gift of the gab. Everyone liked him. His friends were loyal and he could talk his way out of anything. But that... It was no excuse. I know that. And I'm ashamed of myself for what I did to save my own skin.'

They'd all believe his story over hers... She had always been so sure of that. But there was more to it than that...

Russell sniffed. 'It's all been lies. All of it,' he said. 'So I never...'

'No... no... never,' she said softly. 'That did not happen.'

A deep, consuming quiet fell on the three of them as they took everything in. The moment, both perfectly surreal and deeply profound, bestowed her a curious peacefulness.

Vanessa then visualised the people on Whitstable beach

stepping over all that broken glass. Had Russell's mind become similar to that glass after his head smashed against those rocks? *Just broken fragments.* His memories scattered into thousands of tiny shards, jumbled and unfixable, like a huge, complex puzzle that could never be completed. Never be whole again. That would always drive him insane with confusion and frustration. She imagined him trying to slot the pieces back together as he strived to decipher what memories were real and how everything clicked into place.

She thought about Hayden filling his head with lies and twisting events as he shaped and transformed Russell into another version of himself. Like his own Frankenstein's creation. Russell's decent principles, life ambitions and his identity itself were fractured and adjusted to satisfy Hayden's sick desire to have a twin brother he could truly connect with and control. He'd fashioned Russell into a clone of himself. A clone not just reliant on his twin, but one who lived in total admiration of him. To the point where he'd do anything to please him. He'd exploited Russell, and no doubt drummed ideas and stories into his head that left his brother bitter and cold. Hayden had made it abundantly clear that Vanessa was the enemy. And responsible for all the suffering he'd endured.

Russell broke the silence. 'I'll hand myself in... I'll tell them what I did.'

69

H e'd watched a YouTube film about how to escape from a kidnap situation a few years back. Methods to escape from the boot of a car had been featured, and he remembered a few tips, such as breaking through the rear light housing and signalling for help, or by bashing down the backseats using your shoulder or foot. But Hayden couldn't move, and the pain in his feet and ankles was now so unbearable he'd screamed into the binding until he'd almost choked on his tongue.

Now he lay frozen in the total darkness with only the weak blast of the fan wavering over the side of his face as he sobbed. The heavy reality dawned on him: He'd die here. That Jeff character had been a professional. Wherever they'd taken him, he knew nobody would find him. Todd's parting words kept running over in his head, making the urge to scream even more excruciatingly awful.

After everything he'd done for Poppy, she'd turned her back on him. He'd only come back to the States because of that bitch... She was no better than that slag, Essa. Because despite all those insane things he'd gone through back then –

the things he'd done so they could be together – she'd still walked away. His rage waned, and he cried in silent hopelessness until his eyes burnt.

I'm not right... I'm the one that's not right... They all leave me. Everyone important to me... leaves.

Then he got lost in his own bleak, warped mind as he tried to block out the very idea that a small, highly venomous snake lay in wait somewhere in the confined, surrounding blackness.

This must have been what it was like for Russell when they'd left him to die in the dingy, cramped storage area of the foul-smelling, festering stable block.

He pictured himself back in that old, rank place.

'I say we just put him back down there and leave him, Hayden.'

'No, Dom. I can't do that!' Hayden had protested. 'My mum's going out of her mind.'

'His head is mashed. He'll never recover properly. Maybe it'll be the best thing now. You know, the humane thing to do. I'm fed up with having to keep coming right out here. Aren't you? Plus, you haven't given me any petrol money like you agreed.'

'Did you not hear me? No, Dominic.'

'OK, then. Make up some shit. Say... say some piss-head ran him over. Yeah, hit and run. That might work.'

'I've already told her he's hiding up from some dealers from the Springdean. Now she's blaming me! She'd moaned, "My Russell wouldn't get involved with wrong'uns. He doesn't take drugs, Hayden!" I got a right fucking grilling, mate. I told her all those musician types get into gear. It's inevitable.'

Four days later, they were certain they were witnessing Russell taking his final breaths and dying in front of them. After he'd climbed free of the hole, they'd found him lying in a heap, breathing in shallow rasps as he gazed at them in a spaced-out and inert state. Then he'd lost consciousness.

'Does it always take this long?' Dominic had asked. 'It's not quick like in the movies, is it?' There'd been a dramatic change in his friend then, as paranoia and doubt swept over him. 'How long could we go to prison for this?'

'Nobody's going to prison, Dom! Get your shit together.'

Dominic became sullen, distant, and reluctant to help. Started doubting everything. 'Come clean, Hayden. All this to keep him apart from Essa... She's not worth it. Get him help. We'll say we found him like this.'

'Well, you've changed your tune! You wanted to snuff him out the other day.'

'But this is... it's sick... I—'

'He stays here. Got that?'

'He's been crying. Crying and saying he wants his mum. I'm starting to feel guilty. This is messed up, Hayden.'

'I'm starting to think I can't trust you anymore! If we take him to hospital now... What will happen when he wakes up and blabs about what we did?'

'Well, you pushed him,' Dominic had murmured.

That was around the time when Hayden purchased the padlocks.

But Russell did wake up, and when he'd become lucid enough to hold a conversation, Hayden soon established his brother's mind was shot to pieces. He could remember nothing of the encounter on the beach. It turned out he could remember very little at all. Some type of dreadful amnesia had afflicted Russell's mind. *Thank fuck.*

Hayden started weaving his lies from that moment. 'Russell, do you recall the scuffle we got into on the beach?'

No, he didn't.

'You tricked Essa into meeting her. You took her on a date pretending to be me, but she only agreed to go because she wanted to get back at me. She knew from the start you were messing with her! How stupid do you think that girl is?'

'Essa?' Russell had asked in a groggy daze.

'Oh, God, come on, Russ, you must remember what happened. What you did to her.'

'No,' he'd croaked, then squealed in pain. 'Everything is muddled. My head hurts so bad. I feel horrible. I can't see right.'

'She said NO, but you wouldn't listen. When I turned up, you were... you were forcing her!' Hayden pictured himself angrily popping pills from the packaging and forcing Russell to take them as he sobbed and howled like an injured animal. Hayden hadn't let up and kept up the enraged needling. 'You're just lucky it was me that showed up and dragged you off her and not some random stranger, you sick, perverted beast! You forced your dirty little cock inside my girlfriend, you freak!'

'I'm sorry, Hayden,' he'd wailed.

The look Russell had given Hayden in those moments haunted him ever since. That dazed, glassy-eyed expression as his gaunt, weary face dropped and he looked like he wanted to kill himself on the spot.

After he'd finished explaining how Russell had suggested they share Essa, and how she'd run away from him... fled up those dangerous stairs with him in vexed pursuit... how she'd called him a rapist and shoved him from that cliff path... After he'd finished saying *all* that... Russell cried until he'd spewed sticky bile and undigested pills.

'Hey, bro, she led you on... Don't beat yourself up too much. I'm being hard on you, but only so you can appreciate the gravity of the situation. She thinks you're dead, Russ! Essa thinks you died! It needs to stay that way so she doesn't call the police. She's scared right now because she reckons she killed you! But all that will change if she finds out you survived. Do you get what I'm saying here?'

'I don't understand,' he'd whimpered.

'You need to stay dead! Stay out of town. Let me take care of you. Trust me! We have to lie to Mum... You remember her, don't you?'

'I... I can picture her... I think.'

'Good. A start. I will tell her that some undesirables want to duff you up, and that we need to hide you away until the heat dies down. Then, once you're all healed, I'll move you out of the area so Essa never gets to know you're alive.'

Russell, so confused, debilitated and woozy, would've agreed to anything. 'OK, if you think that's best.'

'I do. Now get these pills down you, Russell. You have a fever. If you don't wish to end up in a total state of delirium, take the bastard things!'

Over the years, Hayden had made Russell detest Essa Neal. He'd installed it into his screwed-up brain that she was the enemy. Because if the day ever came where their paths collided, he needed Russell to hate her.

'She led you on, Russ... always remember that. She used *you* to get to me!' he'd remind him often in the early days. 'And she did this to you! She screwed up your life. I don't blame you anymore. You're the victim, not her. You were always the victim in this messed-up affair.'

Russell never fully recovered, and in time, Hayden found it difficult to be around his twin... Witnessing his constant decline depressed the hell out of him... Seeing all the problems that the untreated injury generated. The lame-brained idiot drove him mad. So did the fact that he was responsible. Out of all the dark, twisted and heinous deeds he'd committed in his life – and there'd been many – the suffering he'd let Russell endure after what happened on the beach topped them all.

Hayden felt something touch his leg, snapping him back into the present, and his blood froze in his veins. *Don't think about it... Shut out the world... Shut it out now...* Then in his mind something came into focus... An article... He could see it so clearly now... he could even read it... He'd read it before, many, many times. He knew it from memory.

Case study number six – United Kingdom, 2016.

This, a particularly baffling case, relates to Russell, who fell from a self-made zip line on a beach close to where he lived in Dorset, which resulted in a severe TBI aged nineteen. He consequently suffered constant headaches, terrible mood swings, and personality changes, as well as long- and short-term memory problems, bouts of sickness, neck pain, and narcolepsy. He came to The Darcy Cognitive Therapy Centre over twenty years after his accident. After treatment, Russell's long-term memory did not improve, but his short-term memory has developed incredibly. He has been able to multitask again, and his headaches are less severe and less frequent. He has been able to reduce the medication he takes for depression. Russell often spoke of a heavy, confusing sensation in his head. A ghost in his brain, he'd often referred to it as. A ghost that muddles his every waking thought and jumbles everything up. He described his life as being trapped in a perpetual nightmare. Although the ghost remains, Russell considers his therapy sessions have helped abate this issue and have enhanced his life considerably. He has also spoken of feeling less sleepy, and his sensitivity to light and loud noises has also reduced to a point where he can even enjoy listening to music, something he has been unable to do since the accident. With more sessions, we hope Russell can progress even further, perhaps recovering older memories.

Hayden had put a stop to those sessions. He couldn't have him getting too well, now. Oh, no, no, no.

His mind emptied. But not for long. Now Hayden stood on a podium in a vast television studio, harsh lights beaming in his face, a sea of hard, reproachful faces watching him.

An over enthusiastic, crazy-eyed presenter pointed to him. 'You're up next, Hayden Knox,' he yelled in a hyper, super-fast tone. 'Question one. Which episode of Friends featured the song "*He* pushed me from the cliff"?'

'Um, um, is it... the one with the girl who hits Joey?' blurted Hayden.

'Ah-no. Good guess, but it's the one where Russell gets amnesia. Good try, though.'

The podium slid up. The vast crowd booed, then muffled muttering started breaking out.

'No, no, that's not even a real episode. You've made that up!'

The presenter's wild blue eyes seemed the size of golf balls and he gave a white-toothed smile as he smoothed the lapels of his brilliant-white suit. 'Question two. Which twin did your mother love the most?'

'What sort of question is that?'

'I need an answer, Hayden.'

'Both... both of us. She loved us the same!'

'Ahh, I'm afraid the answer is... Russell. Because, I quote, "My placid Russell has a kind soul. Hayden, however, is a corrupt rogue who screwed up his brother's life with drugs." Oops. Up we go again.'

'No, wait, I lied about the drugs! There were no drugs!'

The podium sped upwards again, causing Hayden to drop to his knees to a chorus of, 'Oooooooooooooh,' from the crowd.

'You're not playing fair!'

'Question three.' The presenter stifled a grin. 'Ahh, nice easy one. Who pushed Russell from the cliff path?'

'Essa... Little Essa... I mean, Vanessa... Vanessa Neal did it!'

The crowd went deathly silent. A sea of vexed, judging stares. He glimpsed a young Dominic watching, his face set in a harsh scowl.

The presenter turned to the faces, a look of joyful apprehension locked on his face. 'Well... is he right? Is he?'

A resounding, 'Noooooo,' rumbled from the crowd.

'The answer is... Hayden Knox. So, incorrect again, I'm afraid.' He turned back to the audience. 'How did he not know that one, hey? You all know what this means.'

The crowd became incandescent with an excited and alarming aggressiveness as the podium moved up again. They chanted, 'Send him up, send him up, send him up.'

Once again, the podium sped up into the air. Oddly, the smirking presenter still stood opposite him.

'Final question, Hayden. What is the full name of the demon affiliated with the alias The Maestro of Life and Death, who is said to be able to grant considerable wealth to those who invoke him?'

'Oh, I know this... It's Luci—'

'Full name, Hayden... I'm gonna have to hurry you.'

'Lucifuge! Yes, Lucifuge!'

'Oh, bad luck... Almost there with that one, buddy. But I needed both names... Lucifuge Rofocale...'

The crowd howled and jeered.

The presenter called for calm, then said, 'Hayden Knox, you have been a terrible contestant on The Podium of Real Truth, and your time on the show, and indeed on this planet, is now up. Goodbye!'

'Wait, wait, I haven't—' He gazed around. The crowd,

though still audible, had been replaced by crashing waves and a scattering of seaweed-covered rocks.

The podium rocked, the movement so sudden and violent it sent him plummeting over the side to a tumultuous, roaring cheer.

Hayden jolted awake from the dream and vomited. The gag made the vile sick retreat back down his gullet and he spasmed in the darkness. He forced himself to stay still, wondering how long he'd been out for. Then another wave of chest-crushing panic hit when he noticed the fan was no longer blowing any air. He now felt roasting, and the urge to fight and start smashing his way out of the car became unendurable.

He saw his mother's face in his head. The image of her haggard face, crow's feet, and puffy eyes became so clear it made him shudder. 'You messed up his life. I know you did! This is karma.'

'I didn't, Mum... He stole Essa... She was mine. He had no right to take her!'

'You're a monster, Hayden Knox. You sucked all the good out of that decent boy. All because of a common slut that didn't even want you... She wanted him! And you couldn't take it.'

Get outta my head. Get out. Please get out. Get the fuck out.

Now another terrible spasm attacked his body. An uncontrollable urge to shift around conquered him. He jerked his legs, causing a blazing pain in his ankles that made him shriek into the binding. *The snake... No, no, no... don't think about the snake...* He willed his mind to roam somewhere else... anywhere else...

The beach... The night of the beach... *God, no, not that either...* Anywhere but the beach. But too late. He could see the waves. And Essa and Russell in a cosy embrace.

He'd changed the story for Russell... and again for

Curtis... He'd even changed the events in his own head. The notion being that by succumbing to a concept so fervently, the truth, over time, would become ambiguous. So he tried to believe with total conviction that his memory of how the events unfolded was true. That he could never be solely responsible. He'd not *made* the pair go off behind his back and he'd not forced them to go to that dangerous, off-limits place. They'd done that of their own accord.

Still, it didn't matter how much he tried to disguise and shape matters to conform to his preferred outcome. One fact remained a constant key truth, and whatever he did to gloss over it, or whatever facts he fabricated, *that* truth would never change. He'd shoved Russell, and meant it. He'd hidden his body away and expected him to die in that filthy old stable block. It didn't matter what he told himself. Nor did it matter that he'd changed his mind and patched Russell up to the best of his ability. He carried out those wicked deeds and could never escape the truth. Now this was his punishment.

I'm sorry, Russell... I'm so sorry... It should have been Essa... I should've pushed her...

Then he felt the snake bite into the inside of his thigh, very close to his testicles, and he writhed into a frenzied, deranged fit. Death couldn't come soon enough, because he could no longer endure a second more of this utter madness.

But death wouldn't come for some time. That grim thought spun in his mind and he knew he'd be insane by the time the end came.

70

Rain lashed against the doors as Curtis gazed around the bedroom, a despondent gloom sliding over him. He still couldn't accept that they'd be moving back to London. He loved this house, but Vanessa had insisted they move on and convinced him it was for the best. He'd agreed with much reluctance. She blamed herself for the terrible fate that befell her friend, as did Jonas. So did he, if he was honest with himself, though he didn't feel they should flee the area with their tails between their legs.

He put his hands on the bathtub and let out a snorting snigger. They'd not even used it once. Vanessa's swimwear was strewn across it, drying from her earlier dip. The bastard thing had been nothing more than her airing spot. He tossed aside the swimming gear, whacked on the taps, and filled the tub with a generous squirt of bubble bath. Creamy lavender and wild iris.

As the foamy bubbles lifted, he added more liquid, and nipped downstairs where he grabbed himself a bottle of champers. Warm, but it would do. It was the bubbly he'd purchased for the night of the dinner party. For their own after-party in the bedroom. Just before the Knox twins came bounding into their lives and sullied their happiness. As he headed for the stairs, he could hear the kids calling for him from the cinema room. He ignored them.

Curtis returned to the bedroom to a frothy cloud of foaminess awaiting him. He tugged off his clothes and sank into the steaming water.

Vanessa emerged from the ensuite in a bath robe just as he popped the cork and let a jet of champagne join him in the bath. She flashed him a perplexed half-smile as he necked the warm fizz and let out a long, 'Aahhh, that tastes like utter shit.'

'Celebrating?'

'Nope. Why would I be? We're letting our dream home go. More... commiserating.'

'Right. How's the tub?'

'A perfect waste of money. So... did you hear?'

Vanessa seized the bottle, took a sip, and grimaced. 'Yuck. Hear what?'

'Jonas said Knox's solicitor is pushing to downgrade the charge from murder to manslaughter on the grounds of diminished responsibility. On account of all Russell's issues... Reckons he'll end up doing a few years in some institute, painting hand-crafted ceramics and chatting about his confused feelings.'

'He's not a well man. If he'd been on his medication... He—'

'Vee, that man was well enough to come into our house and deceive us. He was well enough to help Hayden con us. He was well enough to push...' Curtis stopped himself from ranting. They'd both grown tired of this argument.

'He was doing Hayden's bidding.' She sighed and handed him the bottle back. 'He'd been brainwashed. And whatever they say, Russell did not set out to kill Delphine. Deep down you know that too. I believe him.'

'The guy is a headcase... I should've...' He sipped the champagne and left the sentence unfinished. 'I can't be bothered to even discuss this anymore,' he said with a disgruntled frown.

'I've always told myself that the girl on that beach wasn't me... that Little Essa was somebody else. Just someone I knew. I suppose distancing myself from her was my way of coping.... But the fact is, I walked away and buried my head in the sand. Now others have paid the price.'

Curtis swigged the drink, offering no reply.

'I allowed Hayden to get away with it. Because, ultimately, I was too afraid to go against him. I should have spoken out, but I was too weak. Instead, I ran away.'

'So what, now you owe him? Even after all he has done?'

'I played a part. I'm partly responsible. So yes, maybe I do owe him... something.'

'Does this mean regular visits to see his mum? Why not offer to take care of her until Russell gets out?' scoffed Curtis.

'It was a one-off visit. I felt she needed the truth explained to her. You don't need to go on about it. She's a broken woman. With Russell incarcerated, she's alone.'

Curtis sank deeper into the bubbles. 'And Hayden hasn't contacted her?'

'He used to call her once a week without fail... but he's stopped.'

Curtis thought about the money Hayden had taken from him and tensed up. He only hoped Hayden's silence meant something bad had befallen him. Something awful, with any luck.

'I best check on the kids. I left them watching a film. Enjoy the bubbles.' She flicked some froth into his face and left.

Curtis wanted to grab her arm, pull her into the bath and kiss her, but somehow couldn't bring himself to do it so he let her leave. Instead, he gulped the booze and delved into the bubbles. As the water engulfed him, a dreadful panic rose inside of him and he shot back up, breathing hard and thinking that if a hot bath was freaking him out, how would he ever take himself out on the sea again... *It's those weird dreams freaking you out,* he told himself... He'd been having dreams about drowning often, and others where he'd hurt people... hurt them and found it amusing.

And then the worst dream of all – the one where he'd dreamt of the drink-driving advert. It all played out just as it did on the television, but with Steve in the driver's seat, crushed and broken. Not quite dead, but almost, as he'd gazed at him with a resentful grimace that soon morphed into an ugly look of anguish as he slowly registered his dire plight. As he yielded to the prospect of a long, agonising end trapped in a wreckage of his own making. No... of *your* making, Curtis, he'd confessed to himself. So he'd kept waking up wanting to cry, telling himself he'd been cursed on that damn island.

Now he snorted and guzzled more champagne. 'Stop all this,' Curtis muttered to himself, now thinking how he'd almost plunged Russell into that river... He'd told himself that he'd been protecting his wife, but he'd experienced a tremendous bloodlust. It had fallen upon him, and in that moment pure rage dominated him. He'd sought to purge his enemy, and he'd enjoyed beating the other man to a pulp. If Vanessa hadn't intervened... *No, you should feel proud of your-self for the grit and fortitude you've summoned that night,* he rebuked himself.

Then he thought about Hayden shoving Russell from that cliff path in a fit of jealousy, and a pang of guilt hit him... The boy's life had been shattered over a romantic spat... a bitter rivalry over *his* Vanessa. And he'd come so close to repeating the event.

He shook his head, trying to resist the images, but he pictured Steve again. Alive this time. That big, silly grin and floppy hair with a dodgy side parting. His dad's enraged face came now. His knitted brow and penetrative stare as he'd said, 'You knew Steve was having a few drinks, Curtis. He'd intended to leave his car behind... If it wasn't for you phoning the pub and whinging for a lift, he'd have called a taxi! You caused this!'

Curtis recalled that he'd wanted to say that he'd been too tired from playing football with his friends, but he didn't contest the accusation.

'Why didn't you walk home? It wasn't even far. Why did you have to pester him like that?' his dad had groaned in a bleary mess. Yes, his dad was drunk at the time and later apologised... or at least his mum had forced him to apologise, but it didn't matter... because he'd only said what they'd all been thinking, and he included himself in that.

Curtis knew he'd spent his entire life trying to make up for that mistake by being the hardest, most loyal worker his dad had ever known. By being the best son ever. He'd promised to make his parents proud... He only hoped he'd succeeded.

Curtis finished the rest of the champers and let the bottle fall onto the floor, wondering how he'd possibly hold his marriage together. He kept asking himself, *What else don't I know about that woman?* He kept going over their conversation in Herefordshire and what she'd said before Jonas called.

Things that might destroy our very existence... She'd never elaborated on that...

But he knew deep down in his heart that he couldn't lose her... He didn't care what she'd done, just as long as she stayed with him. That was all that mattered. He detested himself for being such a submissive pushover, but he'd get over it because he adored that woman.

How did Hayden describe her? *Damaged goods...* Yes, that was what he'd said. *Perhaps I'm damaged goods too,* decided Curtis. He guessed he did share one thing in common with Hayden Knox – he too would do anything to keep Vanessa.

71

Vanessa filled two bowls with butterscotch popcorn and fought off the urge to throw the stuff across the kitchen. Curtis's mood since the events in Herefordshire was driving her crazy. A kind, mellow man left Whitstable, and a hard-boiled, surly man returned. He seemed unable to comprehend how she could carry an ounce of sympathy for Russell after all the things he'd done.

It was still impossible to take it all in. How Delphine had died like that, despite emergency surgery for the severe head trauma she'd suffered. Two days after coming out of surgery, when they all assumed she'd come out of the woods – and *bang*. All over. The irony of the situation was not lost on Vanessa. Her past being dragged to the surface had not only caused her friend's death, but it had transformed Curtis... perhaps damaged him beyond repair and altered his amiable nature forever.

Perhaps Hayden had not just taken their money, he'd stolen their future happiness. But she'd do everything in her power to mend their broken relationship so Hayden's actions didn't end up destroying them. Curtis said he'd understood why she'd kept the past from him, but the resentment lingered and kept driving a wedge between them. She got the sense he no longer trusted her. That seemed fair enough.

Vanessa poured a glass of wine and read Russell's latest letter.

"Hearing about my past and learning the way I was before I changed into something... disgusting.... is helping me mend and stimulating my memories. I thank you so much for that, Vanessa. The assistance I'm receiving now is beyond anything I could have ever imagined, and I hope that one day I'll even be able to play the guitar again. If I do, I'll send you a video (if you can bring yourself to watch it). I hope you can.

"I'll never forgive myself for what I did to you and your family, and what I did to poor Delphine. How cruel is it I got to survive such a brutal injury left untreated, yet that poor lady died from a bash to the head? Vanessa, I swear I didn't know she was so badly injured. I assumed she'd just been knocked unconscious and would awaken with a painful lump and a nasty headache. I'm not after forgiveness, because I don't deserve it. So I won't make up excuses and bleat on about how it wasn't my fault... I am to blame. My circumstances do not pardon me.

"But I need you to understand that I wasn't myself. I'd gone to a dark place in my head and my fury clouded my every waking moment. It all seems like a fuzzy dream now. Like much of my life. I'd started to get better before, when I went to a clinic... I wish I'd have kept going, but Hayden didn't allow me to return for further sessions. I now know why, of course. He'd been worried about what they might have unearthed in my memories.

"As for us, I profess that deep down, somewhere in my muddled mind, I perhaps knew there'd been something between us – I'd seen a spark. I was adamant there'd been some hazy recollection of the connection we once shared. I felt it the moment our eyes met when I turned up at your magnificent house. I guessed it was my confused mind playing tricks with me, and that strangely made me really, really angry. With myself, with you, and with your husband. It made me bitter and drew out my hatred. It seemed stupid to even think we were ever in love or something. Ludicrous even. Had you seen it too? *Maybe*... maybe for a second you did... When I watched you from the boat, I sensed it again. When you swam after the boat that day, part of me wanted to stop and let you climb aboard so we could talk... But I let Hayden drive me... I let him steer my course, like I'd always done. I let him stay inside my head and control me. I confess, at the time I enjoyed being him, too... Because I'd always seen him as a confident and dynamic person... I looked up to him.

"Now I know the truth, I'll never forgive him. He's dead to me... And honestly, I think he really is dead. His complete silence suggests that. A part of me wonders why he sent me, and yes, he had money motivations, but I think there was more to it. One theory I have is that he got a real kick out of it. The idea of putting us back together just to see the outcome appealed to his warped nature. One of his messed-up games. To see if I would have a total recall situation. Another is that, deep down, he wanted me to discover the truth because the intricate lie had become too much to bear after all these years. I know the latter is the most unlikely. Nevertheless, I'll try to hold on to that idea.

"Tell Curtis I am sorry for the things I did. I understand that it's unlikely he'd ever forgive me for the torment I put him through, and not to mention pushing him from his kayak and stealing that photo of his brother. I do think that in a different time, and under different circumstances, the two of us could have been good pals. Yeah, stupid thought, I know. I spied on you and your friend Delphine... And I involved your son. That was unforgiveable... I'm a bad person and if they do throw the book at me, I won't complain... because I deserve everything I get... But I am truly sorry. I mean that. I really do."

Vanessa put down the letter. She had never stopped thinking about that night on the beach... or Russell. He'd been special to her, and she'd experienced a connection with him that she'd never replicated with anyone else... not that she'd ever tell Curtis. It would destroy him to learn that. Had she recalled seeing Russell for a few fleeting moments during the night of the dinner party? A brief glance they'd shared? Yes, but she'd told herself that was total madness. Russell had played the part of Hayden so convincingly.

Vanessa took the popcorn into the cinema room, and the intense speaker system rumbled music around the room, making the floor itself shake.

Sofia and Jude, perched in the front leather seats, turned and accepted the popcorn from her with gleeful grins, then returned to the screen to continue watching Disney's *Up*. The beginning always made Sofia sob, and usually Jude refused to view it with her because he was too embarrassed and uncomfortable to deal with his sibling's tearful behaviour; so it had come as quite a surprise when her son suggested they watch it together on the cinema screen. An even bigger surprise was finding Jude giving Sofia a big brotherly hug to comfort her during the early scenes that always set her off.

There is hope for that boy yet, she'd mused with a soft smile.

Now Sofia was giggling at the talking dog as Jude slotted popcorn into his mouth with an amused half-smile.

Vanessa gazed up at the black ceiling dotted with tiny, star-like white lights, and her mind drifted far away. If Hayden had gone, like Russell suspected, then it could be over.

72

V anessa finished her swim and scooped up her buoy. As she waded into shallow waters, she saw Jonas in the near distance but didn't dare call out or alert him to her presence. Instead, she just watched him from the water as he walked past her, enervated and detached. He'd become smitten with Delphine, and now he was alone again.

Vanessa knew of Jonas's dangerous past. In fact, she'd got to learn a lot about him over the years he'd been a client. She knew he was a tough and formidable man. He'd lost many comrades and good friends in his younger years. He'd been to dark places and come out the other side a better person.

Now, he appeared so dispirited it made her eyes swell with tears. Something about the way he'd always carried himself... his body language and exuberant aura, was reminiscent of another significant person in her life. Her dad, Michael. Both men were powerful characters with soft hearts. Both were capable of bad things if the need arose.

Vanessa visualised her dad knelt down by that old shed. The outline of him was just visible in the azure haze of the vivid moonlight. The image would not shift and the memories flooded her like a crashing wave. She could hear him sobbing and saying, 'It's so unfair. Me up in the house having fun. Enjoying my time with Jellybean. Having the best life. Honestly, I am... You know, I've admitted it to myself, at least. That's a start, isn't it? You were right... you always said you'd married a queer... I will not hide from that truth anymore. Sorry, Heidi, I'm waffling... I'm forever reflecting on what might have been...'

Vanessa had heard him sniff as he took a deep gulp on a bottle of whatever he was guzzling...

Then he'd said, 'You know it was an accident, right? I never meant to... If I'd done the right thing... told the truth, who'd have taken care of our baby? Because I wasn't protecting myself. I was never afraid of facing the consequences of my actions... I did it for her!'

That was when it hit her... A primal fear tore right through her in those moments... That was why he hated the garden as much as she did. He'd rarely gone out there either. They never had barbecues or outside gatherings. He never hung the washing out to dry and would always use the tumble dryer. There were no lovely plants or pleasant flowers growing. It stayed a long, depressing patch of unused land.

But the most suspicious thing, which should have been an obvious signification, was the thick concrete block she'd one day spotted under that ramshackle shed when she'd come home from school one day. *How long has that been down there?* she'd wondered at the time.

Vanessa suspected her dad would go down there on occasions for a natter. After a drink, she assumed. That couldn't have been the first time. She must have been fifteen, which meant her mother had most likely been down there since her tenth birthday. The last time Vanessa recalled her visiting the house, although she could never be certain of this. Heidi kept talking about how she intended to start a new family with her latest bloke, Gable, and when she did, Vanessa would be relocating with them to Birmingham. She presumed that was why he did it – *if* she'd got it right... But why else would he have been down at the bottom of the garden talking to her? Why did he pull up the shed and lay a thick concrete base down for an outbuilding used so infrequently?

As Vanessa got a lot older, she decided the troll had been real. But the troll hadn't been hiding children. It had been hiding her mother. A kind-hearted troll that just did that *one* terrible thing because he loved her so much. Because he couldn't stand the idea of losing her to a woman that would end up being a big disappointment to his beloved daughter. Those harsh, jagged thorns that entangled the decrepit structure were the fairies that guarded the sinister secret, and those high fences a barrier to keep out prying eyes.

Vanessa felt she had two choices the day after all the pieces clicked into place, and she deliberated over those two options for days and days before deciding what to do. She could speak with the police and tell them what she suspected. Tell them that her mother was likely dead. Likely sealed in a plastic bag and entombed in a concrete base under the old troll's shed. Her mother, who never cared about her. Never looked after her. Never truly loved her. Or say nothing and get on with life, bury the secret in her head and protect her dad. Her dad who'd loved her no matter what. Who'd do anything for her. Who'd die for her. She'd need to pick a parent and live with the consequences. And she did... but she also made a huge mistake... She'd fallen for Hayden Knox and he'd worked out the sinister secret.

It all came to a head two weeks after the events on the beach, when they'd met in that children's park a few days before leaving Bournemouth. The park, set on the outskirts of the notorious Springdean council estate, was a total dive with broken benches and a wood-chip floor littered with smashed bottles and spliff butts. She'd never forget the revolting shame that flooded her when Hayden pulled her into an embrace and kissed her neck and face. She'd shoved him away. 'Where is he? What did you do with his body?'

'He's gone. That's all that matters. Nobody will ever find him. So let's make this right. It's just us now. Ah, I have missed you so much. I'm going crazy here. I want you so bad it hurts. I love you, Essa...'

'You're insane!'

'No, no, I love you so much and I'm sorry for treating you so bad... Those drugs... that was all Leanne and Dom's idea. They gave you way too much acid. It's no wonder you saw loads of unreal shit! I hate them for that. You're lucky, Essa. The other girl in the car that night, that tart Dom wanted to screw... she got the major jitters and wandered off in a daze.'

Vanessa recalled the prickly girl. The one she'd been glad had left. *Debbie Downer.*

'That stupid cow stepped straight in front of a taxi 'cos she was so out of her nut.' He'd sniggered. 'She ended up in a coma. She's still not woken up yet. So you got off lightly.'

'Oh God, Hayden. That's so horrible. Who is she?'

'I dunno, some moody slapper Dom knows. Tiff, I think.'

'Agh! She's in a coma and you think it's funny?'

'No, no... I don't.'

'At least admit you drugged me. Don't blame them.'

'I didn't, Essa.'

'Admit it!'

'It was just a game. A laugh. I didn't know you'd go all psycho on us.'

'And who was that creepy, tall lad you brought to the church?'

'Essa, I told you before... You experienced a graphic acid hallucination. That's all.'

'Liar! You planned the entire thing to screw with my head! I'm done talking to you. We're finished... for good.'

'Shush. Pipe down. Don't say that. No one needs to know what you did, Essa. I'll never tell a soul. As long as we're together and you're my girl, I'll say nothing.'

'I'm leaving tomorrow. I'm never coming back. Do you understand?'

Hayden had snatched her arm. 'No... You can't... I won't let you... I did this for you... I only—'

'You killed him and I don't think you can even accept that, can you? But you will have to accept it, because I'm going to tell... I'm going to tell the truth and I don't care if you and Dominic go against me. The truth will eventually come out. I'm sure you know it will. It's not fair to your mum... or Russ—'

'You WON'T dare do that!' he'd spat. 'You won't dare!'

Vanessa tried walking away. But Hayden grabbed her, spun her to face him, ripping her T-shirt. He'd screamed in her face so forcefully spittle sprayed over her cheeks. 'I see you for what you are! I see you, I see you, I see you!' He'd kept repeating over and over like a lunatic. Then he'd punched her hard in the chest with his free hand, stealing her breath for a brief moment. 'You're a total bitch, Essa!'

She'd broken free of him and stood defiant and tall. 'I pity you, Hayden Knox. I do. But touch me again and you'll be sorry.'

She'd walked away again, fighting back the tears, and she would never have turned back... had he not said, 'I know your daddy did it, Little Essa.'

Vanessa would never forget that cruel smile on his face when she'd turned back to him. Not ever.

'You can deny it all you want, but *I* know... by the way you talk about her... And that startled face you made when I joked about Michael throttling Heidi and disposing of her body.'

She'd tried to laugh it off. 'Oh, right. It must be true if I pulled a face at your joke.'

'I'd only been pissing about when'd I'd said that, Essa, but I could tell I'd hit on a raw nerve.'

'Yeah, sure...'

'Thing is, I know a bit more about this than you think. Oh yes, Essa; you'd be surprised.'

'Piss off. Stop making up stories.'

'See, now, your mum's new boyfriend at the time – Gable Dankworth, Leanne's old fella – went to school with the guy. It was common knowledge that old Wankworth, as he's also known, had a reputation for being a bit of a dirty nonce. Your mum – desperate piss-head whore she is... sorry, *was*, slip of the tongue – fell for that old beast and deluded herself into thinking he was her ticket away. A nice new family in the Midlands. Convinced she'd hit the jackpot, she thought this Gable wanted her.' A slimy grin had spread across his face then. 'But it wasn't your mum he wanted... Oh, no, not her... Leanne said that manky Wankworth liked 'em nice and young. Between ten and thirteen.'

'Shut your mouth! You're making this up!'

'Nope. Ask around about Gable's reputation. He'd never been convicted... but there were plenty of rumours... And do you know what I think... I think Daddy Michael cottoned on to Gable's plan, and had it out with your dumb mum... and when she wouldn't listen to reason, when she still insisted she'd be fighting for custody over his cherished Jellybean... I think he saw red and... the big bear finally... snapped! Because no way he was ever gonna allow his special girl to be taken away from him... to be led away to live with such a dirty nonce monster.'

'Stop it,' she'd hissed. 'Stop it!'

'People said that Heidi divorced Michael and moved away with Gable and never looked back... but Leanne's dad told her that Heidi never went to find Gable. And Gable, believing Heidi dumped him for some other lowlife bloke she was screwing behind *his* back... never bothered coming back to find her. A rumour floated around that Heidi was sleeping rough on the streets of Portsmouth, but nobody's ever heard from her since... and nobody even seems to care... dirty slag that she was.'

'Goodbye, Hayden... I'll leave you to your crazy theories. Oh, and stop putting those posters of Russell up with your mum... It's sick!'

'You walk away from me, Essa, and I swear you'll regret it. One day I'll make you pay! I'm telling you, Essa. I *promise* you I will!'

She'd shivered and gritted her teeth as adrenaline and rage swept through her body.

'If you go, Essa... if you leave me on my own, then the Whisper Troll will no longer be whispering... The Whisper Troll will be shouting your secrets! I'll kick up such a fuss that people will listen.'

As Vanessa spotted that burly man walking in the distance, the idea popped into her head. He'd not noticed them... not yet... Vanessa had grabbed the safety rail of that metal roundabout, glanced at Hayden and slammed her face into the steel. The loud clomp caused her ears to buzz. Unstable on her feet, she started yelling, 'Ahhhh, stop! Leave me alone!' Which grabbed the approaching man's attention.

Vanessa had to fight through the intense, pulsating pain as she'd glared at a stunned Hayden. 'You wanna play games with me? Fine. Let's play then!' She'd thrust her head forward, showering the boy in claret.

'What are you doing? Stop. Essa!'

As the warm blood trickled over her eyelid and flowed down her cheek, she'd produced a wicked smile, and speaking in a low voice said, 'I can either tell that guy I fell from a swing... or that my ex-boyfriend tried to—' She'd pulled her top some more, revealing her bra strap, and offered him a malicious sneer. 'Your choice.'

'Jeez, Essa... please... don't... That guy will pummel the shit outta me!'

The man rushed over, a stocky guy with a menacing face, flat nose and an intimidating stare. One of the local ruffians from the Springdean, she'd guessed. He rounded on Hayden as he spoke to Vanessa. 'Do you need help, love? This guy do *that* to you?' He'd spoken in a slow, deep voice.

Vanessa had watched Hayden and flashed him a secret, sly grin.

Hayden had squirmed and shook his head in breathless protest. 'I didn't... I didn't do ought... I swear, mate... I swear... she fell... she fell... You fell off the swing, didn't you, Essa?'

She'd let a long, agonising moment pass and said, 'I fell. But thanks for coming to check on me. That was very nice of you.'

'You should get that checked. Looks like you need stitches,' the man had suggested, before giving Hayden a final, baleful glare as he departed.

Once the man had gone, Vanessa scooped up a piece of glass from the ground and, with thick blood dripping from her face, said, 'Open your hand.'

'What? No way!'

Vanessa remembered all those hideous tales her mother had told her... the child-eating troll... the dark fairies that crawled into your mouth... the demons in the cupboards... remembered the fear they instilled in her... 'Take it,' she demanded, keeping a deliberate, mad glint in her eyes.

He'd complied, and she'd balled his hand into a fist, and he'd bleated, 'You're crazy! Ouch, fuck me!'

'I read about this ritual in a book about folklore, legends and cults...' As she'd spoken, Vanessa used another piece of broken bottle to draw a circle around them. 'You'd better listen and take this seriously, Hayden Knox... you really had.' She'd then set about drawing out a crude pentagram icon.

'Ritual? What? Come on, stop it.'

She'd recalled his fear in the decimated church. The Soulmates terrified him. The occult, too. Then she'd muttered in a cold, eerie voice that was not her own, 'We summon *you*, the Demon Lord Lucifuge. We fear your name, as we should... but we invite you to witness this pledge...'

'Who... who the hell is Lucifuge? Essa, shut up!'

To aid the situation, heavy rain fell. A harsh, crashing downpour that came out of nowhere, making the pair of them flinch in curious surprise.

Hayden had watched in mute horror as she'd wiped a gloopy handful of blood from her forehead and grabbed his bloody hand in a tight grasp. 'I confirm that my dad, Michael Neal, knows about what happened on the beach... but he won't say a word. And I pledge never to tell a living soul that Hayden Knox... *killed* his twin brother, Russell... I swear it on this blood oath that I shall take this secret to my grave. I swear it on my dad's soul and on my own. I DO swear it!'

'What are you doing, you mad bitch?'

'Your turn,' she'd snapped, gripping his hand and not allowing him to pull free.

'Piss off!'

'Do it, or I'll start screaming again. Look, someone else is dashing through the rain.'

'Fine... I'll never talk about... about the death of your mum... I'll never discuss Essa's mum, Heidi, with another person. I swear it on... on my soul... and that of my mum's,' he'd mumbled.

'We both understand that if we break our oath, terrible things will befall us,' she'd said, whilst flicking bloody globs from her palm into the pentagram. They were washed away in the wood chippings within seconds.

'You're screwed up, Essa Neal. You can't mess around with this stuff. That's not sensible.'

With a grim smile, she'd snatched his hand back and continued, her voice increasing to compete with the drumming rain. 'So we ask you, Lucifuge Rofocale, to bear witness to our blood oath... and grant you, the Demon Lord, to act as an impartial judiciary, and allow you to destroy and decimate accordingly those who choose to break the pact!'

'Essa... Stop saying this stuff!'

Vanessa then snatched her hand away and peered down at the symbol. 'I don't intend to even utter the name Hayden Knox again!'

Hayden had gazed at his bloody hand like it had sprouted a pair of giant, evil eyes. 'You're a mental slag! I don't even believe any of that satanic bullshit.'

'On your head be it... Lucifuge, the so-called prime minister of the underworld, is known to grant the power of wealth to those who invoke him... to those who are true to their word... but is altogether pitiless to those who break it. So, keep it zipped and you might reap the benefits.'

He'd spat at her feet. 'Dumb slag. Just... drop dead, Essa!' he'd retorted in a cracked voice.

'You don't get to win this time, Hayden,' she'd said, then turned and strutted away, blood pouring from her wound and legs wobbly as she'd gone.

She'd played dirty and won that time. The demon's name, she'd learned about from a J. H. Brennan *Demonspawn* gaming book... She'd known Hayden was far more superstitious than he let on and the creepy ritual frightened him more than he'd care to let on. It had her, too. As she'd strutted on, the bright lightning lit the sky as though the gods themselves were angered, and she'd stopped, shivered and turned to Hayden. Seen the expression of terror moulded on his face. She guessed her face mimicked his.

Once she'd settled in London, Vanessa suspected that her troubled father wanted to open up himself. That he was desperate to tell her about what he'd done all those years back. He almost did once, but Vanessa stopped him and said, 'You should practise what you preach, Dad. Remember what you told me, "Not even your goldfish." Right?'

He'd appeared shocked for a minute. Then he nodded and said, 'You're right, JB. What would I do without you?'

Of course, he knew Vanessa had already guessed what he'd done... They just never outright spoke about the gruesome deed. God, why would they?

Vanessa kept up to date with the happenings at that old house at Redrow Close. There'd been many tenants since they'd left, but the owner, their old landlord, never changed. She'd seen the photos from the last rental advert. Browsed through the snapshots. Saw the old garden. It had artificial grass now, and the old troll's shed was long gone. A decking area now sat atop the concrete slab, and the twisted brambles and shrubbery were all gone, too. She often wondered about the other tenants, and sometimes visualised them chilling down there, sipping a glass of plonk and discussing their day, surrounded by pot plants and bright flowers... unaware what lay a few feet underneath them. That gave her chills. It really did.

Sometimes, she even imagined a world in which her mum was still with them. In that world, Heidi enjoyed spending time with her, Curtis and her grandkids. She loved to take Jude and Sofia camping, and for fun days out to

Legoland, Farmworld and park picnics, the same as Curtis's parents did. Sometimes she'd take Vanessa out for afternoon lunch and they'd enjoy a good catch-up and a long chinwag. On the odd occasion, she'd try to plant loathsome ideas into Vanessa's head, but she never listened to her mum during those moments.

If she could go back and make a different choice now she was older and wiser, would she have talked? If she was honest with herself... *probably not...* But would anyone have listened to her even if she had? Every time Vanessa thought about her dad's dark deed, what happened on the beach, and that dire ritual, it made her blood run cold and her chest tighten. Sometimes she'd become so distraught, her ears would fizz, eyes would blur, and she'd almost collapse in a manic mess.

She'd often considered she was a terrible person and because of that, one day, a day when she was at her happiest, Vanessa's world would crumble and she'd suffer the consequences for her past sins. She'd always told herself she didn't believe in any of that otherworldly stuff – the blood pact, demon rituals and prophecies... But she knew she'd been deluding herself.

This made her mind stray elsewhere... to her friend... Delphine. Her heart ached at the idea of never seeing her again. She'd also conceded to the fact that her death would be another heavy burden to carry.

As a despondent Jonas walked off into the distance, Delphine's words echoed in her head and a terrible realisation struck. An old flame did return... History repeated itself... And they'd brought with them a terrible sorrow from a time long past... All her predictions had come to pass. Another thought, morbid as it was, popped into her head. Did Delphine have a premonition about her own end coming? She dismissed that grim idea. Thinking like that would push her over the edge.

As the gentle waves washed over her feet, she contemplated how close she'd come to telling Curtis everything.

Never tell another living soul, Jellybean. Not ever. Not even if you get close to someone. You must never tell them. Not your children. Not even your pet goldfish.

Not your future husband. Tell... no... one.

She'd understood her dad's words were *not* just meant for the secret on the beach.

In hindsight, she was now glad she'd not revealed everything to Curtis... He didn't need the burden of that black secret hanging over him. As for the blood oath... well, she'd not technically broken her word... Her oath became void the moment she'd learned that Hayden hadn't killed Russell on that cliff path.

Vanessa felt a tug at her arm. With her head stuck in the clouds, she'd not noticed Sofia approach her. She was about to give her daughter a ticking off for coming down to the beach on her own when she spotted Curtis coming down the steps, waving at her.

'I told Daddy I could beat him in a race,' said Sofia. 'But I don't think he tried very hard.'

Vanessa noticed Sofia stepping away from the lapping water, her nose scrunched up in disgruntled unease, and she suddenly hated the other child for drumming that stuff about the pumped sewage into Sofia's impressionable mind.

'Do you believe in fairies, Mummy?'

'What? Why do you ask that?'

'I was watching a cartoon about them. So... do you?'

'Um, I do. Yes. But only the good ones!'

Sofia let out a confused, snorting giggle. 'Are there any other kind?'

Vanessa grinned, shook her head and said, 'No. No, of course not, silly old Billy.' Then she planted a big kiss on Sofia's forehead and in that moment decided she'd concentrate on looking to the future and strive to mend all that had been broken in her world.

As Curtis approached, Vanessa smiled at him. She'd told her husband she would love him forever... and she'd meant it.

THANK YOU FOR READING

Did you enjoy reading *The Visit*? Please consider leaving a review on Amazon. Your review will help other readers to discover the novel.

ABOUT THE AUTHOR

I was born in 1979 and live in Kent with my wife and children. I ran a private investigation agency for over fifteen years, dealing in cases that involved breach of contract claims, commercial debt recovery, and process serving. My agency also specialised in people tracing, so much of my work revolved around tracking down debtors, dealing in adoption matters and locating missing persons. At times, I worked on some pretty bizarre cases and dealt with plenty of interesting and sometimes colourful individuals. Since 2014, I have worked self-employed in the pet care industry, and I am a keen trail runner, mountain biker and kayaker.

I've had a huge passion for screenwriting for many years and started writing novels during the first lockdown. My first novel, *The Tests*, published on Amazon in 2021, was based on a spec screenplay that I originally wrote back in 2009. *The Tests* was then republished with Inkubator Books in 2022 under the new title – *The Wrong Girl*.

My second novel, *The Feud on Dead Lane*, a dark and gritty crime thriller, will be available in early 2022.

If you would like to be informed about my new book releases, don't forget to subscribe to the newsletter @ https://www.robertkirbybooks.com/subscribe

ALSO BY ROBERT W. KIRBY

The Wrong Girl

The Visit

Printed in Great Britain
by Amazon

23325463R00233